Dagger.

Devils Reapers MC

Book Five

By *Ruby Carter*

This Kitten has claws!
Ruby M x

~ Dagger ~

** Warning **

The content in this book is for mature audiences only, 18+
** Contains scenes of a sexual nature, violence, and triggers for PTSD, mental health issues, and suicidal events**

Reader discretion is strongly advised. To donate or access support and resources around human trafficking prevention, please contact 3Strands (3strandsglobalfoundation.org/), Anti-Slavery international (antislavery.org/), or consult the Global Modern Slavery Directory (globalmodernslavery.org/)

***

Model (front and back): Jake Mattila on Instagram- **@jakematti**
Photographer (front): Valokuvaaja Sari Muhonen – www.sarimuhonen.com
Photographer (back): Ukko Juntunen – http://ukkojuntunen.galleria.fi
Editor/Proofreader: Lauren Whale on Fiverr
Proofreader: Hannah Hughes
Proofreader: Patricia Hinojosa
Cover designer: Les from germancreative on Fiverr

~ Links ~

Come and join me on Facebook, Instagram, and Twitter to keep updated with my work!

Just click on the links below!

linktr.ee/rubycarter

https://www.facebook.com/rubycarterauthor/

https://www.instagram.com/rubycarterauthor/

https://twitter.com/rubycarterauth1

The Devils men have an Instagram account!
@devilsreapersmc

~ Dedication ~

To my 'Axe'

Thank you so much for being so patient, understanding and loving. I know I've dipped in and out of the book world over the last five years, but last year into 2020 has been a bit full-on, and I have to admit I have been a nightmare with coming to bed late due to my men being in my head! Thank you for being on this journey with me, listening to me ramble on, letting me blast your head with the plots of each book, and helping in any way you can—especially with medical and biker lingo/info.
I love you so much! xxx

To my readers

I am forever grateful for the amazing reviews, support, and love you continue to give me and my
Devils Reapers men.
Yes, I know this is the last of the Devils Reapers for now, but maybe not forever—never say never.
I hope you enjoy this 'see ya later' to my boys! xx

~ Acknowledgements ~

Lauren Whale - Yet again you have pulled out the big guns and helped me so much with my fifth book! Thank you millions for your inspiring words and continued support! xx

Hannah Hughes, AKA Lil' Magpie - DAGGER is finally here! **cue happy dance!** Thank you so much for letting me share parts of *Dagger* with you, and thank you for your continued support and cheerleading. You rock! Love ya x
I hope you love Dags and Kelly! Xx

Jake Mattila - Thank you for agreeing to be my Dagger, and being so awesome enough to gift me the photos for the cover. You blew me away with your generosity and kindness! I picked the right man for the job, and I'm so glad I waited to find you. Xx

Aleisha Maree, AKA my Kiwi Bird - Know that you are stronger than you give yourself credit for, and that you are one tough cookie! Thank you for your continued support and cheerleading my way to trying a completely different type of darkness. Roll on next year! xx

Naadira at BookedMercy – I'll be forever grateful for your friendship and all your amazing teasers you always bring it. Whatever the teaser/snippet you take it and run with it. Xx

Patricia Hinojosa – Thank you so much for the mind blowing, amazing book trailer and helping me with the translations.
You were an absolute lifesaver. Xx

To my girls, who are my biggest support system, thank you for being my cheerleaders, your continued help, and dealing with my craziness! Love you all loads xx

In no particular order, I'd like to thank Aleisha Maree (my beaut Kiwi bird), Bethany Worrall (my Bee Bird), Hannah Hughes (my crazy-ass Magpie) Shakkia Courtney, and as always Naadira at BookedMercy.
You are all honorary Devils Reapers members. Xx

To my BETAs - You girlies rock!! Thank you for reading so quickly, forever grateful! xx

To my Jam Jar Lovers (Jammers) AKA my Street Team - Hannah, Shakkia, Naadira, Aleisha, Nicola, Erin, Caroline, Alley, Vicki, Leslie, Bethany, Nicole, April, Leslee, Peggy and April.
Thank you for all the support and sharing of my posts. xx
To my Readers Group - Thank you all for your continued support, love, and for sharing my posts xx

To my readers - I am forever grateful for the amazing reviews, support, and love you continue to give me and my Devils Reapers men.
;o)

Contents

~ About the Book ~

If there's one thing I've always known, it's that I need to dominate; in my club, over our rivals, and in the bedroom. I get what I want, and I'm always in control, chasing the pain and pleasure I crave with as many women as I can get—or at least I was, until I met Kelly fuckin' Davis. She's strong-willed, relentless, and she pushes my buttons like no other woman I've ever met. She may be 15 years younger than me, but I can't quench my thirst for her. I want—no, I *need*—to own her ass...

He tells me I'm too young for him and that I shouldn't play games, but no man has ever made this 'little girl' feel like Dagger does. I've needed more of him since the first time he showed me his deepest desires, but he refuses to give into the hunger between us. Luckily, even an ultra-alpha like him is no match for this feisty Latina. I need to be dominated as much as he needs to dominate, and it's time to show him who's *really* in control...

Determined that no woman can tame him, lifetime bachelor Dagger shuns relationships for a life of casual hook-ups with any woman he wants—except one. As much as he tries to fight his forbidden desire for her at first, Kelly Davis has other ideas, and Dagger finds his possessive instincts starting to win out. However, just as Dagger begins to surrender to the chemistry between them, a cruel twist of fate threatens to rip it from him forever.

As MC and Mafia collide and the stakes of club life become higher than ever, will Dagger's desire for Kelly give him the courage to form an alliance from an unlikely source, or will his

need for control spell the end of their connection—and life as he knows it—for good?
Find out in the darkly explosive finale of author Ruby Carter's Devils Reapers MC series, Dagger.

~ Translations ~

<u>Italian</u>

Andiamo a casa a Napoli ottenere. Il getto pronto ad andare stasera. - Let's go home to Naples tonight. Get the jet ready.

Bene - Okay

Buon pomeriggio - Good afternoon

Buona sera - Good evening

Capo - Boss

Cazzo fottuto! - Fucking fuck!

Fica vile - Vile cunt

Gesù Cristo - Jesus Christ

Mia madre - My mother

Padre - Father

Piccolina - Little one

Ricorda il tuo posto - Remember your place

Scusi - Excuse me

Stupidi coglioni! - Stupid cunts!

Uomo minuscolo - Tiny man

~ * ~

Spanish

¡De puta madre! - Fuck yeah!

¡No mames! - What the fuck?

¿Por qué coño - Why the fuck?

Abuelo - Grandpa

Ay Dios mío! - Oh my God!

Carajo - Fuck

Chica - Girl

Coño - Pussy

El cabrón - Fucker

El hijo de puta - The son of a bitch

¡Follarme más duro! - Fuck me harder!

Jesús Cristo de mierda! - Jesus fucking Christ!

La policía - The police

La verga - Dick

Mi amor - my love

Mi mama y papi - My mom and dad

No, salí con… - I went out with…

Niña - Baby girl

¡Puto cabrón! - Fucking bastard!

Sabes cómo me preocupo a - You know how I worry

¡Santo! ¡joder! ¡Moisés! - Holy! Fuck! Moses!

Te amo, cariño - I love you, honey

~ * ~

<u>Russian</u>

Blyad! - Fuck!

Brat - Brother

Doch' - Daughter

Grebanaya vlagalische - Fucking cunt

Malishka - Baby

Mladshaya sestra - Little sister

Printsessa – Princess

~ * ~

"Sometimes you don't realize what you want until you find what you need." – Dagger, Ruby Carter

~ Prologue ~

The stench of blood, urine, and tears hangs heavy in the air, clinging to me and layering my skin and beard. The heat inside this basement is extreme to say the least, and it only makes the odor more pungent. I can only imagine that this is what the Dark Ages smelt like; the scent of fear, despair, and death…

I scan the room for a familiar face—anything familiar, really. Sobbing echoes silently from all angles, the black of the night cloaking my vision so I have only the wall under my fingertips to guide me around the darkened room. Each step I take sounds louder than the last, my boots vibrating off of the cement floor. My eyes are trying to adjust to the darkness, but when it's pitch black outside and even darker inside, what hope do I have? I focus on getting what I came for and leaving.

I turn a corner to my right with one of my brothers behind me. I'm not sure who it is—none of us have said a word since we came in, and we can't even turn a light on. We just need to get in, do what we have to, and get the fuck out of here.

As we round the corner, I feel a whoosh of heat from above me. Squinting up at the ceiling, I can just make out a huge industrial air vent. I know we're close; I can feel it in my bones.

I sidestep away from the wall and see a faint but strip of light on the floor that looks to be streaming out under a door…

Fuck, a door!

The pungent stench of urine and shit gets stronger as I approach. Someone leans over my shoulder and points with two fingers over to the far corner next to the door. I see a familiar blinking red light.

Cameras? That figures, the sick bastard…

"Boss, we have to go, now! We can't fuck around; we don't know if there are more men coming."

A set of footsteps quicken, drawing closer behind me, and Axe pats my arm to talk.

"Dags, I know, brother, but we can't go off half-cocked. We need to make sure the coast is clear."

"We have to go now! Boss, we have to GO!" I declare, not caring about the rare hint of desperation in my voice. As much as I respect my boss, there ain't no man who is gonna lay their hands on what is mine without sufferin' for it. So help me God, I'll slit his fuckin' throat.

Axe glances over me and obviously sees exactly what he needs to see, because he flicks his head at us.

"Move, now! Now, NOW!" Not needing to be told twice, we run up to the door as Axe fires at the camera and it explodes.

We try the door—it's locked. Not waiting another second, I shoot the lock off, kicking the door in with a swift strike. It falls back into the room, and as soon as it does, the smell is enough to put you off going to a public restroom for eternity—a gut-churning stench that burns my nose hairs and makes my eyes water. The putrid smell makes me gag, but the sight in front of me is what makes my stomach roll like waves crashing against rocks—harsh and angry.

The dirty desk lamp in the corner closest to the door illuminates the pure desolation and filth in this small, cramped room. Cages upon cages are lined up against the walls, running the length of the room. The sound of whimpering and crying coming from them increases as we move more into the room. For all intents and purposes, this place is a fuckin' pen, except for the fact that each and every single cage holds not a dog or any other animal, but a woman. Women fill each and every metal cage, even though there's barely enough space to sit on the floor without the top of the cages touching their heads. They all press their bodies right up against the back walls of the cages and ball up into the smallest shape they can. I can't see any of their faces; they're hiding them by tucking them between their chests and stomachs.

I can't breathe, but I don't dare open my mouth; I can feel acidic bile bubbling up the back of my throat, dying to get out. I swallow to force it down. I can be sick after, not now.

Coming further into the room, I start searching at one end, though I don't recognize any of the girls that are cowering and shivering in their cages. My eyes flick from cage to cage, and I notice for the first time that the girls inside are half-naked. I stalk down the room with more urgency in my step than ever now, impatient to get what I came for and get the hell out of this shit hole.

Stopping dead in my tracks, I see the one thing I would know anywhere—the lioness tattoo on that caramel skin. Everything else surrounding me falls away as I zone in, unable to tear my eyes away from it.

If there's one thing I know for certain, it's that I ain't leaving without what belongs to me.

I just hope I'm not too late to save her...

~ Chapter 1 ~

Dagger

She's too fuckin' tempting. She doesn't know what she wants, she's too young for me—I'm gonna be 40 next month she's barely out of diapers—but I can't resist her.

I've been around the block a few times, I never wanted to have an Ol' Lady either. I like my life the way it is; free pussy anytime, any day, anyhow. If I could, I would die a happy man with a pussy on my face, fucking one with my dick, and another on my fingers. There's not a woman out there for me—I'm like an eagle; free, lone, and that's how it's always been.

My mouth waters at the creature standing there in those tight-as-hell jeans in the middle of May, showing off that big heart-shaped ass.

FUCK. ME!

I can't lie, I want to see her bouncing on my dick as I slam into her petite little body, breaking her in. She has caramel skin with long dark mahogany hair framing her face, enhancing those fuckable lips. The sight of her has had me readjusting my dick all day, but on the surface, I'm minding my own business, chatting away to some of my brothers from other chapters after we've finished our rally across three states to raise money for the charity that helped out Bear and Jenna.

I feel her eyes on me. I can't explain the feelin', but it's like the tingling that comes over me when I'm about to shoot my load into some tight snatch. Looking over, I see her deep cocoa eyes devouring me as she licks her lips, seemingly unaware she's doing it.

Fuck me, doesn't that make me want to do shit to her...

When she came onto me at the Halloween party, she was dressed as a lioness from the Lion King, and we were both drunk and chatting around the bar. As soon as she whispered into my ear that she wanted a good fucking, it took all my willpower not to drag her back to my room and show her how a real man fucks, but I had to let her down easy. She was far too young for me—there's about 15 years between us—so I shut that shit down and planned to go and do what I do best; go and fuck some club pussy.

She saw me stumbling down the hall with Brandy that night and tried to hide it, but I saw the baffled reaction come across her face for a moment before she carried on drinking and chatting with the other girls like nothing was happening.

All I knew was that I wanted my dick wet and Brandy's an easy fuck. She knows what I like in the bedroom, too, there's no talking, but plenty of good long hard fuckin'.

Kelly's far too young for the likes of me. She's forbidden fruit...which only makes her that much more tempting...

I think I'm well and truly fucked!

***

Kelly

He's pure filth. Pure, dirty-talking filth.

When he speaks, his voice is like pure unadulterated sex; rough, gravelly and smooth all at the same time, like fine whiskey.

I want his mouth, his body, his sexy-as-fuck beard that I'm dying to ride and leave my mark over...

I'm standing around the rest of the girls at the rally he organized for the charity that helped Bear and Jenna but paying no real attention to the conversation; just nodding and laughing at the right times. The girls are chatting away about the cakes we've served and catching up on gossip between the chapters, but I can't tear my eyes off the man on the opposite side of the road leaning against his aged Harley, that copper hair and matching beard shining in the sun making it look like it has specks of gold.

My gaze roams him from his gorgeous red hair down that muscular body to those long legs stretched out in front of him...and the package between them.

God, I bet he knows what to do with his dick...

The hairs on my arms are standing on end as my gaze flicks back to his handsome face, taking in the shades covering his gorgeous eyes. Underneath them, I know he's looking at me. I can feel those intense green and brown ringed green eyes hungrily roaming my body, making me sizzle.

He thinks I don't notice; he thinks I'm not gonna pursue him like I did at Halloween, but he hasn't met Kelly Isabella Davis.

"Kel' you've got it bad. I thought you said you tried it and he didn't take the bait?" Jade—my best *chica* from another Momma—whispers to the side of me.

I never move my gaze from him, not daring to because I know the current that's passing between us is gonna break if I do. "Yeah, I did say that babe, but when did you ever know me to give up? He was the one who wouldn't stop checking me out at Halloween. He didn't take the bait that time, but I'll just get a bigger line for him to come take a nibble on so I know I'll be able to reel him in," I say with a smirk. "We both know that what I want, I get!"

"What's the plan then?" she asks in a whisper.

I smile at Dagger. "Patience, just patience."

~ Chapter 2 Kelly ~

"Kel' are you okay?" Jade asks me as we finish up helping to set the picnic benches up ready for the post-rally BBQ.

I look up at my *chica.* "Yeah, of course! How are you and Tinhead doing, is his treatment still goin' okay?"

Her face lights up at the mention of her man. Tinhead had a shit time of it recently, and he ended up having to get help for PTSD from being in Afghanistan. Based on what Jade has told me about his time there, he's a fucking hero in my eyes.

"Yeah he's doing good, his treatment's going well too. He had a rough session last week, but we talked through it and he's definitely getting there. It's gonna be a slow process, but I'm so proud of him." Her voice cracks as she says the final words, and I get choked up right along with her. It's so hard to believe that the joker of the club was suffering more than any of us could have imagined.

"Well, you both know we're all here to help you get through it. If either of you need anything, we got it, okay?" I tell her, looking at her pointedly. Jade is stubborn like me, and although some people might think that that would cause us to butt heads, we've never had a cross word against each other. If we did, it would be pretty huge. "What else is there to do except get the food?" I ask her as I lay the last of the napkins on the table.

"Oh, just to go get the man—I mean, *men.*" She purses her lips, trying to hide the smirk forming on them.

"Fine by me! You know me, I don't scare easily." With that, I turn on my heel and stride over to where a group of men are—and where Dagger is propping himself up on the fence at the back of the clubhouse grounds. As I walk closer, I spot Axe, Flex, Dagger, Bear, Tinhead and some of the members from the other four chapters—I only know Red and Rebel from the Missouri chapter by name. They all quieten their talking once I get a couple of feet in front of their circle, and I feel his eyes burning into my skin again, lighting me up with desire.

"I just came over to let you know that dinner's ready."

My eyes flick over to Dagger's, lingering there as I say, "So come and get it." I turn and walk back toward Jade without another word.

I'm only a few steps away when I hear one of them whose voice I don't recognize say, "Fuckin' hell, that ass got me readjusting myself! You gotta tell me she ain't taken."

I inwardly roll my eyes, but keep slowly picking my way around the ditches in the grass. I don't mind that men ogle my ass; I'm used to it. Even women come on to me about it or say they admire and want it.

A moment later, I hear a grumble behind me, followed by the deep gravelly voice that touches every nerve ending in my body. "Nah, she ain't taken, but she ain't free pussy either."

Hmm, who decided that, Dagger? It sure as shit wasn't me; as far as I know, I'm a free and willing woman who wants to sleep with a willing man who's more mature than the ones I've been getting recently.

I thought the mature Russian man who hit on me in a bar a few months ago would be just what I needed, but he soon dropped me after a few kisses and meet ups. Ah well, you win some, you lose some…even if that's only the second or third time that's ever happened to me.

I'm nearly at the gravel when I faintly hear Tinhead ask Dagger, "She's not *free pussy*? Fuck, Dags, you know she ain't going to like being talked about like that. Besides, you can't speak for whether she's free anything or not."

"Fuck if I care. She ain't a club girl, so she ain't free pussy," Dagger replies, his rough voice touching me where I need it most again.

"Everything go okay?" Jade says as I approach, grabbing my wrist. Her eyes silently plead with me to give her the lowdown, but I just shake my head. The smallest smile touches my lips as an idea teases at the edge of my mind.

Hmm, that could work…

"Oh yeah, everything went fine. All right, let's go get something to eat, I'm ravenous."

And not just for food…

***

After grabbing my plate, I'm sitting around one of the picnic benches with Jade to one side of me and Sue the other. Opposite us are Doc, Wrench, and Tinhead.

"You enjoying the party, sweetheart?" Sue asks me as I dig into my big cheeseburger with onion rings, homemade fries, and corn on the side. Sue is the matriarch of the club, and the nicest woman I have ever met. She's so kind, and looks after all the men—and their women—like they're her kids.

Taking a big mouthful of the deliciously meaty, cheesy burger and feel the trickle of meat juices dripping down my chin. Just then, I feel my skin prickle, and look over to the end of the bench. There stands the man I can't seem to stop thinking about, a tray of food in his tight grasp. I carefully grab the white paper napkin tucked under my plate and drag it past my lips and down my chin, refusing to tear my eyes away from his hungry gaze.

"I am indeedy, Sue."

His eyes snap to my lips as I continue to wipe, and I see his nostrils flare at me, then he slams his plate down at the head of the table.

Oh fuck yeah...

My whole body comes alive with need at the idea of him being within touching distance.

This is going to be an interesting dinner.

"How's your business doing, darlin'? You getting many bookings?" Sue enquires, bringing her buttery corn cob up to her face.

I glance over to her. "Oh, it's going really good! Jade's hoping to join me in a couple months—we'll be joining forces to bring together her insane talent with a sewing machine and a sketchbook and my make-up skills. We've been wanting to do it for years."

"That's amazing, darlin'! I can't wait to see you both succeed together. The two of you definitely have the talent for it, and you looked fabulous at Halloween."

My eyes unconsciously find Dagger's again, and I see that he's eating and listening to Tinhead chat. Someone turns the speakers propped outside the clubhouse doors on, and I have to raise my voice to be heard over the blare of the music.

"Well, Jade actually altered my outfit for Halloween—she's the one who cut the middle out of the bodysuit and altered the bottom half to turn it into pants."

"She did an amazing job," Sue beams, and we fall silent as we eat our way through the feast in front of us.

Every so often, my gaze falls onto the man whose stare is setting my skin alight. I just need to get him alone again. I know why he's not willing to give it to what he wants with me, but I don't give a flying fuck about his age. Age is just a number to me, and the only numbers that matter are how many times this man is going to make me cum. I watch him tear at the big chicken drumstick in his hands with his teeth, and the way he devours it has me clenching my thighs tightly together to ease that ache I've had every time I've seen him since Halloween.

This is going to be a fun night. It's still early, and so much can still happen yet…

***

10pm…

"Sssuuue! C'mere and have another drink with us!" I bellow.

"I'm coming, darlin!" Sue shouts back. "You grab that bottle of rum from Tinhead and I'll be right there." With that, she extracts herself from Doc's embrace, straightens him up—he looks like he's had one too many already—and heads over.

As I wait for her, I look over at my girls and smile.

I love how happy they all are with their men. Speaking of men…

My eyes seek out the copper hair I want to see between my legs tonight. I know his game is to avoid me, but we'll see how he does after my little plan is in action…

Just then, I see Red, Rebel, and some of their chapter walk through the main room, with Axe, Flex, Wrench, Brains, and Dagger following suit as they stride to the bar.

"Oh, no luck with the rum, sweetheart?" Sue asks me, standing behind Zara's chair as Zara herself bops around in her seat to the AC/DC coming through the speakers.

I snap back to attention. "Sorry, Sue, I got distracted thinking about work. Don't you worry, you take my seat, and I'll go grab the bottle of rum. Zar', do you want anything to drink? Your usual JD and Coke?" I smile at her.

Before I can resist, she tugs me into her lap, belly laughing as my big ass lands on her thighs. "Kel', this booty is something else, girl! I freakin' love it. Why do you get all this ass when I have hardly anything? Booo!" she slurs out.

A giggle bubbles to the surface, escaping my lips as I decide to give her a real laugh and wiggle my ass against her like I'm gonna give her a lap dance.

"Woohoo! Yes, girl, that's it!" Zara screams, laughing like a hyena between words.

Tears prick my eyes from laughing along, but I recover just enough to slide off her lap. "All right, Miss Hart, I'm gonna go get your drink. Be right back."

As I turn my eyes to the bar, I see Flex, Wrench, Brains, Red, and Rebel's eyes dancing as they grin like Cheshire cats at the little show we just put on. Finally, my line of sight falls onto the one that calls out to me. I don't try to understand it or rationalize it; on paper—or rather, in my parents' heads—a man nearly 15 years older is no match for me, but in reality, I feel a pull tugging me towards him. It's probably just lust and the fact I need a good hard fuckin', but either way I want to go there with him.

At the far end of the bar, Dagger's face is stoic, void of any emotion until I look into those gorgeous green and brown ringed eyes and see frustration and desire shining in them.

Ah, not so immune to my donkey booty, are you Dags?

The men talk quietly amongst themselves as I round the other side of the bar and turn to look at the collection of different bottles on the shelves behind it. The bottles never move, but I can't seem to locate Sue's rum; the Kraken Black. I even risk walking over to the shelves at the far end of the bar and feel his eyes burn into my back, setting my nerve endings tingling.

"Sue! Where's the bottle?" I holler over my shoulder.

"Top shelf at the end of the bar, darlin'!"

I grab a stool from the side of the bar, lift it over the counter, and step on it to retrieve the bottle, then realize what I've done and turn, catching Red, Wrench, and Brains off guard—sure enough, their eyes are level with my crotch, so they all had a pretty good view of my ass moments ago. The electricity that crackles across my skin means I don't need to look to know that Dagger did too.

"Getting a good look there, gentlemen? See anything you like?" I ask, pursing my lips and raising an eyebrow at them. I love to flirt, and what's the harm? I know what men—and women—are like when they see something they want to sink their teeth into, just like I want to with the gruff-sounding man on the other side of the bar. I've got a fucking huge itch, and this man is the only one who can scratch it—I don't know why or how I know it, but he is. Something inside screams at me when he's close to me, and the spot between my legs thrums with need.

"Shit, sorry pretty lady. Actually, no I'm not; you got an ass and a half right there!" Red informs me like I've never heard it before. In truth, I would have loved a little less ass and more *tatas,* but what're ya going to do about it?

I don't mind the attention either—after all, Red's hot. He's Native American, and has long inky-black hair that seems to shimmer in the club's lights, held back by a red and white bandana wrapped around his head. I notice he's got dark ink tattooed up and down his neck, biceps and hands, and when my eyes flick back up to his, I'm surprised. I expected them to be as dark as mine, but they're the color of butterscotch. He really is beautiful.

I don a smile for him. "What can I say, Red? I gotta work with what God gave me. As they say, more cushion for the pushin'." I eye the man next to me as I say the last few words, and I know Dagger is listening. He tries to evade my eyes, but I can see his harden.

I look back at Red, who's resting his arms on the bar in front of him. "While I'm here, gentlemen, what would you like?" I ask, using my head to nod back to the lines of bottles of alcohol. Red's eyes flick over the bottles on offer, and then his gaze lands back on me, scanning my face as the thirst of desire blooms in his eyes. He absently rubs his thumb back and forth over his bottom lip, nearly hypnotizing me, then breaks out into a smile, nodding to a bottle on the second shelf. "Grab that tequila. I need something Mexican on my tongue tonight."

Rolling my eyes at his statement, I grab a nearly-full bottle of the best *Patrón Añejo* we have, sliding it over to him and popping the bottle right in front of him. I bend at my waist so my ass is sticking right out in front of Dagger and I am a hair's breadth away from Red's deep caramel skin. "Here's all the Mexican you're going to get, Red," I whisper just loud enough for them all to hear, then place a chaste kiss on his cheek.

Righting myself to my full height, I make Zara's drink, grab another two glasses and pick up the bottle of rum that Sue loves so much. As I plop my butt back onto my seat, handing Zar' her drink and placing empty glasses between me and Sue, I look between the girls properly and see Sue's, Jade's, and Zara's eyes twinkling with mischievousness. After a moment, the reason for the bottle being so high clicks into place—the little bitches!

I glare at Jade, knowing she's behind it, "You little bitch, really? Gettin' me back?"

"What? A little intervention worked for me and Tinhead, didn't it? This time, Dagger's the one who needs a little push," she informs me between sips of her vodka and cranberry as her eyes dance between me and the bar.

I take a big gulp of the sweet smokey amber liquid Sue has poured me a glass of and let it slide down my throat, enjoying the burning it leaves in its path that warms me as it goes. I gaze back over to the man at the bar as he drinks quietly, then I let my next words slip from my lips, never breaking my eye contact with him.

"Let me do it my way. Like I said, patience."

~ Chapter 3 Dagger ~

Sweet baby Jesus, she tests me at every turn. My
restraint was pushed to the limit as I watched her move
her strong, agile body around the bar with the grace of a
lioness, those tight jeans clinging to every part of her like
they've been painted on. She don't know what she's
doing to me. She may have seen me look, but she has
no idea about the depraved ideas I have. She doesn't
know I would love to see marks across her beautiful skin,
or how I fantasize about her being on her knees, her
arms and hands bound behind her back as I fuck her
mouth.

All the club girls know my particular tastes, and
Brandy understands them more than most. Regular sex
is never enough for us, not really. We are always seeking
more—more orgasms, more restraints, just *more*.

Fuck, when Kelly bent over to whisper to Red, her
ass pulled her jeans taut, practically calling to me to
spank it hard enough to leave bright crimson welts like
homing beacons across her skin. My dick stirred in my
jeans as I pictured it, pushing fiercely against my button
and begging to get out.

Red watched her go, but I know he can't wait until he
gets some of his favorite Brandy, I can see she's gagging
for it too—she's been trying to get some from both Red
and Wrench, fuckin' nympho.

Just then, I feel the gorgeous creature in the tight
jeans flick those deep brown swallow-ya-whole eyes over
at me. I can't explain how, but I know her eyes are

roaming my body like she could eat me up and spit me out.

That little kitten doesn't realize I'm the Big Bad Wolf, and I could eat her for a snack. The silly girl forgets I'm in the mature leagues and she's just a few years into being able to drink.

Pulling back from my thoughts, I swipe my hand down my face and beard, wiping the beer froth off of them.

"Dags, you up for spit-roasting Brandy tonight? She won't leave me the fuck alone, brother!" Wrench says into my ear.

That doesn't surprise me; we've shared her before, and even I have to admit that there's something satisfying about the two of us fuckin' one woman and working together to reach the pinnacle—especially if one of takes her up the ass and the other through her pussy, making Brandy tighter at both ends.

I scan the room again to see whether Kelly has gone, and see that she's moved over to the other end of the room with some of the other women, who are all dancing and grinding against each other.

Fuck, that's hot!

I reluctantly turn my attention back to Wrench. "Yeah, why the hell not? Want a few more drinks first?" I ask from the corner of my mouth. I want that buzz you get off of having a few beers before sex—it intensifies the feeling of my orgasms. I may be an older man, but I still love to fuck like a teenager.

***

"Arrgggh! Dagger! Just. Like. That!" Brandy screams at the top of her lungs as Wrench takes her from the front and I claim her tight asshole. The feeling is amazing. With every push from me and pull from Wrench, we work together to reach our end goal.

I need to get that ball gag out next time; Brandy's voice grates on me even more when she's gaining on her release.

"Fuuuck!" I growl out into the room as I give Brandy's hair a sharp tug back and to the side so her head is at an awkward angle. She won't submit properly, but she loves having her hair pulled like this and the nipple clamps I have put on her. Wrench has the chain in his fist, and he gives it a sharp tug every so often to keep her on the precipice of pain and pleasure. In truth, Wrench doesn't understand it—he just wants to get his kicks. This is what me and Brandy like, so he goes along with it.

Her tight hold flutters and clenches around my dick, and she begs for more, so me and Wrench ramp it up a notch, fuckin' her harder and making her squeal like a pig. I grunt in between ragged breaths as I feel that familiar rush of blood pumping into my dick with each thrust. I slap Brandy's ass as hard as possible, landing slap after slap with each punishing thrust we give her. She throws her head back as Wrench ups the ante with each tug of the chain. Giving a final one, two, and three thrusts I cum hard, lights dancing around my eyes as they roll back in my head.

A moment later, I hear Wrench cum as he rasps out, "¡De puta madre!"

Spurts of my cum keep coming as Brandy screeches, her hoarse voice raspy from cigarettes as her yells fill the room. She collapses onto Wrench in a sweaty heap, and

I slide my almost-flaccid dick out of her, discarding the used condom in the trashcan by the bed as I fall back on the mattress. Wrench lowers Brandy down so she's laying on her back, then does the same as me to stretch his body out before standing up. I glance back down at Brandy. Her dyed blonde hair has started to turn orange and I can see brown streaks through it, but her body ain't that bad for all the use. She's a little skinnier than I like, but gotta go with what's around. Jewel's got a good pussy, but I don't get enough of it, and Candi only seems to like fuckin' Brains at the moment.

"Dags? Take these off, please," Brandy rasps out breathlessly, sliding her naked form next to mine. Her brow and chest are still slick with sweat. Bringing my hand over to her barely-there tits, I unclip the clamps, releasing the metal from her glistening skin. As soon as the first clamp is released she screams like a banshee, and once I've freed the second one, she climaxes again, her back arching off my bed as her fingers skate over her red and erect nipples.

Fuck, there's nothing more beautiful than a woman losing herself in the sensations washing over her...

As soon as her orgasm is over, Brandy falls back on the bed with a soft sigh, laying her head next to my chest. Sweat clings to her hair, and she's still panting.

"Yo darlin', don't be getting too comfy. You know the rules," I mumble out into the sticky warm air of my room.

"Oh come on Dags! I promise I'll be as quiet as a mouse; you won't even know I'm here. It's nearly 3am, and I'm burnt out," she purrs, the tone of her gravelly voice nearly matching my own as she absently strokes up and down my heavily inked chest.

I carefully peel her hand off me and set her straight as nicely as I can—she asks all the fuckin' time. "Brandy, you know my rules. Move ya ass, woman."

Rolling her eyes, she jumps up from my bed and starts shimmying her clothes back in place—not that they hide anything that everyone hasn't already seen.

I slap her ass for good measure. "Now get, Brandy. I'll catch ya in the mornin'."

She grins and sashays her little ass out of my room, leaving me alone with my thoughts. I get under my bedsheets and pull them up to my waist, still naked as the day I was born. I've slept in the nude ever since I was able to—my ma says that if I could have got away with sleeping with no clothes when I was a baby, I would have. As I drift off, I see the most perfect heart-shaped ass ever, followed by shiny dark hair that grazes the band of caramel skin visible under the shirt that ends at her waist.

Mmm, I love it when the little beauty visits my dreams.

Memories of Halloween night fill my head…

We're all standing around drinking, and I'm admiring the others' costumes. Zara is in a catsuit, Flex is in a cheap-ass Batman costume—well, if you can call a Batman t-shirt and a mask on the top of his head a costume—and they're drinking alongside me at the bar. I didn't want to take part in the fancy dress shit, so I'm just wearing my Devils T-shirt and cut. I'm too old for the fancy dress BS…or at least I think I am until the most gorgeous lioness I've ever seen walks into the club. The makeup on her beautiful face is ridiculously detailed—I ain't seen anything like it. She sidles up to me at the bar, squeezing between me and Flex. I can tell by the way she walks that she's already had a couple of drinks by this point.

"All right, who wants to do shots?" she asks us all, pinning me with that stare of hers.

The little girl wants to play with fire, but I'm not about to burn her. Everyone else around me agrees and comes up to the bar. As she moves to let them get to the bar, Kelly's ass is practically flush with my leg, making my skin prickle.

"Nah, you're all right," I reply gruffly.

"Why not?" she asks, her eyes lighting up as they meet mine and flashing with mischievousness.

"'Cause I'm happy enough with my beer and Jacks," I retort.

"You don't think you can keep up with me, is that it?"
Cheeky little witch…

My lip quirks up at her question and I lean close to her ear, catching the scent of flowers and a subtle hint of warm vanilla.

"Little girl, you have no idea. Fine, but I can drink ya under the table."

"Ha! You wish! Let's make it interesting. If I beat you, you take me back to your bedroom and fuck me like I know you've been dying to all night."

Fuck, Kelly, say exactly what you really want! The silly girl doesn't know who she's messing with…

"And what about if I win?" I grumble under my breath. I know what her answer's gonna be; I can see her eyes blazing with lust and desire, and the fact she keeps shifting and clenching her thighs together is making my dick pulsate.

"If I lose and you win…you can still fuck me…and do whatever you want to me. It's a win-win situation."

She squeezes herself and that juicy ass of hers between me and the bar and leans in against my body, her small tits rubbing against my chest, but I keep my arms either side of her. Her delicious scent wraps around me, and I peer down at her, her deep chocolate eyes gazing back at me as they burn with need.

My heart pounds and my dick twitches, needing her to be spread open for me so I can sink it inside of her. "You're asking for trouble, ya know that?" I rasp so quietly that only we can hear it.

Sliding her tiny hands up my tatted arms to rest on my leather-clad shoulders, she lightly tugs my beard, which only makes it harder not to drag her sexy ass to my bed.

"Well, it's just as well I love trouble. You know what? I am *trouble*. So, are we doing shots or what?" she purrs at me, her soft, gentle voice caressing my ears like warm caramel as her tongue skates across her plump bottom lip.

Fuck!

She's petite almost everywhere—her face, her breasts, her waist, her height—but her round ass, her fuckable lips, and her eyes are large and perfect. I see a flash of her on her knees in my mind's eye; butt naked with that sexy ass jutting out, her palms resting on her thick thighs as my dick pushes into those beautiful big lips. I imagine them wrapping around it and sucking me dry.

Sweet Jesus, she's far too close to the fire. She has no idea how badly I'd burn her; I'd ruin her in one way or another…

"All right, let's drink. What's your poison?" I growl.

She turns around on the spot to see the shelves behind the bar—or rather so her gorgeous ass is pressed up against my dick. Fuck! She knows what she's doing, as she stands up on her tiptoes, which rubs her ass against my denim-clad cock.

"Pass the tequila, would ya Brandy?" *she hollers over to the club girl before returning to her usual height, rubbing her ass down my length. My dick twitches in my pants, and I fight with myself.*

I've never wanted to fuck a woman so much, but she's too young. Besides, she don't know about my tastes—they ain't exactly conventional, are they?

My thoughts are interrupted by Kelly pouring the tequila into shot glasses; a couple for each of us. "Here ya go, Dagger."

The sound of my name on her lips has me wondering what it would sound like moaned if I fucked her. I grab the shot glass she's offered me, bring it to my lips, and quirk an eyebrow at her in challenge. "Bottoms up."

I neck back the smooth, fiery liquid, which hits the back of my throat and leaves a burning trail in its wake. As I slam the glass back down, Kelly eyes me suspiciously. "Another?"

I grunt, my eyes never leaving her face. She reacts with a stunning smile, a tiny dimple appearing just underneath the apple of her cheek on one side, her deep brown eyes lighting up with lust again. She's so fuckin' innocent, but I love the cat-and-mouse game all the same.

She passes me the other glass she poured out, and I neck that back and slam the glass down no problem, feeling that burn again as I swallow and look down at the gorgeous lioness.

Her eyes are on fire for me, and roam my lips longingly as they quirk in response to her. She swallows the golden liquid in one glass, then the other, in two swift gulps.

Fuck, that's sexy…

I watch her wince slightly like she just sucked on a sour candy. It's cute as hell.

"Again?"

She responds with an arch of her eyebrow, challenging me. The silly little girl doesn't realize who she's messing with; I've got years and weight behind me, and she's only a little thing. I can't believe she wants to keep challenging me, even though she doesn't care if she wins or loses—the girl's crazy.

I pour us both two more shots each, handing both her glasses to her and baiting her with an arch of my own eyebrow.

The music's loud enough to drown out our conversation, but I see Zara's eyes peek over Kelly's shoulder, and her eyebrows waggle suggestively at me. How Flex puts up with her sass, I'll never know, but what're ya gonna do? She makes my brother happy and she's a good woman—she has a heart of gold.

I glance back to the woman in front of me, locking eyes with her as she necks those shots one after another and slams the glasses back down on the bar.

"Now you go—unless you want to cut out the middleman and just jump straight to your bedroom? Because truth be told…" she rasps, leaning back into my chest, her small hand lightly pulling on my beard, "I've got this itch, and I think you might be just the one to scratch it, ya see."

This girl is forward, and fuck is it goddamn sexy! Her lips are calling to me like a siren in the sea, and her body's thrumming with need; I can practically taste her arousal in the air. I could just…

I shake my head free of the notion of giving in. Nah, she wouldn't be able to deal with the shit I'd be able to do to her body; my mind's made up.

I neck the two shots in one fell swoop, slamming the empty glasses back on the bar as I swallow the liquid down without moving my eyes from her. After a second, I decide to let her down easy. It's for the best; she don't need a man like me, and she probably wants what the other men have got going…nah, that ain't for me.

"Maybe another time, darlin'."

Not giving her the chance to say another word, I leave her standing there and go straight to Brandy, who is standing next to the couch chatting to Jewel. I grab Brandy's arm and march her down the hall to my room, but not before I catch a glimpse of the hurt look covering Kelly's gorgeous face.

"So, what's happening, *chica?* We all on for Saturday? I so need this girls' night out; it's been too long!" I demand down the phone to Jade.

She bursts into fits of laughter, and I feel confusion wrinkle my brow—this girl's gone cuckoo lately.

"When you've quite finished, you can tell me why you're *laughing* at your best and oldest friend."

"S-Sorry, babe. Girl, I know exactly what this need to go on a girls' night is about; you're fucking horny, ain't ya? I saw you at the rally, you were practically foaming at the mouth when Dagger came to the table."

"Oh my fucking God! I so was not!"

"Yes you were Kel', you can't hide that look you get in your eye from me. Admit it."

"Fine, whatever, I admit it. But Jade, the man is *fine.* In fact, he's smoking hot! I can't put my finger on it, but every time I see him, I get fucking wet. I ain't gonna lie, I wanna ride that man like a bucking bronco!"

A moment later, Jade bursts into fresh giggles. "Oh…my…God…Kel'! Stop! You're literally killing me," she howls down the phone at me.

I can't help myself, and end up in fits of laughter too. I know what I must sound like to everyone else, but I always speak my truth and call a spade a spade. Some people call it one of my quirks, and people who don't know me call it being fuckin' rude, but it's just me being me.

"Kel', you do make me laugh. What am I gonna do with you, hey? Look, I get that you've got the hots for him but ain't he, like, ancient?" Jade asks, whispering the last part in hushed tones.

"Jade Smith! I can't believe you just said that! No, he ain't *ancient*, he's mature, like a fine wine or a big T-Bone…one that I want to bone *me*!" I giggle.

"Jesus, Kel'! You got it bad, don't ya? I've never seen you like this."

"I can't help it! I'm horny, and that man… Sheesh, just thinking and talking about him has got my pussy tinglin'. Christ, even my vibrator ain't doing shit for me. I came twice last night,—the first time was long and hard, and the second was like a mini aftershock, it was good—but as I lay there in my bed, I realized I still had this *need*, this hunger that will only be sated when I get a good fucking. Preferably from a rugged, copper-haired, heavily-tatted biker," I blurt out, not giving a damn.

I hear Jade coughing and spluttering in an attempt to regain her composure. "Christ, poor Dagger doesn't know what's hit him, does he? All right, about this girls' night, is it just me, you, and Jenna, or everyone?"

"All the girls, including Sue. She sure can party hard; that woman loves her rum as much as me. And after Halloween, there's no way Dagger knows what's hit him; he probably thinks I'm gonna give up," I tell Jade, balancing the phone between my shoulder and my neck as I try to finish cleaning up the studio. I should have been home by now, but I was too preoccupied with trying to get the make-up out of a hand towel earlier. I love it, but special effects make-up is a bitch to take off and clean up after.

Jade hums thoughtfully. "Hmm...okay, I'll set up a group chat between us girls. I might ask Maggie if she wants to come, she's been quieter than normal. I'll pay for her drinks so she doesn't have to worry about it and just relax; that girl works too much."

"Babe, I hear ya. Every time I'm in the bakery, she seems skittish. It's almost like she's waiting for someone or something to come through the door. She's such a sweet little thing, but after a few drinks with me, you know that girl is gonna end up legitimately corrupted," I chuckle.

"Kel' I would have said anything is possible knowing you, but I would love to see you try with that one. All right, I'll let you finish what you're doing so you can get home. You stayed later than normal tonight; it's nearly 10pm."

"I know, I know. *Mamacita,* chill out, I'm going. I'll call ya when I get home."

"Good, you better. Love ya."

After a final agreement, I slide my phone back into my pocket and finish folding and putting away the clean towels before turning around and grabbing my bag and jacket off the rack by the door. I check my workspace once more to make sure I've done everything I need to before Monday, then I flick off the lights before locking up.

The chill in the late May weather bites from each way down the street, but other than the faint sound of music emanating from the new bar across the street, there's hardly anyone out here. The freshness of the night wafts over me, waking me up a little more. I'm dog tired; I can't wait to fall back into bed and sleep in in the morning.

Rounding the corner to walk further down the street, I pass the lush rose garden that all the local businesses chip in to maintain. Drawn in by the perfume coming off them, I decide to take a quick detour through them, my fingers lightly grazing the edges of the velvety petals. As I lean in to breathe in more of the gorgeous scent, I become acutely aware of either someone watching me or standing behind me. I recall my self-defense classes with Jade, and remember 'face, groin, instep' reciting it to myself in my head over and over.

Whoever this is picked the wrong girl to fuck with…

Slyly reaching into my purse, my hand quickly finds what I want. Clutching onto it with a death grip, I spin around on my heel, then hold my pepper spray outstretched ready to face my assailant

"*Blyad!*" The deep, baritone voice of Mikhail, the Russian I was seeing a couple of months ago, greets me, his ice blue eyes sparkling under the streetlights.

"Mikhail? What the hell?"

"Kelly, do you usually greet friends this way?" he enquires in thickly-accented English. His dark grey suit is the same one he wore the last time I saw him; when he said he'd call then didn't.

"Well, seeing as you're no friend of mine, yes. Do *you* usually say you're gonna call a girl then don't?"

Fuck this type of man, I've been with enough of them and watched enough friends go through this too to give him a second chance.

"*Malishka,* you wound me. Sorry I didn't call you, but business comes first."

His bullshit excuses won't work on me, even if most women would buy them.

"Can you please put the pepper spray down?" he asks in an authoritative tone.

His words remind me I still have my pepper spray pointed at his face, and I lower it to put it away. "Sorry. But you really shouldn't be creeping up behind me—or any woman, for that matter. It's weird," I grumble at him.

Don't get me wrong, I'm not *heartbroken* that he didn't call, but I thought he was majorly into me. He didn't even try and sleep with me first, which is the normal MO of guys I go on dates with.

As I get a good look at him, he pulls a cigarette from his jacket and lights it.

Ugh, yuck! How did I not know he smoked?

I look at him properly now, taking in his grey suit, black shirt, cropped dark hair, strong nose, and of course those piercing pale blue eyes. He's broad all over—kinda like Flex, come to think of it, with the same wide shoulders, but not as tall.

"Kelly, what are you doing out so late?"

I flick my eyes back to his, the smoke of his cigarette swirling around us as the Tennessee breeze picks up slightly. The bitter smoke makes me gag, and I waft it away from my face before I answer him. "I was working; one of the perks of being your own boss, sadly. What about you, Mikhail? Why are you here?" I enquire, confused as to why the hell he would be around the corner from my work.

"I was in the area, *malishka*. Do you want a ride home at least?" he asks as he grazes his thumb over my cheek.

The gesture feels too familiar, even though he's never done it before. I move out of his grasp.

"No, it's okay, I need the fresh air. See ya around, maybe."

Without wasting anymore time waiting for an answer, I turn on my heel and exit the rose garden, intending to carry on walking to my apartment. I'm about to turn the corner when I have the urge to look back. As I do, I see Mikhail standing exactly where I left him, staring after me. I get about a foot around the corner, then sprint all the way home I don't stop; not even when I feel a stone in my shoe. The sensation of discomfort I felt when Mikhail touched me still washes over me in waves, giving me the worst fucking case of goosebumps.

I see my apartment building up ahead and breathe a sigh of relief; I've never been more grateful that my Dad was able to find such a safe place for me than I am now. I burst through the building door with the security pass I have, but decide not to wait for the elevator for my floor— after all, there's only three. It's a fairly new building, and has a handful of elderly residents—in fact, I think I might be the youngest one here.

Mrs. Johnson lives opposite me in 3b; she's an African American woman in her sixties, and the nicest lady ever. She always brings me leftovers of whatever food she's made, and is always inviting me over for dinner on a Sunday. She's always so warm and welcoming that she reminds me of my Mama's family.

I take the stairs two at a time, filled with the same feeling you get when you're a kid and you have to turn the lights off downstairs and run back up to your room because the monsters might get you.

Fear races up and down my spine until I see my deep purple door. Even once I open it and shut it behind me, I flip the peephole up just to double check the stairwell at the end of the hall, staring and waiting.

Fuck, something doesn't feel right…

When I first met Mikhail, he seemed lovely and very normal, but tonight was freaky—and I *know* freaky. I'm into some freaky shit, but not this.

I finally relent and pull away from the door, dumping my bag and jacket on my couch before I drag my tired ass into my boudoir. I love my bedroom; it's a huge room with cream walls which have a slight gold shimmer to them. There's a huge queen-sized bed in the middle of the room dressed with deep plum-colored bedsheets.

Ahh, my happy place…

I strip down out of my clothes, putting them all in the hamper in the corner of my room—I love sleeping naked, or just in my panties and bra. Climbing into bed, I grab my phone and message Jade quickly, as I know I'm going to crash if I call her.

Me:- *Chica, I'm home now. Just got into bed. Love ya x*

Her reply comes a moment later:

My Chica:- *Okay babe, have a nice lie-in in the morning ready for tomorrow's antics. I'll set up a group chat with the girls before you go, hold up xx*

As I finish reading, a new message thread pops up:

My Chica:- *So what time tomorrow night, girls?x*

Zar:- *I can do around 7, if that works for everyone? We can grab some fries and wings at the bar if ya want. Z x*

Jenna:- *7 is good for me ☺ Can't wait, girlies! xx*

Me:- *Girrrrls!! I can't freaking wait! You need to be on the lookout for some sausage for me! ;oP xx*

Dani:- *Freaking hell Kel! I swear a tiny bit of pee just came out! Jesus H Christ. 7 is good for me too. Xxx*

My Chica:- *Only Kelly! Dani, I don't know why you're so surprised anymore, she never seems to get any better. ;oP*

Me:- *I don't see the problem! You girls gotta help a sister out ya know. :oP*

My Chica:- *Well I know you really want someone other than a stranger to satisfy you…;o)*

Zar:- *I fuckin' knew it! Kelly wants Dagger's sausage!*

Sue:- *Oh Lord help him! Kelly darlin', I thought I saw you eyeing him at the rally…I think you two would suit each other to a T ☺ Oh, and 7 is good for me too, girls. Looking forward to it. Xx*

Me:- *Fuck off girls, I can't help it! You know my snatch wants*

that man. I can't explain it,
and I'm not gna question it
:oP he's FINE! Xx

Lil' Maggie:- *Hiya, I don't know if I'll be able to make it tomorrow but thank you so much for inviting me xx ☺ xx*

My Chica:- *Maggie, you are coming! I told you before not to worry about the drinks or anything. Besides, you'll be working Saturday afternoon, so you have no real choice ;o) xx*

Jenna:- *Yes Maggie, you have to come! Please? It won't be the same without you. See it as a work outing, sweetie ☺ xx*

Me:- *Little Sis! You are coming,*
even if we have to force you.
You're a part of this group :o*
I'll do your make-up, and you can
borrow some of my clothes xx

Zar:- *Christ Kel, you have got it bad! Flex told me you ain't ready for Dagger; he's a certifiable lifetime bachelor. Well, ya know what I said to him? 'That's what you thought, you struggled to be with me and now I own your ass' :oP Girl, go for it, there's no harm getting your fill. Mags, you better be there! You know I'll come and grab you xx*

Dani:- *Ditto, Maggie! You have to come, you're a part of our group. Maybe we could find you a nice boy too :o) xx*

Lil' Maggie:- *Okay girls, if you want me there you've twisted my arm. Don't worry about clothes, I'll be okay, but thank you for offering to do my make-up Kell Bell ☺ xx*

Me:- *Not a problem my Lil' Sis, I've got some ace colors I can try out to match that beautiful golden hair of yours. Right bitches, I'm off to sleep, see you all tomorrow xx*

After typing and sending the last message for the night, I close my eyes and eventually drift off, phone in hand and thoughts of those piercing blue eyes that were following me home filling my head. Every time I feel I'm free, they're there once again; following me, haunting me…

~ Chapter 5 Kelly ~

Saturday at 5pm…

I stroll through the doors of Jenna's bakery-come-café, where the girls are in the process of closing up earlier so we can all get ready before our girls' night. I've brought my outfit, plus an overnight bag with a few extra outfits I thought would look great on Maggie just in case, and a make-up case.

"Hey guuurrls! Who's up first?"

Jenna, Jade and Maggie swivel around as I flick the catch on the bakery door to lock it.

"I need to cash up. Jenna, you go first, I'll go after," Lil' Mags says. She's got curves like Jade's, and her ass is not as big as mine, but she's got some big *tatas* on her. We often joke that she's Jade and Jenna's sister as their figures are so similar. Today, her stunning blond hair is up in a ponytail that shimmers in the café's light. She has no make-up on, but is such a natural beauty she could be a model. She's quiet at first; and even though she's definitely getting better with her confidence issues, she still shies away from time to time.

"You sure? I don't mind you going first." Jenna asks as she wraps her arm around Maggie, squeezing her shoulders.

Maggie nods her head and blushes. Bless her, she reminds me of Dani when I first met her. "Yeah, I'm sure. You go first, honest."

"Okay. Kelly, hit me with your talent, babe! Let's go upstairs; I want a quick shower first."

***

"Oh my God, Kelly! You kill me! So what did you say to the girl? Was she happy with the make-up at least?"

"Well, she didn't specify that she *didn't* want to look like the Bride of Chuckie for her wedding day! I fixed it in the end though. You know me, I would never let anyone look bad on their special day. Did you know Dani wants me to do her make-up for her wedding day? They haven't set a date yet, but I don't think it will be long. If Axe had his way, I think they'd already be married. Anyway, what about you and Bear? Is marriage on the cards, d'ya think?"

"Oh God, I don't know, Kelly. I'm happy the way we are, but I love him and he's my forever, that's for sure. I'd be lost without him."

"I know, and I know he loves you fiercely…like a bear! You two are the perfect match."

"Don't get me wrong, Kel', we have our moments, but challenges are what makes love stronger. Anyway, talking of bikers…want to tell me what's going on with you and Dagger?" I meet her eyes and shoot her a knowing look whilst I finish off her mascara.

"Oh no, I know that look, Kelly! Come on, spill the beans," she implores, grinning eagerly as she waits for more information from me.

"Oh nothing…yet. He's playing hardball, but that's okay, better than not being interested at all. I can see he wants me; he nearly fucked me the other night. I don't think he was expecting me to tell him that I wanted him."

"I think Sue is right; you two definitely would make a great match. You've got competition, though," she chuckles.

"Why do you say that, Jen?" I ask as I clean my brushes, occasionally flicking my gaze in her direction.

"Well, from what Bear's talked about he's popular with the club girls—more so than Bear and Tinhead were."

"That don't mean anything, you and Jadey know that. Look at them both now! You know what I'm like, Jenna. I may be stubborn as a mule, but if he wasn't interested, I could understand that and I would step aside. I've seen how the man tears himself up about me up close. He wants me, but won't give into it. He needs to know I'm not easily swayed."

"Ah Kelly, you're so like Zara! Don't let him string you along too much longer, he's 40 soon."

I think on that for a moment.

Hmm, I wonder what they're getting him for his birthday...

"All right Jenna, all done. *Voila*…" I turn to the side so she can see herself in the mirror. She shares Jade's gorgeous complexion; those two have perfect skin and rarely get blemishes, which makes them easier to work on.

"Kelly, wow! My eyes look fudging huge, and I love the color! Thank you! Want me to grab Maggie before I go and change? You know she'll back out if we wait for Jade to be done."

"Your eyes are naturally that big, it's just that you need a little color to make them pop. Great idea babe, go grab my Lil' Maggie."

She jumps up with more pep in her step than before and goes to get Maggie and then carry on getting ready.

God I love these girls; I'm so grateful to have them as my sisters. Having no siblings sure as hell was lonely growing up. I wasn't a typical only-child spoiled brat even though Mama and Dad never let me go without anything; I appreciated—and still do appreciate—everything my parents have done for me, I just wished I had a brother or sister to share it with.

I got my wish when Jade befriended me in middle school, and she's barely been able to get away from me since. When Dad's job had us travelling to DC for a few years we lost touch, but since being back in Dyersburg, I've been reunited with Jadey and my other sister Jenna. Now I have three more sisters in Dani, Zara, and Maggie, and a gorgeous nephew in Ryker, Dani's baby boy with Axe, the Devils Reapers president.

Thinking of the club makes thoughts of Dagger swirl in my head, and I go and grab some of the outfits that I brought for Maggie to busy myself. They're nothing too outrageous, but I want her to let her hair down and see that she's stunning.

"Hiya, Kelly," Maggie's quiet singsong voice greets me from the doorway.

As I turn to meet her eyes, I see her look warily at the clothes and make-up in front of her as she scans the room, overnight bag clutched so tightly in her hand that her knuckles are practically white.

"Hey, little sis. Come on over here and let me work my magic. I won't let you go until you're completely comfortable, okay?" I reassure her. I know I have to filter myself slightly with Maggie; I don't want to scare her with my forwardness or dirty sense of humor. I don't think the girl has ever been kissed, let alone lost her V-card.

As she places her beat-up backpack on Jade's bedroom floor near the closet, she creeps up to me with tentative steps like a newborn lamb walking for the first time, admiring the clothes I've laid out for her. There are some fitted blue jeans in black and acid-washed blue, a selection of crop tops, and a collection of dresses. I didn't bother packing shoes; Jade said she could wear any of her heels as they're both the same size.

"Let's do your make-up first. I think I already know what you could wear."

"Kel…?"

"Yeah, Mags?"

"Could I…wear one of your shirts and some jeans?" she asks cautiously. "I don't want to be any bother."

"Of course! Which color? I have a deep red, emerald, turquoise…oooh yes, the turquoise will make your eyes pop! You okay with that, *chica?*"

"Um…yes please, if that's okay?"

"Of course, Mags. All right, take a seat and take your hair down."

***

"There you go babe, what d'ya think?" I ask nervously.

The fear melts away as I watch Maggie's little face bloom from a look of shock into a huge grin, her eyes darting over her reflection as she takes in her whole look.

I did her make up simply, just accentuating her beautiful features. I framed her eyes with winged eyeliner and a dusting of gold shimmery eyeshadow, complete with pearl eye shadow in the corners of her eyes. Her lashes are so long and gorgeous that they barely needed mascara, and I painted her rosebud lips with a peachy pink lipstick that's delicate but not too pale so she doesn't look washed out against her blonde hair. The black skinny jeans she's wearing are a tad too big on her booty but still look good, the high waist covering some of the gap left by the turquoise low-shoulder crop top. Her double-E boobs make the top ride up higher than normal, but she looks smokin' hot—I'm jealous. Her naturally golden blonde hair falls in soft waves around her face, and Jade's black pumps finish the look. She looks gorgeous.

"Kelly…oh my God…it doesn't look like me… How did ya…?" Her gray blue eyes sparkle as they fill with unshed tears

"Mags, don't cry! Here, have a swig of this," I say, handing her a wine glass of Pinot Grigio spritzer. "If you don't like it, I can change…"

"No, it's not that! I just…don't think I have ever felt pretty before, but you have made me see it. Thank you." Her voice breaks on the last part.

I never cry unless someone dies, but my heart melts after hearing those words and seeing her face light up like I gave her the whole world.

Taking the wine glass from my hand, she necks the drink in one go, surprising us both, then splutters slightly as she hands it back.

Just then, Jade knocks on the door for the millionth time in the last twenty minutes. "Kel'! Are you guys done?"

"You okay now? Look, Maggie, you are *gorgeous,* I promise. One thing I don't do is lie or bullshit. Are you okay if I finish Missus Impatient out there so we can get going? I don't know about you, but I'm starving! I could eat a horse."

***

Around 9pm...

"So, Dani, have you and Axe set a date yet?" Sue asks.

We're sitting in one of the booths close to the dance floor, digging into shitloads of wings, ribs, nachos, and fries.

Dani hums around a mouthful of fries, signaling that she's chewing before swallowing and answering Sue. "That always seems to happen to me! Every time we go out for a meal somewhere, I'm always eating when the server asks if everything's okay, too...Anyway, no, not really, maybe at Christmas or in early Spring. Axe wants to get married any day, really, although he says he doesn't need a piece of paper to prove that I'm his forever. Okay girls, I want a Serious. Girls'. Night. Shots, man talk; you name it, I want it."

"Well, it's just as well it's my round next and I'm doing just that then Dani! Woohoo!" I holler as I slide out of the booth and casually move around to the bar. I know Dani and Maggie hate ordering, but I don't mind.

As I reach the bar, I feel an icy cold hand land on my lower back, touching the skin exposed by the emerald green satin backless dress I'm wearing. It's one I can comfortably get away with not wearing a bra with given its scooped cowl neckline, but the way it skims my pantyless butt and ends mid-thigh leaves nothing to the imagination. It doesn't stop my hackles rising at the contact though; just because you can see it doesn't mean you can touch what ain't yours.

"*Malishka*," a familiar voice purrs in my ears.

Fuck, Mikhail?! One time's a coincidence, but a second? Hmm, I don't think so, buddy.

Tilting my head to the side to meet his cool blue eyes, I greet him just as coldly. "Mikhail, what a surprise," I say, sarcasm dripping from my words.

His hands are still firmly glued to my back as he leans in closer to my ear, the scent of his fresh aftershave surrounding me and the soft expensive fabric of his suit gliding like butter over my bare arms. I get goosebumps, but I don't think it's just that that causes them.

"Kelly, why so cold to me? Do you not wish to get better acquainted while I am still in town?" he asks with that Russian twang.

I'm not gonna lie, he is sexy as fuck, but I don't do creeps, and the longer his hand remains on my back the more I dislike it. It doesn't belong there. He used to do it when we first met up and it was fine, but now? No, just no.

"Mikhail, get your hand off me now! I'm waiting to be served. You had your chance, and I don't give second ones, " I snap at him, trying to make my feelings crystal fuckin' clear.

He still doesn't move his hand, but then I am saved by one of my girls—or rather, he is. Just because I'm petite doesn't mean I'm shy to try some of those self-defense moves I learned out on him.

"You okay, Kelly? This douche bothering you?" Jade says as she comes to stand right between me and

Mikhail. Instantly, he drops his hands and puts them up in a gesture of innocence.

"It's okay, *Mikhail* was just *leaving*." I glare daggers at him, pinning him to the spot as his gaze flicks back and forth between me and Jade.

Just then, Jade shouts back to the table, never taking her eyes off Mikhail. "Dani! Call Axe, the Devils Reapers president! Tell him there's some trash that needs to be *taken out!*"

I see a flicker of movement as Mikhail drains the rest of his drink before buttoning his suit back up and wordlessly striding away and leaving the bar.

As he leaves, I let go of a breath I didn't realize I was holding in.

Fuck!

"Kellybean, was *that* the Russian you told me about?" Jade enquires.

"Yes," I admit. "It was weird; I saw him last night completely out of the blue and then all of a sudden I see him again here too? It's odd."

Jade shrugs at me and leans over the bar. "Can we have 14 shots of tequila—actually, scrap that, we'll take a bottle—salt, and limes, and can we get a bucket of local beers too? Thanks."

"Of course, darling. You girls go back to the table and we'll bring them over. It's too busy in here tonight to wait."

"Thanks Charlie, can you put it on our tab?" I ask the barman.

"Girl, I didn't realize the Russian was so hot! Creepy too, though," Jade says.

"Yeah, he is, I think you scared him off by asking Dani to call Axe," I joke as we go back over to the table of girls. Sue, Dani, and Jenna seem to be slightly tipsier than when we left them, and Maggie and Zara are chatting away.

"Hey girls, we got us shots and a bucket of beers; Charlie's going to bring them over because it's getting busier in here."

As I slide in next to Zara, she hands me my half-full cocktail and I drain it in one smooth gulp, needing the sweet alcoholic zing of my Cosmo, then reach for the last beer of her round, draining some of that down.

"You okay babe?" Zara says as she leans in next to me so I can hear her over Miley Cyrus' *'Wrecking Ball'* playing in the background.

"Yeah babe. Some dude who kissed me a few times and took me out on a few dates then disappeared turned back up yesterday, and he was just at the bar. What's the latest with you and Flex?" I ask, starting to feel the light buzz you get when you haven't been drunk properly for a while and loving it.

Zar' giggles in my ear and slings her arm around my shoulder, trying and failing to whisper in my ear. "Things are soooo freakin' good, Kelly. That man is stubborn, but when I threaten to take away my golden pussy, he drags my ass to bed. We don't really argue; we get our frustration out with each other's bodies instead."

"Fuck! That sounds hot as *hell*, Zara! You're making me ache," I giggle, shifting around in the leather booth.

"Yeah well, I'm sure you got it under control..." She raises one eyebrow and purses her lips at me, a knowing look in her eye.

"Oh yes, don't you worry babe! I have a plan...of sorts."

"Here you go, ladies, " Charlie the barman calls as he comes over and slides the beer bucket into the middle of the table, then places the bottle of tequila, a small container of salt, a huge bowl of lime segments, and shot glasses down next to it.

"Thanks Charlie, you're a star." I give him a cheeky wink, and his eyes travel down my body and back up to my face, lingering on my lips.

Hmm, he is pretty cute. Jonas Brothers, eat your heart out.

Usually, I would fuck him gladly, but he just ain't gonna cut it. I'm tired of boys; I want a man.

He leaves us to it, taking his sweet ass back to the busy bar, but I can feel his eyes are still on me as I swivel back around to the bottle of *Patrón* to start pouring the shots.

"He was cute, Kel'. Why don't you go and get some from him?" Jade asks me from the other side of the booth, smirking at me. The apples of her cheeks are rosy from the alcohol buzzing in her blood.

"He's hot, isn't he? Maybe, babe, maybe." I wiggle my eyebrows back at her as I finish pouring the *Patrón*.

"All right ladies! Shots!" I shout enthusiastically handing them a shot each—including Lil' Mags, who is sandwiched between Zara and Sue, and has hardly touched her drink.

"Lil' Sis, here's your shot and there's your lime. Lick the back of your hand, sprinkle a little salt on the wet patch, lick it off, drink the shot, and suck the lime."

"Kelly...I'm not sure I can do this..." she says with uncertainty.

I mentally kick myself. *Oh fuck, does she think she's gonna end up an alcoholic like her Dad after a couple of drinks on a girls' night?*

"Zar' swap places with me, will ya?" I whisper into her ear, not wanting to embarrass Maggie. She's so shy and sweet; I would hate to hurt her feelings, and I'm fiercely protective of her.

Zara and I slide out of the booth, then I take her place and she takes mine. I grab Maggie's petite hands, which are even smaller than mine.

"Lil' Mags, no one around this table is going to push you into drinking if you don't want to, okay?"

I wait for her to acknowledge what I've said to her, and after a few seconds she silently nods, staring at me.

"Babe, whether you have one drink or ten drinks tonight and get tipsy or absolutely wrecked, you gotta know it doesn't mean you're going to turn out like your Dad, okay? Please tell me you know that?"

"I...I guess, but what if I...turn nasty?" she whispers out under her breath. Even in the noisy bar surrounding us I heard her clearly, so I wrap my arm around her shoulder.

"Maggie, *chica*, that's one thing I know you will never be, okay? What about this? If you look like you've been having too many drinks, I'll tell ya. We all want you to relax and enjoy yourself—with or without alcohol; it doesn't matter. Okay?"

I can see her thinking on it all for a minute, then she gives me a beautiful beaming smile. I swear to God whoever swoops in to grab this girl will have to go through all of us and the Devils if they so much as think about hurting her.

"So how do I take this shot then?" Maggie asks eagerly, her little angelic face glowing back at me as I search those huge eyes for uncertainty. I don't want her to feel she has to.

"Mags, you don't…"

"Kel', I want to experience it, please."

"Okay. Follow me, okay babe?" I inform her.

"All right ladies, everyone got their shot? Like I said Mags, lick the back of your hand, pour a little salt on it, lick the salt off to lessen the burn, drink the tequila, and quickly suck the lime wedge."

She does it perfectly along with the others, and I see her wince and her eyes water.

Aww, bless her…

Tequila is second to water for me; it's what I drank behind the bleachers when me and Jade were teenagers.

"Oh my God Kelly, how can you drink that and not wince or burn your taste buds off?" Maggie asks me.

I smile at her. "Ah, well I am half Mexican after all. How was your first tequila shot? Usually the first one is the worst; it will be better after the second."

***

Around 11.30pm…

"Woohoo! Girls come on, it's our song!" I scream as Ariana Grande starts to sing. The area around the bar is full of people, so I drag Jade, Zara, Jenna, Dani, and Sue onto the dance floor one by one.

"Charlie!" I yell. "Hey, Charlie!"

Fuck, still no good!

"Zara help me out, will ya?" I bellow among the noise, but she doesn't seem to hear me either.

Ah, fuck it!

I go back to the booth next to ours, which is filled with two couples on a double date.

"Hey, can you do something for us?" I ask one of the girls in the group—a pretty little thing with dyed red hair.

"Yeah, what is it?"

"Can you look out for our stuff?"

"Of course, no problem," she says sweetly, flicking her eyes over my body.

Oh girl, you swing both ways, don't ya? I think to myself.

I smile my thanks, then head over and grab Maggie's hand, lifting it in the air as I maneuver through the crowd, swinging my booty and leading us towards the dance floor. As soon as we reach the floor, I tug Maggie into me and start letting my body feel the music, enjoying the moment and the tequila thrumming through my veins.

Maggie just stands stock-still, the rest of the girls dancing around us as *'Dangerous Woman'* booms through the bar.

"Maggie, what is it?" I enquire curiously.

"How did you learn to dance like that?" she shouts over the music at me.

"I didn't! I just close my eyes and let the music move me. Do the same; you can do it too." With that, I close my eyes and sing the lyrics, *"…makes me feel like a dangerous woman…somethin' 'bout somethin' 'bout…"*

As the song finishes, I open my eyes and see Maggie strutting her stuff; she looks sexy as hell.

"Oh my God, Kelly! I have never felt so *freeee!*" she screams at me before bursting into giggles with the biggest smile on her beautiful face.

God I love this girl.

I see Dani and Sue going back to the booth after shaking their booties and turn to Zara. "Where are they going, Zar'? Grabbing a drink?"

She shakes her head, flinging her arms around me and Maggie. "Dani's really tired—Ryker didn't sleep too well last night, he's teething. I think she's gonna get Axe to pick her up, babe. Donnn't you worry, I'll be hereee until the end!" she slurs as the music dips in and out.

Just then, Dani and Sue head over to us. "Girls, I'm gonna go home. I'm so tired, but thank you for an awesome night—it's been amazing. Axe is on his way to come get me."

"That's okay babe, I'm glad you had a good time. We need to do it more, you know. Are you going too, Sue?"

"Yeah I am darlin', I can feel a migraine coming on. I've had an amazing night as well, damn straight we need to do it more."

"What time is Axe coming? Have ya got time for another dance?" I ask over the music and the screaming girls on the opposite side of the dance floor—they're so freaking loud.

"Oh, any minute now. I messaged him about ten or fifteen minutes ago babe," Dani says, checking her phone

"Okay. Come here," I say to Dani, wrapping my arms around her small frame. "Love ya Dan'."

"Aw, love ya too Kelly. See ya soon, okay?"

As she pulls away to say bye to the rest of the girls, Sue swoops in and gives me a huge Mama Bear hug, squeezing me. "Stay away from strange men in bars, Kelly—only trust the ones with beards," she chuckles as she pulls me back at arm's length.

"Very funny, Sue. Well what about Axe and Dani? Axe hasn't got a beard. "

"I don't want one either, I don't want anything getting between me and my woman's lips," Axe interrupts behind us as he slides his arm around Dani's middle. She turns to the side, reaching up a hand and placing it over his stubble, and he leans down and plants one on her. At first you can tell it was only meant to be a peck, but Axe's arm tightens around her and he deepens the kiss, making poor Dani blush to the tips of her ears.

"Fuckin' hell, Axey! Down, boy! Someone throw some cold water on these two," Zara bellows next to me, clapping loudly to separate them as she does.

Eventually, Axe pulls away from Dani's lips with a smack, and she's so embarrassed she hides her face in Axe's t-shirt as if trying to burrow away from prying eyes. In contrast, Axe looks like the cat that got the fuckin' cream.

"You look so happy with yourself, Axe," I quip.

"I fuckin' am." He grins a big toothy smile at us all. Over his shoulder, Doc, Bear, Flex, and Tinhead come strolling through the bar. I glance back at all the women as they get greeted by their men. Zara gets dragged out of the bar giggling, Bear picks Jenna up and takes over her mouth just as Axe did with Dani, and Jade marches up to Tinhead and he threads his hand through her strawberry blonde locks, tugging her closer to his body. Even Doc wraps his arms around Sue's shoulder and plants a gentle kiss on her lips.

For the first time in my life, I'm envious, and I want more than just sex…

"How ya feeling, old man? You're catching up with me, son," says Doc, the oldest member of the Devils Reapers, as he enters the club. He's the closest thing to a father figure I've had since mine died on me and Ma when I was only 15. When I joined the Devils, Axe's Dad took me in and Doc and Sue wrapped me up the Devils' love, and I never looked back.

I look over my shoulder at Doc's weathered, wrinkled face; the same face that's always there to greet any waif or stray that comes through the Devils' doors. He's the best man I know.

"I'm not as old as you, Doc," I grumble as I take another swig of neat Jack, loving the way the honeyed golden liquid slips down my throat and settles warmly in my stomach.

He smirks at me, slapping me on my back before taking a seat next to me at the bar. "Ha! No you're not, son, but you will be soon enough. You're 40 in a week after all. Oh, Sue wanted me to ask you, is there anything you want?"

I glance over to him, confused. "Do I want anything? Presents are for kids like Ryker, I don't need 'em. As long as there is booze, a party, and free pussy, I'm good," I tell him, my lip quirking at the thought of free pussy for a moment until the pear-shaped jailbait I can't get away from springs to the forefront of my mind. I shake that thought off.

I'm never going there, ever.

"Well, we'll see what we can do son, okay?" He drains his Bud, claps me on my back one last time, and takes off down the corridor to his and Sue's room.

Glancing back around the main room of the club, I see the clock on the wall off to my left.

Fuck, its nearly 3am, how long have I been sitting here? Even the club girls aren't around.

I rub my face.

Fuckin' hell Doc, like I needed reminding that I'm getting older next week.

My Ma wants me to spend the day with her, but I'm reluctant to. I'm a shit son and I hardly see her, yet still she don't mind. She calls, but I ain't seen her for two months with all the shit like gun deals going down in the club. She doesn't always like my choices, but she understands them. She knew when I joined the club all those years ago that I needed the structure and balance I just wasn't getting at school.

I drain the last of my Jack, pulling my ass up from the bar stool and double-checking that the main door is locked, then peering at the video feed of the gates to make sure they're locked before flicking the main light off and dragging my ass off to bed. I would grab Brandy for a quick suck-off, but her door is closed as I pass, so I guess it's me and my hand tonight, and the only eyes I will be seeing are the caramel-hued, almond-shaped, and forbidden ones in my mind. I already know I'll be cumming over the thought of that heart-shaped ass pushed down flush into my bed and bouncing around as I pound into her tight, juicy cunt.

Fuuuck, I'm a dirty old man!

***

My 40th birthday…

"Are you going to get your ass out of your room or what, Dags?"

Axe has been pounding on my door since 9am, and now he's resorted to bellowing. I've never been an early riser; shit, he never used to either, but ever since he and Dani welcomed Ryker, he's been an early bird. I eventually get my now-old ass out of bed and run my fingers through my hair—it probably looks like a fucking bird's nest. Pulling some boxers on and glancing down, I readjust my morning wood so it's less obvious before opening the door to my Prez, who's now standing on the opposite side of the hall, leaning against the wall.

"Boss?" I grunt. I'd have thought It's too fuckin' early for club business but nothing surprises me anymore.

"You're up, finally. Come on man, get yaself dressed and meet me in the main room," Axe says before stalking towards the bar area.

I close my door and amble back to my bathroom to have a quick shower.

I guess I better wash my fuckin' hair to be clean for my birthday…

Fuckin' hell, I sound like Ma! She always said the same thing.

I quickly stand underneath the hot water before it turns frigid—the hot tank never lasts long in this place. The water sloshes down my hair and over my body, and I watch it slowly drip off my dick, which jerks at the sensation of a droplet hanging off the head.

Fuck, that tickles!

I grab my body wash, rubbing some into my palms before sliding it under my arms, down the dusting of hair on my chest, and washing my balls and dick.

Fuck!

As I touch myself, images of Kelly enter my mind. No sooner have I shaken them off than she's back, presenting her ass for me to paddle, spank, and do with it what I please. Before I know it, my hand is practically choking my dick as I pump faster and harder with every stroke like I'm squeezing the cum out.

The vision morphs to one of her chained to my bed spread-eagled, her arched back exposing her wet pussy for me and the fucking beautiful sight of my spank marks blooming on the side of that perfect ass of hers. I speed up again, feeling that familiar zinging up and down my spine that goes straight to my balls. At the same time that I claim Kelly in my vision, I cum with a roar, my release shooting into my hand and up the shower wall.

Fuck, I haven't come that hard in years, especially not tugging myself off!

I bow my head, resting it on the tiled wall in front of me as my breath heaves and I try to calm my racing heart.

Once I have my breathing under control, I rinse the rest of my body and wash away my cum, watching it swirling around and eventually being swallowed up by the drain. Climbing out of the shower, I dry myself vigorously before towel-drying my hair. After swiping the condensation off the mirror, I get a good look at the 40-year-old man staring back at me.

Hell, where did all that time go?

It doesn't seem like two minutes have passed since I joined the club, and now look at me.

My hair is all over the place from being towel-dried, so I hang the towel back on the heated rail and start to comb through my copper-colored hair. I may look scruffy, but I know how to take care of it. Until yesterday, I had to brush properly to keep it from matting, but since Zara gave me a haircut, I don't have to deal with that anymore. I wasn't planning to go this short, but she's left the top long enough to part and style, which I do. Part of me misses it, but not as much as she already does; she was nearly in tears while cutting and shaving, and she kept saying that I needed to donate it. Truth be told, I didn't know you could do that, but I told her sappy ass to keep the cuttings and do with my hair what she will.

Rubbing my hand across the bristly hairs on the nape of my neck feels so good that I know I should have done this years ago. The summers around here are gonna be a lot cooler on my neck, that's for sure.

I pick up the beard scissors by the sink and decide to take some of the length off my beard too; I don't want to look like Santa, but I can't get rid of all my beard either. After some thought, I decide to trim six or seven inches off so that it's about two inches longer than my chin.

A few minutes later, I admire the finished result—it looks good, but I've decided I need to get a tatt on the side of my scalp. There's too much bare skin for my liking now, but being covered in ink since you were able to get your first tatt will do that to a man. My hands, arms, and upper chest are covered, and I've got a full leg piece that even covers my knee; that fuckin' hurt like a sonofabitch.

I decide that I best get my ass moving before Axe comes and finds me again, so I brush through my newly-cut beard and pick up the trimmer. I'd better make an effort for my birthday at least; I couldn't give two fucks the rest of the year.

***

I dress in my favorite classic Harley t-shirt that Ma bought me last year—I love it as it's got *my* bike on the front; the exact model down to the year. I don't know how she got it, but she did. Pulling my cut on, I button up my jeans before shoving my size 11 feet into my boots.

Well, it's now or never. I hope the fuckers haven't made too much of a big deal of my birthday.

As soon as I leave my room at around 10am, I can hear the faint sound of people whispering—or at least trying their damnedest to keep their voices down. It doesn't help that one of the voices is Bear, and he can't whisper for shit.

As I round the corner and head into the main room of the clubhouse, everyone in the club jumps up and shouts "SURPRISE!" at the tops of their voices. A huge banner is hanging from the ceiling, reaching from one end of the bar to the other. Balloons are gathered in each corner, with huge 4 and 0 balloons at the far end of the room next to a table.

I don't know which way to turn or what to do until Bear comes barreling over to me, nearly knocking me clean off my feet and hugging me so hard I have to fight to stand up straight. "Happy birthday brother!"

"Fuck, I said I didn't want a fuss! I guess this is all *your* doing?" I direct a pointed look to Dani, Axe's woman, Zara, Flex's woman, Jenna, Bear's woman, and Doc's Ol' Lady, Sue.

"Uh, if by 'this' you mean throw a surprise 40th birthday party for you, then yes, we did. Come on old man, we got some celebrating to do!" Zara claps me on the back before stalking over to the bar, where shots are poured and beers are already chilling.

I glance back at Flex, my VP. "You need to spank her more brother," I tell him.

As soon as the words hit his ears, he smiles slyly, his lip curling upwards. "Brother, that's the problem, I do! She loves the push and pull of it. Come on, we thought we'd start the morning with a couple of drinks then have breakfast—the women have made you a fucking banquet."

I can't help shaking my head at all the fuss the others are making—give me drinks with my club, and I'd be a happy man. I'm a creature of habit who knows what I like and what I don't.

"Drink later, it'll get cold. Come on, Dags." Zara beckons me, so I cross to the other side of the bar and go through to the kitchen.

The countertops are covered with every breakfast item you could think of, including stacks of pancakes, waffles, bacon, eggs, cereal—there's even fruit, although that must be for the girls, as none of my brothers or I have eaten that stuff since we were made to by our Mommas when we were kids—even Sue doesn't try anymore. All the women inside beam at me as I walk through the door.

"What would you like to eat, son? I'll grab it and bring it over," Sue says.

"Fuck, I could get used to it being my birthday after all if I'm going to be waited on. I'll take a shit ton of eggs and bacon and some pancakes."

I make my way to the kitchen seating area at the other end of the room, sitting next to Bear. He's already got a heaped plateful even though the other men are just filing in—that's probably down to his missus, Jenna. I have no idea where the big fucker puts it all to stay so lean; he might be a big muscly bear, but he never seems to gain any weight.

"Here ya are son, enjoy. Any of the rest of you want or need anything else?" Sue asks the rest of the men as she places a massive plate of food and a glass of juice down in front of me.

"Just a bit of sugar darlin'," Doc tells her with a big toothy grin, his legs spread wide where he sits between Axe and Flex.

Sue shakes her head in embarrassment, but she doesn't deny her man and goes to sit in his lap.

Looking down at my plate, I can tell the girls have gone to extra effort to make the food-look good—and boy, does it. I dig into my man sized breakfast, the salty, crispy bacon melting on my tongue and cutting through the sweet syrup and silky soft pancake coating my mouth.

Fucking hell, that tastes good!

I swallow it all down in no time and take a swig of my orange juice.

"Fuck that was good, girls! Ya know, you didn't have to do all this," I grumble. I don't mean to sound pissed off, but I don't like people to make extra effort for me.

"Well it's a good job the rest of us have to eat too. Stop being such a stick in the mud, Dags. You're only 40 once, so there," Dani retorts as quick as a whip, sticking her tongue out at me.

"Sweetness," the Prez warns her.

"Don't you 'sweetness' me, Axe. I'm just speaking the truth, so hush."

"Woman, you did *not* just tell me to hush like a damn child!" he growls with a hint of playfulness as he strides over to his woman. He stops a foot away from her, but it won't be long before he closes the gap; we're all used to the Prez and Dani going crazy over each other.

"Yes I did. Don't start all that macho Alpha crap," she tells him.

Sure enough, as soon as she's finished, he strides forward and wraps his arm around Dani's middle, tugging her body against his.

"Quit hating; from what I remember this morning you were *loving* all the Alpha I put in you."

I chuckle to myself at that. *Fuckin' hell!*

"Ewww, Axey boy! Do you have to say that shit around the rest of us?" Zara protests.

Axe rounds on her with a grin. "You can't say *shit* after I've heard you and Flex going at it. You're as bad as me and Dani." He claims Dani's lips, and I hear her whimper once as she pulls away.

My dick stirs at the thought of a woman whimpering for me like that.

All I need for my birthday is a good fuck…or a threesome with Wrench or Brains and one of the club girls.

My thoughts are interrupted by the deafening rumble of what sounds like a fighter jet landing out in the compound.

I leap out of my chair, ready to follow Axe outside and investigate, when I realize no one else is moving from their seats. I turn on the spot to look at the rest of my brothers with a confused frown and see that every single one of them is beaming. Dani, Zara, and Sue are even bouncing on the spot like little kids.

"Boss, what the fuck? Are we going to see what it is?" I ask.

Axe, Doc, and Flex all get up and walk towards me with shit-eating grins.

"Dags, brother, do you really think that we are just having breakfast and a few drinks for your *40th fucking birthday*? Nah, brother! The Missouri, Alabama, and Kentucky chapters are arriving throughout the day, and tonight, we are having a party to end all parties. Doc and Rebel are puttin' on a BBQ, and we are having a huge spit roast in the backyard," Axe explains.

"And not the ones you're used to, brother," Tinhead shouts as he walks through the kitchen door with a smug grin and his arm tightly wrapped around Jade. I'm shocked, but pleased to see he looks lighter in himself since starting treatment.

"You fuckers! You…you motherfuckers!" I bellow, trying and failing miserably to keep the smile from my face. This is why I love this club; they're my brothers, my sisters—my family. My brothers' women scream in unison, and every single one of them wraps their arms around me.

Glancing over to Doc and Axe, I shake my head in complete shock at what they've planned.

"Prez?"

"Yeah Dags?" he smirks,

"I hate you, boss," I grin back at him.

"Yeah, yeah, brother—you want me to beat your ass for that before you enjoy your party? Come on, let's go see which of the chapters are here," he tells us as he heads to the clubhouse doors to meet everyone.

I follow him out, still hearing the rumbles of bikes coming through the compound gates. I don't believe him about inviting all those other chapters until I open the clubhouse door and see all the bikes already parked up. Fuck, there's got to be at least 50 already, and more are coming through the gates.

Fucking hell!

The morning sunlight blazes down on us all, reflecting off of all the different colors and makes of bikes, which are lined up and looking like a Harley Davidson warehouse.

Rebel and Red are the first to come barreling up to me, lifting me clean off the ground and carrying me back into the clubhouse as the rest of my brothers come piling back into it, following us in. Once we're all inside, I get placed down on the couch and given a liter of beer to drink on my own.

Fuck, I haven't had a good session like this in a while...I can tell this is gonna be a good day—and a good fuckin' night!

***

Around 8pm...

Sweet Jesus, I already thought it was going to be a good night, but this is the best fucking night in a long while. The drinks are flowing—including all my favorite beers and whiskies— and the food is out of this world; steaks of all kinds, marinated meats, and burgers with different types of cheese. I'm a happy man.

I sit outside in one of the many camping chairs next to the picnic benches. I've got Brandy draped over one side of me, Jewel on the other side, and Candi rubbing her ass against my crotch. I'm tipsy at best and full-on drunk at worst, but that doesn't stop me from draining the beer I hold in one hand and then tugging on Candi's hair so her body is pressed against mine. Fuck, she looks sexy like that. Maybe it's my full belly, the beers, or maybe all the shots I've downed, but this is the life; I don't think it could get any better.

I lean back against the chair, my eyes almost closed, when I see the woman who's been haunting my dreams, tempting me in so many ways.

It doesn't matter that I have three women wearing skirts that are barely covering their pussies with tits spilling out of their tops literally hanging off of me; when she stalks towards me, my dick jerks, suddenly hard as fucking steel up against my jeans. She looks like every man's idea of motherfucking heaven—including me.

I'm done for…

Chapter 8

Dagger

From the moment I see that gorgeous, cock-pulsating lioness moving towards me, my eyes don't leave her body, and I think I may cum in my pants like a damn teenager.

Unlike the club girls, it's not what she's showing; it's what her clothes are accentuating. She looks absolutely fuckin' mouthwatering. Her long dark hair is loose in waves down her back that bounce as she walks, and she's wearing a black crop top which shows off a band of tanned skin at her midriff. A leather jacket with studding over the shoulders sits on top, paired with cherry-colored wedged heels that have gotta be at least five inches high. The best part is her leather-effect skin-tight black pants, which hug her butt and make it look out of this fucking world, reminding me of my daydream of taking her on my bed, ass begging to be spanked as I take her over and over, bringing her to the brink of her orgasm. It's like she walks over to me in slow motion, that juicy-as-fuck ass bouncing around like a peach.

My cock reminds me how hard he is as he pulses and twitches up against my zipper. Suddenly I feel claustrophobic with these girls on me.

Candi must feel my dick harden, because she pushes back on it, grinding her little ass on me.

Fuck, that feels good! Shame my dick don't want anyone else but that sex-on-a-stick Latina chatting and drinking with Jade and the other girls…

Before I know it, I'm up and out of my seat. I don't stop to check if the club girls are okay, grunting out an apology as I make my way over to where the rest of my brothers are drinking, stalking past Kelly and the girls as I do. Both groups are hanging near the makeshift bar they built outside, where Tinhead and Wrench are taking turns serving. My eyes hardly move from the owner of that plump behind, but I go over to stand next to Bear and he hands me a Bud.

"How's your party, birthday boy? You get lucky with the club girls?" he chuckles, slinging his meaty arm across my shoulders and tugging me further into his hold. He always gets like this when he's been drinking, but tonight I don't care. I mirror the action.

"I am having a fuuucking amazing night brother. Good booze, Doc's barbecue, Black Sabbath and Motorhead blaring from the speakers, *and* I'm getting some pussy tonight. So yeah, as 40th birthdays go, I think this would rival others," I tell the others, my voice slurring as I've not really stopped drinking all day. It's been steady drinking all day and fast, hard drinking all night—a bit like how I fuck; except the fact that I can drink what I want, but I know I shouldn't fuck the woman I want. She's the one I want to strip bare and paddle the ass of red raw—but I can't. She's the one I want to dominate in every hole she has—but I won't.

She's too fuckin' young; she deserves someone her own age like Wrench, but that fact doesn't stop me readjusting my hard-on anyway. It's a damn good job the floodlights illuminating the yard aren't shining over here, because everyone would get a great eyeful of this dirty old man leering over a girl who's almost old enough to be his daughter.

Fuck, that thought makes my balls shrivel up—it should wilt my dick too, but the fucker's still trying to get to his target.

"Dags, brother! How ya doing?" Red calls as he starts walking over with the rest of the Missouri group he was just talking to, including Rebel. Our group has now swelled from the five of us to ten—Doc's still over at the BBQ. "Happy 40th old man! You good?" he slurs at me, slapping his hand on my shoulder.

I try to bite my smile at his drunken state back long enough to answer him. "Red, I'm fan-fuckin'-tastic man, how are you? You guys enjoying yourselves?" I ask, trying to be polite. I don't have much to say at the best of times; small talk ain't my bag.

"Yesss brother, the food is hitting the damn spot. You up for sharing some of the club girls later?" he asks in a deep whisper.

I pretend to think about it, but I already know the answer will be no. Normally I don't mind sharing girls with a brother; Wrench and Tinhead both know my tastes and have never judged me, but no one outside of our chapter has seen that side of me.

"I'll think about it, Red—let's see if we're still standing by the end of the night first. Hey, when you leav—"

I'm abruptly interrupted by the music being turned off, then Dani shouts at the top of her voice, "Can I have everyone's attention?!"

With a bit of alcohol in her, her confidence really does go from strength to strength. She's gotta be one of the strongest women I know, but to be honest, all the Ol'

Ladies are strong in different ways. Glancing over to my Prez, I see his eyes flare with pride—even in the dead of night, I notice that his heated stare hasn't moved off of his fiancée and Ol' Lady.

"Dagger, can you come forward please?" she asks a little softer now, a cheeky smile gracing her lips.

Fuck, now everyone's staring at me like I'm in a goddamn zoo.

I amble up towards her, standing under the floodlight as the rest of my brothers, the Ol' Ladies, and the club girls from all the chapters gather around, surrounding me.

I have Axe behind me, and Flex is the other side of me, grinning from ear to ear like a damn fool.

Dani starts again, blushing as she does, "Well, as you know, it's Dags' 40th birthday, which is why we're all celebrating today. We all know you hate this sort of thing, Dagger, so without further ado..."

I follow Dani's eyeline to see Jenna and Jade walk purposefully over to me with a huge ass cake with 4 and 0 candles sticking outta the top.

Oh goddamn it, I haven't had a birthday cake since I was a kid!

Everyone around me erupts into singing 'Happy Birthday' to me until the cake is close. As I look at the flames, my eyes collide with those of the lioness dressed like a biker's wet dream. Her plump lips break into a saucy smile, and I don't know how long my stare is on her, but I become aware of the fact that the cheering has started and take that as my cue to blow out the candles, covering the remains of my beard but never taking my eyes off hers for a second.

Once the candles are out, I glance down at the cake the girls have made—I never truly got to appreciate it lit up because I was too busy eye-fucking Kelly. I see it's a scaled-down version of my bike; same model number, same color…it's the fucking bomb! I smile my thanks at the girls—they're both used to me being of few words now and beam up at me.

"Now, we all got you something that I think you're gonna really appreciate…" Dani says excitedly as she flicks her head to the side and Axe walks over to her. He reaches down behind the speaker and produces a flat, rectangular present wrapped in gold paper, handing it to me before giving me a huge hug.

"Happy birthday, brother! Enjoy!"

"Thanks, Axe." As I start tearing the paper off it, I spot a layer of bubble wrap. After unraveling it, there in all its glory is a framed platinum disc of Black Sabbath's 'Paranoid' album signed by everyone—including Ozzy.

"FUCKING HELL yeah! This is incredible!" I can't tear my eyes from one of the best presents I've ever got, admiring the autographs and the shiny silver disc reflecting the floodlights. I turn toward the rest of my brothers with a huge grin, not being able to hold it in even if I wanted to.

"Dagger, your face is lit up like a kid at Christmas, bro. It's fucking the dog's balls, man!" Bear pulls me back into his grasp as Jenna, Jade, and Sue go to the makeshift bar to slice up the cake for me, which is plenty big enough to feed more than all these greedy fuckers here.

I get so busy showing everyone the disc that I don't realize until it's too late that the one woman who I was hoping to avoid any more interaction with is flush against my side, the scent of vanilla and mint mixed with rum wrapping around me as she whispers into my ear.

"Happy birthday, Dagger," she says in a breathy, sexy voice that goes straight to my hard-as-nails dick,

Christ, I'm glad it's dark out...

Even though everyone is watching us, I feel her luscious lips place a chaste kiss on my cheek, then she leans in against my body and pulls away slowly and hesitantly, exhaling heavily in my ear in such a way that I nearly cum right there and then.

Her next words are spoken in breathy, hushed tones. "I've got your birthday present ready for you to unwrap...me."

Hell if I know why, but the sexiest piece of ass here wants to play with fire. The thought of her being mine to dominate makes my balls tighten.

Fuuuck!

***

Kelly

I walk up towards Jenna, Jade, and Sue, who are standing at the bar cutting up Dagger's cake.

"Girls, could I have a big corner piece of this cake?" I ask as my heart races like it's competing in the Kentucky Derby.

Fuck, fuck, fuckity fuck!

I know Red, Bear, and Axe must have heard what I said as soon as I moved away from Dagger's toned body, and even though I wanted to plant one on him and demand he take me back to his room and fuck me until the morning, I couldn't. As much as I'm myself around him, there's always something else there. Normally forwardness wins out, but for some reason this man is like kryptonite to me, so I've pulled back a little. Jade would be proud—well maybe.

"Kellybean, what did you do?" I look over and see that Jade is on the opposite side of the bar, looking out onto the crowd. I watch every move of her eyes as I work out what to say.

"Nothing! Well, not really. why?" I fib as I gnaw on my lips—a nervous habit I used to have when I was a kid.

"Well how come Dagger and some of the men— including Red, Wrench, and some other guys from the Missouri and Alabama chapters, are looking this way as they're talking—a lot."

My eyes widen. *Shit!*

"I don't know what to tell ya. I whispered into Dagger's ear. I told him happy birthday…and something else." I say the last part in hushed tones.

"Oh, sweet Jesus biscuits, Kel'! When have you *ever* been able to whisper? Never, that's when! I bet when you say you 'whispered' you were loud, especially given that you have been drinking. That thrown in with how much you want to bed Dagger? I bet you were more than two decibels louder than normal." She rolls her eyes at me and carries on cutting the cake up, just as Dani comes back around the corner from checking on Ryker, who's asleep in her and Axe's room. She reattaches the baby monitor to her belt loops and looks at me.

"What's this? You want to bed Dags?" she attempts to whisper, failing miserably.

Oh shit, maybe Jade was right.

"Oh God, don't you start, Dan. I can't help it! That man…God, everything about him is sexy and makes me want to jump his bones. I think he wants to play the game, but like I've told Jade here and Jenna, there's more to that man. Something about him calls to me."

"Wow Kel', I just thought it was just a sex thing, but if you get all that from his vibes before you've even kissed him then don't give up," Dani tells me as she grabs a couple of slices of cake on paper plates before walking straight over to Axe to hand them to him and Flex.

Anyone watching them could see that they're immensely in love as she reaches up to give her man a kiss on the lips and he threads his fingers through her loose hair, deepening the kiss as he conquers her mouth, eventually letting her go. She shyly comes marching back over to us, now flushed pink. You would think she would be used to it by now, but clearly not.

"Zar'! Can you come and help?" Dani shouts over to her bestie. They're a bit like how me and Jade are together, they love and respect each other fiercely even though each have gone through their own battles.

Zara marches over with Jewel, who she was talking to when Dani called. I try not to hate the girl—who is actually okay—but I do hate the fact she was all over Dagger when I got here after my last booking. My stomach twists in disgust. It's not her fault, but she still chose this life—some don't get that choice from what Dani and my Dad have told me. Some club girls and other women get forced into the life of a slave, trafficked, and sold like cattle. It's absolutely sickening.

"Reporting for duty, Dani. Pass a couple of slices to me and Jewel. We'll go over to our men first, and if we all spread out, we can get through them all pretty quickly."

Before I can stop myself, I blurt out something that makes me look pretty pathetic and kind of like a lovesick puppy. "Can I take one of those to—"

Zara interrupts me before I can complete my sentence. "Dagger? Yes, you can. Maybe you should feed it to him in his lap too, as his birthday treat. Men love that shit, babe…or is that pussy? Food, sex, beer; they love it all," she laughs. Zara is a nut like me and I love her for it—we get on like a house on fire.

She sashays over and whispers in my ear, "Girl, whatever Dags has told you about him staying away, he hasn't been able to tear his eyes away from you all night. He's a thickhead of a man, and I know I said to you about his age and all, but the girls can testify to what I'm sayin'. Even with your back to him, his eyes have hardly strayed from you and that ass of yours."

"I doubt that, but I hear ya, Zar'," sighing. "I don't know what the problem is; I'm not asking for him to marry me, just a hook up, maybe more if we both want it after. I'm not gonna lie, babe, I can only get off to thoughts of him going down on me with that beard," I admit, releasing my secret that's technically not a secret at all. The girls all know I want him—even just a taste…

"Girl, I hear ya. Fuck, when Flex went down on me for the first time, the sensations were out of this world, and the rough texture of his beard rubbing in between my thighs felt amazing…"

Ay Dios mío! She's turning me on with her words…

My thighs clench, and I suddenly decide I'm too hot in this June heat, so I peel my jacket off, slinging it over the end of the bar.

"Oh my, Kelly! I love your top," Zara tugs me hard against her, turning me around so my back is to her as she admires my sheer black lacy top. This style looks even better with us both being able to go without a bra—having smaller *tatas* will allow ya that.

"It's gorgeous, ain't it? I have it in a couple of different colors, you'll have to borrow some."

"What was that you were saying about me between your thighs, Sugar?" Flex growls as he wraps his big arm around Zara from behind. I don't get a chance to really laugh or spur them on, but as he captures her lips, all my nerve endings come alive; chills running up and down my spine and up the back of my neck. That ache's back in full force deep in my stomach. I glance in Jenna's, Jade's, and Sue's direction and Jade's eyes widen, telling me who is behind me—not that I need it, I can feel him.

I grab ahold of the huge piece of cake Jade's just cut in my little hand, swiveling around on the spot until my eyes collide with a broad chest clothed in a black shirt with a Harley Davidson stretched across it. His worn leather cut rests on top, telling a million different stories of his time as Sergeant-at-Arms and as a biker. I risk a peek up at the man in question and notice his head. I was too nervous about coming onto him to see it before, but he's shaved it close around the edges and back with the rest of his gorgeous deep red hair flicked to the other side.

Oh my God, why the hell would he…?

I can't help my hand from reaching out—not that I would truly stop myself from touching him, if I'm honest.

I tentatively rub my palm over the shaven part of his head, but I don't move my eyes from his, seeing for the first time that they're practically forest green in the darkness. As my hand reaches the base of his skull, my fingers thread through the longer, thicker locks of hair at the back and I tug them gently, which only makes his eyes burn brighter. With that, I leave him standing there as I stroll over to the picnic benches, wanting to be on my own. I only get five steps away from him before I feel a large, calloused hand clamping around my wrist, burning the skin there. I send a little smile up to God in thanks that he reacted and keep on walking.

I think I have won, and am almost to the picnic benches when I am slammed up against the side of the clubhouse wall and met with the fiercest stare you will ever see. I might have bedded plenty, but I have never seen such pure lust and hunger in any other man's eyes than the ones shining back at me. They call to me and my soul, reaching deep inside of me…

"Don't play games, little girl. You like something, you take it," he growls out at me. His reaction is completely not what I was expecting.

"I'm not playing games, Dagger; I have been blunt and clear about what I want, and I know that you want it too."

"Yeah, I'll admit you have, but you can't play the same *games* I can *play*—trust me on that," he says in a low voice, the stress on his words sounding menacing.

"What kinda games? Are you into dead people?" I blurt out.

I see him recoil as if I've slapped him the moment he registers what I have said. "What the fuck?" he grumbles at me.

"Well, are ya?" I push him again. I hope he *ain't* into necro-what's-it, but I gotta be sure.

"Hell. To. The. Fuck. No!"

"Okay, well then what? You gonna murder me?" I counter, hoping he'll at least clue me into what he means.

"Fuckin' hell! Maybe, if you don't quit fucking around with these shitty questions."

I raise my eyebrow in a question.

"No, I ain't gonna kill ya…not yet at least. Happy?"

"No, not yet. That depends on you." I inform him softly as I graze my fingers up his arms, giving him goosebumps in my wake, All the colors on his skin are slightly faded-out with age, the tattoo outlines mostly gray rather than black.

"What about me?" he says as he glances down at me.

My heart gallops in my chest, and I have to wet my lips before I can speak. His eyes follow my tongue across my lip, and I see his jaw tense.

"It depends. Are you going to let me give you your birthday present at least?" I ask, never daring to take my eyes from his.

"What is it?"

"Just me feeding some cake to the birthday man."

"Okay. Do it here then, Kelly."

Fuck, the sound of my name has never sounded sexier on his lips, the roughness of it hitting me at my core.

Still grasping the cake in my death grip, I see that some of it has slipped onto the floor, but I have enough to feed him. I scoop some up with my fore and middle fingers, placing them gently to his strong, kissable lips. They look slightly rough with age, but that just adds to the beauty of him and my need to feel them on me…

He looks down at my fingers for a few seconds, then up to my eyes, slowly, deliberately, and sexily parting his lips so I can slide my fingers into his hot, warm mouth. He wraps his long, strong tongue around my fingers, sucking them clean as I pull them out with a pop. My heart races, wanting him more and more by the second. I go to scoop some more up for him, but he takes hold of my hand, stopping me in my tracks.

"My turn," he growls.

Fuck, I bet I could orgasm just with his voice in my ear...

I pull my hand away even though his touch still burns, and he grabs the plate and scoops a decent amount up with his own fore and middle fingers before placing them against my lips, mirroring me.

"Open up," he rasps out to me.

I comply instantly, and he places the creamy sponge cake on my tongue. I clamp my lips shut and begin sucking the cake off his fingers. I swallow the cake, but carry on sucking, running my tongue in between his fingers and wrapping it around them. Our eye contact never wavering, I pull his hand so his fingers pop from my mouth. Just when he thinks I'm done, the tip of my tongue snakes out of its own accord, grazing the pad of his middle finger. When I nibble it, he pulls his hand free of my hold, but the electric current racing through me doesn't stop, running from the top of my body to my toes, before zinging back up between us.

His eyes roam my face, and his nostrils flare to a point I would think would be painful. Without saying a single word, he flings the cake with force through the air so it lands near the picnic benches.

I don't get to ask him why he did it before he pushes his whole body up against me and captures my lips like a starving man, stealing my breath from my lungs. He pinches an erect nipple that's pushing through my top and tweaks it, sending a rush of my own juices to the inside of my thighs.

I can't help the moan that rips from me as Dagger's tongue invades my mouth with more force and dominance than I thought was possible.

I weave my hands through the back of his hair, tugging on it, and am rewarded with a growl that vibrates through my whole body, feeling delicious. He pulls away slightly from my lips, leaving me—*us*— completely and utterly breathless

Resting his forehead against mine and still breathing hard, he rasps, "Fuck…too…fuckin'…young!"

"No…I'm…not…I want you…Dagger!" I pant back at him.

"Fuuuck! Fuck!" He lifts me up under my ass. "Wrap your legs around me! I'm gonna show you why you shouldn't always get what you ask for, silly girl," he growls.

"Dagger…Take me back to your room. Now!" I demand in his ear as I bite down gently on the thick vein pulsating in his neck, then lick the place where I have just bitten.

He responds with a deep, throaty, animal growl.

God, I hope he does more of that! My clit's throbbing…

My heart leaps as he marches us through the main door and straight to the bedrooms.

YES!

~ Chapter 9 Dagger ~

The way she sucked my fingers and used that velvety soft tongue of hers has precum leaking out of my dick still as I march through the club with her around my waist. The fuckin' spitfire is pushing me to this, but we'll see how she deals with what I'm gonna give her—and pull from her.

My dick pushes right up against the zipper at the thought, but the fucker can wait a little longer before I sink into that fuckin' body of hers.

I stride faster, eating up the space between us and my bedroom as the hellcat nips and nibbles up and down my neck. I still have ahold of her gorgeous butt, and my fingers bite into it reflexively.

Sweet Jesus, the flesh surrounding my fingers feels amazing; I'm loving the feel of her ass against my palm.

As we reach it, I kick open my door, carry her inside, and slam it shut with another kick. As soon as I let go of Kelly's butt and let her slide down my front, her hand reaches for my dick.

Holy Fuuuck!

Acting on instinct, I grab her wrist, flexing my fingers around it. I feel the heat radiating off her and glance at her face—her cheeks are flushed, and her eyes are dilated to hell.

She needs to see that I can ruin her and burn her with the way I play, because fuck, this little girl won't be strong enough to survive me…

"What do we have here, Kelly? You want me? If you want this to go well, you *will* trust me with your body. That's the rule; take it or leave it." As I circle her body painfully slowly, I graze the rough pad of my thumb against the curve of her delicate neck and all the way down her shoulder, pushing the thin strap down.

Her skin breaks out in goosebumps, her breathing so heavy she's practically panting.

Jesus, she's responsive…

Pressing my lips against the shell of her ear, I rasp out, "Ya see, the thing is, I know your body better than you know it yourself. I can bring you to your knees, little girl…so what d'ya say? Give yourself over to me…"

Her breath hitches, giving me all the answer I want, but I need her words. I need to take her and show her she can't have me more than once because she wouldn't survive the second time.

"Say it, Kelly…I can smell you want it." Fuck, I'm being a bastard to her, but I can't help it—I'm like a dog in heat. I smell it, I want it, I need it.

Just then, I hear the shaky whisper of an answer, but it's so quiet I would have missed it if I exhaled. "Yes."

"What was that?" I demand; not needing the clarification but wanting to be a bastard again.

"Yes. I give myself over to you."

I stand stock still behind her and bask in the euphoria I feel at those words for a moment.

My dick jerks forcefully, demanding to take over. It needs to calm down, there is no ABC with this shit—especially not the way I want, need, and have it. No, we are going straight to XYZ.

"Good. Now put your hands behind your back!" I say harshly. There's nothing nice about me when I'm like this, never has been. She's getting the full shebang.

She hesitates at first, so grabbing a fistful of her hair, I pull her head back. Tilting it to one side, I bite down on the curve of her neck, intent on leaving a harsh mark to warn her about not complying, "Don't hesitate again. I told you to do something, and you gave yourself over to me, so I expect you to carry it out. Now, do I have to show you how I punish bad little girls?" I grind out between clenched teeth. I'm on the verge of pushing her on the bed and wrapping my hands tightly around her neck as I use her body for a fuck toy, never letting her cum.

Pushing my front against her back, I feel her clamp her hands together behind her and graze them down my denim-clad dick.

I have to hold my breath back to gain some composure, then bending my head, I kiss her shoulder. "Good girl. Now stay that way."

I turn my back on her and go to my closet, kneeling down and pulling out exactly what I was looking for. I lean back on my haunches to see if Kelly's moved, and see she hasn't even moved an inch; her hands are deathly white she's holding them together so tight.

I creep over towards her, and glide the cool metal of the handcuffs across the bare skin, making her jump as I run them over her arm, shoulder, back, and then the other shoulder and arm. I reach around the front of her body, dropping the handcuffs right in front of her face so she sees what they are before bending over her body again so I can hear her ragged breathing.

"These are to go on your wrists. You can tell me to stop at any time, and I will drop anything and everything I'm doing. I will only give what I know your body wants and can withstand. I'm gonna ask you again, Kelly; will you give yourself over to me?"

As much as I want—fuck, *need*—her, I'm imploring her to say no.

She won't understand this, she's too fucking you—

"I give myself over to you," her breathy words cut my thought short, then tug and wrap around my dick.

I don't say a word, and she continues to stand stock-still in the middle of my room, still facing the door with her hands clasped together.

Moving to stand in front of her, I go to the door and lock it, swiveling on the spot. I lean back on it and fix my stare on the little girl who's just been snared in the dragon's lair.

Her eyes go round as dinner plates, bigger than I've ever seen them before, but that's not what has caught my attention—it's the fact they're glowing gold.

That means...fuck! Her eyes change color when she's aroused!

The tip of her tongue snakes out, wetting her lips, and with that movement, I know what I have to do. She needs to see it all...

"Take your clothes off!" I bark at her.

Her mouth pops open in response.

Sweet. Fuck, my dick's gonna look perfect in there...

"I said, take your clothes off! I told you, no hesitation. Don't make me have to remind you again, or I *will* punish you!" I growl at her.

She gulps loudly, kicking off her red heels instantly before stepping out of them, making her even tinier than she already is. She starts tugging her leather-effect pants off next, never removing her eyes from mine. Inch by fuckin' inch, she pulls those pants down to reveal her gorgeous tanned skin.

I growl when I see she's completely commando underneath them.

Sweet Jesus, I don't think my poor dick's gonna last three pumps by the time I get to fucking her!

She eventually has to bend down to take her pants off the rest of the way, still not removing her eyes from mine

A moment later, I see her bare heart-shaped ass. It looks perfect, just like my daydream!

Fuck!

As soon as she's tugged them off, she rights herself again and my eyes roam her body, drinking her in.

As I reach it, my gaze homes in on the prettiest pussy I've ever seen. Her clit is already protruding, peeking out of its hood.

Fuuuck, she's on the edge too.

Flicking my eyes back up to her face, I see she's nibbling at her bottom lip. I raise my eyebrow at her in warning, and as soon as she sees it, she whips her black shirt off, her luscious hair bouncing around as she does. She throws it on top of her pants, which lie in a heap on the floor.

Her eyes light up as I take a step in front of her, never taking my eyes from her. Her little nipples are erect and pointing right at me, and I gently brush the handcuffs against them, making them painfully hard, and Kelly lets out a moan.

Ahhh, that sounds so sweet…

"Turn around," I grunt.

She complies quickly, turning on the spot so I can get a great look at her ass.

Fuck, it's exactly how I imagined it; both cheeks plump and protruding outwards until it tapers off at the top of her thighs. The sight of her naked form and long dark hair as I slap the handcuffs on her wrists held behind her back has to be one of the sexiest visions I've ever seen.

I can't help myself any longer; the monster inside me is clawing to get out. I've been patient and gentle so far, but seeing her at my mercy has him clawing to the surface.

I grab a fistful of her hair, pulling her head to the side and back towards my chest, then rub my hard-as-fucking-steel dick against her butt crack through my jeans. The minx pushes up against it with a whimper. "Do you feel this, you naughty girl? Bend over and spread your legs."

I reluctantly let go of her silky soft hair, letting it slip between my fingers, and she complies instantly.

"Wider!" I growl.

Kelly does as I say, her stance widening even though she's still bent at the waist. I have a full view of her glistening wet pussy, which has made the inside of her thighs slick from her arousal.

Motherfucker, I haven't even touched her yet! She's gonna go off like dynamite.

Unbuckling my belt and popping my button with haste, I let my jeans drop in a sigh at my ankles followed by boxers, then wrap my fist around my dick. The ache is bliss, and my hand is slick with the precum leaking from my dick. I spank the flesh of Kelly's ass, making her body jolt and her gasp in either shock or surprise at the sting— that was a slap made to hurt.

I trail a finger down her thigh. "So wet...is this for me, little girl?"

"Y-y-yes." she gasps.

Choking my dick, I rub my precum around the edge of her pussy lips. As soon as I do, her whole body convulses.

"Ahh, Dagger!" Kelly rasps out, and I'm greeted with the sight of more of her gorgeous cream seeping out of her.

This girl gets more surprising by the minute...

I reach out and run the fingers that have been in her mouth from me feeding her cake up and down her slit, rubbing her clit, then pulling back. I do it again, and this time her legs shake, threatening to give out. I smear the cum I have on my fingers all over my dick, glazing myself with her juices.

"Get on your knees."

She drops to the carpeted floor obediently.

"Now turn slowly and come and kneel right in front of me like a good little girl."

She does exactly as I say, my aching, pulsating cock jerking more in my fist as she turns around, giving me the full beautiful view of her whole body.

Her gasp at my dick is welcome, her eyes burning into me as I fist my cock, jerking it every now and then. My eyes hover over the mocha colored nipples that are begging to be bitten hard.

Her slight body entices me even more than I care to fuckin' admit. I take in the way her hips flare out before moving my eyes down to her thick thighs and admiring the hypnotic lioness tattoo with its mandala backdrop on her gorgeous thigh. I can tell she's trying to reach her pinnacle, as she starts clenching and rubbing her thighs together.

Time to put a stop to that…

"Spread your legs. You will not cum," I grunt to her as my eyes meet hers before the heavy-lidded dark orbs start devouring the sight of me and my cock. I see her do as I ask again and smile.

"Do you want my cock?"

"Yes!" she rasps out. Her breathing grows more rapid, and she wets her lips painfully slowly.

I take one large step up to her so my cock is only a lick away from her lips. "Your lips were made to suck cock, you dirty *slut!*" I snap, pushing her to jump up and run out of here—she doesn't know how close to the fire I'm pulling her.

I wait for a millisecond, letting that term sit with her, but after that, I don't give her any more time to retreat. Like a fucking dirty old man, I fist my cock again and again, right in her face. Her mouth instinctively pops open—she seems completely unaware how of just how fucking dirty she is in the best way.

Moments later, I paint her lips with a shitload of precum, making her look like pure filth. Her tongue snakes out to lick some of it off.

"Don't! Leave it how it is!" I bark at her.

Her eyes flash up at me, but she obediently puts her tongue back in her mouth,

I repaint her lips brutally, pushing the head hard around her lips. When I'm done I leave my dick right at the opening of her beautifully shining lips, not moving an inch despite the pure desire to shove myself right in her mouth and force her to take my cum all the way down so it sits in her belly.

As the thought flits across my mind, her soft, heavy breathing quickens against my cock, driving me insane. Another trickle of precum runs out of me, and just like that I shove my dick right into the little slut's mouth.

Fuck!

I push straight to the back of her throat, fisting her hair to guide her hot mouth as I pump furiously in between her lips.

"Fuck yeah! You like that, you dirty girl?" I grind out, taking her over. She's completely at my mercy, and I fucking thrive on it.

Her silky warm mouth and her tongue wrapped around my dick feels right, and she sucks hard like she's sucking the life out of me, but I'm already searching for more, always seeking that familiar tightening of my balls.

Kelly pants in between each suck and lick. Flicking my eyes back down from the top of Kelly's head, I pull my cock nearly out of her mouth, but the sexy bitch tries to suck me back into it like a vacuum.

Damn that's fucking hot!

Kelly must sense how much it turns me on; she takes more of me back into her greedy mouth, sucking hard, and looks up at me. Sweet Jesus, her eyes are blazing hot with desire and desperation…

Just like that I cum harder than I have in all my years fuckin'. It barrels out of me as I give a guttural roar; streams of my cum filling her mouth until it slows to a trickle.

I tug my dick out of her mouth, watching some of it leak out of her pouty lips. I go to tell her to drink all my cum down, but I stop short as I see her do it, never taking her eyes off mine. To top it off, the sexy bitch sneaks out that gorgeous tongue, swiping up the cum that's started to drip towards her chin.

As I come down from my high, I look back down at her—*really* look at her. She looks so small and fragile; what is it about this little girl—and she is a girl—that makes me want to fuck her senseless strapped up with rope or handcuffs on every limb?

A wave of pure guilt and shame crashes over me, and I tug up my boxers and pants, shoving my semi-hard dick into my pants but not bothering with buttoning them up. I leave her where she is without a word, marching into my bathroom and slamming the door.

I stand in front of the mirror staring at myself, absolutely disgusted at what I see glaring back at me.

You sick motherfucker! What the fuck have you just done? She's practically young enough to be your fucking daughter!

Fuck, that thought makes me feel physically sick.

Motherfucker, just fuck!

I splash my face with icy cold water. God, I don't think I've ever felt so dirty and old than at this moment...so why do I have to keep pushing images of her on her knees sucking me off inside that sweet, hot-as-fuck mouth out of my head?

What the hell has just happened?

I'm on my knees, butt-naked, handcuffed, and in the middle of Dagger's room.

I should be doing a happy dance at the fact that I finally got to be in the bedroom I have been dreaming about since October, but now I'm not so sure. He just stormed off into his bathroom without saying a word to me, not even checking if I was okay or anything. I don't get what's wrong with him; one minute he was loving it as much as I was, and the next…

I have just experienced one of the most erotic sexual experiences of my life; and we haven't even had sex, for fuck's sake!

What the hell am I gonna be like when we do? He's gonna have to mop me up off the floor. That is, if he ever comes out of that damn bathroom so he can finally fuck me senseless over his bed. Jesus, I'll take it any way he gives it to me…

I replay the scene of what just happened over and over in my head as I sit back on my heels, the coolness of the metal handcuffs touching the hot bare skin of my ass. When he clamped them across my wrists I couldn't believe it, though I always thought the man had a naughty twinkle in those sparkling green-brown eyes. Seeing him take authority over me and my body was so foreign to me, but hearing the need in the rasp of his voice told me that he thrives on it, needing it more than I can imagine.

Every time I lick my lips or dab my tongue on the corner of my mouth, I can still taste him blooming on my taste buds. I was expecting the normal salty taste, but Dagger tasted sweet and salty like popcorn—warm, comforting, yummy and so moreish that I don't ever want to get rid of this taste.

As the minutes tick by my knees start to grow numb and feel strange. There's no rhyme or reason to why I haven't got up or dared to move, yet something has me stuck in the same place, not moving an inch.

If he doesn't come out after 30 Mississippis, I'm gonna try and move my ass to go and find the sexiest man alive who has the most beautiful cock I've seen. Long? Tick. Juicy? Tick. Thick? Tick. Most of all, I loved the two prominent veins running underneath his cock. When I pressed them with the flat of my tongue, it sent him spasming in my mouth as he growled above me.

When a man takes pleasure from my body the way Dagger just did, there's no wonder I am so on the edge. If a cold breeze blew on my clit right about now, I'd combust.

1 Mississippi…

I listen out for any noise coming from the bathroom…nothing

2 Mississippi… nope
3 Mississippi… zero
4 Mississippi…nada
5 Mississippi…zilch…

***

26 Mississippi…no
27 Mis——

I stop when I think I hear the door open, as I have with each number, feeling myself get more annoyed at the big douche for leaving me here like this. I hear the slapping of his boots coming out of the bathroom, his footfalls softening as he steps on the plush carpet of his bedroom and stops all of a sudden.

The burning sensation returns, running up and down my spine, and I know he's shocked at me still being in the same position. The carpet behind me dips slightly, and I feel the fibers moving under my feet, followed by tugging off the handcuffs to where he wants them. Still not a word has been said between us. As soon as he finally unlocks the handcuffs and pulls them away from my wrists, I jump up from my spot—before realizing my feet have gone completely dead. Pins and needles shoot around them and I try to swivel around to face him before my legs start to give way.

"27 fuckin' Mississippis I've been sitting here like a damn fool, Dagger! 27 Mississippis!" I shout out, hopping between each foot as I speak. If I put my weight down on one leg for too long, I know my legs are going to give way. Fixing my glare on him, I'm beyond pissed at him for treating me this way; I won't let a man treat me like shit. He's rubbing and tugging at the back of his neck, not really looking at me—I hate that.

"Look, Kelly…"

"Don't you 'Look, Kelly' me! What are you playing at, Dagger?" I bite back, thankful that my voice isn't wavering. I slap my hands on my hips, so annoyed at him that I totally forget about my feet and one gives way. I end up landing at an awkward angle across Dagger's bed with the rest of my body on the floor.

"Fuck! Babe, you okay?" Dagger asks above me as all I can do is inhale his bed sheets.

I feel warm, rough hands go around my naked body, and Dagger pulls me up so my back and ass is up against his front.

God his hands and strong arms wrapped around me feel amazing…No, fuck that, you're pissed at him.

I bring my elbow sharply into his gut.

"Oof!" he grunts.

"Yes! Get off me! Are you going to tell me what all this was about?" I start gesturing around us as he runs his palm down his face, pulling on his beard and growling as he does.

Even though I'm annoyed at the man, I can't deny that that noise hit me right in the most delicious places.

He turns on the spot, giving me his back as he ducks his head. Despite my anger, I take a moment to admire his wide broad back that looks muscular even through his t-shirt and cut. It tapers down a pretty firm-looking ass for a man; not that he's ever gonna be able to compete with me and my donkey booty.

Hearing him exhale brings my attention back to the back of his head, which is still turned away from me. "Out with it, Dagger, come on! What the hell was that all about?"

"I told you not to play games. I warned you, didn't I? Well, this is me; this is how I *play*. I don't do plain old normal sex," he grumbles at me as a strange look flits across his face.

"I'm not talking about tha—"

Before I can finish, he interrupts me, "Would you put some clothes on?! I shouldn't have done what I did with you."

I totally forgot I was butt-naked for a minute, but I don't give two shits; I've never been ashamed of my body at all. After straightening my spine, it only takes a few steps until I am pretty much toe to toe with Dagger, peering up at him as he tries not to stare at my body. I can see the inner battle he's having to not move his line of sight from my eyes.

"What is the issue here, Dagger? Are you gonna tell me that what we just did didn't feel amazing? Is that it?"

"Yes," he replies with a grunt.

"Yes, it felt amazing when I was sucking your balls dry, or yes, you're gonna tell me it didn't? Which is it? Because I'll tell ya what, Dagger…it felt amazing to me." I reach out to his hand, grabbing it quickly so he doesn't get a chance to retreat. His eyes are still straining to keep eye contact and not wander.

Cute.

I place his hand at the top of the inside of my thighs, swiping it through the wetness and pressing it over my pussy, holding it in place. "That's how amazing it felt to me, Dagger. I don't normally get wet over just sucking a man off."

He tugs his hand away and I hear him growl at me as he takes a step back. What the hell?

"Look Kelly…whatever *this* is," he motions between us with his fingers, "This is as far as it's ever going to go. You're too young and I'm too old."

"Bullshit!" I bark at him.

"What?!" he demands.

"Bull. Shit! You're speaking absolute bullshit. I don't give two fucks about your age; if that was the case I wouldn't even be here. I don't get what everyone's hang up about age is!"

"It's fucking wrong, you're in your 20s, you're barely legal and I've turned fuckin' *40* today, Kelly! Jesus!" he grumbles, tugging at the back of his head and averting his eyes to fix them on to the floor.

I scan over him as I pull my top on and tug my pants back on. He doesn't look up, just props himself up against the wall with one leg bent behind him.

Now dressed and with one shoe in hand, I search the floor for my other shoe.

Shit! Where is it? Near the door?

Nope…

Bending down, I see it under his bed and kneel on the floor to quickly grab it before I turn to get the hell out of dodge.

As soon as I do, I hear a sharp inhale of breath, and once I grab my shoe, I peer back over my shoulder at Dagger.

What I find there stokes the flames that are still fucking burning for him, the jerk. He's standing a foot away from me, his heated glare on me and my ass…

Hmm, so I'm not young enough not to admire my booty…

Straightening up, I bend one knee again slightly for long enough to slip my other shoe back on, and then readjust my top before I leave. Just as I get to the door, my hand tightly gripping the handle, I turn on my heel, facing him again. He's still in the same place I left him.

"I'm 25, not 18, Dagger! One thing you need to know about me—and you listen up and listen good—is that I *never* give up…Go ahead, keep telling yourself that you don't want this—that you don't want my lips wrapped around your cock again, that you don't remember the fact I know you want to fuck me senseless. But don't expect me to stop, and don't keep using the excuse of my age, because that's bullshit and you know it."

I don't wait for a response before I go to exit his room; I've got one foot through the open door when I turn to look over my shoulder, burning holes into his gorgeous eyes. If I could pull out my camera and take a picture of his face right now I would—it's priceless.

Just before I slam his door behind myself, I say, "Oh, and who the hell said I wanted plain old normal sex?...Maybe I like to *play* too. Did you ever think about that?"

~ Chapter 11 ~

Dagger

"...who the hell said I wanted plain old normal sex?...Maybe I like to play too. Did you ever think about that?"

Her words echo in my head as she slams the door to my bedroom and I hear her walking away, those sexy-as-hell shoes clicking against the floor. Did she mean what I think she meant?

Thinking it over, she didn't freak out, scream, or act out when I slapped on the handcuffs. She took to it well...too fuckin' well, actually...

Ah fuck it, I ain't gonna overthink that shit. It is what it is, she's too fucking young and I'm too old for her, even if I am dying to sink myself back between those luscious lips that sucked me dry. Just the thought of them has my dick hard and ready to go again.

Jesus Christ, I'm like a teenager!

I pull my phone out of my back pocket to check the time.

Ahhh, it's still early, and I'm not even drunk yet!

Sliding my phone back into my pocket, I march out of my room, through the fairly empty main room, and back to the warm June Tennessee heat in the back of the compound. Walking past the birthday cake on the floor, I round the corner to where the chapters are gathered. Some men have fallen asleep on the lawn chairs—I can see Doc nodding off in one already. Rebel and Red are tag teaming Brandy and one of their club girls in one corner—I think her name is Vix. Her and Brandy are getting fucked in the ass and playing with each other's pussies.

Fuuuck! That shit is hot!

I can see Vix's blond hair whipping around her face as she bounces on Red's dick. Fuck, if she's not too used up after they're done, I might have a go with her and Jewel.

I glance over at Bear, who's got Jenna pressed up against a tree and is whispering sweet nothings in her ear.

Fuck that relationship shit. One woman is never gonna be enough for me, I'd grow bored and fuck it up. Besides, I like being a lifetime bachelor—even if Ma still keeps on about me getting a nice woman.

Pushing the thought away, I decide to do what I'm good at; fuckin' and fuckin' hard. I go straight up to Jewel, who's rubbing her hand up and down Wrench's lap as he palms her tit. I don't bother waiting for him to finish; it's my birthday.

"Brother, will you be alright if I take Jewel off your hands?" I ask.

He just lifts his chin in agreement, and she happily slides off his lap and slips her hand into mine. I tug her towards a spare chair next to Brains and Candi, then collapse into it. At that exact moment, I see caramel eyes glaring over at me from the makeshift bar, the floodlights shining around her and making her look like a sexy fuckin' angel.

Shit! I thought that when she left me, she left the club, but no. Her eyes fix on me as I pull Jewel into my lap—I'm so fixated on Kelly that I barely even feel Jewel rubbing her ass up against my dick. Those deep golden eyes burn into me as she talks to Jade and the rest of the women, but when Jewel pulls my hard dick out of my jeans, she tears her gaze away from me and turns back to Zara, twisting her body away from me.

I can see she's pissed, and I just know she's fighting with herself not to come over and tempt me with the sinfully sexy body under those clothes. The image of her on her knees flits through my brain and I groan, my head dropping back as Jewel starts to jerk me off. My dick is pulsating; desperate to be inside something warm and tight.

"Dags?" Jewel breathes heavily in my ear.

I lift my head to look at her. She's not a bad-looking woman, but definitely older than Kelly, that's for damn sure. She's gotta be 29, 30 maybe.

"Yeah?" I grunt out, annoyed that she's stopped jerking me off.

"Want me to suck you off? You seem tense," she tells me, then carries on jerking me off and starts nibbling on my neck.

I think about refusing at first, but I know Kelly is over there—maybe seeing this will open her eyes to the fact that this is me, and I ain't gonna change for any golden pussy.

"Yeah, fuck it, I am tense and it's my birthday. Go get me a couple more drinks, and then I want your mouth on my cock. Go!" I bark at her. I can be a bastard sometimes. especially when I'm horny as fuck, but Jewel obediently sashays her little ass over to the bar area to get drinks, walking right past all the rest of the women chatting.

I see Kelly glance over at me with a hurt look and I smile back at her.

That's right. This is me; I'm Dagger, I'm 40 years old, and I want an assortment of pussy.

My smile slips as I hear a tiny voice screaming, *Even if yours is golden and the best tasting I've ever had!*

***

Kelly

I get that he's not comfortable with my age, but I'm 25, nearly 26, and he's only 15 years older than me for Christ's sake!

My eyes are locked on him and Jewel, and he stares straight back at me, daring me to come over and say something. I ain't gonna give him the satisfaction. He can't tell me what he did with me in there wasn't right, and if he thinks so, he's fucking deluded.

He has no idea how wrong he is. I've asked countless dates, boyfriends, and one night stands to do exactly what he did with me in his room, but they've always been like the slowest horse in the derby—never able to cross the finishing line.

I've always wanted to feel the freedom of someone else being in control of my pleasure. I don't even know when my taste turned that way, but it has. Unlike for most women, it's nothing to do with '*50 Shades*' or '*Secretary*'—even though they are both hot.

Ever since I was young, I've always been careful to be a certain way and keep control of what I do and how I feel. Because I care what the world outside my family and friends thinks of me, it's a well-rehearsed performance I hardly ever let drop. But the thought of letting someone else take over my wants and needs the way Dagger did…it sets my whole body on fire. I can still feel the wetness pooling in my pussy.

I wasn't ever fully satisfied with my previous partners because they didn't understand my needs, and at one stage I signed up to a dating site to my tastes, but I didn't want a relationship like that. I'm too free-spirited to be a 24/7 submissive, but I want someone to take care of me and help me drop the mask. Dagger gave me the tip of the iceberg of what I could have tonight, and I want the whole glacier now. I know he would dominate my body like he did my mouth.

My stomach drops when I see Jewel get his dick out—the dick I had in my mouth and swallowed cum from not long ago. I know I have no claim over him, but the sight stings, especially when I can still taste him even after all the Jack Daniels shots and Cuba Libres Tinhead made me. Men say that each pussy tastes different, but it's the exact same for men too. I remember one man I slept with tasted so sour I thought my taste buds had shriveled up.

I can't watch anymore, so turn around to actually listen to the girls' conversations, feeling guilty when I see the expectant look on Zara's face.

Oh shit, did she say something? Think, Kelly, think!

"Kel'? You all right?" Dani asks me, swirling her drink in her hand.

"Yeah, sorry. What were you saying?" I ask the girls, looking between them.

Jade's eyes widen knowingly. "I KNEW IT! Oh my God! Nooo! You didn't?!" she nearly screams in my ear.

My eyes swivel to look at her; she looks like she's about to explode with word vomit. She gives me a gleeful grin, then the crazy girl starts bouncing up and down screeching in my ear, "Did you?! Did you *do it*?"

"Jade, you're gonna have to calm the hell down! What are ya…?"

"Did you have sex with Dagger?!" she blurts out.

The rest of the girls gasp, and I hear Sue chuckle.

Tinhead, Axe and Flex groan in the background—fucking hell, that girl was not quiet—and I swear I hear Tinhead say, "Knew the old Dags had it in him!"

"Jade!" I shush her through clenched teeth, grabbing her arm so my fingernails bite into her skin. A quick glance back tells me Dagger was too busy talking to Jewel to notice. "No, I didn't have sex with him…but I fucking wanted to!" I let out the last part on a sigh, not realizing I've said it until it's out there in the open, but not being able to shove the words back in my mouth.

"Oh okay…hold up, so what did happen? You and Dagger disappear, then you reappear and so does Dagger not long after. Come on, Kelly; when have you ever not spilled the beans?"

I know she's right, and I need to hear what Sue says about it all—she's known him the longest.

"We didn't have sex but I…I sucked his dick, okay? It was more than that…but I can't really explain it. Out of nowhere, he started going on about my age—he's so hung up on the fact he's older that he can't—or won't—see what's right here ready for the taking. I ain't him, but if I was, I would be taking my fill."

"Wowzas! I wasn't expecting that, Kellybean. Was it intense? He seems the type—the quiet ones usually are,"

Jade asks, throwing her arm over my shoulder as the girls huddle closer to me.

"It was *so* intense, Jadey. It felt like there was electricity running through me. "

"It's not like Dagger to have reservations, Kelly. For as long as I have known that man, he has taken what he wanted and given what he deemed fit no matter the circumstances. Not having sex because of the age difference is a new one..." Sue says, trailing off thoughtfully.

"I can't change my age any more than he can. *His* age doesn't bother *me*; it never has. I don't see numbers when I look at him, all I know is that I'm drawn to him. I can't explain it..."

"None of us can explain it, and we have all had the same affliction with our men. Just wait him out Kelly, he hasn't torn his eyes off you since he sat down with Jewel; I thought you were going to catch on fire his stare was so intense. Maybe he's not so hung up on the age gap after all. With that nugget of hope, baby girl, I'm gonna go and get my old man and get into bed. Night night, sweethearts," Sue says, giving us all her famous Momma Bear hugs before she heads inside.

I take a thoughtful sip of my drink. *Hmm, so there's hope yet...*

***

"Oh, for fuck's sake," I hear Jewel curse behind us. Glancing over my shoulder, I see that she's knocked over one of the beers she just opened.

Really Dagger, sending her over here? Could you be any more blatant?

I see she has an unopened bottle of Jack and four beers—well, technically three beers now.

Jenna goes over to help her clean the makeshift bar top and opens a fresh beer for Jewel. "Here ya go hon, d'ya need any help carrying them over?"

"Oh, no thanks Jenna, thank you for the offer though. I'll catch you girls later; I've got the birthday boy to look after."

Jealousy floods down my back like a bucket of ice-cold water. I fix a stare on her, watching her juggle the drinks over the uneven grass as she holds her skimpy top up and heads right over to settle in Dagger's lap.

I go to turn toward them, but Jade stops me

"Kelly, don't. He ain't worth it, he's drunk. Forget it okay?" Jade tells me, wrapping her arm around me.

Shaking my head free of the hurt, I twist out of her hold, march back to the bar, and grab the tequila. I might normally hold it well—better than well, I *am* Mexican—but this many drinks in, it's a surefire way to get the party started and forget everything—I know how it's gonna go down.

"LADIES! TEQUILA!" I holler in a sing-song voice at the top of my lungs. I'm louder than usual thanks to the alcohol and hurt running through my veins, but I don't care. I need to drown out these thoughts of Dagger, so the louder the better.

***

"Yes Zar', shot, shot, shot! Yes! Woohoo!" we all scream.

Flex, Axe, Bear, and Tinhead are all admiring their women, and I don't know if he's staring at it or what, but my ass feels hot.

Is that normal? It can't be. Fuck, all I wanted to do was drink and forget him…

"Kel'—*hic*—it's your go!" Zara tells me.

"Doubles! Doubles! Doubles!" the girls chant.

I look round at them all. Jenna had to stop after one round as she can't stomach anymore, and Dani's propped up against Jenna, egging me, Jade, and Zara on.

I snatch up the bottle, shaking it.

I guess that's about double…fuck it.

I finish the bottle in two big gulps and feel the exact moment it hits the pit of my stomach, mixing with the rest of the booze there in a way that makes it churn.

"Jeeezus Kel', you okay?" I see Jade's face, my vision blurring around the edges as I stumble over to the grassy area. I feel her arms wrap around me as she tries to pull me back to the club, but my feet keep moving.

She tugs at me again, her words slightly muffled. "What a fucking bastard…come on babe, you don't need to see that."

I'm not sure what she's talking about; everything is so freaking blurry, merging into one colorful mess…at least until I see a flash of dark copper hair.

I can just about make out the outline of the old steel drum the club uses as a fire pit behind him, flickering flames lighting his hair up like the sun.

"Fuck, harder! Harder!"

Before I can see where the cry comes from, I feel myself trip over something that I realize a moment later is Jade's foot.

"Oh shit, sorry."

"What ya sssaying ssssorry for Jadey?" I slur out, glancing over my shoulder at her.

I see her eyes grow round with alarm as they flick between me and whatever's in front of me. Turning my head back around, my eyes land on Dagger's boots, which are only inches away from my face. I hear him grunting and moaning just like he did when I was sucking his beautiful cock just hours ago—the same beautiful cock that fills Jewel's mouth.

Shit! Shiiit, I feel sick…

The effects of my drinking come to the surface, and my mouth instantly fills with saliva, making me heave.

Oh shit! No, not now!

Before I can stop it, the acid bile bubbling in my stomach erupts like Krakatoa and Mount Vesuvius combined. I empty the whole contents of my stomach on the grass just left of Dagger's boots, but I still can't stop heaving and retching, my stomach finally protesting all at the tequila, Jack and Cokes, wine, and cocktails, as well as the birthday cake Dagger fed me.

The next thing I know, someone's holding my hair back away from my face—how embarrassing.

As the music blares on, I realize that the 'couple' by my head have stopped grunting and moaning.

How considerate of them…

The hand holding my hair disappears, reappearing again on my back a moment later.

"You okay?"

My whole body freezes. *Dagger* is the one rubbing up and down my back!

He stops, picking up on the change in me. "Kelly?"

I turn and look behind me through my eyelashes, noticing the concerned look on Dagger's handsome face.

Bastard…

"Kelly, are you okay?" Jade says as her voice draws closer to me.

I don't look at her, unable to tear my eyes away from his face even if it is blurry.

"Yeah Jadey, I'm okay."

"Here babe, I got you some water and some tissues."

I see Jade handing them to me, but Dags snatches them out of her hands before I can take them, uncapping the water bottle, he balls up a tissue and drips some water on it.

What's he doing that for?

He takes my chin between his thumb and forefinger, tilting it up and gently holding me in place as he dabs at my mouth with the tissue.

"You got some puke here. Stop pulling away, I don't care. With the amount you were chugging, it's a wonder you haven't got alcohol poisoning…silly little girl."

"Don't! Don't ssssay that, Dagger."

"You've done enough, move," Jade snaps, making him drop my chin, a frown marring his brow.

I smile weakly up at her. "Thank you for the water, Jade. Can you take me to your room?"

"Yeah, come on. You can sleep there; Tinhead and I will take a guest room." She reaches down, grabbing both of my hands as Dagger stands up to move out the way.

I know he's right and I was silly to get so drunk, but I was and still am mad at him for the way he's treated me.

Jade wraps her arm around me, and I feel Dagger's piercing gaze on my back for every step Jade walks me back to the club. I stumble around the corner, relieved to be away from the onlookers—well, mainly Dagger's sexy piercing glare. As I collapse against the gravel wall, I see that Jade has a cruel smirk on her face.

"Jade? What is it?"

"No matter how much what happened between you and Dagger hurt you—which you *will* tell me all the details about tomorrow, by the way—I think you got your own back perfectly on him."

"What're ya talkin' about babe? I'm too drained to think; the bastard forgot aftercare earlier."

Jade beams. "He was so close to cumming, but you stopped him when you puked. HA! You truly cockblocked the asshole and gave him blue balls!"

~ Chapter 12 Kelly ~

Jeezus, my head is pounding!

I roll over in bed—a bed that definitely isn't mine judging by the sinking middle of the mattress—then crack one eye open to find the room is mostly in darkness apart from a dim table lamp and a pool of bright light in the far corner of the where the curtains on the window stop short.

God, I'm gasping for water! My mouth feels like a camel's toes…

I try and wiggle up into a sitting position, then look over and notice the Tylenol and big glass of cold water on the nightstand along with a cute little message on a sticky note.

'Kellybean,
Hope you're feeling better, come find me and the rest of the girls in the kitchen when you're awake. Love ya xx'

Grabbing my cell off the table and bringing the screen to life, I see it's 9:43am. I inwardly groan at how lousy I feel, but I could murder some food and a huge-ass mug of coffee with sugar and a little half-and-half to wake me up a bit.

Shuffling my ass off the bed and standing, I proceed to sip the cool glass of water, which is cold and delicious on my dry throat. Thirst quenched, I swallow the two Tylenol and shuffle my pants from last night back on, spotting a shirt that Jade left for me at the end of the bed along with a pair of cherry-red sliders—she's the best. The sliders are a size too big, but the shirt fits perfectly, and at least I don't have to walk out of this room with last night's outfit on.

In the bathroom, I splash my face with cool water and check the state of myself in the mirror above the basin. I don't look as bad I thought I would, apart from big panda eyes—I'm just grateful I didn't put on heavy eyeshadow last night.

Grabbing tissues from the box on the counter, I make quick work of wiping under my eyes, and remember I have a few of my trusty make up essentials in my purse, which has been helpfully placed to one side of the sink. Grabbing that, I reapply some cover-up under my eyes and put on some pearlized Chapstick and some blush cream, dabbing it on the apple of my cheeks.

After cleaning up, I decide that I'd better go and show my face—otherwise I'm sure Jadey will come for me herself. Double-checking my reflection and readjusting my top to give the 'girls' the best look I can with what I have, I grab ahold of my purse again, hoisting it over my shoulder. After walking out of the bathroom, I make sure I haven't left too much of a mess in the room.

Once I'm satisfied it's not too bad, I stride through the door and back into the hall. The rich, salty smell of bacon and eggs fills the air, and I can hear distant, muffled talking coming from the kitchen. Following the sound, I walk in to Sue talking about what she has planned today.

"I've gotta go get some more groceries first, but how about I make my famous homemade chili?"

"That sounds the bomb," Zara grins. "What about—"

"Sue, sign me up for that bad boy, but I may have to take mine to go—I need to get back to the shop," I interrupt her as I enter the kitchen.

Jade and the rest of the girls turn around to see me walk in.

"Oh, look what the cat dragged in. Come and sit down, young lady, and tell us what happened last night. First, what would you like to eat, sweetheart?" Sue asks me as she comes over, wraps her arm around my shoulders in a motherly hug, and pulls me toward the big table my girls sit at. I plop my ass onto the free seat next to Jade and Zara.

"Hey. How are ya feeling, Kel'?" Jade asks, giving me a lopsided smile and tilting her head to one side. She's wearing cute cut-offs and her favorite cherry-red tank top, and her wavy hair is tied up in a loose bun,

"I'm okay, babe, honestly. Just feel slightly humiliated at puking right next to Dagger's feet."
I turn to Sue. "Sue, can I have some eggs and bacon? Thank you."

"Yeah, sure sweetie. Would you like some coffee too?"

"Please, with creamer and sugar," I respond, giving her a smile.

"Oh Kelly. Don't be, he won't have cared about anything other than his blue balls from what I hear..." Zara quips.

Dani hums. "I think you're *kinda* right."

I turn to her. "Why only kinda?"

"When Jade took you back to her room, Dagger abandoned his pursuit of getting his dick wet and tried to drink himself into oblivion—although that was before I got into bed."

"Yeah, Dani's right—we went to bed after her and Axe, and he was still at it with Jewel nowhere in sight. God knows how that man can drink so much," Jenna interjects.

God, I don't want to think about him and Jewel together. Kill me now!

I don't reply to any of them, and thankfully Sue comes back over and slides over my plate of food and cup of coffee in front of me and squeezes my shoulder before going back to cooking. I start stabbing at my eggs, practically inhaling them. They melt in my mouth, and rich creaminess hits my tongue—they taste so good.

Swallowing my mouthful, I grab my cup of coffee and gulp half of it down before changing the subject from Dagger and Jewel. "Why the hell are people so obsessed with age? Is it a bigger issue for everyone else than it is for me? I'd get it if I was 14 and he was 40, but I'm 25 for fuck's sake!" I say, waving my forkful of salty, crispy bacon at them.

"Oh sweetie. That man is just like all these bikers once were—they soon get their heads outta their asses," Sue tells me from across the kitchen. "Doc was a stubborn mule with me too at first. I was working at the local grocery store he came into, I asked him on a date, and he told me he wasn't the right man for me, but he still kept coming into the shop, so I persisted. Eventually, I wore him down, and then that stubborn mule claimed me right there and then. He put me on the back of his bike, and I've never looked back since. Even when we found out I couldn't give him children, the Alpha biker in him came out in full force, and he said he was too selfish to share me anyway…even though I adopted Axe, Flex, Dagger, Bear, Tinhead, Brains and Wrench when they came into the club. I love all of them boys like they were my own, and so does Doc."

"Aww Sue, I love that Doc gave in and was too stubborn to let you go, but I doubt me and Dags will ever get to that. Even so, I can't stop thinking about him and how he makes me feel. I don't get like this over just any man."

Jade nods. "It's true, Sue. Me and Jenna were saying last night that we've never seen her like this before."

I can't meet the girls' eyes, and decide to eat the rest of my breakfast in silence and get gone—I need to get home and sort shit out.

***

"*Hola Mamá. No, salí con Jade.*"

"*Sabes cómo me preocupo a Kelly,*" my Mom tells me.

"*Mamá,* stop speaking in Spanish! It's not fair on Dad," I chastise her. Even though my Dad can speak perfect Spanish, I still think it's rude.

"Your *Papi* can understand, you know this full well, and you know I love to use my mother tongue. So where did you go with Jade?" she enquires.

She and my Dad have always been overly cautious with my safety—they say it's because of me being the only child and Dad being a cop in the next town over. While I could be annoyed that they forget I'm 25 with my own apartment and business, I would never forget what they did for me in setting me up with both. I will always be forever grateful.

"We went to the club for Dagger's birthday party. It was…a really nice night. What are you up to, *Mamá*? I'm just in the shop going through paperwork," I ask, keen to stop thinking about the kind of night it really was as a pang of hurt tears through me.

Being typical *Mamá,* she ignores my question and goes straight for the mention of a man's name.

"Dagger? What kind of name is that, *Niña?* You like him, yes? What are you doing working on a Sunday at 11:30? *Niña,* you know you shouldn't be working on Sundays—you work too hard as it is."

I inwardly groan.

"*Mamá*, it's not his *real* name! It's a road name for the club...Don't worry about me working too late, okay? I find working in the salon easier than at home, I can concentrate more and everything I need is here—I have all my receipts and my appointment book. So, what're ya up to, Mom?"

"Kelly Isabella Davis, do not avoid the question. Do you like this Dagger or not?"

"Maria Isabella Leticia Davis," I counter, mimicking her. We do this a lot, we're both stubborn as each other. "Drop it, okay? You're not getting any more information off of me, and if you don't let it go, I won't come over for dinner tonight..."

I know it's a catty thing to do to her, but my threat is empty—Sunday dinners are our family thing, and I would never not turn up.

"*Niña*, don't try and threaten your *Mamá;* you know as well as I do you that will be here at six o'clock sharp, my young girl. Your *Papi* will be home from a night shift soon and he's gonna to be asleep until four, so I need to vacuum before he gets home, but I'll see you tonight, baby."

"Okay *Mamá*, see you tonight. *Te amo.*"

"Te amo, cariño."

After ending the phone call, I just stare at my phone, still in shock at my mom's prying. I can't believe her sometimes.

I looking at the clock on the wall with a sigh.

It's nearly lunchtime and I still have so much to do! I'd better get on with it...

***

"Despacito, Quiero respirar tu cuello despacito. Deja que te diga cosas al oído. Para que te acuerdes..."

Luis Fonsi blares out of my car speakers as I pull up on my parents' driveway, letting the quiet neighborhood know the loud *Mexicana* is back. It's a good neighborhood and we have good neighbors, but that doesn't mean I don't see them looking at me and silently wondering why I can't be quiet like my *Mamá* whenever I visit.

Yeah, that's never gonna happen...as she and Dad always say, I have enough of the loud Mexican personality in me for the both of us.

I switch off the engine and jump out next to my Dads new navy Chrysler SUV. He always has such nice cars that no one ever believes he's a police officer, but he just works and saves hard. I grab my sandals from the passenger seat, shoving my bare feet in them before I walk toward the house. The garage door is open slightly—just enough for someone to bend under, which means Dad must be doing something.

"Hey Dad! You in there?" I holler.

I'm just about to stoop and clamber underneath the door when it starts moving upwards to reveal the best man ever and my first love—my Daddy. His black hair is slightly sprinkled with salt and pepper patches either side of his head these days, and his tanned Floridan skin is even darker than usual. In fact, he could easily pull off being Mexican himself. His deep navy-blue eyes crinkle at the corners as he smiles at me.

He's why I have never settled for anyone less than I think I'm worth—he and *Mamá* have shown me the importance of being with someone who makes you their world and looks at you the way they both look at each other after all these years.

"Baby girl, you got here early! Come and give ya Dad a hug. You okay?" I hear an extra hint of curiosity in his tone, which means that Mama has been in his ear about me. They just need to chill out.

I get pulled into a big bear hug and wrap my arms around his waist. His familiar scent greets me, reminding me of a lifetime of hugs from scraped knees, broken arms, and being bullied at school.

"Yeah, I'm good Dad. So what's for dinner this week? Chimichangas?" I ask as I pull away from him.

He has that look in his eye I know well from seeing it whenever I was hiding something from him—mainly Brett, my first boyfriend. I couldn't help it, every boy at school was scared of dating me because of my Dad. I expect him to grill me about Dagger, but to my relief, he doesn't.

"Nope, monkey, not chimis. We are having steak, baked potatoes, salad, and slaw," he beams at me like a kid in a candy store.

One thing guaranteed to make my Dad happy at dinner is my *Mamá's* steak and baked potato dinners. She marinates the meat in her special secret sauce—me and Dad don't know what's in it, but it's smoky, sweet, and spicy all at once, and it makes the steak melt in your mouth.

"Mmm. What are you doing in the garage anyway?"

"Just sorting through my toolbox for something. Go in and see your Mom; she'll only come looking for you."

He gives me a wink and jokingly digs an elbow into my ribs to get me to go and see my Mom.

I smile and head towards the garage door that leads to the house. "Okay, okay, I'm going. How long are ya going to be?" I enquire with one foot on the stairs to the kitchen, looking back at him over my shoulder.

"Not long…ten minutes or so," he replies back as he carries on rifling through his toolbox.

***

"*Mamá*, I can't eat anymore! Why can't I give Pedro the rest of my steak? He wants it, don't ya Ped'?" I look down at the family dog we adopted when I was 16, who waits patiently at my feet for any tidbits I might drop. Pedro is a Pitbull-Beagle mix; he has the cream and pale tan coloring of a Beagle, but his body and face structure is a blend of both breeds. He's loyal as they come and not a fan of strangers, especially men. He's also inseparable from my parents—except for when I'm over or there's food.

"*Niña,* no! He'll get fat, and at his age any extra weight isn't good for him. You know that."

I give my *Mamá* my own puppy dog eyes, batting my eyelashes, but she just rolls her eyes at me. She really is just like an older version of me, and we even look similar; we have a lot of the same features and we're the same height, but her boobs are a couple of sizes bigger than mine. Where my dark hair is far past my shoulders, hers is cut into a long bob. Our donkey booties are the same, even though she swears hers has more 'shelf' to it.

HA! In her dreams.

"*Mamá*, he deserves a treat; he hasn't seen his big sister for a week. He's missed me!"

"Haven't you, Pedro?" I say to him, giving him a big kiss on top of his cream-and-tan head and leaving a huge red lipstick mark on his fur.

I glance back up to my Mom and see she has a bemused look on her face. Spearing her last piece of steak, she lifts it up to her lips and lets it linger in front of her mouth, then looks quickly at my Dad and says, "So, *Niña,* are you gonna tell me and your *Papi* about this man called Dagger?"

Two weeks after my 40th birthday party…

"Settle down, you miserable bastards! We have another sale of the merch from Matteo taking place at the end of next week—they're wanting to take about 500; 200 Glock 44s, 150 of the G45, and 150 of the .357 SIG's."

Axe looks at me. "Dags, you'll be coming with me, Brains, and Tin. We'll be leaving north out of the compound. Flex, you'll go with Bear, Wrench, and Doc; I want you to leave south out of the compound seven minutes later. I doubt anything will happen while we're gone, but I want the club on lockdown until we all get back just in case. After church is done, I'll tell all the women and club girls out in the main room; Rebel and Red are coming down in case of trouble as we'll all be at the deal. Matteo is planning on being there for the deal as well—he said his contact is a bit temperamental but has known him a while. We'll be meeting him there too. Any questions so far?"

Fucking hell…our second encounter with the Italian Mafia boss, Matteo Giordano.

He's classically Italian-looking, with dark hair, dark eyes, and the even darker soul of a man who has killed at least a thousand men and tortured thousands more. Some might say he's dead behind the eyes, but I have seen many men with that look, and Giordano's are different. He has dealt out death as casually as if he were dealing out a deck of cards; appearing detached, cool, unemotional, and glacial. That man has no fear behind his eyes; just the cold-blooded calm of a calculating predator. From what I've heard, his approach is merciless; no sympathy given, he just neutralizes threats like a machine that's been programmed that way.

"No questions about the plan here boss, but how many of the guns we got left after the deal? We good?" Tinhead enquires while playing with his bike keys, tossing them back and forth.

"We have about 3200 left, so we're doing really well on numbers. Ideally, I want them all gone within six months, because I don't want to draw any more attention to the club than we have to. I ain't about going to jail and leaving my woman and boy for years. We just gotta take our time and do it carefully. The meet up is at 9:30pm sharp at a location about an hour and 20 minutes away on the Mississippi River. That's it for club business from me, anyone else got anything they want to bring to the table?"

One by one we go around the table and respond "No" to Axe's question, and once Flex gives the last response, he slams the gavel down on the worn-out wooden table.

"Go grab yourselves a drink; I'll be out soon to talk to the women regarding the lockdown next week."

We all get up now we've been dismissed and filter back through to the main room to drink together.

***

Grabbing myself my last ice-cold beer of the night and some salted chips, I see that it's getting close to 10:30pm. I need to crash soon, but I'm horny as fuck.

I park my ass back on the corner couch in the main room, settling next to the club girls hanging around Wrench and Brains. Watching Jewel's ass shimmy and shake as she dances near Wrench is definitely not helping my horniness, especially since she is wearing pale blue denim cutoffs that show off her bouncing ass, reminding me of Kelly...

Shiiit!

My head flops back to rest on the back of the couch and I take another swig of the sweet blend of hops. I clench my eyes shut, and as the nectar slips down my throat, I swear I can feel Kelly's pussy walls fluttering against my fingers...

If only I took my chance to go all the way and cuffed her to the bed...

I picture her with spreaders holding her open for me and a love egg in her tight pussy, anal beads peeking out from between those lush ass cheeks. If I could just fuck her, this infatuation would be over and I could sink my dick into some club girls without imagining her face.

Fuuuck, tonight is gonna be a long one for my hand...

***

A week later, en route to the gun deal...

"Yo boss, those coordinates Matteo's right-hand man gave us lead us to County Road 404 just off of Donaldson Point," Brains' voice crackles through the speakers in my lid. We have just left the compound, and I'm riding behind Axe. Brains and Tin are in the cage behind us, and we are looping around and meeting the rest of our brothers on Route 155.

"Okay, Brains. Radio silence from now on unless 911, okay?" Axe replies curtly. I can feel the tension coming off of him in waves. It's not Matteo himself—he took a liking to Axe during the last deal, to all of our surprise. Instead, I think it's the fact that Matteo has warned him about his contact.

After a few minutes, we meet up with the rest of our brothers with no problems. I pull back to let Flex pull in front of me, then I drift to the side to let Bear into the formation. As I do, Axe comes back on the radio.

"Any problems?" he says. I know from experience that he's asking about police presence or other followers.

"None at all, boss," Flex replies over the radio, and then we are back to radio silence. We can all take a breather and enjoy the ride more than we did when we last met up with Matteo, that's for damn sure.

***

Axe comes back on over the radio as we pull off of MO-WW onto Highway AB. "Remember what I told you. I know you will all be on the lookout anyway, but stay extra vigilant—we don't know who this buyer is. No one leave their back exposed, okay? All right, we need to travel a little farther up here, and then there's a clearing just up on the left to pull into. It's behind a forest area away from the main county road."

Flicking my eyes down to my display, I see that we are twenty minutes early for the meet.

Great! We can scope the area out.

Pulling off the county road leading to the 'clearing' Axe mentioned, I see that it's essentially a dirt road surrounded by bushland, trees, and forest. This is a good spot. The mild night is exactly what I love about riding—

the cool air washing over my face and now-shorter hair and beard feels great in this heat.

Axe and Flex pull into a spot hidden off the dirt track that's only reachable by bike or car, parking up behind a huge-ass ancient tree. Bear and the rest of my brothers follow suit, parking as close together as they can, and I slide in last before Wrench slots the cage next to Axe.

After we've all pulled off our lids, Axe turns to us all and says, "Let's go and take a piss before they get here."

Axe goes first, then Bear and Wrench, with Doc following after. Flex, Tin, Brains and I wait for them to return.

"How ya doing there Dags? Not as bad a ride as the last time we met the Italian Mafia boss, right?" Tin quips as he steps down from the cage. Brains does the same, and they both slide their guns into their back pockets.

"Oh, hell yes! Anything's better than that long-ass journey. Who are you thinking will turn up first?" I ask my brother.

"I think the 'Boss' will, going from past experience. He runs a tight ship by all accounts; Brains did some more background checks on him."

"Yeah, Tin's right. I'm waiting for my contacts in the FBI and Interpol to get back to me with some more information on him. I'm looking forward to some interesting reads; we only have basic stuff right now." Brains glances over my shoulder.

"Ah, the Prez is back. V.P., you want to go?" he asks Flex.

"Yes," Flex strides over to where the others are just coming back from, catching Axe on the way and slapping him on the back as he walks to another spot to piss.

***

It's not long once we're all back to our spots before we see flashes of head lights coming through the breaks in the tree branches.

"I see about three sets of headlights coming up the track, boss. Want me to flash our headlights so they see us?" Tin asks, leaning against the side of the cage,

"Yeah Tin, just once, but slow, yeah?" Axe replies without looking away from the headlights coming closer.

Tin does what Axe instructs him, and we see the headlights start to pull into the clearing where we are waiting.

As much as I'm wary of Matteo Giordano, I breathe a sigh of relief when we see his entourage of Maserati SUVs roll to a stop opposite us, I'm not a huge fan of cars, but fuck, you gotta be blind or stupid or fucking both not to appreciate the hell out of his cars. They're black, sleek, powerful, and understated. You might think a 'Boss' would drive a Ferrari or a Lambo, but they draw too much attention; Maseratis are understated.

The driver doors on the left and right cars open and Leo steps out of the left one. He's Matteo's second in line, underboss, right-hand man, or whatever you want to call him, and he's a tall fucker—much bigger than Flex, easily 6"6'. He's also bulkier than all of us put together—and not from eating too much pasta, that's for damn sure. For some reason, his haircut is a lot shorter than the rest of the entourage.

Nico jumps out of the right hand car and goes to open the back right door of the middle car just as Tomma exits the other side of it. He's got the same build as Tinhead, but a similar haircut to Nico and Lorenzo that appears to be a necessity to be in the Giordano Mafia family.

Nico's about Bear's size, also with the shared Giordano military buzz-cut, and looks similar to Lorenzo—so much so that they could be twins. Lorenzo himself gets out of the middle car's driver's side door and comes to stand in front of the car.

Axe steps forward as Matteo the Italian Mafia boss exits the car through the door Nico holds open for him. He's dressed in all black, his elegant suit sharply contrasting our rough-around-the-edges look. He saunters over to meet Axe, and Flex and Leo step forward to talk to each other.

Once their greetings are over, Axe shouts over his shoulder, "Dags, Bear, Doc, Tin, Brains, Wrench, here," a look of concern written all over his face.

I flick my head over to the others, and Bear catches my eye, his expression resembling my thoughts exactly as confusion mars his brow.

We stride over to meet the rest of the men, me silently flanking Flex as the rest of our brothers gather around us.

Leo stands next to Matteo, and I notice he's dressed more casually than his boss in an all-black shirt and tie combo instead of an expensive designer suit.

"*Buona Sera*, gentlemen. As I was just telling Axe, this contact I have set up with you tonight is abnormally…what are the words…unstable and erratic. You may have heard of him; his name is Raúl Ramírez. He's the leader of the Mexican Cartel, and an *uomo minuscuolo* with a tiny brain—don't be fooled by the way he looks. He uses his own supply, which makes him extremely dangerous and volatile."

"Boss, I can see some headlights coming—he's here," Tinhead informs us all.

"One more thing. Don't make any sudden movements around him…He's always on edge," Matteo cautions us as he straightens his expensive suit jacket and flicks some invisible lint off of it.

My eyes move from Matteo the Mafia boss to my own boss, giving him the side eye. His eyes meet mine before making the slightest movement towards Bear. As he steps forward to stand next to Matteo, I do as he told me and slip into line behind him and Bear, whilst Flex moves to stand in front of me in our usual bike formation.

We stand there a moment, watching and waiting within the forest clearing under the canopy, until all of a sudden four Land Rovers pull into the small clearing, monstrosities compared to our bikes and Matteo's understated cars. With custom paint jobs and shiny chrome rims, these things are pimped out to high heaven. They park at the end of the makeshift entrance to the clearing, effectively blocking us all in.

I risk a glance to my left at Bear and see he's not liking this at all either. I take a look to my right and catch Tinhead's eyes scanning every inch of the scene in front of us. I know he's solid in these situations, especially after he battled some mental wounds not long ago, so it's clear to me that he's sizing up our options, exits, and best strategy.

My focus is brought back to the scene ahead of me by the sounds of car doors being slammed. I move my gaze back over to our 'guests' and watch as one by one each drivers' side door opens and what I can only describe as 'thugs' exit. They're not dressed in suits like the Giordano guys, just black combat wear, including black military boots and black camo jackets. The third car's left back door opens last, and out steps another big fucker—this one similarly dressed to Matteo's right-hand man Leo. He's completely shaved, with cartel tattoos creeping up his neck. On the side of his head sits a massive black Mexican sugar skull with something crawling in and out of the eye sockets.

He steps around the front of the pimped-out matte black car with chrome rims gleaming even in the moonlight, before opening the other back door. Out steps a man I wasn't expecting at all; a small, skinny, slimy-looking worm.

Jesus, Matteo wasn't wrong about him smoking his own supply, either; his eyes are bloodshot to hell, red-rimmed, and flitting all over the place. I can see he's fidgeting with something shiny like silver in his hand, but I can't pinpoint what. He steps further into the clearing as one of his henchmen signals to Matteo and Axe with a flick of his head and they both step forward. Thankfully it's a small area, so we can all hear every word that's being said.

As much as I doubt Matteo is scared of Raúl, I know that we could have been, so I gotta take my hat off to Matteo; he didn't have to warn us about his contact.

Fuck, we were not prepared for this shit! Yet he still warned us…Why do I get a feeling this meet is as important to Matteo as it is to us?

"Raúl Ramírez, may I introduce Axe, president of the Devils Reapers MC in Tennessee. Axe, this is Raúl Ramírez, leader of the Ramírez Cartel."

Axe outstretches his hand as Matteo finishes, and the skinny runt just looks down at Axe's hand dismissing it like it disgusts him.

"Giordano says you have some guns for me. Is that right?" he sneers at Axe like he's inferior. It's like he can hardly be bothered to be here—but in truth, his facial expressions are all over the place anyway.

Axe lifts his hand up to signal to us to go grab the guns out of the cage, when all of a sudden, the thugs' guns are cocked and pointed straight at Axe.

"*¡No mames!* Is *this* Giordano?!" Raúl roars, his maniacal eyes bulging out of his sockets. His face reddens, but a sheen of sweat gathers on his forehead and temples.

We all draw our guns—including Matteo's men—pointing them straight towards him and his crew. My stance immediately changes so I'm ready to shoot my gun at a moment's hesitation, my legs spread as wide as my shoulders and my shoulders themselves back.

"Put your guns down. Now!" Matteo shouts out to Raúl's crew, but they don't waver.

He pulls out his own gun and raises it to point it straight at Raúl, lifting his chin higher. "Tell your men to stand down, Ramírez. Now! Or I shoot!"

"*¡No mames!* you brought *la policía*? You trying to set me up?!" Raúl screeches.

The man's off his head!

Raúl starts waving his gun around in the air, pacing up and down and making jerking movements here, there, and everywhere.

I watch Leo inch closer to his boss' back, obviously ready to drag him behind him if things go off.

I start inching closer to Axe. I have nothing to lose except my Ma, whereas he has Dani and Ryker to think of. Besides, who the hell is gonna miss my ugly face? An image of the tiny submissive temptress pops into my head, but I shake it away as I step closer to Axe.

"Stop right there, ya *cabrón!*" Raúl screeches like a wild banshee at me.

I stop dead in my tracks, staring at the sniveling cunt—after getting this tiny bit closer, I can see his nose is running and his nostrils are red from all the blow he's done in the car.

"Ramírez! Calm down, *stupido!* This is not *la policía.* You insult me by saying this! *I* invited you here; *I* am Matteo Giordano. Axe is a business associate of mine, and he does have some merchandise for you, but I won't repeat myself. If you and your men do not put your guns down in the next *minuto* I will give the order! Do. Not. Test. Me! You *stupidi coglioni!*" Matteo growls at him, his already thick Italian accent growing stronger. He's furious; his nostrils flaring and jaw clenched, the little cunt must be stupid or have a death wish to anger Giordano. Raúl is still not to be trifled with, that's for sure, but if I was a betting man, I would put all my money on Matteo. After all, Raúl may be unpredictable because of being off his head on coke, but it also means he's more likely to make mistakes.

Matteo is outraged, yes, but calm, and he has a vicious look in his eye. I bet he never backs down from anyone who tries to start a situation with him, no matter who they are. Axe was lucky not to get on his bad side.

The atmosphere still hasn't shifted; the anger radiating off Matteo towards the Mexican Cartel boss is intense, and Raúl's eyes stay cold for another moment before he seems to sober up and waves his men off with a flick of the wrist. They do as their boss instructs, but Matteo waits until all the guns are down and tucked away before speaking again.

"Bueno, Ramírez. Now, let's get on with this. The sooner this deal is done, the sooner we can leave and you can give me my end of the bargain."

~ Chapter 14 Dagger ~

We pull back into the compound a little after 11pm with more money to add to the bank and 500 pieces of merch lighter. I park next to Flex and just sit on my bike for a while.

"You coming, Dags?" Bear asks as he rounds my bike.

I nod. "Yeah, I'll be in in a minute, brother."

I gaze across the compound and see Kelly's car parked next to Jenna and Jade's Beetle.

Fuck, what's she doing here? I bet Jade or Zara invited her to get under my skin, the witches…

Zara in particular has been onto me for months— when I asked her to cut my hair, she kept asking whether I was cutting it for someone special and smirking.

I shake my head; I need a drink after that highly-strung night. I unhook my leg from my bike and saunter back into the clubhouse, which is filled with the sound of Black Sabbath's *'Iron Man'*

Ahh, my heart song. I love it.

Rounding the corner to the main room I see Zara and Dani bellowing the lyrics out into each other's faces as Axe and Flex smirk at them from the bar.

"Dags, I got you two Buds! you look like you need them, brother," Bear hollers over to me, his arm wrapped around Jenna's waist possessively.

I walk over to the bar and pick them up. "Thanks, bud, you got that right. I'm going to go drink them on the couch."

I love my brothers and all, but I do like the quiet too; I enjoy sitting in solitude and clearing my head—well, as much as anyone can in a noisy club.

Plopping my old ass on the middle seat of the empty couch, I prop my feet up, keeping one bottle of Bud in hand and the other on the table in front of me. My body relaxes into the smooth, soft leather and I've just decided to close my eyes for a split-second when I feel the couch cushion next to me dip slightly and a hand run up and down my left arm. Brandy's distinct perfume surrounds me in a thick cloud.

"Penny for your thoughts, Dags?" she enquires huskily as she carries on stroking my arm and pushing her fake breasts into it. I open my eyes a crack and look through the slits of them at her.

"I'm all right, Brandy, it's just been a long-ass day, I'm just going to chill out, drink a couple of Buds, and then crash," I mutter to her around the bottle of Bud in my mouth.

One thing Brandy doesn't get is subtlety; she keeps rubbing herself up against me. I'm about to push her off my leg when I hear Kelly's giggle growing louder from opposite the bar.

My eyes catch sight of the temptress. I can't seem to tear my stare from after a second, and I watch her stalk across the main room, her shiny long black hair bouncing around her shoulders as she walks. She's wearing the tightest red leopard print dress I ever saw paired with black glittery wedged shoes that she crosses at the ankles as she perches her juicy ass on the bar stool.

Fuckin' hypnotic!

Seeing movement, my gaze flicks down to the ice-cream bar she's lifting to her lips in her right hand, and watching her eat it has me harder than forged steel. She starts licking the chocolate ice-cream from base to tip, then the she-devil of a siren lures my focus in further— not with her song, but her oral skills. She's deepthroating that motherfucker like the pro she is, swirling her tongue around it from base to tip, then going back to deepthroating it nice and slow.

Doesn't she realize everyone's staring at her? Wait, of course she does—she knows exactly what she's doing. Even the other women are looking over.

Brandy groans. "Shit! If that girl sucks ice cream like that, I would love her to lick me out! Fuck, that's hawt!"

She has no idea what that mouth can do…

The memories of my party come flooding back, and I can almost feel her lips wrapped around my shaft, taking me right to the back of her throat…

Shit, I'm readjusting myself just watching her devour that ice-cream!

I down the rest of my beer and grab the other one, and I'm about to shoot up out of my seat to go back to my room when Zara shouts over to me.

"Dagger! You coming over for another drink? There's a tequila here with your name on it."

Catching the cheesy-ass smile covering her face, I remember that I've gotta get Flex to tan her ass until she learns to help herself. I am about to turn on my heel to go back to my room anyway, but then Kelly turns toward me on the bar stool she's perched on. She has an enticing look on her face, those huge, mesmerizing eyes luring me in, and the sight of her lips still wrapped around the tip of that goddamn ice-cream has me rethinking my plans.

Downing some of my Bud, I saunter over to the bar where Zara and Flex sit next to Kelly, grabbing the shot Zara poured me off the bar as Kelly keeps her prolonged eye contact with me.

"So, are we all doing shots?" I grumble out to anyone who will answer, but my eyes don't move from the temptress in front of me.

Her gaze moves to my lips, and I watch her cheeks flush as she pulls that ice cream out of her own plump pouty lips, drawing the stick out from her mouth painfully slowly.

Fuck! I need to get back in that mouth again…

"Yeah, let's do shots then, shall we?" she tells me with a quirk of her manicured eyebrow.

I raise my shot in answer and she picks up hers.

Zara beams. "You're sticking around for a few drinks all of a sudden then Dags? Hmm, funny that."

"Woman, you're getting yourself into trouble! Stay for a few, brother," Flex tells me as he slaps me on the shoulder, making the aged leather of my cut creak.

I lean back so I'm close to his ear and mumble, "Brother, you *need* to spank Zara more. Wanna borrow some of my paddles?"

Chuckling, he responds as only Flex could, "Dags, you're thinking exactly what I'm thinking, but my Sugar needs a level 5 paddle."

Laughing back, I sit straighter and lift the glass to my lips, locking eyes with Kelly in an unspoken signal. We both down the shot, and I enjoy the smooth trail of fire burning down my throat.

"Want another one?" she asks me, batting her big beautiful eyes at me.

"Just make sure you don't have a repeat performance of the last time you had tequila, little girl," I retort, flashing a smirk at her.

She blushes slightly, but grabs the bottle again and promptly refills all of our glasses.

"Ready to go again…little girl?"

I love seeing the need burn in her eyes with each thigh squeeze she gives as she squirms in the bar stool, and watching each breath hitch as I repeat the name to her.

Fuck, that's beautiful.

"One, two, three. Go," she prompts us all to down our shots, then does so herself and leans back. "Woo! *¡Carajo!* That nearly hits the spot…but I need something a bit more…mature."

She turns, flashing her deep gold eyes at me and showing me they are ablaze with arousal. I would have to be blind not to know what she wants—standing this close to the woman, I can practically taste it. My dick stirs as my mind flashes back to the sweet nectar in between her juicy thighs.

"Maybe you should try some of the oldest Macallan whiskey we have then…72 years old, old enough for you?" I mumble over the lip of my beer bottle, taking a long swig as her face breaks into that sexy smile of hers, that dimple under her cheek on full show

She leans forward enough so that I can see down the top of her dress, and I spy that she's braless.

Fuck, she knows I'm gonna look, and don't I feel like a dirty old man for doing it…

My dick isn't in agreement; he wants in, pulsating as her soft, sultry voice touches my ears.

"Dagger...the only mature thing I want inside me is the man standing right in front of me, but he'd rather almost fuck another woman than *play* with the one he really wants. Such a shame..." I feel her small hand rub up my thigh, inching closer to my cock until she's almost touching the tip.

Fuck!

"Little girl...I'm too fuckin' old for you. Do you really want me to tie you up, shove a ball gag in your mouth, and fuck you raw until you can't take anymore? If you want it, I can give it to you, but that's all this can be."

I feel her nails dig into my inner thigh, and her lips are a hair's breadth away from my cheek as her voice tickles my inner ear.

"Dagger, don't pretend that you haven't dreamed about this good little girl and her golden pussy since you had your first taste; I can practically feel your cock twitch every time you look at me. Now take me back to your room and fuck me raw like we both want. I hope you have an extra-large gag, because I'm going to be screaming your name loud enough for the whole damn club to hear."

I grab her hand off my thigh, placing it over my rock-hard cock. "Feel that? That's one of many things that's going in your pretty pussy tonight," I growl out under my breath near her ear.

I hear her breath hitch, and tugging on her arm, I lower her off the stool so she stands in between my thighs. I keep a firm grip on her with one hand and down my beer with my other, slamming the empty bottle on the bar before swiftly standing and tugging Kelly behind me straight towards my room. Kelly follows obediently, trying to keep up with me. I'm going to show her exactly what I was trying to keep her from…

Pushing her up against the front of my bedroom door, I grind my dick against that ass that drives me wild. "I hope you're ready, little girl, because after I'm done with you, you're not going to be able to walk straight. Now get the fuck in there, strip, and kneel in front of my bed with your hands behind your back. Then. You're. Mine."

***

The air in my room is thick with anticipation and desire. I admire Kelly's butt-naked form as she kneels in front of my bed, hands clasped behind her back and resting at the top of that luscious ass facing me.

I've been standing here staring at this picture in front of me for about 20 minutes, and my cock's painfully hard seeing her like this—like the perfect little submissive. I see her shifting her knees uncomfortably on the hard floor. I could have put a pillow there, but I wanted to see that ass wiggle.

Pushing myself off the wall, I stalk towards the girl who drives me wild and pushes my buttons. As she hears my boots thud on the floor right behind her, I see her back straighten and her hold her breath. My hand finds the back of her hair, stroking the silky strands in between my fingers until I reach her scalp.

"So, are you ready for what I can give you? You need a safe word, so pick one. If anything gets too much, use it and I will stop what I'm doing no matter what, okay?"

"Yes. To all of it."

"You need to trust me; that's only way this is gonna happen, because I ain't about to hold back. So, what's your safe word?"

"I trust you to give me what I can take. My safe word is tequila."

I chuckle at the word. "That's good to hear, because that's exactly what I plan to do. I like your choice, though. Because you came into the club with no panties on tonight, you deserve five hard spanks—remember that word."

I remove my hand from her hair, casually go back over to the drawers on the other side of my room and open the bottom one, pulling out all the items I need to hand tonight. After fisting my favorite riding crop in one hand, gathering everything else in the other, and reclosing the drawer with my foot, I walk back to stand over Kelly.

"If I give you a request, I expect it to be upheld straight away. If you can't, use your safe word and we stop altogether. Are we clear?"

"Yes."

"Good. Now stand up and bend the top half of your body over my bed so your sexy ass is sticking right out into the air."

She does exactly what I ask of her with no hesitation whatsoever.

My palm finds her big butt cheek, squeezing it until I can see the indents of my fingertips in the caramel skin. Removing my hand, I pick up the riding crop—it's my favorite. Because I've had it a long time, the leather is worn and buttery soft, but still strong.

I drop it on the bed right beside Kelly so she can see what I'm gonna use on her. "Do you see that? That's what I'm gonna use on you three times; I'll use my hand for the last two. Now is your chance to say if you can't deal with that, Kelly."

"N-no, I want it," she stutters, the desperation and slight nervousness clear in her voice. Her eagerness has my dick aching painfully.

"That's a good girl. Ready?" I ask her.

She nods her head, so I decide to spank her once across both cheeks, just hard enough to make her skin sting.

SMACK!

"Use words, Kelly. I need to be able to hear you."

"Y-yes. Yes, I'm ready," she corrects herself quickly.

Hmm, a quick learner…

No, this is a one-time thing; just enough to get her out of your system.

"Good girl," I praise her under my breath as I pick up the crop. I'm trying to keep my eagerness under wraps from this woman, but she's under my skin.

"I want you to count with me, Kelly. Count the lashings," I instruct as I feel the crop mold into the palm of my hand like an extra limb.

SMACK!

"One," we say in unison.

SMACK!

"Two," we say louder.

Kelly's voice doesn't waver even though I spanked her harder than the first time. She's taking it really well, better than I would imagine, but this last strike with the riding crop is gonna sting.

I swing my arm back so that the riding crop whips through the air and lands right on my intended target across the top of the crack of her juicy ass. Seeing the blood rush to the surface under her skin is a beautiful sight.

"Thr-three!", she exhales, clearly catching her breath.

I drop the riding crop on the floor with a thud as I caress her ass with the palm of my hand. "You did so well. Are you ready for two more with my hand?"

"Yes, I am," she replies instantly

"Good girl." Giving her behind a final rub, I swing my hand up and strike her again, straight on the juncture where her ass meets the flesh close to that sweet pussy.

SMACK!

"Four," we count in unison again, but this time I hear the hint of something carnal in her voice. I don't want to wait to hear it again—her moans are mine for the night.

I swing my hand back up in the air and let it land back at that juncture, an inch closer to her pussy this time.

SMACK!

"Five!" Kelly cries out.

The heat radiating off of her is enticing me in, so I relent and push two fingers straight inside her pussy. She's soaked, hot, and her walls are fluttering around my fingers. I start to feel her hips move and push against them, so I quickly withdraw my fingers to halt her chasing her orgasm.

"Who said you could move your hips? *I* decide when I let you cum, not you. Do I need to spank you again...little girl?" I growl through clenched teeth.

She doesn't respond, so I tug on her hair, yanking it enough for her to feel the pinch. She responds with a hiss and answers me eventually, but it comes out sounding like a question, "No?"

"You seem unsure; maybe I should remind you. I'm going to spank you twice again to do so. When I ask you a question, I want an answer straight away or I'll keep spanking you until you do."

I feel her squirm under my palm.

Hmm, the little minx wants this...

I strike her with two slaps that land one after the other across her ass.

"Do you know why I spanked you again, Kelly?" I ask.

"B-Because I didn't answer you w-when you asked me a question, " she stutters out, her body above the waist now face down on my bed.

"That's right. This sight right here—your ass up in the air with red welts and my handprints across it—is beautiful!"

I stand back and take in the sight of her caramel skin glowing from sweat and the slaps of my hand. Reaching behind me, I grab one of the items I got out earlier to try out on her before stroking my hand down her soft bare back, watching her muscles flex and dip as I reach the base of her spine, stopping right at the top of her ass crack. I slide the tip of the black dildo between her wet, juicy lips, collecting her honey on it, then tease her little bundle of nerves. Hearing her gasps and moans reminds me how loud she was last time.

"Ahhh...don't...stop...Dagger!"

"I don't intend to. Instead of gagging you, I want to hear all the moans and cries I pull from you. I want to hear my name torn from your lips as I make you cum. Now be a good girl and don't move." With that, I wrap my fist around her long hair, tug it to one side, and push the dildo all the way up inside her.

"Ahhh...fuuuuck! Dagger...ahhh!" Kelly screams out, trying not to writhe or whip her head back. I turn it for her and see her eyes are now as wide as dinner plates, but she hasn't seen anything yet.

"What did I warn you about, Kelly? I told you you didn't know what you were getting yourself into. Wrap those lips and tongue around these, little girl, because your ass is about to get full."

My ass is about to get full?

I don't get time to think more about it before neon-yellow spherical anal beads are pushed into my mouth.

A look of pure lust and dominance shines in Dagger's mesmerizing eyes, devouring me. He never breaks his stare as he pushes the beads past my lips. His own lips part, and I hear him exhale on a sigh as he tugs them back out of my mouth, the first one exiting with a loud pop in the deathly silence of the room as my heartbeat gallops in my ears.

He casually pulls the next biggest bead out of my mouth, repeating the same painfully slow process over and over until the last one is out of my mouth.

"You ever had your ass played with, Kelly?" Dagger rasps out so quietly I would have missed it if I wasn't staring at him intently.

The atmosphere in the room is full of anticipation by the time I eventually find my voice. "Not really. I want it though. Dagger."

"Good, because I'm going to do some playing. I hope you ain't planning on sitting down tomorrow—you're going to feel me inside you for weeks," he practically growls at me through bared teeth before lining the end of the beads up with my butthole.

I instantly freeze and tense up as they make contact, going rigid. Dagger caresses my butt, then swipes the beads up and down my ass crack until I can feel my saliva sliding in between my ass cheeks—it's the strangest feeling.

"Relax, Kelly; you have your safe word if the sensation is too much, but I know you're going to love it."

I relax enough to appease him, silently staring at him over my shoulder. He raises the corner of his mouth at me in the smug smile I've noticed he does when he thinks no one else is looking.

"That's a good girl, now turn back around."

I do as he says, but the logical part of my brain protests.

What's wrong with me? Why ain't I fighting it after what he did before? I would never...

All thoughts evaporate as I feel the squirt of cold lube on my skin, followed by Dagger's fingers sliding it around my butthole, and then the pressure of his thumb being pushed inside of me. I cry out as he adds his finger into the mix.

"Ahhh, fuck!"

"That feel good already, Kelly?"

"Yes!" I exhale on a ragged, heavy breath, feeling my pussy clamp down onto the dildo still deep inside of me.

Sweet baby Jesus, this is going to be hard, but I want it. It goes against everything I ever thought I wanted, but my body is taking over.

Dagger squirts more lube straight into my butt, the sensation making me moan.

"Ahhhh!" The sensation is strange, but really good. I don't get to think about it any longer before the first bead is being pushed inside of me.

Oh my God. The fullness is...is wow!

"How do you feel, Kelly?"

"G-Good. Yeah, really good," I reply, my voice shaky.

"You're doing well. Don't forget your safe word." With that, he pushes the second bead deep inside of me. As the pressure increases in my pussy in response, I can't help squeezing the life out of the dildo.

"Ahhhh Dags...fuck!" I flick my hair to the side as my back arches, sweat starts to gather at the base of my head.

Dagger bends over my back, his denim-clad hard dick pushing against the beads still hanging between my butt cheeks. He latches his teeth onto my shoulder, and I gaze at him in a misty haze.

His stare is so intense that I don't see him reach around to pluck my hardened nipple until he does, and my body flexes in response.

"Ahhh, fuck me!"

"That's what I plan to do, but first I am going to put all these beads inside of you...You're not going to cum until I tell you to anyway, you're going to wait for my command. Can you do that?"

"Dags! Are you fucking serious?"

"I don't joke, Kelly. Do it for me and you'll be able to cum after. I want to see you take my orders."

All the alarm bells I have in my head are going off, but my mouth runs before I can stop it.

"Yes," I say on a breathy sigh.

"Good girl,"

A moment later, the pressure of his cock leaves my skin and he's pushing the third bead deep inside me painfully slowly. My pussy clenches down on the dildo tightly again.

"Jesús Cristo de mierda!"

The sweat dripping down my spine slips slowly down my curves to balm my full ass, and I feel another squirt of lube fill my butthole, followed by the pressure from another—much bigger—bead being pushed in.

"Deep breaths, Kelly; this is the second largest bead. Relax, and remember you have your safe word. What is it?"

"Tequila," I rasp out.

"Good girl."

As much as it would annoy and grate on me if it was anyone else, when Dagger says the phrase with huskiness in his voice, it hits me in all the right spots—making me even wetter than before if that was ever fucking possible.

As I exhale and relax, Dagger takes the opportunity to press the second largest bead inside of me.

Still feeling the sweat trickling down my spine painfully slowly, I am almost overwhelmed by the fullness of my pussy and my ass feels.

Dagger smooths his rough hands down the planes of my back, then grabs my butt cheeks and shakes them, sending exquisite sensations and sensitivity ricocheting through my whole body.

I don't think I can take anymore—my body sags against Dagger's bed sheets, which are now wet, hot, and sticky from my sweat. I don't get any respite as Dagger fists my hair tightly, yanking my head to one side so I can see him through the curtain of hair over my face. There's a carnal look of pure craving in those eyes that stare back at me.

I feel his other hand rub into my thighs, and he grazes his knuckles over my sensitive clit, making my eyes roll back into my head in pure bliss. He grabs the free end of the dildo which is still buried inside me to the hilt, tugging on it to withdraw it, and then working it in and out of me as the pressure and fullness from both holes threatens to become overwhelming, making me feel like I'm dreaming. The desire and longing I have to cum is too hard to describe—almost beyond words.

As if sensing my desperation, Dagger leans down. "Don't think, just feel, Kitten. Just feel," he rasps in my ear as he keeps pushing the dildo in and out of me, working me up to a crescendo.

I know I am about to blow like fucking Krakatoa; my head and back are twisting like I'm a woman possessed....and then suddenly, Dagger's hands and thrusts disappear completely. I whip my head around to look at him, and glare, about to give him shit when he locks eyes with me, smirks, and shoves the last bead straight into my ass, making my head spin.

My head is so fuzzy I swear I can hear some poor animal in pain somewhere, screaming and wailing, but a moment later, the penny drops.

What the hell...? Fuck, that noise was me!

"Fuck, ain't that a thing of beauty! What a sexy, fuckin' beautiful sight! Sweet Jesus, you're so needy and full of nothing but the dildo in your pussy and the string of beads hangin' out of your ass!"

"Daaagger!" I screech out in response. My pussy is pulsating, and I can feel the beads stretching me every time I breathe.

"Hold on, Kelly, because I ain't done with you yet. Remember you have your safe word."

My eyes don't move from where he stands at the end of the bed. He drops his jeans past his knees, then starts fisting his cock and tugging on his balls as he stands over me.

God, if you're up there, you seriously did good with this one, but if you don't kick this man's butt for keeping me a quivering mess who's about to combust for so long, I will kill his ass…after I fuck him silly.

"Turn back around, Kelly. Do I need to use the handcuffs on you again?"

"Fuck no. Just fuck me, Dagger!" I grind out as he drops his head back, rolling his neck as he speeds up his assault on his dick and then fixes me with a heavy-lidded stare. Just then, he lets his cock go and I can see a big juicy pearl of cum shining under the dim lighting of the room. It's calling to me, tempting me.

Flicking my eyes back up at him, I watch him remove his t-shirt.

¡De puta madre! This dude better not flake out on me, or I'll go all Misery on his ass.

To my relief, he flings it to the floor and removes the rest of his clothes eagerly.

YES!

I admire him as he stands there fully naked, the warm lighting illuminating each intricate tattoo that graces his skin.

Starting from the top of his right hand, I notice a stunning picture of a woman's face which creeps up his arm before turning into flames that cover the rest of it, the oranges and blacks intertwining with one another. Gradually moving over to his pec, I notice a huge skull that takes over the whole muscle, although if the detail on it turned out to be that stunning, I would put it over a large area too. He has another skull taking up his entire left pec, merging into black swirls and jagged lines that go down his entire left arm then morph into a grey and black shaded rose.

My gaze pulls away from his torso, travelling down his thick, muscular legs. One's bare, but the other one is a full leg piece—even his knee is covered with flames, skulls, and crosses. A huge-ass tiger's face sits right on his thigh, filling the width of the muscle; shaded and detailed with such intricacy that it looks about to jump off his body.

Hmm, we both have big cat tats…

"Woman, have you finished gawping? I did ask you to turn back around."

Shit, I was so in the zone admiring him that I couldn't think straight!

As soon as I turn back around, he's on me like the fierce alpha tiger taking his tigress for mating. He slides his whole hand around the length of my hair, wrapping it tightly around his fist. Next, he removes the dildo, but not before pumping it in and out of me a couple more times. It lands on the floor with a thud, the atmosphere crackling between us as electricity shoots all over my body.

I hear the familiar sound of a condom wrapper tearing, my pussy flooding with excitement as I wait for him to roll it on.

When he's done, Dagger angles my neck to the side again, commanding my body. It instinctively knows what to do and how to respond to him, bending to his will.

His simple words from earlier echo around my head. Just feel…

"Keep your eyes on me, Kelly."

I don't dare remove my gaze from his, and a moment later, I'm rewarded with the feeling of him pushing deep inside me, knocking the wind out of me. There's no warning; he pushes, and I simply take it. He bottoms out, and the force of him doing so jolts the beads that are still buried deep in me, making the breath catch in the back of my throat.

"Do you feel all that, little girl? Are you ready?"

"Yes," I'm hardly able to gasp out.

He needs no more encouragement than that before he starts to move—and I mean really fucking move; most men my age wouldn't be able to do this.

Withdrawing from my body, he almost pulls out, leaving only the tip in, and then slams into me with such force my body rocks. He pounds me again and again, never relenting beyond loosening his hold on my hair. Every time he pushes inside me, he brushes against the end string of the beads, and between them and having his cock inside me, I'm fit to burst.

My legs start quaking and shuddering from the intensity of my impending orgasm, and I start begging him for it—I don't care. "D-Dagger. I need…I need…"

"Little. Girl. I. Know," he rasps out in a feral growl above me, thrusting into me between words. Both of us are left groaning and moaning as he becomes more savage with his thrusting. He grabs a fistful of my hair, and his other hand bites into the flesh of my hips as he roars, "Come! Now!"

As he cums loudly into the room, I let go of all the tension I've been holding back and let out a scream as an earth-shattering, life-changing orgasm rips through my body like a tornado through a town.

"Carajo! Carajo! Jes—ahhhh!"

I don't get to finish my sentence before I feel Dagger tugging the beads outta my ass one by one, creating an intensity of feeling I have never, *ever,* experienced before. In this moment, I know for sure that this man was made for me.

My whole world tilts, and my legs buckle under me. I smoked a little weed back in college, but shit, I feel like I'm on the strongest dope ever, floating along in outer space—it feels like my body isn't my own.

I feel Dagger stroking my hair to the side as he lowers me on the bed on my back. I go to thank him, but I don't think I can speak even if I try. I feel the sensation of sheets being moved from under me, and then myself being covered by them as Dagger wraps his arms around me. I can't seem to concentrate on anything, feeling like this is all a daydream of sorts.

What the hell is happening to me?

"It's okay, Kelly. I'm here, okay?" Dagger murmurs as my whole body relaxes and my eyes close, bringing me utter peace.

***

"You're awake. How ya feeling?" Dagger says, his voice vibrating in my ear, I blink a few times, trying to focus on the light that's still on in the corner.

Fuck, did I pass out?

Looking down at the naked body under my hands, I stare at the skull tattoos again and see the dusting of hair on his chest for the first time up close. My tongue snakes out and sneaks a quick lick of his nipple, making him jolt in surprise.

I sit up and gawp at the man next to me. "Oh. My. God! My freaking dream came true!"

"I see you got your voice back. Tell me more about this dream," he smiles.

Why did you have to say it out loud? Fucking hell, Kelly!

"What was that?" I reply simply.

"How d'ya mean? My comment just now, or what you experienced a couple of hours ago?" Dagger smirks at me, sitting up at the same time to reveal more of that gorgeous body

I risk a glance at him under my eyelashes. "Damn you, Dagger!" I scold him.

He says nothing, just carries on smirking that sexy-as-hell smirk at me. I go to shove at his chest, but he catches my wrist.

"Now now, little girl. Behave, or I'll have to spank you again. So, are you going to answer me? Which was it; my comment or what you experienced?"

"What I've experienced, obviously. What was wrong with me after? Why did it feel like I was either high off the best green ever or floating around out of my body?" I ask.

He doesn't take his eyes from my face, but they don't give anything away. His expression is unreadable most of the time, unless you catch it in a rare moment when his guard's down. Finally, he breaks the silence, casually stroking the back of his hand back and forth up and down my arm.

"It's not drugs, it's the sex—this life's drug, I guess you could say. But this kind of sex ain't for you, I can tell by that look in your eye. I've seen it many times before, Kelly."

"Don't come at me with that utter bull, Dagger! Do I look like I was born yesterday?"

His facial expression doesn't waver; stoic as ever. "Kelly, look; this ain't going to work, whatever it is. Just leave it."

He whips the bed sheet back and climbs out of bed, stomping over to his clothes that are in a heap on the floor, then starts shoving his long legs back into his pants.

I ain't gonna sit in bed being one of those sad bitches begging for it, and I recognize bullshit when I see it—my Dad taught me well. I make quick work of shoving my own clothes back on, and am mid-way through pulling my dress back over my head when I feel Daggers callused hands on my arm, stopping me.

"What, Dagger?" I snap at him, not giving a fuck. "I ain't gonna beg you for anything, but I recognize your bullshit when I see it. This is nothing to do with your lifestyle, and don't use the age thing again, because it clearly wasn't an issue when you were fucking me raw. Be straight up and honest with me; I wanna hear the truth."

Dagger tugs at the back of his head, threading his fingers together at the base of his skull.

How can he still look sexy as fuck? Damn him.

"I can't give you forever, okay? I can't give you the happily ever after you want, Kelly. You're too young for the likes of me, trust me. I've seen all the games and tricks women pull when men say that shit, so you won't fool me with any of that. It's better this way; one fuck and that's it."

"Who the hell d'ya think you are, Dagger?! Who the fuck said I wanted forever?"

God, if only, I add silently.

"Who said I wanted happily ever after? As for the 'games and tricks' that women pull, I have been on the receiving end of the same tricks that men have pulled on me to excuse their shittiness, so cut the crap! You're doing a lot of assuming in that thick head of yours, Dagger. When you wake up and want to explore the connection we have just experienced, you know where to find me, but if you think for a second that I would trick you or play games with you then you don't know jack shit about me. You should know I can't lie or fake shit; it's always got me into trouble."

I look away from him as I finish pulling on my dress, then shove my feet back into my shoes and stride out with my back ramrod straight, leaving him alone in his room to stare after me.

Stubborn-ass man!

~ Chapter 16 Dagger ~

One week later…

"Dags, hand me the hammer, would ya?" Bear hollers at me from the top of some ladders above the counter as I walk through his Ol' Lady's bakery-come-café. I'm still wondering why the hell I agreed to help him out; I wanted a nice chilled-out day in the backyard of the compound, and was planning to maybe go and see Ma.

I can't help sighing inwardly at Bear's request; if I'm being honest with myself, I know exactly why I'm standing in the rarely-empty bakery helping one of my best buds carry out repairs.

"You here to help me, or just stand there watching a real man do all the work?" Bear quips, a smirk plastered across his big bearded face.

"Yeah, yeah! You wish you were a real man, Bear, shut ya mouth. What is it you need to do anyway?" I ask as I walk over to fuckin' moaning Minnie.

"Jenna asked me to take down this old sign and put the new one up on a brand new shelf before the old one falls. So, ya gonna hand me that hammer or what?"

Grabbing the black and red hammer off of the counter and handing it to Bear handle-first, I smile as he snatches it out of my grip, then stand back, watching him use the claw end of the hammer to unhook the nail from the wall. I step back underneath him just in time, not needing to be told what he needs as he drops the old, rusted nail into my palm.

"Which nails d'ya need to put the new sign up?"

"Pass me one of the anchor bolts in that pack next to my coffee mug, would ya?" He points at the plastic bag with two big anchor bolts inside it, and I hand them to him.

"Anything else you need, Your Highness?"

"No, not for this. Could you take the new shelf out of the packaging so we can put it up before unboxing the new sign? Looking at this shelf, the wood surround is all buckled because of the steam and heat from the coffee machine, so we might need to move the new one." Bear looks down at me briefly, then says, "Jenna don't know I'm doing all this today, by the way. She and Jade have gone out for a girls' seeing as I asked them to shut the café for a surprise—they didn't want to do it, but this needs to be done."

"Sounds sensible to me, brother. I'll handle this shelf for you; do you want a coffee after?" I ask him as I move everything I need for the new shelf onto one of the plastic-covered tables.

"I could murder another coffee. Well, I'd prefer an ice-cold beer, but maybe after. I'll probably get some loving from my woman too." He turns to look at me. "Speaking of women, what's this I hear from Jade about you sticking it in Kelly? I thought you were adamant you weren't going anywhere near her?" he chuckles.

I shrug my shoulders, looking over the thick glass shelf and assortment of screws and washers I've fished out of the box before I grumble out into the silence of the bakery, "Fucking women."

I turn so my ass is leaning against the table. "What do ya want me to say, Brother? That she didn't give me the best blow job I've had in the longest time? And that's even after I tried to show her how what my sexual tastes were to scare her away and prove to her that she was too fucking young. Hell, she still is, but she tempted me so fuckin' much the other night that I caved. I took what I wanted and gave her exactly what she needed. There's no point talking about it now anyway, I told her straight that it was just a one-time thing, but I feel like a creep for going there."

"Hmm, funny," Bear retorts with a smirk.

"What's funny?" I snip back at him, growing annoyed at all this talk about women.

Bear's smile doesn't waver. "Nothing, brother. You unwrapped that shelf for me?"

I don't miss the attempt to change the subject. "Quit with the games, what the fuck is funny? Come on, spit it out, Bear—I can see you have something to say."

"I just think it's funny how you talk about her age and how you feel bad for going there, but you haven't said that it felt wrong or you regret it. If you were *really* hung up about her age, I figure you would have. You also started off by saying she gave you the best blow job you've had recently, and I know you're no stranger to 'em. Seems to me that you're attracted to her, and she's clearly liking your old ass because you didn't scare her off. Maybe you're scared of what it all means? Just my thoughts, man."

With that, Bear gets down from the ladder and starts moving around behind the counter to make us coffee, leaving me staring at the empty shelf I've just unwrapped and put on the counter.

Bear's words hit me like a bomb, and I'm left wondering what the hell it all means, but I know he's not wrong. Kelly and I are both helplessly attracted to one another; every time we're in a room together, I can't help but seek her out, and every time I do, her eyes are on me.

Even so, I can't stop thinking about the age difference and the way I treated her during our scene last week. I know pushing her too far and rushing into it without setting many ground rules was the worst thing I could have done as an experienced dominant, but fuck! I wanted to play properly, and it was easy to get carried away.

She was the perfect submissive—she was eager to please and she listened to my commands, taking everything I gave her in her stride. Yes, I wanted to scare her by giving her a sensory overload, but I wasn't expecting her to actually *take* it—I kept reminding her about her safe word because I expected her to use it. Instead, she ended up all the way in subspace. After the scene was over, I tucked her in against my side to bring her out of it, but she ended up falling into a deep-ass sleep for about an hour while I rubbed salve over her juicy red ass.

God, it took all my will to not take her again there and then, but I needed her to be able to consent just as much as I needed to give her proper aftercare—both are equally important in my lifestyle.

I've woken up with a hard-on every day this week after dreaming about how she looked with those anal beads stuffed into her ass like a turkey at Thanksgiving. Even now, I recall my handprint on her ass, pushing those anal beads into her ,and my dick fucking her hard as I fisted her hair. She looked absolutely perfect.

"What ya thinking so hard over there, Dags?"

I shrug.

"Look, you gotta make the decision on what to do, but I don't see Kelly growing bored anytime soon. From what I've seen, she's as tenacious as she is petite, and has a very similar mentality to Zara and Jade. I'm just warning you, brother, I hope you're ready for that. Anyway, what d'ya want in your coffee?"

"I know. I hear ya brother, I hear ya. Just give it to me black." I grumble back at him.

I remove my cut, slinging it over the back of the booth holding the glass shelving. I start to unwrap the screws and parts for it, but I'm not really concentrating on what I'm doing—my head is filled with thoughts of Kelly's juicy ass.

"Here ya are, man," Bear says as he slams my cup of coffee down next to me. I grab it and slug some of it down, needing a caffeine hit.

"So, I was thinking we'd take down that big old-ass shelf first, remove the old screws, sort and prep the new screws, make the new holes, and grab something to eat afterward? I think Jenna's got some cold meats in the fridge in the kitchen—we could have subs and some chips?"

I nod, taking another deep slug of coffee—I've necked nearly half a cup already. "Sounds good to me brother. Let's get going; it's nearly 2pm, and if I'm starting to get hungry, you gotta be starving!" I say, giving his shoulder a shove.

***

"Dags, this shelf is gonna look the dogs' balls when we get it up; Jenna is gonna love it. Thanks for helping me with this, brother, it would have been a pain in the ass to do on my own. I owe you one."

"You don't owe me shit, brother. You know I got your back." I slap Bear hard on the back, but it doesn't move him—he's built like a truck. He's not always been so strong emotionally, though, and there have been times when I was there purely for him to use as his punching bag, but I'd do it again to see my brother with the woman he belongs to. Jenna is as strong as they come—in fact, all the women in the club are as strong as the men they captured the hearts of. Finishing the last of the soda I grabbed to drink with lunch, I climb the ladder.

Once I'm up there, Bear hands me the screwdriver and I start unscrewing the old rusted screws.

"You were right about these screws—they're shot to hell. So we're drilling new holes next to the old ones then filling the old ones?" I ask, peering down over my shoulder at where he stands at the bottom of the ladders.

"Yeah that's the plan. Hold up, my phone's ringing." He digs his still-vibrating cell from his pocket and checks the caller ID. "It's Jenna, you got this?"

"Yeah, answer her. I'm good," I tell him as I carry on lubing the nails holding up the old shelf.

As I work, I overhear Bear's part of the conversation between him and Jenna. "I'm just doing a few things at the bakery with Dags…Yeah, he's here now, why?...Oh okay. Just leave it, Cupcake…I know you do. I love you too, baby. See you soon."

"How are you getting on, Dags?" Bear shouts to me after hanging up the phone.

"I've removed one side, I`m gonna do the other side now. You want to do the middle so you can hold the whole thing up and then lower it down to me?"

"Sounds good to me," he tells me as I'm stepping down the ladder.

He grabs one side of the ladder, I grab the other, and we start to move it to the other end of the shelf. Once it's underneath the screws, Bear passes me the oil and screwdriver I've just been using, and I climb up and get started on the other side. Once that's done, I come back down the ladder and we move it again, positioning it under the middle screws for Bear.

"Can you pass the oil?" he asks from under the beat-up shelf that looks as old as the building. I pass him the canister and the screwdriver, but as he starts unscrewing, I hear a crack.

"Shit, what was that?"

I stare up at the thick glass shelf Bear has ahold of and see a crack running from one side of the shelf to the other. "Bear, stand there and don't move. The shelf has a huge-ass crack running through it. You hold one end and I'll try and bring the other side down, okay?"

"Yeah brother, can you reach it?"

I take a firm hold of the end of the shelf furthest from Bear. "Yes, I've got it. All right, now start lowering it down." I stand under half of the broken shelf, guiding one end with an open palm under the other ready to grab it.

"Here it comes, Dags," Bear informs me, trying to maneuver his half down to me inch by inch until I catch it.

"Got it, brother!"

Just as I shout up to Bear, I hear the bell above the bakery's main door open and swivel my head around to catch a glimpse of Jenna, Jade…and the mouthwatering siren staring right at me with those enormous eyes. Her warm caramel skin is flawless even without a scrap of make-up on. She wears black wedged heels, a purple dress that stops mid-thigh, a stunning smile that I see is fading now she's clocked me, and she's got her hair piled up high into a bun that sits on top of her head with a couple of lose strands hanging down. She looks beautiful.

She turns on her heel, about to grab the door handle, and completely forgetting what I'm doing, I shout at the top of my lungs in an authoritative, harsh, and commanding tone.

"Stop!"

She halts straight away, responding instantly to my tone. She may come across as loud and unfiltered, but in this moment I know she needs the kind of control that she can't get with other men. She willingly hands control of her body over to me again like the perfect submissive she is.

~ Chapter 17 Kelly ~

"Stop!"

My body responds instantly, stopping on instinct. My back is straight and my body is frozen as I face the bakery door, wondering why I didn't listen to my gut instinct when Jenna got off of her phone call to Bear. I thought it was weird that she was adamant I come back to the bakery for a midafternoon treat after our trip. As soon as I walked through the fucking doors, I could smell his subtle aftershave among the lingering hints of coffee in the air.

I grab the door handle for a second time when Dagger speaks again, "Kelly, don't..."

There's a commotion, a cracking sound, and then the room is filled with the sound of shattering glass as Dagger cries out in pain.

"Ah fuck! Motherfucking shit!" he hisses, making me stop, spin around, and look at the man I have been pining after for months; the man who gave me the most mind-blowing sexual encounters I have ever experienced.

His hypnotic stare is fixated on me, but mine drops to his right hand, which is pouring blood all over the floor. I remember every part of my first aid training at the hands of my Dad all at once and stride over to him, finally reaching him and grabbing his tightly clasped fist. I don't dare look back up at him this close; his intense stare has already got my skin prickling like crazy. My skin becomes more alive with every light touch as I grab his fingers, unfurling them.

I hear Bear and Jenna rushing in and out of the kitchen looking for supplies.

"Have you got antiseptic wipes or spray, Jen? And a clean cloth or towel to wrap it with, please?" I ask calmly, still not removing my eyes from his fist, which it takes both of my hands to cup.

Eventually, I pry his fingers open enough to reveal a huge gash running from in between his thumb and index finger straight across the middle of his palm. There's only about an inch and a half of skin left untouched on either side.

"Here you go, Kelly."

I look to the counter and see what I've asked for. Grabbing the antiseptic wipes, I finally sneak a quick glance at the man who makes my thighs clench, my pussy quiver, and my heart race.

"This is gonna sting," I say, locking eyes with him properly for the first time since I first saw those forest-green eyes,. I make quick work of cleanup as I lower my eyes again and swipe the cut, going with the broken skin so as to not cause more damage. As I do, I feel his arm stiffen, and he winces. Once I've cleaned the main cut up, I grab the clean cloth to wrap around the open wound, then I put pressure on it again and hear him exhale heavily.

"You okay?" I ask, taking another peek up at him.

He gives me a look that's half grimace and half smirk before replying, "Yeah. Fuckin' peachy, Kitten."

"If you could use your other hand to put pressure on the gash and keep your wounded arm straight up in the air, it will stem some of the blood flow. You need to go to the emergency room. Come on, I'll drive you."

"Nah, you're all right, I'll call Wrench and ask him to take me in the cage," he grumbles out at me.

I stand back away from him long enough to grab my purse from where I dumped it on the counter to get to him, then fix him with a determined glare.

"Honestly, I don't mind. Wrench is gonna take about 20 minutes to get here and then you gotta get over to the emergency room on top, and you need to go now. Come on, I'll drop your ass there. Bear can come so he can hold your hand." I raise my chin at him in defiance to see if that makes Dommy Dags come back in full force—chance would be a fine thing.

The look in his eyes changes slightly, his stare hardening under the heavy lids. The atmosphere between us starts to crackle as he replies, "Like I said, I'll get Wrench to come with me. I don't want to put you out, little girl."

Fuck this shit, I ain't gonna pander to him!

"And like *I* said, it's fine!" I snap back at him. "I can drop you off at the emergency room and pick you up after. I had an appointment to speak to Dani about her bridal make up, but I can do it tomorrow. What is it, are you worried about being alone with me in the car or something? Don't worry, I won't jump on you wounded—I don't want you thinking I'm gonna *trick* or *play games* with you." I hoist my purse higher up on my shoulder, letting my hand rest on my hip.

He just stands there, scanning my face like he's looking for weakness.

Well, he ain't gonna find it.

"Dagger, brother, Kelly's right. The sooner you get fixed up the better; your sorry ass is still dripping blood all over the floor," Bear points out, and I silently thank him for being the voice of reason. "Go with her, I'm gonna stay here and finish up."

Dagger breaks eye contact with me and looks at his hand, where the blood is starting to seep through the bandage.

Seeing this, Jadey goes up to Dagger and flings him another clean dish towel. "Here you go, Dagger."

Not giving him another chance to argue, I turn on my heel, walking out the door. Once I'm outside, I remember he won't be able to open the door, so kick it open with the back of my heel and stare out into the fairly busy street, waiting for him to exit but trying not to let the swarm of butterflies go too crazy in my stomach as I think about being in the car with him.

I'm about to shout out over my shoulder and ask whether he's coming or not when I hear the tell-tale sound of his biker boots squeaking on the tiled floor. He brushes past me a moment later, my skin coming alive from that minor contact.

Fuck, what the hell is it gonna be like in my car?

Not wanting to dwell on it, I let go of the door and start walking with urgency toward my car, which is parked across the street behind my shop.

***

The journey over to the emergency room wasn't as bad as I thought it would be, but the atmosphere was still thick with tension and unspoken words. Dagger didn't say anything the whole time, just sat there with his head back against the headrest, unmoving.

Every time I twitched or shifted in my seat, I felt his eyes on me, making the hairs on the back of my arms stand on end as I tried to concentrate on driving. I've realized that ever since we had sex, I have the urge to bow my head or throw my head back in pure ecstasy whenever I feel his gaze on me.

We're standing in a queue at the reception desk in the emergency room, waiting for him to get booked in. Luckily, the waiting room doesn't look too bad—there are only two people in front of us. The familiar hospital smell hangs in the air even here.

"Do you want me to help you with filling the forms out?" I ask as the first of the two people in front of us leaves.

"Oh, you're talking to me now? I thought you'd gone mute," Dagger grumbles under his breath.

Annoyance flares inside me. "No, I've not gone mute, but what do you expect me to say, Dagger? Do you want me to beg you to think about what you said last week? Nah, that ain't going to happen, old man."

"I seem to remember you begging me before just fine. Why are you really here, Kelly?"

"Hell, I don't know, Dagger, I came for shits and giggles!" I say sarcastically. "Why do you think? No matter how you think of or treat me, I don't like seeing you hurt. I just want to get you fixed up, and then I'll drop you back off at the club and you can carry on living your bachelor life. How about that?"

In response, Dagger leans down to my ear, his breath on my skin sending shivers up and down my body and making me fight back a groan.

"Tut, tut, little girl. You trying to make me hard? Your defiance makes me want to push you up against that desk and tan that ass of yours, then fuck you so hard I leave you breathless again."

***

Three hours later...

"So, Mr. Thomas, how exactly did you do this?" the doctor who's examining Dagger's hand asks.

In the last three hours, I have found out his real first and last name by filling out his insurance forms for him. He definitely does _not_ suit Derek, that's for sure.

The doctor looks to be in her early to mid-30s, and she's beautiful—skin smooth as butter, mousy blonde hair tied up in a high ponytail as she bends over Dagger's hand, inspecting the wound.

My eyes are fixated on his hand, but I know he isn't checking down her scrubs—I can feel his blazing gaze on me.

He eventually speaks up when the doctor looks up at him expectantly. "I was helping a friend of mine to remove a glass shelf that had broken, and it slipped out of my hand and sliced me as I tried to save it. Can you fix it, Doc?"

I can see he's in pain; even though he doesn't make a sound, I see his arm flinch every time she pokes and prods the gash.

As she swivels back toward her desk to type up some notes, she says, "Luckily for you, Mr. Thomas, yes I can. I just need to test if you have any nerve damage as the cut is quite deep. I don't think you do, as you've moved your hand in reaction every time I've touched it, but it's something I have to check. Do you have any numbness in your hand, including your fingers?"

"No."

"I know your hand hurts, but do your hand, fingers, or thumb feel weak at all?"

"No, Doc."

"That's good. Then the only bad news I'm afraid I do have to give you is that we are going to have to stitch you up as the cut is deep and the edges of it are jagged. The good thing is that we can give you some pain relief to help during the process, and once you're bandaged up, you can go home. You'll have to come back or make an appointment with your primary care physician after 7 to 10 days to get the stitches removed."

"So you can't just glue it up?" Dagger grumbles. "How am I gonna ride my bike?"

I see the doctor's shoulders visibly sag at the thought of giving this dominant, already-grumpy biker more bad news, so I decide to step in, knowing how to deal with him.

I look at the ultra-alpha male and in a firm tone tell him, "It looks like you can't, so just put up and shut up and let the doctor do her job. She has a whole waiting room full of patients out there."

I don't know whether I'm sassing him or speaking my mind, but whichever it is, he just stares me down with a raised eyebrow. I'm not scared of that look…he should know the Dom clawing under his skin excites me.

I see the doctor eyeing me, silently warning me not to anger him, and I smile. "Don't worry, I know how to handle his grumpy old ass."

"So, are you going to take the drugs and get stitched up?" I challenge him, raising an eyebrow back in his direction.

A cocky smirk graces his lips again, bringing my skin to life and causing a swarm of butterflies in my tummy.

The connection is right there between us both, and how he can deny it is beyond me. I may be younger than him, but this has never happened to me before, and I don't think it has to him either.

Never breaking eye contact with me, he says over to the doctor, "You get me the drugs, Doc, and you can use me as a pin cushion."

"See, was it that hard?" I ask him as I beam towards where he sits on the hospital bed.

As soon as the doctor leaves the cubicle to get what she needs, he snatches my hand, pulling me toward him with such force I practically land on him,

"What are you doing, Dagger?" I say, trying and failing to hide the surprise in my voice.

He places my hand over his rock hard denim-clad cock, and on instinct I squeeze.

"You feel that? Keep talking back and I'll drag you to the bathroom and stuff it down your throat—don't think I won't," he hisses, letting go of my hand and shoving me upright as we hear the doctor.

"Knock, knock."

She rolls in an IV stand with a bag of something hanging off of it, then gets to work moving things closer to the bed and pulling the bed light from behind Dagger to position right above him. I shuffle over to sit back down in the corner so the doctor can get on with what she needs to.

"You're not allergic to any opiates like morphine?"

"Nah, I'm all good with that stuff," he replies.

"Ah, good. I hope you're not scared of needles either, Mr. Thomas?"

"Nah, I…"

He doesn't get the chance to finish the answer before the doctor proceeds to put a canula into the top of his left hand and starts to hook him up to the IV. I start seeing the liquid drip down into the line.

"I'm just going to put some numbing cream around the area where I'll have to sew, okay? It will work fairly quickly, but in the meantime, I've hooked you up to some morphine. That will work quite quickly too."

***

One hour later...

"Come on Dags, get your ass into the seat. Here's your seat belt. Can you belt yourself in, or do you need help with it?" I ask the patient. He has had to have 14 stitches in his palm, but there's a bandage over it, and he's nicely drugged-up thanks to the morphine.

"I got it, I got it," he says, eventually getting his ass into the seat. Once I'm happy that he's not about to slide out of the car, I shut the passenger's side door, round my car, and jump back into my seat. My butt almost touches the leather before I feel Dagger's good hand under my ass.

"Dagger, move; I can't drive with your hand on my seat, " I say flatly. I'm tired, hungry, and I just want to drop his ass back off at the club, dive into a Chinese takeout, and crash.

"Sit on it, little girl!" he orders me the way I like with a slightly amused lilt to his voice.

"Would you quit calling me that!"

Don't. Ever! I fuckin' love it; it makes me feel dirty!

"Never. Now do as you're told, and sit on my fingers!" he growls out in a rough voice that sends shivers up and down my spine, the look in his eyes warning me not to argue.

"How the fuck do you think that's going to work with driving?" I bite back at him. I love giving him shit; something about rebelling against him and pushing his buttons calls to me—although part of me also wants him to drag me out of the car, bend me over the front of the cab without caring who's watching, and fuck me raw to get me back into submission.

"Not my fuckin' problem. Sit on them and drive. Now! I need to get back to the club."

Before I know what's happening, I do as he says then clip my seat belt in, put the car back into reverse, and pull out of the hospital parking lot. As I head out of the hospital grounds and straight into the traffic heading back into the center of town, I feel Dagger's long, thick fingers wriggling under my dress, swiftly moving my G-string to one side. Before I know it, he's two fingers and two knuckles deep inside me, stealing the breath right out of me.

"¡Santo! ¡¡joder! ¡Moisés!"

As the lights turn red, I glance over to the invalid to my right to see his eyes are an intense shade of dark green and his nostrils are flared wide.

"So. Fuckin'. Wet. So tight. You speaking Spanish is hot as fuck," he growls at me, making my pussy clench down on his thick fingers. I can't help squirming in my seat, eager for more—more movement, more friction, more *anything* if I'm being honest with myself. As I pull up to the lights, he curls his fingers inside me, hitting that spot. I moan uncontrollably, but decide not to make things so easy for *la verga.* How can he tell me we can't carry on and then play with me like this?

"Now who's playing the games with me Dagger? Men! You're all the fucking same…"

Except you were definitely not the same in bed, that's for damn sure… a voice in my head adds.

Any other woman would have told him to take his fingers out of her, but I'd be lying to myself and him if I pretended I didn't love that they are inside of me. Just before I see the lights change, I shift in my seat and start rising and falling onto his fingers, fucking them once, twice, and thrice for good measure.

I think I'm as nasty as he is, and I can't even say that I actually give a fuck about it…

***

Parking the car in front of the clubhouse and turning the engine off, I look over to the invalid who passed out about five minutes away from the club and remove his fingers. Much to my dismay, I didn't get to finish myself off.

La verga!

"Dagger?"

When he doesn't respond, I try giving his shoulder a shove.

Nope, nothing.

Pulling out my phone, I dial Jade, who answers after four rings.

"Kelly! How's the grumpy patient?" she chuckles down the phone at me.

"Jade, are Tinhead or Bear there? I'm parked outside the clubhouse doors and I've got an unconscious Dagger in the front seat. I'm gonna need someone to get him settled in his room."

"Sure babe, I'll grab a few of the guys. I saved you some food, are you coming in or do you wanna take it to go?"

"Is it okay if I take it to go? I just wanna take a bath and get into bed; I'm pooped. What is it, anyway? Please say it's Jenna's chicken and rice and bean salad!"

"Yup, sure is. I saved you a leg, much to Bear's dismay. Hold on, I'll come out."

Less than two minutes pass before Jade, Tinhead, Bear, and Flex come out to get Dagger out of my car.

Once the men are gone, Jade plops into the passenger seat, putting a hand on my arm as I stare after Dagger. "You okay, babe? You look more in a funk than when you left with Dagger earlier."

"I'm fine, it's just that he's a dick. I know he wants me, Jade, I'm not crazy."

"No babe, you're not crazy. Bear, Dylan, and I were talking about it, and he does want you—I can see it and so can Dylan. Just give him space, but make him chase you. I may have an idea for that..."

~ Chapter 18 Dagger ~

The next morning…

"What the hell?" I grumble into my pillow. My mouth feels like a sandbox.

I raise a hand to clear my face and eyes of sleep, and roll over onto my back as I'm rewarded with a sharp stab of pain.

"Ahh, fuck!"

As my hand throbs, I remember going to the emergency room and pry my eyes open to see that there's a bandage wrapped around my hand and I'm still fully dressed minus my cut and boots. I promptly forget about my hand and sit straight up in bed, and the movement makes me grimace.

Hell, what happened? How did I get home?

The last thing I remember is getting stitched up and Kelly helping me into the car…

Fuck, she pushed my buttons last night in the emergency room! I swear she was sassing me on purpose.

As I swing my legs out of bed, my head starts to swim a little, and I look over at my nightstand to see a glass of water and Tylenol. I snatch them up and swallow them, looking back at my cut-up hand.

I can't believe I got distracted by Kelly. As much as I want her—and I *do* want her—I know I need to stay away from her; but lately it feels like she's haunting my ass.

Looking at the time on my phone, I see that it's only just past 9, but decide that I'd better get ready. I already know that the shower's gonna be a bitch, so I'll forgo that until I've spoken to Doc.

***

I round the corner into the main room after taking nearly a half-hour to put some fresh clothes on.

"Yo Prez, is Bear here?" I holler out into the main room where Axe, Dani, and little Ryker are playing on the floor, stacking blocks.

As Axe pushes them over, making Ryker laugh, he looks up at me and signals for me to come over with his chin. "Yeah he is, brother, but he's not up yet. He brought your bike back early this mornin'. How's your hand now?" he asks with concern, looking down at it.

"Ah, I was gonna ask about my bike. It's painful, but I've had worse, boss. Doc up?"

"Yeah brother, he and Sue were in the kitchen last time I checked. Tell him we have church at 12, okay?"

"Will do, Axe."

Just then, I notice that his Ol' Lady is smirking at me. "You okay, Dani?"

"Oh yeah, everything's fine, Dagger, all good over here. How about you? Is your *other* hand okay?" Dani asks, a small smile gracing her lips as her cheeks heat up.

"Uh, yeah, it's all good and in working order. I'll catch you both later."

I turn on my heel to leave, and I make it about a foot away before I hear the Prez's Ol' Lady say, "Yeah, that's what I hear too…"

Why's she actin' so weird? I'd better check in with the boss later about that.

I carry on heading to the kitchen, and even though it's open I overhear shit I don't need to.

"What can I say, sweet cheeks?" Doc's low voice rumbles, "After all these years, you sure know how to turn me on."

Sue giggles in response, and I decide to make myself known before things get hot and heavy, coughing dramatically as I reach the doorway. I know they still have sex, but they're practically my parents; I don't need to hear or see it.

Sue whips her head around toward the door, face flushed and looking complexly flustered.

"Oh Dagger, sweetheart, you're up! How are you feeling?" she asks, fiddling nervously with her mussed-up hair as she leaves Doc's arms to head to the stove.

Doc appears cool and unfazed, stroking his long beard.

"I'm good, my hand's hurting but I've had worse. Doc, have you got any ideas about how to shower? You might have told me yesterday, but I can't really remember much of what happened—just the drugs and stitching and getting into Kelly's car. I don't know how I got back into the club...or into bed, for that matter," I explain, scratching the back of my head with my uninjured hand.

"I would suggest wrapping a plastic bag around your hand and only having quick showers until I can take the stitches out. As for not remembering much, morphine can do that. Have you had any trouble urinating, chest pains, breathing difficulties, or itching? We were worried about you; Bear, Flex, and Tinhead had to carry you into the club from Kelly's car."

"Nothin' like that, Doc. Ah, that makes sense...she still at the club?" I try to hold back the eagerness in my voice, but I don't think I do a very good job of it, as Sue peers over her shoulder at me.

Damn it!

"Sue, you okay?" Doc asks his Ol' Lady

She looks back over her shoulder at me again, then huffs and turns back around to face the stove, arms crossed over her chest. I know that look of disappointment well, I've seen it a lot over the years. It's been directed at myself, Doc, and my brothers—hell, even the club girls.

What did I do?

"Why do you want to know if Kelly's here, Dagger?" she asks curtly.

"To say thanks for taking me to the emergency room."

Liar! my subconscious screams inside my head. It's right; my logical brain might know I need to stay away, but my instinct doesn't want to let her go.

Fuck...

"Did I do something last night?"

The look I get from Sue at my question tells me that I did, but hell if I know what.

After shooting me a scrutinizing stare, she finally relents, her shoulders sagging. "You really don't remember?"

"I really don't. Like I said the last things I remember were being at the hospital, getting the drugs, my hand getting stitched up, and Kelly helping me into her car. The rest is a hazy blur."

"I think you need to speak to her about it to be honest, Dags. I don't know the complete ins and outs of everything that's going on with you two, but I do know she likes you a lot. if you don't want to go there, you need

to stay away, and for God's sake don't hurt her
.otherwise you will have all of us Ol' Ladies to contend
with. God knows what Jade would do to ya," she half-
chuckles with a sympathetic look in her eyes.

***

"This is her apartment building, Jenna said she's in
3a. Want me to wait down here for your sorry ass?" Bear
says from the driver's seat in the club's cage, giving me
the same look as Sue did.

"Yeah. I doubt she will wanna see me, so I'd be
grateful if you could hang down here. If anything
changes, I'll call ya."

"Okay, brother. See ya in a bit."

I give him a curt nod, then use my left hand to get out
of the passenger side of the cab like I'm back to front. I
step onto the sidewalk and round the front of the cab,
then walk up to the apartment block door and press the
buzzer for 3a.

I hold it down for a few seconds with no answer, and
am just about to walk away when a breathy voice comes
over the intercom.

"What?" Kelly exhales breathlessly.

Just then, I notice a tiny camera hidden in the panel
and speak directly to it, hoping being able to see me will
help.

"Kelly, you gonna let me in?"

"Why should I, Dagger?"

"Because I need to talk to you about last night," I say,
waving my injured hand at her.

After a few silent seconds, she finally relents and
presses the buzzer to let me up.

Entering the building, I waste no time eating the stairs up with my strides. As I reach her floor, I see *'3a'* embossed on a deep purple door and notice a small camera is pointed at her door.

Looking over to the other apartment door opposite, I'm surprised to see they haven't got one.

Hmm, weird…

I step up to the door and knock, then step back, bracing myself for the tornado that is Kelly to knock me on my ass. It takes her a couple of minutes to answer the door, and when she does, I can't help but admire her, even though she's only standing there in her sweats. Her hair is piled up on top of her head in yesterday's updo, and she's absolutely stunning—even more so with the morning sunshine reflecting off of her dark mahogany hair. She's beautiful, even if she does have one hand planted defensively on her hip and a pissed-off look in her eye.

She quirks a perfectly-manicured brow at me. "You wanted to talk, so talk."

"Can I come in?"

Rolling her eyes at me, she walks back into her apartment, which I see opens out into an open-plan kitchen merging into a lounge area. I follow after her and slam the door shut.

When I turn back around, she's standing in the lounge, her arms folded over her chest accentuating her small waist.

"Get on with what you have to say, Dagger."

"Look, Kelly, I don't know what happened after I got into the car with you—"

"What? Are you fucking serious right now?! You told me the other week that you know the 'tricks and games' that women play, so who are you trying to kid? Quit fucking with me." She stomps over to the other side of the room, the anger practically vibrating off her in waves.

What the hell is she talking about?

I stalk over to her, grabbing her by the shoulder and spinning her around to face me. Pain shines in her eyes, and seeing it there hits me like a punch to the gut. I know I somehow caused this.

"Talk to me," I implore her, grasping her chin so she has to look right at me. She visibly gulps, then wets her lips. As worried as I am, I can't help following that tongue of hers.

Sweet baby Jesus!

"Do you really not know what you did last night?" she asks me, skepticism lacing her tone. It's almost like she doesn't trust me, and yet she trusted me a week ago to do things to her no other man will have ever dared to. What the fuck did I do to break that trust?

"All I remember about the hospital and getting into the car—the rest is hazy. I would never lie to you, Kelly. You need to believe me the way you did when I took control last week and you gave me your absolute trust," I say.

My eyes don't leave hers as she searches for a hint of deception—I know she won't find it, and there's no evasiveness there either. After talking to Sue, I know I need to put some distance between us and make amends for whatever I did, but I wouldn't lie to her.

"Fine...I believe you. So you don't remember telling me sit on your fingers as I drove the car home, or the fact you stuffed two of them knuckle deep inside of me as I drove your drugged-up invalid ass back to the club?"

She tries to tug her chin out of my grasp but she ain't getting away that easy. I normally wouldn't care this much about a woman thinking I'm a bastard—if it ain't got anything to do with fuckin', it usually doesn't bother me—and all this feeling shit is alien to me, but the hurt in her eyes has me wanting to take it away. My good hand holds the nape of her neck, bringing her flush against my body. I inhale her coconutty shampoo, and her defensiveness melts away as she leans up against my body, fisting my t-shirt.

"Kelly, I genuinely can't remember doing that. I'm sorry." Wanting to break the tension, I add, "...but did you at least get off?"

I can't help but bite a smile back as I am shoved away by the feisty woman in front of me, her caramel eyes ablaze and shooting daggers at me.

A second later, she steps back up to me, her arms flailing here and there as she yells, "You jerk! You fuckin' asshole! No, I didn't, ¡puto cabrón! I might want your ass, but I ain't desperate enough to ride your fingers while you're *fucking unconscious*. You know what I did?" She leans in further, so close I can practically taste her.

"What's that, Kitten?" I ask her in hushed tones. I can see by her flushed cheeks and ragged breathing that she's all worked up, and so the fuck am I. I remember well what it feels like for her pussy to be wrapped around my dick, and her being so close has lit my own arousal like a flame.

The sexy minx reaches up on tiptoes, breathing her next words into my ear in a husky whisper. "I came home...grabbed my vibrator...turned it up to the top level...and came. Then I did it all over again."

"That right? So, you were a naughty little girl?" I smirk. "Jesus, Kelly, I came here to apologize, not fuck ya."

"I know that, but what better way to apologize to me for being a dick than to fuck me again? Come on, let your body do the apologizing for ya."

Before I can say anything, she lands a chaste kiss on my lips, deepening it after a moment by nibbling on my bottom lip to seek entry to my mouth.

I freeze, waging an inner war with myself. As her hand palms my denim-clad cock, my dick wins out, and my hand fists the hair on the nape of her neck as I plunder her mouth with my tongue, needing more from her. This little sorceress has cast her spell over me, and I can't seem to quit her, let alone want to. Flex and Bear were right—I'm fucked!

As I tug away from Kelly's lips, I know that we both know where this is headed—neither of us can stop it any more than we can stop a river from flowing.

"Bedroom," I growl, reluctantly letting go of her head.

She pulls me down a small hallway to the open door at the end. The walls of Kelly's room are painted cream, and there's a huge-ass bed in the center of the room with stark white bed sheets and a deep purple comforter over the top.

Pulling me to the end of the bed, she starts tugging at my zipper, urging me on as her fingers brush against my boxers. I know this is gonna end up wrong, but right now, in this moment, I want this woman more than I've wanted any in my 40 years. Something is gnawing at the back of my head, but I ain't ready to scratch at it…yet.

"Strip. Now."

I see her body relax slightly at my command, as her big eyes have turned gold with desire again. A split-second later, she starts stripping, but the quick, practical way she does it tells me that she has no interest in making it the main event.

Taking a step back to get the full picture, I take in the small triangle of hair on her pussy, her beautifully-shaped thighs, and that stunning lioness tattoo with a mandala behind it. Her skin looks as if she's been airbrushed, and she's the perfect pear shape. I just stand still, devouring her with my eyes until she speaks up.

"Dags...you haven't said anything in a while," she says uncertainly.

Flicking my gaze back up to meet the insecurity in hers, I kick myself. *Fuck, what was my face doing? She's covering herself up.*

"Kelly, you have nothing to hide your body for; you're stunning, and everything about you is good enough to eat...in fact, that's exactly what I'm planning." Growling at her under my breath, I give her a little shove so she lands flat on her back, her feet draped over the edge of the bed. "Lay there with your knees bent and open your legs."

She does exactly what I asked of her, and I watch her peel her legs open to reveal her pussy, which glistens from her bundle of nerves right down to her hole.

Her breathing hitches, and I watch her skin start to glow as she blushes. She's a fucking masterpiece if there ever was one.

Discarding my cut and dropping it on top of her clothes pile, I drop to my knees, hooking her legs over my shoulders and tugging them tightly to my back.

"I want you to be loud; I want your next-door neighbor to hear you. Now hook your ankles behind my head and hold the fuck on."

Without further warning, I face plant straight into heaven, feeling Kelly clench her thighs against my head as I do. I gather the nectar she has from her hole, swipe it up, and spread it with my fingers, nibbling my way straight to that perfect bud that's protruding out at me and begging to be sucked. Coming up for air, I look up at Kelly and see that her nipples are erect. I give them a little tug, making her gasp and quiver.

"That's it, little girl. I wanna hear those moans."

"Dags...I can't. She's the sweetest old lady."

"Kitten, I don't care—I want her wishing she took her hearing aid out."

Tugging on her nipple again, I delve back into her juicy pussy, this time adding my tongue into the mix as I swipe her juices with my fingers and drive them into her hole back and forth, back and forth, which gets her mewling like a cat. I can hear her swearing in Spanish as she scratches and pulls at the bed sheets.

I latch onto her clit and shove my fingers deep inside of her pussy, making her scream as I feel her pulsating around my fingers, clawing for friction.

"Ahh, Dagger! Fuck me! Fuck me!"

"Not until you come around my fingers first; you wanted my fingers last night, so now you get them. Fuck them, little girl, I want to see your cream streaming down my hand," I urge her, then go back to sucking on her clit as I continue finger fucking her how she wanted me to last night.

Every now and then, I look up to see her writhing around, tits in the air. God, she looks so fuckin' perfect my dick can hardly wait his turn.

I fuck her faster, making her clench down on my fingers, "Ahh, yess! Yes! Fuck! Faster!" she screams, shuddering.

I have her exactly where I want her, and up the tempo to take her over the cliff. Watching her cum last time was mesmeric. I pump my fingers in and out of her faster, reducing her to a babbling, moaning mess. Her hand fists my hair fiercely, and as I feel her thighs starting to wrap around my head tighter I gain more momentum, sucking and gently biting down on her divine clit.

I hit the jackpot as Kelly screams bloody murder into the air, which is heavy with sex, arousal and her rich scent. "Yes! Y-E-E-E-S-S! Daggger!"

I raise my head above her sweet-as-fuck pussy and watch the bewitching scene of her cumming, admiring her as she trembles and quivers from the aftershock.

"Perfection, Kitten. Absolute perfection."

***

An hour later...

"Brother, I thought you were gonna be ten or fifteen minutes! You look like a man who got a good lay, so does that mean you're back on?" Bear asks me as we drive back to the clubhouse.

"We didn't really touch on that...we were too busy touching everything else," I admit, grinning. "What can I say? She gets under my skin and I can't help myself. Fuck...I don't want to hurt her, but I can't promise her what you and the rest of our brothers have with your women. What the hell am I gonna do?"

"Dags, man, get your head out of your fucking ass! Has she asked for more? Because not once have I heard her say shit like that."

"I know, brother, but I can't be sure. Fuck, I don't want all this drama. I just want sex; none of the feelings crap or lovey-dovey shit. She's never asked for that, you're right; all she has said is that she wants to explore the connection we have. Neither of us know why it's there, but it is."

"Well, there's your answer, but you're so stuck in your ways that you forget she's not club pussy you're free to pick up and drop when you want. You and Flex are too alike, brother! She could be good for you; you never know until you try."

10 days later...

"Doc, would you hurry the fuck up and get these stitches out already? They're driving me nuts. I'll take the fuckers out myself just to get on my bike again."

"Dags, man, calm the hell down! I can see you're agitated, so hold your hand out. You'll feel some tugging and it might sting a little, but that's what the beer is for."

"All right, got it."

Doc comes to sit in front of me with a pair of small scissors, starting to cut the stitches on the side closest to him, then wiggling and tugging to get them free.

"That's one done. You up for the get together later on?" he asks, clearly eager to keep my mind off of what he's doing.

"Yeah, it should be good, but I want a long ride in town first if you're up for it? I need to let off some steam." He's already down to the third stitch; I didn't even feel the second one come out.

"Got nothing to do with not getting any for over a week, has it?" he quips, not taking his concentration off of my hand.

"I don't know what you're talking about; I've just not been up for it. Not being able to use my hand kinda puts me out of commission. Don't you worry; once I get my hand back, I'll be taking all the club girls back to my room."

I hear a heavy exhale as the words leave my lips, and look up from my hand to be met with Jade's deathly glare.

Oh fuck!

"Really, Dagger? Is my best friend aware of what you're planning?"

Sighing, "Jade, look, me and Kelly are just having a bit of fun; she knows what I'm about."

I regret the words as soon as they spill out of my mouth—in truth, we didn't really talk about it. Instead, we talked with our bodies, fucking each other senseless. The last time I saw her, I had to get her to ride me. She looked like a goddess with her hair whipping back and forth as she took my dick.

"Oh, okay. I'll be sure to remind her of that later. Doc, did you want anything from the bakery?"

Just like that, I'm clearly dismissed from the conversation.

Ah fuck, I don't need any headaches!

If I'm being honest, it's no wonder I haven't gotten any for nearly two weeks with that sexy Kitten tempting me in my mind every night. Me and my good hand have been the best of friends while I picture her.

"I'll take a couple of those muffins Sue likes. Thanks Jade."

With a final shake of her head at me, Tinhead's Ol' Lady and Kelly's best friend walks out of the club in a huff.

Doc gives me a knowing smile, then turns his attention back to my hand. "Don't worry about it, Dags, I know everything you said before Jade came in was all talk. You'll get there too, son. It won't be long."

Huh? What's he talking about?

I'm about to ask him what he means when Axe comes over to check on me. "How's the hand looking, Doc? Is he gonna have to be put out to pasture, ya think?" my Prez smirks at me with a chuckle.

"Cheeky fucker, being 40 don't stop me healing," I argue, elbowing him in the ribs as Doc continues to work on me.

"Ah, that's what I like to hear, brother! Want to ride out once your stitches are out?"

"Hell yes, that's just what I was saying to Doc a minute ago."

"You're nearly done, Dags. Got the last couple to take out, then you just need to do some clenching exercises on your hand before you attempt to ride," Doc tells me, not looking up from my hand.

Axe is staring down at it too. "You won't be helping out in Jenna's bakery anytime soon then? No career change?" he jokes.

We all start laughing, and I shake my head.

"Yeah boss, I've decided to transition from club life to serving you coffee. I'd scare all of Jenna's customers away!"

Axe smiles and shakes his own head, turning for the door. "Come and find me when you're ready to ride; I'm just gonna go check on Ryker."

"Alright, last stitch," Doc announces. "This is a big one, so it may hurt, okay?"

"Doc, it can't hurt any more than the cut did. Just get it over and done with."

Nodding, he starts cutting and tries wiggling it free, but at first there's no give. Eventually, he tugs harder, and then yanks it free.

"Fuckin' hell Doc, you weren't kidding, were ya?" I look over my hand and see that a few spots of blood have pooled along the dark pink scar running the length of my palm. "Looks good though, thanks."

He responds with a big smirk. "All in a day's work for a bikers' club."

***

Around 4pm...

The ride out through town is so freeing that it feels like a balm to my soul. We get about halfway through our route before my hand starts to burn like fuck—it's not as far as I wanted to go, but I ain't about to damage my hand again and go another two weeks without riding. I promise myself that the only time I'm gonna stop riding again is when I'm dead and buried, but even then they'll have to prize my dead fingers off my baby.

"Looks like you have company, brother," Axe says over the speaker connected to our lids as we pull into the clubhouse.

Looking around his bike as he parks up, I spot Kelly's car next to Jenna and Jade's Beetle.

Fucking great!

I park next to Bear and Flex's bikes, kicking the stand up on my bike and tugging off my lid.

In my peripheral vision, I see Axe, who's looking between me and the clubhouse. "Brother, what is going on with you? You don't touch a club girl for weeks, and now you're getting visitors? I've never seen you like this" he says, a quizzical look on his face.

"Axe, I don't even know, but I'm trying to be gentle and let her see I ain't the one for her, I don't know how to do just one woman; when have you ever seen me in any kind of monogamous relationship?" I ask with an exasperated tug on the nape of my neck.

"Sounds familiar to Flex and Zara's scenario. He had his wife's death, but you got your own barrier to contend with; and I ain't talking about the age difference—it ain't bothering her, and it clearly ain't bothering you as much as you say it is. If it was, you wouldn't have dragged back to your room...twice."

I meet his eyes as we both dismount, shocked.

I didn't think any of my brothers had noticed I'd given in twice...fuck!

"How the hell? Dani?" I ask him as we carry on walking to the clubhouse's main door.

Slapping me on my shoulder, he nods. "Yeah, my woman wanted my opinion. I gotta say, after seeing you two together, you seem to just fit."

I walk back through the noisy clubhouse, the atmosphere buzzing with the sound of Nikki Minaj and the smell of alcohol.

My eyes zone in on the ass I'd know anywhere, and I see her facing towards the bar, chatting excitedly to Jenna and Zara. She's got those skintight leather-effect pants she wore on my birthday, and I find myself admiring the way they seem to mold to her ass like they've been painted on her.

Her scarlet shirt is cut off at her midriff, exposing a strip of her tanned skin, and her hair hangs loose in her natural waves, the club's lights making it shimmer. As my eyes skim down to her feet, I see she's wearing a pair of killer heels with studs on the narrow heel.

Fuck! They're hot as hell!

I know I must have been staring for a while when Axe's low baritone voice hits my ear. "Brother, if you're not interested in her, you need to tell her and be ready for another man to step in. Are you ready for that? Because I bet Wrench, Brains, or even Red would gladly step in."

I can't help the growl that emanates from deep in my gut at that bombshell.

Shit!

For a moment, I think I'm in the clear, but then Axe steps into my line of sight and shoots me a shit-eating grin, shaking his head as he heads towards the hall leading to the bedrooms. The look tells me I just failed his test.

Motherfucker!

"Dags, how was your ride out? Does your hand feel better?" Bear calls out from the far end of the bar, a beer in one hand and a cupcake in the other. I see heads flick in my direction at the mention of my name, the dark-haired beauty standing at the bar gawking at me in my peripheral vision as I stride over to Bear.

"Bud, the ride was exactly what I needed. I had to turn back once we got into town as my hand started to burn, but it feels good to get back on my bike."

"I'm glad, brother. You drinking, or you gotta take painkillers?"

I can't help glancing back at the woman who makes my body hum with need, but after a second, I tear my eyes away and answer Bear.

"I'll take a Bud for now, but Doc says I gotta be careful. I'm just going to grab some food and my drugs. I'll be back in a few."

I head for the bedrooms, walking past Kelly and Jade. As I do, their conversation stops abruptly, and I feel the tension coming off Kelly in waves.

"All right, Kelly?" I ask casually.

In response, she turns away and replies sharply, "Yeah, I'm perfect thanks. Just peachy!"

I know she knows what I said about the club girls—there is no way Jade hasn't told her what she overheard—but I decide to grab my painkillers before jumping into that. Rounding the corner to go to my room, I hear them talking again. Jade must have said something Kelly didn't like, because when she replies, her tone is indignant.

"He just needed to get his dick wet, and I needed to get my pussy fucked! There's nothing else to say, Jade. Can we change the subject now?"

***

Two hours later...

I'm sitting here nursing a beer that I've had for the past 20 minutes. I've already had one, but I've decided to make my second last on account of the painkillers. My brothers and I are chilling on the corner couch, chatting and taking it easy. Wrench is already on his way to being wrecked, and Brains has fucked off to his room to get some, but the rest of us have our feet up on the table in front of us. Our usual rock music stops suddenly and some Latin music comes on. It's turned up full blast, and I glance over to see the rest of the women are in the corner dancing around. I try to keep my looks over into the far corner to a minimum, but I can't help but glance over every time I hear that filthy-as-hell laugh.

"Still not locked down Kelly yet?" Flex mumbles to me, dropping his head closer to my ear so I can hear him clearly over the noise.

"Flex, no offense, but I ain't you, brother. I've been single all my life and don't know any different, so why change the habit of a lifetime?" I ask as I take a slurp of my beer, sneaking another sly look at her from the corner of my eye.

"I hear ya, Dags, you're preaching to the choir, but if or when you do decide to admit it, you need to know that that shit is gonna knock you on your fucking ass, brother. Trust me, I wasn't ready for it, but when I gave into my feelings, the fact that I would never need another woman was crystal clear. Take it from someone who went down a similar road."

"Fuck's sake, V.P., you, the Prez, and Bear have all had my ass about this."

"That's because they've been there too, brother. Whatever you decide, we got you."

I can't deny anything without lying, but—

"Hey."

As a familiar voice stops my thoughts in their tracks, my body freezes and then thrums with energy so palpable I'm eager to swing my eyes over to where she's standing. Giving in, I look up to see a tipsy Kelly staring down at me, gnawing on her plump bottom lip.

Wrench gets up and goes over to turn the music down, and I feel a stab of annoyance as I see his eyes flick down to look at Kelly's ass as he passes her but refocus my attention on the beauty in front of me.

"Hey yourself."

"How's the hand?" she asks in a husky voice.

"It's getting there," I tell her, flashing her the angry red welt across my palm,

The tension between us is so palpable that you could cut it with a knife, but I hate that it's there, caused by the unspoken words—the unspoken *truths*—between us.

"I think we need to talk," we both say in unison.

I pick my beer up, take her hand and lead her to my room, closing the door behind us.

In response, she flashes a dazzling smile at me that's not quite wide enough to make her dimple pop out, but eases the tension somewhat.

She breaks the silence first as I pick my beer back up, blurting out exactly what she wants. "I want you to fuck me again."

Her words nearly make me choke on my drink, and I end up spluttering in surprise. There's no-one quite like Kelly—she tells it how it is with no bullshit, just straight up unfiltered.

"W-What? How is that gonna help matters?"

"Because you need it, and I want it."

I rub a hand over my face. "Kelly, you don't know what you're asking. We'll talk about this tomorrow."

"We will not, because I know *exactly* what I'm asking, Dagger...I want you to tie me up, fuck me, make yourself cum before allowing me to, and take what you want," she purrs, leaning down close to my face so I can see underneath the red crop top she has on. She's braless and turned the fuck on; her nipples are as hard as diamonds and pointing right in my direction.

Fuuuck!

My dick's starting to throb with the need to fuck her again, spill my cum all over her body, and mark her.

Shit!

As hard as it is, I pull my eyes from her deliciously delectable body, staring over at the opposite side of the room and dismissing her.

"Little girl, don't start what you can't finish. You don't know who you're dealing with," I grumble over the lip of my beer bottle, taking another swig of the lukewarm nectar.

Her eyes scan mine, falling to my lips as she smirks at me. Cocking her hip, she leans in close to my ear and says in a sultry, husky, determined voice, "No, it's you who needs to realize who you're dealing with. I know I can bring you to your knees...*again*...you just gotta let me. Do you remember how my wet lips were wrapped around your cock on your birthday? How I took *all* of it, right to the back of my throat, and sucked...every...last...inch, then took all the cum you gave me and swallowed it? I bet that if I slid my hand inside your pants right now, your dick would be throbbing in my hand, begging for me to take it back into my mouth."

She turns on her heel and stalks off, and I watch that ass go towards the door. She isn't wrong about my dick being hard for her, but the idea that she could bring a man like me to his knees is bullshit...

My reply makes her hand freeze on the handle. "I'm too old for you and you're too young for me, just let it go. What we had was me fucking you out of my system, that's all."

"What a load of utter crap! I don't care about that age bull you keep telling yourself is a problem, Dagger," Kelly snaps back over her shoulder at me. She's glowering, trying to hide the wounded look in her eyes, but I see it loud and clear. I could kick myself for it, but I know I have to do this.

"Look, we can't be any more than this, but it was fun while it lasted," I spit. Seeing her wince at my words like they're venom stings me too, but they are out there now.

I open the door myself and stride out, and she follows, then screams at me, "Fine, suit yourself! See ya around, asshole. I'll stick to my battery-operated cock; at least a vibrator doesn't break your heart!"

She lifts her chin and swivels around on her heel, and I stare after her as she goes back into the main room, probably walking straight up to Jade, Zara, Jenna, and Dani.

Grabbing the fresh, icy-cold beer Flex extends to me as I walk back into the main room and sit back down a few moments later, I don't say anything until I've finished it and he's handed me a new one.

He opens his mouth to speak.

"Don't say it!" I snarl before he can manage a word.

He raises his hands in surrender, and I drain the rest of my beer next to him, Wrench, Axe, and Bear—but my eyes can't seem to focus on any of my brothers. I keep looking over Axe's head, staring at that sexy woman.

Our age gap will be a problem for her; if not now then down the road, I tell myself.

"You all right there, Dags? You've been staring at my head for the past five minutes," Axe enquires after a while.

Glancing back down to meet his eye, I see his eyebrow is quirked up as though he's waiting for an answer from me.

Oh shit, what were they talking about?

"Yeah sorry boss, just distracted...what was that?"

Axe shoots me a puzzled look. "Distracted, hey? Everything okay?"

"Yeah, all good. So what is it you were saying?

"I was just saying that me and Dani have set a date for the wedding in March next year so Ryker's old enough to stand next to me during the ceremony. She wants the works; shirts, ties, suit pants. You down for that? I promised my Ol' Lady that I'll make it happen, after all." The stern look he gives me tells me that if I say no or bitch about it my ass is getting a beat down.

I inwardly groan about it, but out of all of the Ol' Ladies in the club, I will do it for Dani. "You got it Prez, anything for your and Dani's big day."

***

"You shouldn't have drunk so much on those painkillers, Dags. Take it easy for the rest of the night otherwise the floor is going to come up and meet your face soon," Doc informs me from the couch.

I haven't really moved from this spot all night, just drinking and trying to ignore the temptress over in the corner. The girls have a monopoly over the music, but no one else seems to mind. Zara, Jenna, and Jade giggle at something a tipsy Kelly just said and she changes the song to one of my favorites, Black Sabbath's *'Iron Man'*.

The iconic guitar riff booms through the club, and as Ozzy's voice hits my ears, all the girls swivel towards me. Kelly starts singing at the top of her voice, never breaking eye contact with me.

"Has he lost his mind?
Can he see or is he blind?
Can he walk at all?

Or if he moves will he fall?
Is he alive or dead?
Has he thoughts within his head?"

Before I can react, she turns back on her heel singing the rest of the song towards the girls and swigging her drink down.

I smirk at her little show, tilting my head to one side towards Doc.

"I'll be okay, Doc, I'm gonna crash soon, don't worry about me, brother."

The song changes, but the music is still blaring. I watch a drunk Wrench and Tinhead talking to the girls as they sing and dance to some new song. Then, I see Wrench wrap his hands around Kelly's waist, tugging her against his body, and instantly feel fury boiling up inside of me and my back teeth start grinding against each other.

"Dags, you can't blame either of them, ya know? You told her…"

"I know exactly what I told her, Doc. She can do what she wants." As the words leave my mouth, I know they are absolute bullshit, and so does Doc—I see him look at me like a chastising father, but what's done is done.

I stand up about to go to the bathroom before going back to my room—I don't need to see this shit. As I get to my feet, I witness Kelly strolling towards the hall leading to the bedrooms with Wrench's arm wrapped around he as he whispers shit in her ear.

My body tenses on instinct, and my heart starts racing in my chest.

I'm gonna kill that little fucker!

As they disappear into his room, something flips in me and I stalk after them, punching my fist into the drywall next to the bar.

My lip curls as I hear her giggle—the giggle that's meant for me—and I storm towards Wrench's room, kicking Wrench's door open with such force it bounces back off the wall.

Kelly doesn't flinch; she just lays there smirking with an eyebrow arched, but Wrench practically jumps out of his skin. I see she's sprawled out on his bed with her legs wrapped around head. His pants are hanging loose and undone, and she's still got her top on but her pants are gone.

"You! Pull your pants up!" I roar at Wrench, seeing red.

"You! Pull your pants up!" Dagger growls at Wrench, furious.

Poor Wrench, he doesn't even realize that he's a pawn in this game between me and Dagger. I can't believe Dagger's reacting this way though, what did he expect after what he said in his room or what he said to Doc about the club girls? Did he really think that Jade wasn't going to tell me?

"Dags, what's up? Kelly told me she's free," he says, a look of pure confusion and shock maring his handsome face. I feel bad for dragging him into this, but after what happened out there, I had no other choice than to resort to shock tactics to get this stupid red-haired biker to see what everyone else can.

"You. Get up and cover *my* pussy up, now!" he barks at me.

I'm covered with my thong still on—even if it is practically see-through—so I lean up on my elbows and argue back, knowing what that does to him.

"What's the problem, Dagger? Can't I finish what I've started?" He never breaks eye contact, but his nostrils flare and his jaw clenches at me.

Even though I know better than to remove my eyes from his, I glance down to his crotch area and see that he's as excited by this little show as I am.

I remember that Wrench is still in the room watching the scene play out between me and Dagger, so I decide to push Dagger's buttons further—if it means getting what I know we both want, then I don't care about the consequences. I spread my legs wide enough so both men in the room can see, and hear both of their breaths hitch at the wetness on the sheer material, showing them my clear arousal.

I hear Dagger growl and readjust his cock, but he never takes his eyes off me and my body, which is the perfect invitation for the next stage of my plan. I reach up, slide my thong to one side, and glide my fingers through my wetness. It enthralls me that Dagger is watching me take pleasure in exposing myself to another.

"Enough!" Dagger roars. My body listens to him, and I freeze mid-swipe.

"Wrench, get the door and follow me," he growls.

Wrench does exactly what he says and grabs the door, while Dagger tugs my ankles to the edge of the bed before scooping me up in his strong arms. I instinctively wrap my legs around him and bury my face into his neck. Finding a bead of sweat there, I lick it painfully slowly and am rewarded with a growl.

Wrench follows us and opens Dagger's door, trailing in after us and turning on the light without saying a word.

I can feel Dagger is close to the edge—tension bunches underneath his muscles, and I swear he's about to break his jaw from clenching it so damn hard. He lets me slide down his body so I'm standing right in front of him, and Wrench stays in the corner, watching on and flicking his hooded eyes from me to Dags.

"Wrench, brother, you can stay and watch if you're game—this is the first and only time you get to. But know this..."

Dagger tugs on me so my back is flush up against him, my ass rubbing against his dick. He wraps his arms around my body, palming my boob through my shirt, then tugging my thong to one side to show Wrench my pussy. "This right here is mine. She belongs to me; she has for a long time."

The words I've waited so long for him to admit make my heart warm with pure adoration, but I don't really get to take stock of them before he rips my thong off and swipes through my wetness once, twice, and a third time, making me arch my back so my head sits on his shoulder, mewling like a cat and swiveling my hips to gain more friction.

I don't hear Wrench move an inch or say a single thing, the sexual tension in the atmosphere is so thick I can taste the testosterone in the air. Like a bitch in heat, I am thrumming with need for my mate to take me. Now the one I have wanted for so long has claimed me, I don't care about anything past embracing this delicious moment.

Swiveling me around in his tight grip, Dagger walks me over to his bed, perching on it with me standing in between his legs. Then, he grabs onto my butt, squeezing it almost to the point of pain, which the whore in me only wants more of.

He pulls me onto his lap so I have to drop my legs to either side of him and my pussy is right above his denim-clad cock. Needing him, I grind up and down on him. His hand glides underneath my shirt and palms and squeezes the flesh of my boob, then zones in on the peaks of my nipples, tugging gently at first and then sharper, making my back bow.

Fisting the bottom of my top, he starts to tug it upwards. I peer under my eyelashes at him, seeing his heavy-lidded gaze of anticipation clear as day now.

I revel in it. If I could, I would bottle up and bathe in his clear desire and craving for me.

His need goes right through me, sending intoxication rippling through my body, which only sets the inferno inside of me burning hotter.

I lift my arms up in the air so Dagger can remove my top with ease, and he wastes no time baring my tits for his pleasure. In my peripheral vision, I see Wrench come closer to the end of Dagger's bed, getting a good look as I grind against Dagger's hard dick.

"Brother, you can watch, but you ain't touching what is mine again. Ever," Dagger growls from the back of his throat. My heart buzzes with excitement on hearing those words again.

"Remember, you have your safe word if you don't want him here, but I know you do, Kitten, I can feel your heat on my dick. Now give me your lips!"

I stretch up so my nose brushes up against his, the need for each other strong through our touch. I linger there for a moment, memorizing the fire behind these green and brown ringed eyes before I finally let my lips fall onto his, electricity crackling between us. Like a dying man wanting a drop of water, his thirst is fervent and frantic as his tongue plunders my mouth, impatiently demanding mine as we devour each other and needing to fuse us back together.

As I let him dominate my mouth like he dominates me in the bedroom, I grind down hard on his cock, then sneakily reach down and start popping his buttons. My fingers fumble with the fastenings, and I'm bursting with need for him to take me again. I've missed this—I've missed *him*.

Eventually pulling apart, I rest my nose against his, his warm breath tickling my face as I stare back into his eyes and carry on my pursuit of getting his cock free for me to ride him.

As soon as I pop the last button, I have to fight back a low growl as I see he's gone without boxers. I fist his cock and pull it out, and as the air touches it, I see a single milky drop spilling over the edge of his veiny, juicy dick.

I keep my eyes on Dagger as my thumb swipes through the wetness, coating the whole pad of my thumb with precum.

A growl rumbles from Dagger's chest. "Look at Wrench, little girl, then push that thumb into your mouth nice and slowly and suck on it how you suck on my dick. Show him what he's missing."

The deep baritone of his order sends an electric sensation shooting down my spine towards my clit.

Carajo, that's hot…

I turn my head and push my naked breasts into Dagger's chest; the delicious softness of his t-shirt rubbing on my sensitive nipples.

As I turn my head, my eyes lock on Wrench, who hasn't moved from the edge of the bed, the desire and lust beaming off him sending a ripple of want through me. He may never have been a real option for me, but he's still hot as fuck, and the thought of him watching me and my man turns me on.

I casually lick and suck on my thumb as the distinct flavor that is Dagger blooms on my tongue, bringing back all the memories from the first time I took him in my mouth and stoking the inferno that grows every time I'm around him. As I continue sucking, I put on a show for

Wrench, capturing my thumb in my mouth and grazing my teeth against the pad in slow motion. I push my thumb deeper into my mouth, flicking my tongue against it as I suck hard up and down it before pulling it out right to the tip. I swirl my tongue up, down, and around it.

I notice Wrench is moving his hand furiously, and peeking down, I see he's jerking himself off. His cock is nice and thick, and darker than Dagger's. My tongue snaking out, I turn my attention back to my man and suck my thumb clean, holding Dagger's blazing eyes as I roll my hips against his cock.

Before I know what's happening. I'm being lifted off my feet and his wallet is being stuffed into my hand. "Condom! Now!" he demands, slamming his mouth back on mine brutally hard enough to bruise my lips. Gasping for lungfuls of air as I reluctantly pull away from his lips, I find the bright red condom wrapper and open it with my teeth, wasting no time before rolling it over Dagger's luscious cock.

"Now fuck me and feed me your tits!" he growls at me.

"Yes, Dagger," I purr, lining up my dripping pussy to his angry, pulsating cock. I wrap my hand around it to steady it and waste no time before I rise up on my knees and sink myself onto it straight down to the hilt, knocking the air completely out of my lungs.

"Fuck! Fucking perfection!" Dagger growls into my neck, his bristle prickling the sensitive skin there. "Kitten, don't go shy on me now, I'm showing my brother what no man is having but me. This is the first and only time I'm sharing your orgasms with someone else. I can't promise you a future, but I will never watch someone else have you. Your orgasms, your moans, your kisses—everything belongs to me! Now fuck your man!" he growls between clenched teeth

"Yes! They always have belonged to you."

With that, I rise up and ride him, taking him slow at first, which earns me a hard and delicious spank on the ass that zings straight to my pussy.

Using his shoulders, I press down and pull up, bouncing on his dick and taking him again and again. This is gonna be quick because I've missed him and his cock so much, but I don't let up, determined to please him. However long this lasts between us, I will make sure he never forgets my name.

"Ahhh, Dagger, I'm so close!"

The air in the room is thick and heavy with our combined pants and heavy breathing. Just then, I hear grunts, and swinging my head away from Dags, I see Wrench fisting himself painfully tightly with his head thrown back.

"See how Wrench is fucking his hand so hard? It's because of you, Kitten; he knows he's never getting anywhere near your pussy. This golden cunt is mine!" He reinforces his words by jerking his hips, meeting my thrusts with everything he has until we find our perfect rhythm, just fitting together.

"Ahhh fuck, baby!"

We moan and hiss out into the room, and I feel myself near the nirvana I always get with Dagger. It's not a coincidence, no other man has ever been able to make me come the way he does.

Dagger bites down on the nape of my neck where it joins my shoulder, sending me off into an explosion of a climax that has my whole body tensing. I finally collapse onto Dagger's chest as my pussy keeps clenching, milking him. My whole body is alive, and my chest is pounding wildly. I hear Dagger groan loudly in my ear, and look up to see his eyes roll back in his head as he pushes into me one last time.

"You're mine, Kitten!" he growls animalistically, and I feel his cock throb inside me as he cums.

Once we're both spent, my whole body sags against him, feeling electric. Every nerve ending is on high alert, and I swear that the lightest touch could set me off again.

There's a shuffling noise behind me, and I turn back around to see Wrench cleaning himself up with some tissues from Dagger's nightstand and shoving his dick back in his pants.

"Woman. I'm gonna say this one time and one time only. Quit looking at Wrench's dick, otherwise I'll paddle your ass," he grinds out as his semi-flaccid cock jumps inside of me, making me clamp down on it.

"Tut, tut, little girl."

I peer up at him with a big smirk, not wanting to break our bubble by moving.

"Dags, we cool, brother?"

I look over at him to see that his dick is back in his pants, and he's looking nervously over at where I'm butt-naked on a semi-naked Dagger.

"You gonna try to stick it in Kelly?"

"Dags!" I chastise him, slapping him lightly on his chest.

"What? I need to know if we are going to have a problem. Told ya, Kelly, your pussy is going nowhere near my brothers."

"Haven't you been paying attention, Dagger? I have said from Halloween I've wanted you; that's why I asked you to fuck me! If I wanted Wrench, I would have gone there already," I bite back at him.

He raises his eyebrow at me as he realizes he's been played, and Wrench breaks the silence.

"We're all cool, Dags, I'm not going to try and stick it in Kelly. She's all yours, brother."

"Good. I'm hers too, I just needed this little girl to play games to wake me up to the fact," Dagger says softly.

Wrench leaves, and Dagger swipes his thumb across my bottom lip, gazing at me like he finally understands our connection. I slide off his lap, disconnecting our bodies, and my pussy burns from his hard fucking.

Dagger swings his legs off the bed, discards the condom, and slides back into next to me. He instantly wraps his arm around me as I stare up at him, discarding his shirt so I can lay my head on his now-naked chest. His sweat glistens in the soft lighting of his room as he plays with my fingers, interlinking our hands. I snatch his injured hand up and place a gentle kiss on the center of it, right over the raw welt.

"How's it feel?" I enquire, still not quite believing that we are here enough to talk about it.

"Still aches now and then. It looks worse than it feels."

Nodding thoughtfully, I peer back up at him with a dirty smirk playing on my lips. "So when can I say it?"

"What's that, baby?" he says, smiling down at me as he tickles my side, making me squirm and sending me into fits of giggles.

"I told ya so!" I squeak out.

~ Chapter 21 Kelly ~

Four weeks later — Ryker's 1st Birthday...

"Morning. I know you're awake, your ass keeps grinding against my dick." To prove his point, Dagger humps my ass, sending my body into overdrive.

I finally give up on going back to sleep, rolling over to face the man who has either been in my bed or had me in his every night since he got his head into gear.

His face lights up in that trademark Dagger smirk. Since we have been 'together', he's been more relaxed, although he still gives off scary vibes if we go out somewhere where people don't know him. We haven't had any problems yet, although that might be because we haven't really done much talking apart from with our bodies...

The more time I spend with him, though, the more invested I am in us. I just want to know he has the same ideas about this as I do. He said no man can go near me, but what about another woman going near him?

"What are you thinking about so hard over there? If you need to ride my dick again, that can be arranged, but we'd better get up and help with the party set-up first, otherwise Axe is gonna have my ass," he chuckles out as his arm reaches over to the nightstand next to him to show me the time on his phone.

It reads 8:22am, but we've already been up for hours. He woke me up around 4, clawing two orgasms from my body as he held my hands above my head and fucked me senseless. I fell asleep on him, then woke him up around 6:30 for more by sucking on his dick. Once he woke up, he used his belt to tie my hands behind my back as he finger-fucked both holes, and then allowed me to cum before he took me again from behind. My body aches and stings from the spankings he gave me, but it's always worth it.

"Well, you'd better get your ass in that shower then. I'm gonna go grab something to eat before I take mine."

I go to roll out of bed, but Dagger's hand wraps around, tugging me back so I fall back onto his chest sideways. "Kelly, is there something you need to say? Say it."

"I don't know, Dags, it's just...what are we doing about us? What are we?" I ask as I gnaw on my bottom lip. Unable to look him in the eyes, I fidget with the bed sheet as the room grows silent.

Dagger sighs. "Kelly, I don't know what to call it, but know you're the only woman in my bed just as much as I'm the only man in yours. That's how it's gonna be, okay?" he asks, tipping my chin up so my eyes meet his.

It's not the answer I was hoping for, but it will have to do. I feel unsure about everything right now, which is totally not like me.

I need to go and speak to Jade; she always knows what to say...

"Yeah. I'm gonna go grab something for breakfast, babe. Want me to grab you something?"

He searches my eyes for a moment, then asks, "Can you grab me some sausages and toast?"

"Yeah, sure." I jump out of bed, shove my legs into my sweats, and when I struggle to find my shirt from last night, Dags throws his at my head.

"Here, catch," he sniggers.

"You jerk, Dags!" Pulling it over my head, I snatch one of my shoes off the floor and fling at him, unable to help the giggle that bursts out of me despite my worry.

His face is a picture, the pure dominant coming out in the way he growls at me, still laying there in bed.

I quickly exit the room, sniggering on my way to the kitchen, where to my relief I can smell food and hear my girls.

"Morning bitches! How are we all today?" I ask the room as I walk in. Sue and Zara are cooking, and Jade and Dani sit at the table. After strolling over to grab a plate, I head over to the hotplate by the stove.

"Well, good morning to you too. You look awfully refreshed this morning—wouldn't you say so, Jade?" Zara smirks over her shoulder at me.

My gaze goes to my best friend, who beams back at me. "Oh yes, definitely rested, what with all those screams of '¡follarme más duro!' and…what was it, Zara? 'Kitten, take it all!'?"

I stick my tongue out at her and flip her the bird, making her and Dani collapse into hysterics.

"Hilarious, you dicks! You're just hating on me; all I did was come in here to get some breakfast and some advice!"

I snatch a up few sausages and pancakes, drizzling some syrup over them for good measure, then plop down into an empty chair next to Jade.

"I thought everything was going great with you and Dagger?" Zara quizzes me, worry etched on her face.

"Oh hell yes, things are pinch-me fantastic!"

"But?" she enquires, turning to face me with spatula in hand.

"How d'ya know there's a 'but'?" I sass her as I munch on a sausage.

"Oh trust me, she always knows," Dani pipes up over her mug of tea, rolling her eyes.

I snigger back at her.

"Well, is there?" Zara asks as she comes over to me with her hand on her hip, her platinum blonde hair bouncing around as she does.

"Fine! Yes. But it's nothing major…or at least I don't think it is. I asked him what we were. I'm not a label kinda girl, but I want to know that he isn't gonna stick it anyone else while we're together."

"That's fair enough; I was the same with Flex. He fucked around like Dags, but anything more than sex was cheating on his wife's memory. With Dags, I can only go by what I've heard and seen. Sue used to call him a permanent bachelor, but maybe not so much anymore. What did he say?"

"Hmm, I guess. He told me that he didn't know what to call it, but that I was the only woman in his bed just as much as he's the only man in mine."

All the girls look at each other silently, and my heart drops.

"What? Spit it out! Tell me," I insist, fighting a sudden wave of frustration.

"It's not the worst thing he could have said—I was expecting him to call you his 'fuck buddy'. Just do what you do best, Kelly."

"What's that, Zar'?" I lean forward at the suggestion, eager to hear how I can make sure of where we both stand. For my part, I would never go anywhere else…the man is a God!

With a mischievous grin, Zara beams from ear to ear at all the girls and then back at me, then says five words which make us all collapse into giggles. "Bring. Him. To. His. Knees!"

***

After finishing my breakfast and getting Dags' too, I walk back into his room expecting to see him fully dressed, but it's empty. I place his foil-covered plate of food on the nightstand, then hear that the shower is still running.

Zara's words echo in my head, so I strip out of my sweatpants and Dags' t-shirt, dropping them on the floor outside the steam-filled bathroom as I enter. The dull hum of an extractor fan resounds in the far corner, and I see him through the condensation on the glass panel. The morning light shining through the glass illuminates every ripple of muscle, and I watch the cascading water of the shower flow over his hair before dripping down the slope of his lean back and sexy tushy and spilling down those ropy, powerful thighs. The water clings to his lightly tanned skin, the definition in each muscle making my mouth fill with saliva.

Even though he made me cum so many times last night and again this morning, I burn for him again.

I don't think I'm ever gonna tire of this man…

Before I get caught gawping, I step into the far end of the cubicle, the zing of electricity at him being so close only matching the excitement swirling in my stomach as I come up behind the man who makes me ache inside, making him jolt slightly in surprise as I slide my hands over his slick, inked arms before driving them up his wet, slick, tattooed back then moving them around to his chest. I press my face against his back, and my tongue snakes out instinctively, licking some of the water droplets that have mixed with his sweat. His body automatically relaxes as he places his rough, tatted hand over mine.

"Baby, what are you doing here?" he says, the softness in his raspy voice sending delicious sensations over me that hit the spots he knows better than anyone, including my vibrator.

"I'm here having a shower with you, but first..."

I kneel down on the wet shower floor, tapping the inside of his legs.

Dagger automatically shifts his stance so his legs are spread enough that I can squeeze through while still remaining on my hands and knees. I peer up underneath my eyelashes, my hair plastered to my back from the waterfall pouring over me. God, he looks magnificent, his soaked copper hair hanging loose.

I scan down his body, taking in all the tattoos covering his defined chest and admiring the way his sinewy arms seem to stand out even more under the flow of the water.

I sneak out my tongue, flattening it against his already-hard cock that's jutting out towards me.

"Mmmm...baby, didn't you get enough of my cock this morning?" he grumbles under his breath, caressing the rough pad of his thumb against the apple of my cheek before he slides it against my bottom lip that's still wrapped around his cock, the roughness sending tingles straight to my pussy.

He pushes his thumb in my mouth, and I smile and pull away.

"Never! I always want your cock, you know that. Plus I wanted to shower with my man..."

I try out the last words, letting them linger in the air to see if I get any reaction—we've used them before, but only during sex. Not seeing any panic, I carry on sucking his cock, but Dagger has different Ideas.

He steps back away from my mouth, tipping my face up. "Kitten, you have to realize that I've never done a straightforward relationship. I can't promise you what my other brothers have got, but I promise you that I'll try. I'll try harder than I fuck. Even if I can't give you what you want, I can give you what you need," he chuckles, steely determination in his eyes.

"Dags, I get it, I just need to know where we stand. If you say you're willing to try, then that's more than good enough for me...but if you have a need to stick your dick into something other than me while we're together, you need to tell me and end it before you do. If I find out you're sleeping with other women as well as me, trust me, you will be a eunuch eating your own cock for breakfast. Are we clear?"

"Crystal, Kitten."

"One more thing. I need to know...why do you call me Kitten?"

"Haven't I told you this? Because. I. Am. Obsessed. With. Your. Pussy...and the woman who it belongs to. Now, don't make me ask twice, take my cock like the dirty girl you are!" Dagger growls from above me, fisting my hair tightly. "Suck *your man* off before his balls explode and he becomes a fucking eunuch on his own," he laughs, the sound rough, gravelly, and sexy as hell.

I see that familiar sparkle in his eye that appears when he gets something he wants, and I hope to myself that that will always include me...

***

"*Happy Birthday to you, Happy Birthday to you! Happy Birthday dear Ryker, Happy Birthday to you! Yay!*" We all sing in unison for Axe and Dani's son.

He giggles from where he's perched on Axe's hip, staring at the big '1' candle on top of the amazing cake Jenna made him—it's a huge monkey that looks just like the one he's had since he was born that he takes everywhere with him.

Dani walks off towards the kitchen wearing a cute turquoise fit-and-flare dress that perfectly sets off her dark hair and coloring and makes her look a million dollars, and her make-up—done by *moi*, of course—looks *perfecto*!

As she passes me, she looks over her shoulder and asks, "Kel'? Can you help me with the cake?"

"Of course, beaut'!"

I leave the rest of the girls and head to the kitchen after Dani, but just as I get to the door, I feel the heat of my man's stare on my back. Sneaking a look over my shoulder, I see him staring at my ass hungrily for a second before his eyes snap up to my face.

He looks at me with the same stoic look he always wears when we're around others, but I shock him by rolling my tongue inside my mouth and pushing it right up against the inside of my cheek. Just like that, he drops that façade he's perfected for me and only me as he breaks into a dirty grin and shakes his head at me.

Jackpot!

I give him my back again, feeling the heat return as I carry on heading to the kitchen to help Dani. As I enter, she's standing inside with a smirk and Ryker's cake on the counter, untouched.

As I realize that she didn't need help with the cake at all, she practically launches herself at me, squealing.

"Oh my God Kel', tell me everything that happened earlier! Dagger hasn't been able to tear his eyes off you all afternoon! Babe, I've got a great feeling about this."

I can't help grinning like a Cheshire cat back at her and start doing my happy dance around the kitchen, which includes some slut drops and dirty dancing.

"It went well then?" Dani giggles.

"Yes. There are no words at the moment, but he said exactly what I wanted to hear. Normally I would be skeptical at a man committing, but knowing Dagger and the way he is, what he says is what he means, and wants…and that's me, *chica!* I can't believe I finally got my man! Oh, that reminds me…do we have any Nutella?"

I smile at her and give her a wink, sending her into more fits of giggles.

~ Chapter 22 Dagger ~

Three days later…

I meant my promise to Kelly that I'd try, and I hope she knows how hard I *am* trying. Old habits are hard to break, and I've been this way since I was a teen. Relationships never interested me; if I could get my balls emptied and find someone to explore my tastes in the bedroom with, that was enough.

I wasn't looking for a woman, but then she came along being stubborn as hell and not taking no for an answer. I've been giving her space and watching her with her girls like a respectful partner would, even if I've wanted to march over there, drag her back to my room, bend her over the bed, and use that new toy I got on her every time I've seen her with others. I need to see her as Kelly, not as a pussy I can dominate whenever I want.

It took me a lot to stay in the same spot when she pushed my limits by imitating her sucking my cock, but I did it. That girl fuckin' loves to test me, and I fuckin' love being tested, but she doesn't try it as much as she would if I was anyone else.

I know she needs me to take control as much as I need the structure of controlling someone. She gets me and understands me and my needs, and I understand her need to be dominated and have her control taken away without ever actually giving it up. She's always in control of her life, her career, and herself, but it puts her under so much pressure that she needs me to take over her desires in the bedroom and just be in and enjoy the moment, feeling what I give her. She revels in it, and it's more than sex for us.

I'm chilling at the bar, and it's gotta be around 10 or 11 now, but my Kitten still hasn't come to me. Taking a big swig of my Bud, I gaze over to the far corner of the room where Zar', Jenna, and Jade are. The club girls sit in the opposite corner, and I can hear Brandy slurring and bitching about me being off limits now, so I stop listening to her whiny ass.

I'm just about to go over to ask the girls whether they've seen Kelly when Sue and the sexiest woman alive walk back in the room together, looking thick as thieves. She's not realized where I am, and I stand and watch as she peers around the corner to look over at the couch and then glance in the far corner at the club girls.

She flicks her head back around, the worried look in her eyes instantly softening as her gaze meets mine, and then her beautiful mouth breaks into a full beam. Stalking over to the temptress—my Kitten—I push her up against the wall behind her. Her breath hitches as she peers up at me, her eyes growing bigger than I've ever seen them as I push my now-hard cock up against her. I thread my fingers into the hair at the base of her skull, tugging so it pinches. Hearing her hiss at the pleasure and pain is even more enticing.

"Little girl...where have you been?" I rumble out under my breath. I'm close to my limit of waiting, and she can feel it too. She's been holding her breath, but eventually exhales as my dick rubs on her pussy, teasing her.

"Why? Did you miss me, Dags?" she teases, licking those perfect plump lips of hers.

"Yes!" I growl as my patience snaps and I pull her arm, dragging her all the way back to my room. As I swing the door open, I see my Kitten has been busy.

So, she wants to play…She's always so in tune with me.

This woman never stops surprising me…

***

"I see you want to play. Are you trying to top me? Trust me, Kelly, that ain't ever gonna happen," I bite at her more forcefully than I intended, making her look like I slapped her.

"What? No, of course not. I wanted to play, but also we haven't spent much time together today and I appreciate you giving me my space…even though I thought you were about to eat me up at dinner when I had that pickle," she chuckles.

That fuckin' pickle!

I was jealous of it being in her mouth, and it didn't help that the minx was nibbling on it like it was my dick whilst staring right across the table at me. I was so close to jumping across the table to get her. I can't help myself; everything that woman does is sexy as hell.

"So…I see you've been going through my closet?" I ask her authoritatively, never removing my eyes from her or her sexy-as-sin body. I watch her reaction carefully as I pick up the first object she's placed on my bed—my well-used dark brown flogger—gripping it with one hand. I spank her lightly on her denim-covered ass, making her jolt and snap out of the trance she was in looking at the bed and bringing her back to the here and now.

"Little girl, you want to play with these?" I ask in a commanding tone.

"Yes," she says simply in a breathy gasp. My dick's pushed to the point of pain against my jean buttons at the way she sounds alone—the fucker is gonna have indents on it by the time I let it out.

"Good girl. You wanted to play so we play…hard! Once you're naked I want you to stand next to the bed bent over at the waist and holding your ankles."

Longing shimmers back at me in her eyes as she absently licks her bottom lip, breaking out of her daydream to carry out my demands.

I stand back watching and admiring the scene as her clothes are hurriedly discarded like the whirlwind she is to reveal all that delicious skin that belongs to me. As her ass comes into view, the temptress stares at me over her shoulder, grasping the string of her bright purple thong so it cuts into the tanned plump flesh. The growl that rips through my chest at the sight makes her eyes flare with desire.

Eating up the space between us in a few strides, I fist the material tight within my hold, pulling fiercely as my other hand wraps around her and pins her to my body, so my cock is snugly cocooned in between her ass cheeks. Leaning down, I latch onto and claim her mouth as our tongues get reacquainted. She's the oil to my flame, making me burn blistering hot.

Her taste of candy and peppermint blossoms on my taste buds as our mouths plunder and explore each other, hungry for one another like it's been months since they've been connected.

My hand seeks out the hard peaks of her pebbled nipples, which are already eager for attention. I pluck them between my forefinger and thumb like the sweetest cherries, playing with and grazing them while I'm still taking my fill of Kelly's mouth. This woman entices and plunders not only my mouth, but every part of me—including the heart that's laid dormant like Pompeii for the last four decades.

She purrs, her whole body vibrating and reminding me not only of my need to dominate her, but her need to be dominated.

I reluctantly tear my lips from her, then place a chaste kiss on her nose. "Woman, quit distracting me and finish what I asked," I grind out as I turn on my heel, trying to resist the urge to take what I want from her here and now.

Kelly grins at me, then bends over holding her ankles, her delicious ass pointed straight up into the air looking like pure perfection.

Exquisite.

I stride back over to stand four inches away from her, staring with fascination and deep hunger, and appreciating her gorgeous body.

The sight is bewitching and completely enticing. "Good girl, now spread your stance a little…and a little more? That's it, perfect. Remember you have your safe word, Kelly, you need to use it if it gets too much as I won't be able to read your face. Tell me you understand."

"Yes, I understand, Dagger," she replies to me in a low, breathy, eager voice.

That's my girl, be excited…because I am too, darlin'.

I make quick work of discarding my own clothes, eagerness and electricity thrumming through my body that's rife with need and want. It's thick in the air too. I need to be inside of her, but hold back as she needs this as much as I do. My cock stands to attention, pointing right at her and bobbing around in eagerness.

Picking up the flogger, I know I need to build her up to strikes, so I swipe the leather strips gently across her ass, loving how it jiggles as I do. Building up the anticipation for her, I repeat the motion again, swiping and grazing the soft leather strips from left to right across those ample blushing globes. I decide to kick it up a notch and push her a little further down my darkened path. If she wants to go there with me, then I'm submerging into my world tonight…

Pulling my arm back, I bring the strands of leather down so they snap on her ass, still fairly light but making her yelp out in surprise,

I wait for the safe word to escape out of her lips, but it doesn't. The sound of heavy breathing in the room is broken by my voice. "Again?"

Please don't turn me down…

"Yes! Oh God, yes, Dagger! More! I need more. I want to feel it on my ass as I walk," she pants out breathlessly.

I swipe my fingers through her slit and find she's totally drenched, even though I've barely got started. I can't resist letting my cock swipe through her wetness too, letting him get in on the action even though it's not his turn.

I hear Kelly mewl and gasp at the skin-on-skin contact on her pussy. "Ahh Dagger, yes!"

"Not yet, little girl," I say, forcing myself away from her alluring arousal by taking a reluctant step back. I bring the flogger back down on her backside with the same force, landing one, two, and three blows over each cheek and seeing them bloom with welts. Sweat starts to gather on my temples from exertion.

"Bend over the bed, Kelly!" I bark out, my sexual frustration held back but hanging by a knife's edge. I'm so close to just taking her before I give her what she needs and deserves from me, but I don't.

"More! More!" she screams out, flicking her hair back so it sticks to the sweat that has started to roll down her spine. "Dagger! Don't stop! I want it harder! she begs me as her ass bounces in the air.

If my Kitten wants harder, I'll give her harder…

My eyes dart down in between the apex of her thighs, and I see her arousal glistening in the soft light from the corner lamp.

I tear open and roll on a condom, then grab the other object she got out of my closet—a wireless double love egg which I bought especially for Kelly, even though it cost a few hundred dollars. Gathering some of the arousal off of her inner leg, I coat the toy in it and it slides right home.

I feel Kelly freeze at the contact, then drop her head into her chest, relaxing more as I position the smaller part over her clit.

I decide I'm gonna have some fun before I fuck her and bring her to the edge, so I grab my phone and link the app I downloaded up with it. I start it at the lowest setting to get her started, and it's so quiet I don't even hear anything until Kelly's breathing starts becoming labored and I see her fisting the bed sheets.

Fuck!

My dick is aching with desperation to get back inside her, but I busy myself with flicking my hand over the button to increase the intensity again and again. Soon, all I can hear are Kelly's gasping and steadily louder moans.

I give us both a breather for a few seconds, then turn up her egg to level three, making her scream breathlessly.

"Dagggggger!" she screeches, her voice growing hoarse.

Not giving her much chance to get her breath, I spank her with the flogger, striking across any flesh that wasn't touched by the previous whipping over and over until my hand gives out and drops it.

As the last of my resolve evaporates, I pull the egg out and toss it on the floor, not bothering with turning it off before I ram my dick straight inside of Kelly's tight, soaking wet pussy. I fist her hair, fucking her with everything I have, and she meets my every thrust. I know I'm close, but I hold back, needing to feel her shatter around me first. Tugging her hair tighter, I jerk in and out, burying myself right to the hilt and hitting the exact spot I know will send her over the edge.

As soon as I hit it once, twice, then thrice, she explodes like a firework, clamping down on my dick, screaming and gasping as we pant together. Trying to milk me dry, she clenches back down on my dick, which sets my own orgasm off. That spine-tingling, ball-aching, out-of-this-world feeling ricochets through my whole body and I empty my load.

"FUUUCK! Kelly!" I howl out through gritted teeth as the aftershocks ripple through my whole body.

My legs give out and I fall on top of her, sending us both into fits of laughter that leave us both panting as I roll us over so I'm spooning her. She falls asleep with my arms still wrapped around her, our hearts still pounding.

Even though I know she's napping, I kiss her whole face, peppering pecks over her as I slowly and gently disconnect my cock from her. Easing myself off the bed, I go grab a warm cloth to clean us both up with and some lotion from my closet to use on her ass. Walking casually back over to my sleeping beauty, I can't help staring at her in her light slumber. I clean my dick with one side of the washcloth, and then hold Kelly's legs open with one hand, placing the warm cloth over her pussy and cleaning her up gently and carefully, needing to take care of her. I roll her over so she lies on her front and admire my handiwork, the ruby red welts decorating her tawny-colored ass like a work of art. They're beautiful, scattered in each direction—if it wouldn't hurt like a bitch, I'd bite this ass.

Just staring at my marks all over her makes my dick come back to life in full force, but I focus on aftercare and squirt a generous amount of the soothing lotion into my palm, smothering her whole ass with the cream then carefully rolling her onto her side so I can lay underneath her. I lower her head back on my chest, letting her sleep while I place kisses on top of her head and tell her, "I got you Kitten, I'm never letting you go."

***

30 minutes later...

"What *was* that?" Kelly asks, breaking the silence in the room as she peers up at me, her face rosy with sleep. She offers me a lop-sided smile, still trying to wake up.

I gaze back at her, smiling as she swipes at the drool that's pooled on her chin from sleeping on me.

"Hey, sleeping beauty. What was what?" I ask, thinking she's talking about the tattoos she's staring at.

"I felt like I was having an out-of-body experience; flying, maybe. I had it the first time we had sex, remember? What is it, some kind of sex drug?" she grins at me, that dimple clear under her stunning smile.

"It's kinda like a drug, it's called subspace. It's basically a sign that a sub has reached peak submission. Some people become nonverbal, some act feral, and some experience an out-of-body euphoric experience like you. The feeling will always lead to a crash, though, which is why a good Dom does aftercare like I did by holding you while you slept and rubbing cream up your ass."

"Wow! I wasn't expecting that! I'd heard about subspace in books, but the feeling…it's…all you said and more. It feels like I'm on drugs. Hold up, did you say, 'cream up my ass'? You jizzed all over my ass to help with the marks and stings?" She screws up her face, the expression on it one of pure confusion.

"Nah! I put lotion on your ass, the aloe vera helps. What am I gonna do with you, Kelly Davis?" I grumble out, still staring down at her.

She beams up at me with a mischievous glint in her eye, and I shake my head. "Get that look out of your eye, little girl, you need to rest. You mentioned about having space over the past few days, but you gotta know that I didn't stray."

"Well that's great news, Dags, but what else is there? You look like you want to say something else."

Sighing; her observations are always on fucking point with me.

"Yeah…well, I never even *thought* about another woman. I can't promise I won't fuck this up, but I need you to know I only want you, Kitten. I'm excited to see where this goes, and I hope that I don't end up fucking up what I have with the one woman I want more than I've ever wanted anything…"

Just then, her past words come back to me from nowhere, and I trail off in shock.

Oh shit! She was fucking right! She was the one who brought me to my knees all right!

"So what colors are you wanting me to try out on you? My treat, seeing as you're helping me tidy the studio on your break. It's the least I can do, Mags," I tell her.

As she eventually succumbs to my stern glare with a nod, I go to grab a few eyeshadow palettes and a selection of foundations, then bring them back over to where she's sitting, putting them on the ledge in front of the mirror that hangs on the wall in front of Maggie. She's as cute as a button with her gorgeous natural blonde hair and big piercing blue eyes.

"Thank you for this Kel', you sure you don't mind?"

"I'm sure, I wouldn't have said otherwise, *chica*. Do you want a natural look or a heavy metal grunge look?" She stares at me for a moment, wide-eyed, then starts to chuckle, shaking her head.

"Natural it is."

I hardly chat when applying make up for a client to be able to concentrate and regulate what I'm doing, but with friends, not so much. I've nearly finished applying her foundation and I see Mags looks completely relaxed, so I decide to make conversation.

"So how are things with your dad?"

She instantly freezes, and I see the shutters starting to come down in her mind, so I blurt out, "I know you don't like talking about it, but you know you can tell me anything. Even if you just need a break, let me know. We're all here for you and we care about you."

"Thanks Kel', I really appreciate that. I appreciate all of you girls, including your men—even if Dagger still scares me. Seeing that he makes you happy makes me happy too."

"Aw hon, you have nothing to be scared of with Dagger...between us, he's a pussycat really, but don't go telling anyone, okay? Otherwise I'll never hear the end of it!" I tell her, and we both end up a giggling mess. Picking the eyeshadow palettes up, I show them to her so she can pick her shade. She chooses the one I thought she would; a creamy gold shimmer so subtle you'd only notice it if the light catches it.

Sweeping it over her eyelids, I ask a question I've been curious of the answer to for a while now. "Mags...can I ask you something? You don't have to answer if you don't want to," I add, remembering to tread careful with her—she's not Jade.

"Yeah, sure," she informs me, her eyes still firmly closed.

"Have you had sex?" I ask more bluntly than I intended to.

Fuck! Great one Kelly!

I feel her tense up, holding her breath, and a stab of guilt fills my chest.

"Oh my God, Mag—"

"No," she answers in a barely audible whisper.

When I speak again, I'm more collected. "It's okay, Maggie, you just haven't met the right man to give your V-card to, that's all."

I give her a little reassuring squeeze of the shoulder as I walk around her chair to do her other eye.

"I haven't had a date with a boy since I was in high school; I've been kissed and that's about all. When a boy asked me to go to prom, my Dad flipped out and got…in a mess, so I decided not to go in the end. It doesn't matter though, whatever."

My heart aches for my Lil' Mags. Going to prom is a rite of passage, and I bet she's not even been on a date because her low-life dad, if you can call him that.

***

After giving her a little makeover to cheer her up, Maggie admits her Dad's getting worse at home. I tell her to go grab her things and come back to mine, but she keeps telling me she's fine and it's not his fault, it's an illness.

I get it; if my *Mamá* or *Papi* were addicted to alcohol and gambling, I would find it hard to deal with, but they'd still be my parents. They wouldn't give up on me, so why would I give up on them?

"What time are you meeting Dagger?" Lil' Mags asks me as we're walking back from my studio.

I almost don't hear her as I'm busy organizing receipts for my taxes on my tablet, but I look up and smile. "Oh, in about an hour. We're having lunch at a drive thru, and then we're going to go catch a movie he's chosen…so more than likely some godawful horror film because he knows I hate them. What time are you finishing work today?" I ask as we near Main Street, heading for the crossing,

"Oh that's sweet, I'm so pleased Dagger finally got his act together! Don't let him make you watch a horror if you don't want to though. I'm finishing at 6, it's Saturday so I'm closing. Jenna's hoping to try some new coffee syrup flavors out, though, so I'm looking forward to that," she informs me, her little face beaming at me. Her natural makeup looks amazing, making her killer cheekbones and those rosebud lips pop.

Thinking about our movie date has me super excited, so I pull out my cell and message my man:

Me:- Babe, can't wait 2 see u, excited for our date :oP…What's the movie we're seeing? *50 Shades*? ;o) LOL xx

My Dags: - Kitten, I can't wait to get my hands on you. It's been a long ass day. *50 Shades*? Wtf? I ain't seeing that shit; that dude's a fucking pussy. He's not got anything on your man! X

I can't help smirking at his response.
Only Dagger…
Just then, Maggie breaks my thoughts of him. "What movie are you seeing?" she enquires, raising her head and pretending to peer over my cell like a goof.

I shake my head and chuckle as I link arms with her. We're about the same height, so it's a helluva lot easier with her than Zara, that's for sure.

Coming up to the crosswalk, we wait for the traffic to slow and finally stop.

"Come on missy, better get you back to work before—"

I get interrupted by a booming voice behind me. "Excuse me, do you know the way to Dyersburg Hospital?"

Pivoting on my heel, I see a man hanging out of a black van advertising an out-of-state plumbing company staring right in my direction.

I glance at Maggie, but she just shrugs at me. I take the lead so we can both cross the street quicker once we're done. I approach the lost driver, reassuring myself as I get up to the driver's side that he doesn't look like a mass murder.

They never do... I hear my *Papi's* voice say in my head.

He's middle-aged, wearing work overalls, and is bald apart from a few hairs on his head. Why men like him don't just shave it off is a fuckin' wonder to me. I decide to speak for us both, as I know how crazy shy Maggie is around men.

"Hey, you said you wanted the hospital? Keep going straight down Main Street, turn left about a block down and keep going for another four blocks, then you'll see a big sign f—"

I stop in mid-sentence as I see something glimmering on the seat. I know a gun being carried casually is not uncommon in Tennessee, and I've been around guns all my life. What with my Dad being in the police, but on the seat...in a plumber's van?

Staring at it and then back to the driver, I see his once-friendly expression has changed to an indifferent glare. Alarm bells in my head scream for me to run, and I swivel on my foot about to snatch Maggie away when...

"Ahh fuck!", a sharp sting biting my neck.

I try to push Maggie out of harm's way or scream to warn her, but my voice sounds so weak already.

"Maggsss..."

My vision around the edges of my eyes starts to blur, and I feel a huge hand clamped over my mouth. My whole body's dragged along the sidewalk, which starts to swirl around me, moving in slow motion. Another set of arms are wrapped around my legs fiercely tight, then I feel rope being tied around my ankles, constricting them. I try as hard as I can to see a tiny glimpse of my fuckin' kidnapper, but whoever is behind me has other ideas, facing me roughly at the back of Maggie's golden locks.

She's slumped over, her arms twisted behind her back at an awkward angle and tied with thick industrial-looking rope…

All I can think of in this moment is how I am missing out on a date night with my man. Then everything goes black…

I'm waiting outside the bakery for Kelly. I texted her 10 minutes ago to tell her I was outside, but she's still not come out. The movie starts in 30 minutes, and she wanted to grab something from the drive thru on the way there, so I decide to go and see what's keeping her so long.

The cheeky minx will pay for it in the bedroom tonight…

Hopping off my bike onto the near-empty sidewalk, I head through the bakery and am greeted by a flustered-looking Jade serving the last of the customers before they shut shop.

Spotting me as soon as I walk through the doors, she shouts over the noise of the coffee machine, "Ah, decided to bring her back have you? You two are as bad as teenagers. Has she got our best barista with her too?"

Frowning at her question, I scrub at my beard. "Sorry Jade, you've lost me…I'm here to pick up Kelly, isn't she here?"

My eyebrows knit together as I glance around the bakery trying to understand if I misread her text. I pull out my phone and check my messages; she definitely asked me to meet her at the bakery.

"Huh? What d'ya mean, Dagger? Her and Maggie have been gone ages. She took Maggie over to her studio to give her a little makeover on her break and they've not come back since; I just assumed they were with you. Can you check her studio? They're probably still there because Kel's talking Mags' ear off." she chuckles as she serves another customer.

"Yeah, I'll go over. I'll come back either way to let ya know, okay? See ya in a few."

I can't help but worry; Kelly's pretty good at being on time and if she's late she normally messages me or calls. I try her phone again as I cross over at the lights, but it rings out and eventually goes to her answering machine. As I round the corner leading to the back of her studio, I see Kelly's car is still here. She's going to leave it here overnight while I take her on the back of my bike—my first time ever riding with a woman as well as her first time riding with me, but she doesn't know that yet.

I go to the front of the studio, which has frosted windows so people can't look in but plenty of natural light still gets into the studio. I rap on the door loud enough that people further down the street are twisting their heads to see what the noise is.

"Kelly! Maggie! Are you in there?!" I holler at the door as I continue thumping, but nothing.

What the hell?

Picking up my cell, I ring her again and again but it keeps going straight to a answering machine after ringing out.

Fuck! Where are you, Kelly?

***

As I walk back through the bakery doors, I see it's a lot quieter now, and Jade and Jenna both swing their heads toward me wide-eyed like rabbits caught in the headlights.

"Dagger? What is it?" Jade asks, her brow wrinkling with worry.

"She's not there. Neither of them are, Jade. The studio's shut up, but her car's parked out the back like she was going to do tonight. I've called her phone half a dozen times too."

"What?! What do you mean? This is weird, Dagger..." She trails off as I hold up a hand to stop her.

"Which way does she walk to the bakery from her studio?" I ask as I peer out of the window over at the crosswalk and the traffic cameras.

"Across the street and then past the salon next to her. Why?"

"Try not to worry, I'm just going outside to use my phone."

I don't give either of them time to respond to me before I stride back out of the bakery to sit back on my bike. I can't stop staring at the crosswalk as I wait for Axe to pick up.

"Yo, Dags," he answers, sounding surprised. "I thought you were meant to be out with Kelly?"

"Boss, she and Maggie ain't here. This ain't like either of them. I know something's off. I just know it."

"Brother, what do you want me to do? Want me to get Brains to check any cameras in the area?" Axe asks, suddenly all business.

"Fuck yeah. I wasn't sure if he could hack the traffic cameras, but if he can, ask him to check the ones on the crossing closest to the bakery and her studio."

"Yeah he can, I'll get him on it once I get off the phone. Get Jade to check with her parents; don't they live in the suburbs? She's probably up there."

"Nah brother, her car's still parked behind her studio."

"Okay Dags. Check in with me and give me an update if you hear anything. Want me to send Bear over to the bakery?"

"I will do Prez. Thanks, brother. Yeah, maybe. You know I'm not good with keeping the girls calm."

"We got this. Speak soon."

***

Walking back into the bakery, I see Jade on the phone, Jenna looking on as she serves the last customer. Both of their faces are masks of pure worry.

Fuck, maybe I wasn't gentle enough with them when I told them she was missing. I ain't got time for feelings. I just want to find Kelly, then I'm gonna tan her ass for a month.

"You trying Maggie too?"

"Yeah. Her phone's doing the same as Kelly's ringing out and going straight to a answering machine."

Fuck this shit!

I go through the doors to the kitchen for some quiet and to call Axe back to chase him. It's barely been five minutes, but I need to know she's okay. He answers after two rings.

"Dags?"

"Axe, Jade's tried Maggie's phone too and nothing; it just rings out and goes straight to a answering machine too. Could—"

"I'll get Brains on it after the camera stuff, brother. Don't worry, we *will* find her."

"Axe... she knows how important communication is to me, and as much as I've never had a relationship before, I know I haven't fucked it up yet. If I had, she would be here giving me shit, and something in my gut is screaming at me that this isn't normal. You know when Dani went missing?"

I hate to ask, as it's a hard topic for him to talk about—hell, it hurt me too when I found out what Dani had gone through with that sick psycho—but I need him to know how bad I feel about this.

"Yeah?" he says, his voice turning dark. I know it pains him; it would me too if it was Kelly.

"I have the same intuition you did. I know Kelly, this don't feel right, and my gut has never failed me once in all the time I've been in the club."

There's a slight pause over the phone until he breaks it. "I'll get Brains to work his magic tracing their phone. I believe in your gut too, though, it's got us out of scrapes a couple of times over the years. Get Jade to check in with Kelly's parents in the meantime, and call me if you get anything else."

"Yeah, sure boss."

Ending the call, I exit the kitchen and find Jade, who's cleaning the tables down.

Cutting straight to the chase, I inform her, "I need you to ring Kelly's Mom and Dad to see if she's there. Axe has got Brains checking the traffic cameras on the crosswalk and tracing both their phones, but in the interim I need you to call her parents."

"Yeah, of course Dags. I hope she's at her parents'," she whispers.

"Me too Jade, me too."

***

"Hello, Mrs. Davis? It's Jade...Oh I'm good thank you, I was wondering if Kelly was there? I can't seem to get ahold of her...Oh, she's not? Okay, have you heard from her at all?...Okay. Oh, I'm sure it's nothing. Have a nice evening; see you soon."

Jade ends the call and shakes her head at me, and I feel like a caged tiger. At this moment, I need the open road, and I need Kelly.

Fuck! Where the hell is she?!

"Dagger? I'm seriously worried now; this isn't like either of them," Jade says, her voice wobbling.

Ah shit, I can't do emotions, or women crying...

"I know. I am too, Jade, but I promise you I will find them both. Me and the club will do whatever it takes to get them back," I say in a steady tone to bring her some reassurance, even if I don't feel it myself.

I'm about to grab her to give her a tight hug when my phone starts going off. My heart leaps as I run into the kitchen and pull it out of my pocket, quickly falling again when I see it's Axe.

"Boss?" I answer in a clipped tone

"Dags...I need you back at the club. Bear is coming over now, he'll be there soon to bring the girls over too," he informs me flatly.

"Fuck, boss, is it bad?" I ask aggressively. I'm tightly wound like a coiled viper, ready to strike and sink my venom into whoever is to blame.

"Brother, just get here," he says, then the line goes dead.

"Fuck!" I growl.

I swipe my hand over the kitchen counters, smashing all the dirty dishes onto the floor. My rage is at boiling point, and about to go over the edge at any given moment. I tug and pull at the back of my neck to the point of pain, feeling my lips curl as I try to get myself in check. The women don't need to see me like this, and Kelly certainly doesn't.

I grind my back teeth to gain composure, and as I turn around to go back out of the door, I see Bear in the doorframe, a look of pure desolation in his eyes. We don't say anything, but as I go to walk out of the door, he wraps his arms around me.

"Brother we'll find her. You know we got this. I'm here for you; whatever you need I'm there."

I can't answer him—when I'm fuming, there's no talking to me. The only thing that helps me clear my head is getting on my Harley.

I just give him a curt nod and stride back out of the bakery, heading back to the club to face whatever fate has dished out for me.

***

"Come in, bud," Axe says as he opens his office door. Flex, Tin, and Bear follow me in, all surrounding me as we stand behind Brains on his multitude of computers, one of which he's linked up to the big TV attached to the wall.

"Dags, me and Brains have already watched this, but no one else has seen it. I don't want you thinking you're the last one to know. Press 'play', Brains."

"You got it, boss."

Brains does what Axe says, and at first the footage is unclear, but then I clock Kelly and Maggie coming into view of the camera at the crossing. I watch on at my woman walking towards the crossing, looking down at her phone and smirking—a glance at the time on the footage tells me that it's around the time she was messaging about the movies and '50 Shades'. Maggie says something to her as she stands next to her. Whatever it was, Kelly just shakes her head, laughing and linking arms with her as they wait at the crossing.

Kelly says something to Maggie as a black work van pulls up at the lights. A man inside shouts something at her and Maggie, and Kelly turns back around to see if he was talking to someone else, but Maggie just shrugs. They both walk over to the driver in the van, then Brains presses 'pause'.

"Why did you do that?!"

"I need to zoom in on the van and men to see if you recognize them at all," Brains replies levelly.

"Okay, okay. Get on with it."

It takes him all of two minutes, during which time we've all inched closer to the big TV, needing to get a good look at these fuckers who've got my woman.

When I get my hands on them, I'm gonna make them pay...

Brains presses the 'play' button again, and I see that Kelly is talking to the driver—it looks like she's giving him directions.

The camera can't seem to get a clear shot of the driver, but I see that he's maybe around my age, bald, and wearing some kind of uniform. As she's talking, something she spots makes her freeze, gawping at it. She turns to look back at the man, but at the same time, unbeknownst to her and Maggie, two men appear from around the back of the van—I can only assume they were riding in it. They're wearing matching overalls, so I think that's what the driver must have on too. The driver's posture seems to have changed since Kelly saw what she saw.

Watching the whole scene unfold is like watching a movie. Kelly swivels around to try and grab Maggie's hand just as one of the men puts something in her neck. She tries to push Maggie out of the way but looks to have no real strength doing it, and then she's calling Maggie.

Watching her like this, I have to block off the fact that she's mine. I need my head straight and my self- control back.

She looks completely helpless, falling over, then the man who injected her with what must be some kind of sedative clamps over her mouth as her arms flail all over the place. She's dragged the length of the van and off camera, then they do the same to Maggie. A passer-by runs over and looks to be shouting at the men, but they pay him no mind, then walk out of shot.

"I'm just going to show you the other camera, which had a view of the back of the van. Hold up…there we go."

I clap Brains on the back as he pulls up the other footage. I don't understand how he does it; I'm just motherfucking grateful that we have him, because the club would be lost without him.

As the other camera starts to roll, we can see for definite that the two men who were on the outside got out of the back of the van before rounding it to get the girls.

As we get to the part where Kelly and Maggie are bundled into the back of the van, the man who was dealing with Maggie at first starts tying Kelly's legs together.

What the fucking hell?

The men load the girls in then jump in the back of the van themselves. As soon as they're in, the van is speeding like hell through the lights to get out of there.

The next thing I know, Brains is going back and replaying a few frames, then going back and replaying them again. Seeing something, he zooms in real close and freezes over the image of the man in the van holding Kelly while the other one ties her legs. For some reason, he seems to twist and turn out of the way of the camera more than the others do.

What the hell?

"Bear, Tin, can you call Jade and Jenna in here?" Brains instructs curtly, never taking his eyes from the computer monitor. Axe nods, deferring to Brains' instructions, and both Tin and Bear return with a petrified Jade and Jenna.

Deep inside me, my own fear threatens to break free, but at the moment I'm trying not to feel. I need all the facts before we act.

Brains presses a few buttons, zooming into the footage and then running it through some program that makes it a hell of a lot clearer with no pixelation.

Brains turns to the girls. "This is the video from across the street from the bakery, and the facts are these at the moment; Maggie and Kelly have been abducted by three men in a van. That's all the information we have so far, and we need your help to see if you can identify any of these men. Could either of you tell me if you recognize any of them?"

I can't tear my eyes from the screen to look at their reactions, but I hear gasps, crying, and Jade choking out, "Oh my God, Dylan! They must be so scared."

"It's okay babe, we'll find her. I need you to watch and see if you recognize these men, okay?" Tinhead tells her softly, responding to her with all the emotion and feeling I should have earlier.

As for me, I'm numb. *These fuckers have my woman, and I need to get her back!* is all I can think.

"Okay," Jade replies, sniffling behind me. In my peripheral vision, I see Axe flick his chin twice at an expectant-looking Brains to start the footage up again. Brains plays the video twice more, and is about to play it a third time when Jade interrupts with steely determination in her voice that reminds me of her best friend.

"Hold up, Brains! Can you zoom in on his face? Him, the man who injects and turns away from Kelly?"

Brains does so, replaying it once again.

Jade exclaims three words, and as soon as they are out of her mouth, simultaneous hope and fury starts to bloom in my chest. "Yes! That's Mikhail!"

"Who the *fuck* is Mikhail?!" I growl at Jade, my anger simmering on the surface like hot fat in a pan, ready to spit at anyone who dares to stand close enough.

I see Tin glaring at me like he could go toe to toe with me right now for yelling at his girl, and I raise a brow at him in challenge. He may be 14 years younger than me, but I could take him easy.

Fortunately, Jade doesn't react to my anger, forcing us both to back down. "He's a dude she met up with a few times until he didn't call her back. I'd know that nose and those blue eyes anywhere. He showed up when we were out a couple of months back, and he wouldn't leave until I threatened him…with getting the Devils Reapers involved," she admits in a whisper.

Annoyance floods me that I'd never heard of his man before, but I know now isn't the time to get hung up on her dating history. "Jade, you need to give me her Mom and Dad's address," I snap at her.

"What? Why?" she asks, her eyebrows pulling together in confusion at my demand.

"Her Dad's a cop, yeah? Well, maybe this Mikhail was a low life he put in jail who's after revenge? He's got my woman, and I'm gonna fight tooth and nail to get her back," I say, verbalizing my innermost thoughts.

No one bats an eye lid at my declaration, then Axe pipes up, "Brother, that's a long shot, but at the moment I guess it's all we have. Take Tinhead with you."

"Axe, I can do this on my own," I reply, feeling exasperated, but his unwavering stare tells me to get in line and follow orders.

"I know you can, Dags, but we got you," he tells me in a gentler tone than his expression, slapping me on the back with a force that means finality.

"Okay, I'm in too. I'll take you; they know me," Jade pipes up, her head held high as she swipes the fallen tears from her face.

I'm about to tell her I want to go alone, but Brains interjects, "I'll send these pictures to your phones. I'm running the plates on the van, but I reckon they're either fake or stolen for certain."

Not wasting any time listening to anymore shit, I don't even wait to see whether Tinhead or Jade are following me as I stride back through the main room. As I pass, I can hear the whispers and sniffing of the women—her girls, Jade must have told them—and I'm just about to walk out the door when Brains hollers at me.

"Dags! Send me Kelly and Maggie's numbers and I'll trace them. You said their phones are still on, so if they're carrying them still, we can find them."

I agree with a nod of my head. Exiting the clubhouse, I stride right over to my bike. I should probably stay and form a plan, but I don't need to be cooped up chattin' in the fuckin' club right now.

"I'll send you the numbers, Brains. Thank you so much," Jade replies for me as she and Tinhead follow me out.

Good, one less thing to worry about. Now to go and meet my woman's parents…

***

Around 8pm...

The inky darkness of nightfall welcomes us a s we pull up to Kelly's parents' house. There's almost no light up here beyond the hue of the city in the distant horizon and the stars flickering above us.

Their house is a big family home with tan-and-gray brickwork and a huge-ass oak tree in the middle of their lawn that's gotta be easily a few hundred years old. The house has a wraparound porch and a big-ass drive which has two cars parked on it; one a dark-blue Chrysler, and one a red coupe.

Good, they're home at least.

Parking my bike up behind the club's cage, I sit there for a minute trying to compose myself. Ordinarily, I hate the police and they hate us, but these are Kelly's parents, so I need to reign that shit in and control the monster in me still clawing to get out.

Jade interrupts my thoughts by hopping down out of the cab of the cage and waiting on the sidewalk for Tinhead to get out to the truck. Tin climbs out, and I follow his lead as he locks up. Tugging my lid off, I place it over my bike as I dismount, following them up the path to the huge house. As we near it, it only becomes larger and more impressive to my eyes.

"Dagger, let Jade do the talking, okay? You're too close to the edge right about now, brother, plus she's known them since she was a kid," Tin warns me.

My teeth are clenched so fiercely I swear my jaw is about to snap in two, so I just give him a short nod, never taking my stare from the dark cherry wood door with its ornate brass knocker and glass panel at the top.

Jade wastes no time running up the few steps of the porch and knocking the knocker three times, waiting less than two seconds before she does it again more frantically.

"Red, it's okay. Let them at least answer first, okay? C'mere babe," Tinhead wraps his arm around her shoulders in an attempt to soothe the petrified look in her eyes.

I can't comfort her because I know my look is probably the same, if not downright maniacal.

I don't get to think on how this is going to go anymore before the door is swung open by a woman, who is an older version of Kelly. She's the same height and shares the same looks, although her hair isn't as long as Kelly's and has been dyed.

"Jade? What is it? Have you been able to find my *Niña?"* she enquires, her eyebrows drawing together with concern. She looks from Jade to Tinhead to me, and then back at Jade.

I look over at Jade and see that she's already trying not to cry. "Can we come in? We need to ask Mr. Davis something."

"Jade, you're scaring me. What is it? And who are these men?"

"Please? I don't think you'll want to give the neighbors a show. I'll explain everything once we come in."

"Of course. Please wipe your feet as you come in; I'll go grab Jacob. Don't worry, Pedro is locked in the kitchen eating his dinner."

She gives me and Tinhead a wary look before she turns away, although me more than Tin. I try to ignore the pang of hurt I feel at the look. I'm used to it, but coming from Kelly's mom, that shit stings. This is not how I imagined meeting her parents to go.

Kelly's mom leaves the door open wide in a silent invitation as she jogs down the hall in search of Kelly's dad. I push Tinhead out of the way and follow Jade into the house, where I'm greeted by the most amazing smells emanating from the kitchen—the air is filled with the scent of spices and what I think is chicken cooking.

As we stand waiting in the entrance, I clock pictures of a younger Kelly with huge oval-shaped eyes and a beaming smile that's missing her front teeth, holding onto her Mom and Dad's hands. I don't get to look over the rest of the collection hanging on the wall before I hear heavy footsteps marching down the hallway straight toward us.

As I turn, I'm met with the sight of the man in the pictures. His hair is as dark as his daughter's, aside from a few small graying patches sprinkled at the sides of head. At first glance, his dark hair and tanned skin could easily pass as Mexican too, but I recall Kelly telling me her Dad was American and from Florida ,which explains his darker tan.

"What's the meaning of this, Jade? Maria is scared half to death! Who are these bikers you've brought with you?!" He spits the words like venom, only adding to the wound we're all afflicted with.

I grind my teeth together, no longer giving a fuck about what this man thinks of me, then growl, "This biker right here is your daughter's man." I stab my thumb against my chest, hoping the sharpness of the gesture will help to keep my anger in check. "We're here to see if you can help us."

I cast my gaze over to Jade, silently lifting my chin to encourage her to tell them.

"Mr. and Mrs..."

Before she can continue, Jade gets interrupted by a frustrated Jacob Davis, who rounds on me.

"Back up a fricking minute! Did you just say you're *with* my daughter?! Over my dead body, buddy! You're practically my age! What are you, some kind of pervert?"

He closes the gap between us, fisting my cut in his grasp as the anger vibrates off of him. I don't even flinch; I've been treated like this by cops before, and name calling doesn't bother me...unless it's Kelly doing it.

I stare straight into his furious glare, suddenly completely stoic in the face of his anger. "Yes, we're together, and that shit ain't about to change, but right now, that ain't important. What is important is you helping us to find your daughter and her friend."

My last words cause him to loosen his hold, but he still glares me down before giving me a final shove.

"What do you mean 'find her'? Jade?"

His eyes scan over to her, and I can see tears welling up in her eyes...

Gnawing on her lips, she finally blurts out, "She and our friend Maggie have been...been abducted." She's just able to get the final words out before breaking down into full-blown tears, leaving Kelly's Mom and Dad just looking completely bewildered and lost.

"W-what? What do you mean? She has her pepper spray, she's prob—"

I cut the cop's ramblings off by grabbing my cell phone out of my back pocket and pulling up the photos that Brains sent over to me.

"Do you recognize any of these men?" I demand as I thrust my cell phone under his face.

Taking it off of me, he carefully inspects each picture. Not a flicker of recognition comes across his features, and he shoves the phone back in my face.

"No, none of them, why would I?" he asks disgustedly as he goes to his wife's side. Kelly's mom is a blubbering wreck, holding onto Jade as they try to console each other.

"Well, because Kelly knew the man in the last picture, and he's one of her abductors. We didn't know if he was someone you'd arrested or had conflict with seeking revenge or something."

I put the pictures back under his nose, pausing longer on them all and especially on the last one.

Jacob just shakes his head.

"H-How do you know Kelly knows the...the last man?" Kelly's mom pipes up, pulling away from Jade's embrace to peer up at me warily.

"Because Jade identified him," I inform them both.

"Yeah, his name's Mikhail. He's Russian."

As soon as the words are out of Jade's mouth, Kelly's Mom freezes completely, her mouth twisted in a look of pure horror. Her eyes widen, and she turns to her husband, locking eyes with him and shaking her head back and forth as she hyperventilates and starts fanning her face with her hand.

Kelly's Dad's whole posture has turned rigid, his nostrils flare, and he grinds his back teeth.

I don't get to ask what the fuck is going on before...
Bang!

Maria's body slams down onto the floor.
She's fuckin' fainted. Fuck!

***

"How long was I out, *mi amor*?" Maria whispers up from the couch in their vast, expansive lounge complete with high ceilings, dark wood furnishings and terracotta-painted walls that you would be forgiven for thinking are in Mexico or Spain.

Jacob hasn't stopped glaring at me since we've been in here, but the sound of his wife's voice snaps him out of his stare-off with me, and he turns back to her.

"Only a few minutes sweetheart. How are you feeling?" he asks as he bends down so they're face-to-face.

"F-Fine. Oh Jacob, our *Niña!* We need to find her before that monster…" Trailing off, she begins to gasp and wail into his shirt, gripping a fistful of it hard.

"What monster? Does someone want to fill us in on what the hell is going on? Do you know something that could help us find Kelly? Tell me!" I roar.

Fuck, my patience is hanging on by a thread; I can't handle this anymore!

I start prowling up and down the length of their couch waiting for someone to spill the fucking beans.

Tinhead clasps a hand over my shoulder, tugging me close to him ."Brother. Dags, try—"

I meet his gaze with an intense one of my own, and he reels back at the look on my face.

"Don't you fucking dare tell me to calm down, Tin! Are you telling me you wouldn't feel the same if this was Jade we were talking about? Because that's a load of bullshit and you know it! I just want to find Kelly!" I bark back at him, the atmosphere suddenly cooling around us as I hear Maria shifting to sit up on the couch.

I turn my glare back to Kelly's parents, who are now sitting next to each other as they clasp each other's hands. The horror, fear, and worry from before is still there, but something else flickers across both their faces.

As I notice that their lips are pressed together in matching grimaces, I know the shit they have on this Mikhail is big. I didn't get this far in life without being able to read people and trust in my gut, and it tells me that whatever has caused that expression is the key to everything.

Maria takes a long look at all of us, then says, "You need to sit down. We'll tell you everything."

~ Chapter 26 Kelly ~

14 hours later…

My eyes are so heavy I don't think I could open them if I tried.

Fuck, how much did I drink last night?

I try and fail miserably to grab or touch anything around me, and am startled by the sensation of something cool against my arms.

"Ssshh Kelly, you have to be quiet," Maggie's soft voice filters through my ears, her words coming through muffled like I have cotton balls stuffed in them.

Maggie?

I take a deep breath in, the stench making my stomach roll as the reek of piss, shit, and vomit linger over us.

I feel a small, sweaty palm clasp over my mouth tightly, which only has me flailing my legs trying to kick out at the owner…or at least try, as my arms and legs aren't moving.

Grasping the hand over my mouth, I try to claw it off me with everything I have, but the hand only holds me down more. "Ssssh Kel'! Please, they'll come back. Please be quiet."

As it dawns on me that the hand is Maggie's, I eventually calm down and feel her other hand stroke my hair.

Who will come back? Where are we?

"That's it, Kel'. Deep breaths, keep calm. Can you talk yet?"

Talk yet? What the hell…?

Without warning, my eyelids are being pried open and I instantly recognize Maggie's little face, but as she comes clearer into focus, I realize that her shy, sweet face is full of pure fear and horror.

I try to open my mouth to ask her what's wrong, but nothing comes out.

"Don't worry, you'll get your speech back soon, mine still hadn't come back until earlier. Try not to panic, Kelly, just rest up. The girls closest to us have been here for a week, and they've told me what the guards' daily routines are. We have time to talk about this when you get your speech back."

What the hell is going on? What does she mean 'the other girls'? Where the fuck are we, and what mother fucking guards?! ¿Por qué coño can't I speak? I inwardly scream in my head.

Some would call it a blessing, like Dagger.

Oh God, I bet he's losing his shit…

I try to remember anything that could give me any idea what's going on or who the people who have us are, but nothing. I try to speak, to ask Maggie if she's learnt anything else from these 'other girls', but the words vibrate around my skull. I'm screaming them in my head, so why won't they come out of my mouth? Why can't I hear them?

I realize that I can no longer see Maggie and feel panic setting in as I look back and forth, searching for her.

She finally notices and comes back into my line of sight again, and I relax a little, although I notice how small this room is…

Wait, it's a fucking cage!

Maggie's voice returns to my ear in whispered tones, "Hey, Kel', it's okay, please stay calm. It's okay, I'm right here. Deep breaths. I know it smells terrible in here, but I can't let you have a panic attack on me. Please."

She never moves her eyes from mine, holding them until she realizes my breathing has evened out. "That's good, hon. You should get your speech back first, which shouldn't take too much longer, then I will tell you everything. You have to try and keep quiet, or whisper if you really have to. The longer we pretend we're unconscious, the longer we have to plan to get out of this…place," she implores, her voice sounding strong even for Maggie. Her eyes tell a completely different story; they're filled with pure terror. She leans back against the bitterly cold metal cage and moves my head and neck so I'm leaning against her shoulder and won't end up with a crick in my neck. Whatever the hell this is, wherever the hell we are, I know my man won't be far behind.

***

"Wake up, Kel'! You need to wake up now," Maggie whispers into my ear with urgency.

My eyes spring open and search for her in the darkness, finally settling on her face at the other end of our small cage.

"W-w-what's going on, Mags?" I'm finally able to croak out. My throat's so sore, but thank God I can talk. I try and sit up, but everything still feels so heavy and floppy.

"Oh, thank God you got your voice back! How ya feeling, honey?" she asks me as she crawls back over to me.

I take in her whole appearance, realizing much too late that what I first thought was smeared mascara under her eyes is actually bruising. Not only that, but her bakery sweatshirt is torn at the collar and her black pants are filthy with dirt and God only knows what else, especially given that the strong smell of piss and shit stink up the air and it's dark enough that we could be laying in anything.

I gag involuntarily at the thought.

Oh God, now is not the time to be sick, Kelly…

Maggie reaches me and starts helping me to sit up as best I can.

"Can you feel this?" she asks as she pinches my arm, pulling at the skin and making me tense.

"Yeah."

"Good. Can you move your limbs?"

"I think so," I tell her. I try, and while I can't sit up fully yet, finally being able to move my legs, feet, and arms means that the feeling of complete helplessness leaves me at last.

"Where the hell are we?!" I demand, hearing a hiss in my voice that even catches me off guard. I instantly soften my expression in silent apology as my eyes meet hers.

"I don't know. All I can gather from the other girls and what I've witnessed is that the men who come in here have their faces covered apart from their eyes. Brittany in the next cage to us says that they're either Russian or Polish; she's been here a lot longer than us…"

Her eyes instantly go over to the next cage, where a person who I assume is the girl she called Brittany is staring wide eyed at us, her face void of any emotion—of any *thing*. She's barely Maggie's age—if she's lucky—and slender. I can already tell she's too slim, even if I can only gage it by the look of her clothes and what I can see of her limbs underneath.

"She told me we get food and water once a day and have to do our business in the corner of the room over there when they let us out." Maggie points to the far corner, which is dark, dingy, and barely visible in the darkness.

"When do they usually come by? Morning or afternoon?"

"She said mid-afternoon, she thinks, but the guards haven't been in yet."

"I'm just trying to gage how long we've been out and how far away from home we are," I inform her.

She just nods at my answer, and I see she's got a far-away look in her eyes, staring at the far corner.

"Hey, what is it? We're going to get out of this; you know that right?"

"I'm fine, just…you have Dagger looking for you, but who the hell is going to be looking for me? My Dad won't be, that's for sure."

"Come here, my Lil' Mags." I wrap my arms around her as she starts to sob quietly but uncontrollably. "I can't speak for your Dad, but I know all the girls will be looking for you too. Don't worry, okay? I'm so proud of how calm you stayed while I was a mess and unable to talk. I told you before you don't give yourself enough credit for how strong you are, didn't I?"

She carries on sniffling into my hair as I soothe her stroking her head.

"Sorry...I was really worried when you didn't wake up around the same time as me."

"*Chica*, don't worry, okay? We'll wait for the food to come and see what we can find out about them. Are we in some kind of basement or warehouse, do you think?"

"Brittany seems to think it's the basement of a house. She said you'll hear people coming and going and doors being slammed upstairs at certain times."

"Okay, we'll hold out until we hear them too so we know the routine. We have people coming for us, and whatever this is, we will get out of it, Mags."

***

About six hours later...

"Pssst! Pssst!"

I peel my sandpaper eyes open groggily.

Did I imagine that noise?

"Pssst! Pssst! Hey!"

Rubbing my eyes to clear my vision, I look around the spot where I've been lying on my side. I'm facing Maggie, who is still sleeping.

"Hey you, new girl!"

I still can't see the owner, but I answer back in the direction the voice has come from. "Yeah?"

"They haven't brought food or drink in yet, but they did come in a while back. I was pretending to be asleep, and saw them come over to your cage. They stood over you speaking in some Eastern European language. They didn't stay for very long, but were talking as they left, which they don't do usually. Things are different since you and your friend got here."

"How? Did you see us arrive?" I enquire.

What the fuck is so special about me and Mags?

At the back of my mind, I recall all the stories *Papi* has told me about women being sex trafficked to America to find a job, money, or a better life than they had before as a warning to be careful.

With her blonde hair and blue eyes, Maggie fits the bill perfectly for those sick psychos…

I can't think like that. I have—no, I *need*—to believe Dagger is searching for us, scouring the earth for me.

The thought of not seeing him again makes my heart ache, my chest tightening further at the realization that may very well happen.

The girl speaks up again even though one of the girls near her is shushing us, shifting towards me so I can spot her. "In the hours before you arrived, there was a new man who came in with the guards. The atmosphere was tense, and the anticipation rolling off the guards was clear even in this shit hole. Three men brought you in; they were wearing coveralls, and it was dark but I could see their eyes smiling when they put you both in your cage."

Do I dare ask her the question that's been echoing around my mind?

"What…happens to you all?" I ask warily.

"Whatever they want. Best advice I can give you to get through this is to go to your happy place in your head and play dead like one of those animals that do it to survive in the wild. It's what I do," she informs me, sounding fairly blasé about it, which shocks the hell out of me.

"Oh God, I'm so sorry you have to go through that... I hope you don't mind me saying, but you seem very calm about it all, and I wish I knew how. Who the fuck are they, anyway?"

"Don't be, you're not doing those things to me. I'm anything but calm, but there is no point dwelling on it. I'm blocking it out; I got it locked up tight in my mind for when I get out of here to tell the police though. I don't know who they are; I've never even seen what they look like. Every time they've raped me I've been blindfolded."

Fuck! Rape? I won't survive it...I have to get back to Dagger.

I try to disguise my shock by introducing myself. "My name's Kelly; what's yours?"

"Ashlee. Try and get some rest and pray we get some food and drink tomorrow, Kelly," she says in a whisper.

"Yeah...night, Ashlee."

***

We've been awake for at least five or six hours judging by Brittany's guess and what I can see of the "daylight", if you can call it that—unless my eyes have finally adjusted to the darkness.

I can see how big the room is—or rather isn't— as well as the amount of cages that line the entire length of the room, pushed right up against the walls.

As I look at Brittany, I realize that she reminds me of one of those girls you see in TV ads asking for donations for a third world country.

Ay Dios mío, she's not slim, she's nearly skeletal! She's pale and gaunt, with every bone and every feature standing out.

Looking over to Ashlee's cage, I see she's got a stare fixed on the door opposite her. I follow her eyeline and see that she's watching the light and shadows that cross the chink visible under the door. She doesn't move her eyes from the spot for ages, the occasional blink the only sign she's conscious.

"Kel'? If we don't get out of this, I just want you to know that I have loved being your friend." Maggie's words threaten to stop my heart, and when I meet her eyes, they are full of sincerity as well as the tears glimmering in them.

I pull her into a tight hold, hugging her tightly as the cramps from hunger take hold of us both again and I hear Maggie's stomach growling.

"Don't talk like that, Mags. We will get out of here, I promise you."

God, we have to! I add silently.

"Come on, try and lay down for a bit," I encourage her, laying her on her side, but she just stares up and the grimy, repulsive ceiling. I lay down beside her, interlinking our fingers as we both rub furiously against our empty stomachs, silently hoping to hell that this is all some kind of twisted nightmare…

***

"You. Come with us!" a thickly-accented voice booms down at me,

Doof!

The dull blow of his foot causes blistering pain to burn from my ribs, knocking the air out of my lungs. As I gasp for air, I peer at the figures in front of me, dressed in black combat gear complete with balaclavas. Both the figures glare down at me expectantly, and that's when I notice the front of the cage is open.

"Come now!" the one who kicked me yells at me again.

Fuck being treated like this! If Dagger knew what I'm about to do, he'd go nuts…

"No! I'm not going anywhere until you feed and water us. Then I'll go with you!" I bite back at the men, holding my own and giving them both a steely scowl.

No words are exchanged, but I see the man who kicked me give a nod and then march out of the room, leaving the second man standing guard over my open cage.

Small fingers wrap around mine as Maggie whispers in my ear, "Just go with them, find a way to escape and get help."

I'm about to respond to her when the first man reappears with bowls of soup and bread stacked on a serving cart along with bottled water. After the first man nods at it, the second slams our cage door shut, and starting at the end closest to the door, the men start dishing out the food and water until they reach mine and Maggie's cage and hand a bowl of soup and some bread to Maggie before thrusting some water and bread in my direction.

I check the thick quarter-baguette over to make sure there is nothing in it, then do what every hungry person does and stuff it in my mouth, not giving a fuck. I don't get to take a slug of water before I'm dragged towards the door and a blindfold is strapped around my eyes forcefully, making the whole scene before me disappear into blackness.

Fingers dig into my slender wrists, wrapping them together with rope, and I'm tugged along, blindly walking where they pull me.

We must walk for five minutes—give or take, as time seems to be moot at this point. Eventually, I'm pulled to the bottom of a set of stairs, neither man saying a word to tell me where or when to step as they drag me up a set of stairs—I count 15.

I hear the click of a door, and as soon as it's opened, a gust of warm air billows around my face, smelling of lemon-scented furniture polish and floral perfume. I get yanked further into the room using the ropes binding me, and one of the men pushes me backwards. I instinctively try to save myself, but fall back on to a soft seat.

"Come on, get this over and done with. Do what you want, you sick bastards!" I shout into the room. I don't miss the way that my voice seems to reverberate off the walls.

Am I in some kind of library?

I don't get to think about it before the blindfold is whisked away from my face, my eyes rapidly squinting in the bright glare of the massive office space. I blink a couple of times to regain my sight and get accustomed to the brighter surroundings before flicking my eyes around the room, but when I do, everything seems to freeze, my heart seizing as my eyes focus on the figure in front of me.

My pure rage comes tumbling out of my mouth a moment later as I scream at the top of my lungs, baring my teeth.

"You! What the flyin' fuck, Mikhail! What the hell is this bullshit? Just because I didn't go home with you after the club the other night or take you up on your offer to 'get acquainted', you think it gives you the right to fuckin' *abduct* me? You sick freak! I hope you know you're in for a world of pain when my—"

"Enough!" A harshly-accented voice booms into the room, cutting through my tirade at Mikhail.

Whirling around, I'm met with the sight of a tall, slim man with broad shoulders, mousey-blond close-cropped hair and dark blue eyes that match his pin-striped suit. His eyes glide over my whole body from my hair to my bare feet, casually assessing me with a dirty smirk.

"Who the fuck are you? If you think for a second that I'm letting you lay a finger on me,captive or not, you'd better think twice, *carajo,* because I aced my self-defense lessons," I spit, lifting my chin at him and daring him to try it. Who the fuck does he think he is?

"Pssh…" the man scoffs, dismissing my words with a flick of his fingers. "Mikhail did as he was told, and from what he tells me, you enjoyed the attention. You women think you're always in charge. HA!"

"What are you talking about? What does he mean, Mikhail?" I ask them both, my head flicking back and forth between them. I'm completely at a loss.

"*I* told him to meet you and get to know you and your habits…" The man trails off with a smile, then says, "Apologies, where are my manners? Hello, *mladshaya sestra*. I'm your *brat.*"

"Look, dude, I don't speak Polish or Russian or whatever language that was."

"I said, 'Hello, little sister. I'm your brother'."

24 hours prior...

We head back from Kelly's parents' with information overload. Every detail of their life has just been blown wide open, but I can't wrap my head around it, and we're no closer to finding Kelly for it.

God only knows how she is...

I gun it back to the clubhouse, weaving in and out of the traffic to get back to Brains.

I didn't stop to say goodbye to her parents and left Jade and Tinhead to handle pleasantries, telling myself that I'd rectify all the shit that transpired during our unexpected first meeting tonight later on. At the moment, all that matters is to get more information about this Vadim Lebedev and find out where the fuck he has taken my woman.

I run at least half a dozen red lights to get back to the club, although I'm almost glad I have this ride to get my head straight for the onslaught that's to come. I go straight through Main Street, the sight of her studio striking me like a bullet to the heart.

I wish I'd just told her I'd pick her up from the studio on my bike instead of asking her to come to the bakery so I could make some big fucking gesture about her being the first woman on the back of my bike...

I shake my head clear of those thoughts almost as quickly as they come; I need to get my shit together and my head in the game.

Pulling through the clubhouse gates like a bat out of hell, I park my bike next to Bear's, kicking the stand out and dropping my lid on the seat without really caring where it falls. I run straight into the clubhouse, which is pretty much deserted in the main room. Glancing at the clock behind the bar, I see I spent over three hours at Kelly's parents' house—it's 11:35pm, and the only people in the room are Wrench and the club girls.

"Yo, where's Prez and Brains?" I shout over the music blaring out of the speakers.

"Dags! Axe is at home after Dani called him a few minutes ago, and Brains is in his room. What is it, brother? What happened at Kelly's parents?"

I don't bother to answer him—I ain't got time to chit-chat. Pulling out my cell, I call Axe, growling in frustration as the line rings out.

Fuck!

I call again, prowling the entire length of the bar as I do. After the second ring of my third try, Axe's voice comes over the line.

"Dags, what you got?"

"Boss, I need you here; I have the information we needed. Kelly's parents had a bucketful of shit that we didn't know about, and we have the name of the person who most likely has Kelly and Maggie."

"I'll be there in 10 minutes. Give the name to Brains, get him searching it."

"Okay, boss."

After ending the call, I stride straight over to Brains' room, thumping on the door, which is whipped away from my fist on the third bang. Behind it, I'm greeted with the sight of Brains' trademark baseball cap turned backwards on his head the way it always is when he's working or thinking.

"Brains, Axe is coming back over to the club so I can fill you both in on some shit we uncovered from Kelly's parents, but before he gets here, I have a name for you to search. You may need to go to your contact in the CIA for extra info, but I'll explain everything when Axe gets here. The name is Vadim Lebedev. Did you trace the phones yet?"

Brains nods soberly. "We traced them and found both of them dumped about two blocks away from the crossing. Sorry, brother. I'll get straight on that name, but I'll need you to leave the room for me to make contact with my source in the CIA. Not even Axe knows who it is."

I do my best to ignore the wave of panic that rises in me at the knowledge tracking Kelly's phone turned out to be a dead end.

"Okay, Brains. How long will it take?" I ask. My whole body feels like it's on a tightrope; one more blow and I know I'm gonna fall into hell, and that shit ain't gonna get Kelly back.

"All depends on what shift work he's on and if he's on duty or asleep. Either way, he comes through pretty swiftly."

Nodding at his answer, I leave his room and wait in the hall for Axe to arrive. I know I'm being an asshole to everyone around me by being sharp with them, and I know it's not their fault, but if there's one person that understands how I'm feeling right now, I know Axe will get it 100%. I can't stand the helplessness of this fucked-up situation, and it is motherfuckin' fucked up.

***

I give Axe and Brains a brief lowdown on the information we got from Kelly's parents and they take it all in, staring and gawping in bewilderment.

I finish my account and look between them both. "Yeah, so that's pretty much it. We need to find Kelly as soon as possible even more now. Brains, what did your contact say?" The impatient tone is clear as day in my voice as Axe and I lean closer to Brains' computer, eager for any information he can feed us. I'm praying for anything that can get me even an inch closer to her. I can't sit or stand still with the impatience, even being in a room is setting me more on edge.

"He's not answered me yet, he must be busy, but when he sees I've been trying to reach him he'll call back. I'll let you know when I make contact with him."

"Okay." The word sounds weak, but what else can I say or do at this point?

I just hope that my Kitten is okay.

"Brother, go get some rest," Axe orders me.

"Axe, I don't think I can even sit still, let alone lie down and try to sleep."

"Dagger, that's an order. Brains will come and get us both if he has any information—I'm staying here tonight just in case," he instructs me sternly as he crosses his arms, raising an eyebrow at me in challenge.

"Fine, I'm going, but you better come get me straight away as soon as he makes contact!" I holler at Brains over my shoulder as I'm being shoved out of the door and pushed towards my room by Axe.

I crash through my door, collapsing on my bed, where I'm immediately greeted with that floral scent of Kelly's wrapping around my senses, my body relaxing at her perfume despite my concern for her. It calms and excites me at the same time, bringing up a memory from a few days ago when I had been out at church and came back into my room either expecting to find her in the main room with her girls or waiting here, but not in the way I found her. Closing my eyes for a few minutes, I can't stop the grin breaking out on my face as I replay the memory in my mind.

"Kelly? You in here?" I holler out into the empty room, putting down the drinks I've brought in from the bar on the nightstand as I clock the light shining in the bathroom. "Kitten? You okay?"

In answer, the door flies open and there standing in front of me in the doorway to the bathroom and completely ass-naked is Kelly. Her breasts, pussy, and her ass are painted with what she rightly told me is her second favorite thing in the world one night after playing—Nutella.

"Little... girl... what have you been up to?" I say in a low voice as I prowl towards her, stalking her and circling her like my prey.

Fuck...this woman!

"I just thought I'd let you enjoy one of my favorite things painted on one of your favorite things...me!" she giggles, her laughter turning into high-pitched squeals as I lift her over my shoulder, not caring about my t-shirt or the bed sheets.

One thing's for certain, I'm eating chocolate ass, pussy, and titties tonight...and not necessarily in that order, because my mouth instantly zones in on her chocolate-covered pussy.

Fuckin' heaven!

***

4am—10 hours missing...

"Dags!" Brains hollers through my door.

I roll over with a groan, glancing at the time and seeing it's still fucking early. Realizing that there's only one reason why Brains could be waking me this early, I jump out of bed and swing the door open to see him standing on the other side with a haggard look on his face, his eyes bloodshot and ringed with red.

"My contact called back. He's been crazy busy at work, but he said he knows the name, which is a good thing for us. It means he can find him on the database, and he's doing it during his shift so will get the information to me ASAP. I've told him it's urgent, but all we can do is wait. Just thought I'd let you know, brother," he says on an inward yawn.

"Thanks, man. You told Axe?" I reply in a gruff voice.

"Nah, I decided to tell you first; he's probably passed out by now anyway. I'll keep you posted if anything else comes through," he informs me as he slinks back towards his room.

Kicking my door shut, I fall back into bed, unable to stop thinking about her and hoping to hell she's okay. From what her mom said, this Vadim is a sadistic cunt...

***

8:20 am – Over 14 hours missing...

I'm standing in Brains' room with him, already showered and dressed. I came straight here after my shower, having been awake since 4am and unable to shut off my thoughts—even Kelly's lingering scent wasn't able to soothe me this time. Instead, I lay there thinking, wondering what other information might be about to turn up…

"How did you sleep?" I ask Brains, half-expecting the answer—I can see he's dog tired.

"Shit, in a word! Not gonna lie to ya, I had one ear open listening for my phone to go off. I'll sleep when I'm dead, right?" he chuckles at his half-hearted joke, but I don't have the energy. I'm already hanging on by a thread.

One of Brains' phones starts vibrating on his computer desk. He grabs and answers it straight away, facing towards his computer. All I can do is hold my bated breath, staring at the back of his head.

"Hi…Yeah, no problem, I get it man. So…fuck!"

He looks around to me and gives me a nod, then carries on with the rest of his conversation.

"All right. That's what we were told, we just wanted to make sure our information was correct…Yeah, send it over…Speak—Huh? Really? That might work…send all you have. Speak soon."

Brains spins back around in his chair to face me. "We need Axe, brother. My contact is sending all the information over to my secure email, but he says it's quite the interesting read."

"Fuck! Good, I'll go tell Axe."

Leaving Brains to his computer, I go on the search for Axe. I storm through the main room, then the kitchen, before eventually finding him in his office.

"Boss! The contact has just called Brains and is sending the information on Vadim over."

"Thank fuck!" Axe declares as he rounds his desk, leaving whatever he was doing to slap me on the back. "We will get her and Maggie back, okay? I know how it feels, you know I've been in your shoes."

"Flex! Gather the men! We got a 911 in Brains' room. Now!" he barks at my V.P. who just came out of the kitchen.

Without missing a beat, Flex strides straight to the main room to gather my brothers.

I head back into Brains' room to see that in the short space of time I was gone, Brains has decorated the once-blank whiteboard that fills the length of his back wall with documents, pictures, and arrows that point to information.

Axe strides in on my heels. "Brains, I've ordered all the men to come in for this, but any questions anyone has can wait until after you've brought us up to speed."

Right on cue, all my brothers come filtering in, and Bear and Tinhead make a beeline for me.

"How you holding up, brother?" Bear asks, the concern clear in his tone.

"On the edge." It's a short answer, but it sums exactly what's going inside of me right about now.

"You all know why you're here—Wrench, I assume Flex would have told you what transpired last night when he came to get you. We reached out for information on our prime suspect, and Brains' contact came back to him not long ago. Brains, hit us with it, everyone else, no questions until after."

Brains approaches his whiteboard. "So, here are the facts so far. We believe Kelly and Maggie have been taken by a man called Vadim Lebedev." He points at the picture of the man that's been pinned in the center of the whiteboard. "It's been confirmed that he is a member of the Russian *Bratva,* but not only that—he's the *Pakhan,* the leader. From the information, he may well reside in Florida, but that's all we have on residence. He has also obviously been raided in the past by the CIA and FBI, and there are allegations of involvement with the sex trade and sex trafficking women on those documents."

My heart starts to sink, the mania inside of me taking over as the words 'sex trade' and 'trafficking' threaten to have me clawing at my skin. I stare at the man in the photo on Brains' screen. He's of slim build, has short mousey-blond hair and blue eyes, as well as a thick, ugly-as-fuck scar that runs down from his jaw on one side, curving around the column of his neck.

"Fuuuck! We can't take on the Russian Mafia alone— we have no idea who or even what we are dealing with. Look at Raúl! If Matteo hadn't been there, fuck! I think we all would have been dead right about now," I say, breaking the deafening silence that threatens to suffocate me. "Prez, we need to reach out to Matteo at least—he may know something after running in the same circles. I know it would mean us owing him, but this is on me—I'll do whatever I can to pay it back," I announce, directing the last part to the whole room, not just to Axe.

Axe shakes his head. "No. She may be your woman, but this is on all of us! We're a family, and family sticks together—stronger together. Who would have thought it, the one fuckin' man I thought would be an eternal bachelor—?"

Before Axe can finish, Brains clears his throat. "Uh, boss? Funny Dags should mention owing Matteo something; I don't think we'll need to. My contact did some digging into Matteo for me a while back, and I asked him to keep a background check running for insurance purposes in case anything went wrong during these deals. My contact told me earlier that something other than standard Mafia shit flagged up," he interjects, making all our ears prick up as we turn towards him.

***

10am - Over 16 hours missing...

After hashing the plan out with all the men then putting a plan B in place just in case, we've finally got it sorted. We are all gathered around the church table, with the speakerphone in the centre of the table almost ringing out. The number we were given after the first gun deal isn't Matteo's direct line, but it does go straight to his number two, Leo.

Finally Leo's voice greets us. "Speak," he says, his deep voice thick with his Italian accent.

"Leo, this is Axe. Is Matteo free to speak to me? It's urgent."

Leo doesn't respond; we just hear a lot of rustling, background noise, and muffled rapid-fire Italian before Matteo's smooth voice fills the line.

"Axe. What seems to be the problem?"

"We need your help. One of my men's woman and her friend were abducted yesterday."

"I see…Why should I get involved in such matters?" he replies thoughtfully.

"Well, the person we believe has taken her runs in the same *circles* as you do. He's a pretty big boss, and we have no idea what to expect of him. It'll be walking into the unknown for me and my men unless you help us out."

"What do I get out of it? I'm not a charity; why should I get my hands dirty and risk creating a war for something that doesn't involve me?" he bites back, suddenly sounding irritated and annoyed.

"What about redemption? Justice? Revenge?

"They're all the same. Spit it out, Axe. What do you know?"

"I have it on very good authority that you have a huge price on the head of the same man that took our women."

We're met with deathly silence for a few seconds, but when he speaks again, intrigue drips from his words. "I have many enemies."

"What about a certain Russian…Vadim Lebedev?" Axe asks.

Matteo growls and swears in Italian, then says, "You have my men and my thanks, but I want to kill the *cazzo fottuto*…"

"No!" I shout down the phone, not caring that I'm breaking rank. That bastard is mine!

"Do not test me. He is the debt for my men, and now I know he's back on American soil, it won't be hard to get to him myself. In the meantime, your women will disappear."

Glaring at the phone, I relent and nod at Axe in agreement.

"Deal. You get to kill him, and we get your help and men. We have information that he's in Florida, but we have no address," Axe tells him.

"Leave it with me, Axe. I have a few acquaintances in Florida who will be able to sniff him out. In the meantime, I'll arrange for the jet to get us there. Gather what you need and be ready to go as soon as you can. Leo will send you the details of where and when to meet us. *Ciao."*

As the line goes dead, Axe wastes no time turning to us and giving orders. "Brains, Bear, I want you with me and Dagger. Go get your shit together. We're going to Florida."

~ Chapter 28 Kelly ~

"What?! Are you fucking high? You have the wrong girl; I am not fuckin' Russian. Do I look Russian to you? You need to let me and my friend go."

I try and struggle out of Mikhail's hold that is still firmly wrapped around my wrists, tugging on the fucking rope before using what is probably the last bit of energy I will ever have to swing back my elbows and hit him right in the stomach.

"Oof! *Malishka!* Fuck! Do not struggle, this will only get worse for you." Mikhail kindly informs me, thinking he's doing me a favor.

Fucking jerk…

"You are my half-sister, and by having the same blood as my father, you are *Printsessa* to the family name. Your mother fucked my father, and you are the result of that," the man claiming to be my brother bites back at me as he rounds the vast table at the end of the room.

Mikhail pulls me along to stand at the edge of the table so I'm close enough to breathe in the same air as this cuntwaffle. He has serious problems if he thinks my *Mamá* would cheat on my *Papi;* they love each other fiercely.

As I glare down in disgust at my captor, I try and wiggle free of the viselike hold Mikhail has around my arms. He brings me flush against his body, and I feel the sick fucker's hard-on pressing up against my butt cheek.

"Enjoy it while you can, *que coño.* That's as close as you're getting to this booty," I snarl as I try to struggle out of his grasp.

"Keep it up, *malishka.* You're just grinding that big ass of yours up against me," he retorts with a sneer, making me stop my struggling instantly. The thought of any man except Dagger touching me like that again makes my skin crawl.

The sicko in front of me leans back against his desk chair and casually shoots me a maniacal grin as he absently rubs his palm up and down the arm of the chair, a contemplative look hiding the anger on his face, but not his evil demeanor.

"What do you need to see to believe that we share the same blood line? A DNA test? Or would you like to meet your *real* father?" the little weasel asks with a smug look on his face.

"What the fuck are you talking about? My real father is…"

"Jacob Davis," we both say in unison.

"Yeah, yeah, I know that's what you have been told, but who you thought was your *Papa* really isn't!"

I lean over the desk away from Mikhail, struggling as I try to reposition my arms, which are still twisted at an angle behind my back. I feel my lips pull back, and I bare my teeth again, sneering with contempt at the *coño* speaking utter bullshit about *mi Mamá y Papi,* the anger rolling off me in waves as I scream in his face, the sound resonating around the vast room.

"I told you, you sick *hijo de puta!* My father is *Jacob Davis!*"

Suddenly, the door flies open, the force sending it bouncing off the wall as it reveals an older man who roars in a thick accent, "No, *Printsessa,* I'm your *Papa!*"

***

The man who has just barged through the door looks like an identical-if-older version of this *hijo de puta* who's declaring we're related. The man even wears a similar-styled suit to the dick sitting at the desk in front of me, but in black.

He glides into the room with authority and purpose, walking straight over to the man in the chair. The man who was seated vacates it promptly, standing to one side as the crazy man who reckons he's my dad sits down in it, lifting one leg and crossing it over the other as he looks pointedly at the man next to him.

"Ivor, are you not treating your *sestra* correctly? I warned you to play nice."

"I apologize for meeting you like this, Kelly, but your *brat* is right, you are my child," he informs me as he absently picks imaginary lint off his pants before fixing his stare back on me. That's when I notice he has a gnarly, angry-looking scar that starts an inch away from the corner of his lip, running down his jaw and one side of the column of his neck.

"My name is Vadim Lebedev, and I am the *Pakhan* in the Russian *Bratva*—the leader of the Russian Mafia. Hasn't your mother told you about our time together?" He chuckles. "Of course she hasn't, she was full of such…spirit and fight when I *acquired* her. It follows that she'd be denying and defying me even now."

As realization starts to dawn, I don't think I can actually speak. My mind and heart are frozen to the core, and I don't dare to breathe in case they shatter.

I don't want to hear what he has to say, either—a small part of me believes that it's true, but 90% of my mind is screaming, *'No! It's all fake, these men are frauds who have no place in my life.'*

"You still seem unsure that what I am telling you is correct. That's fine, but I speak the truth. I can prove that with time, which we have plenty of now."

What? Is he crazy? He really thinks I'm down for this shit show?

When I don't respond, he starts up again, his eyes scanning and lingering on my body, then snapping back up to my face. "You look so much like her—you have the same figure. Has she ever told you about how she came over to America?" he smirks, the grin spreading across his smug ugly face.

"Shall I tell you all about it?" he asks.

I can tell by his tone that that's a rhetorical question, but spit a response anyway.

"No, you're all right, buddy. I'd rather not hear all the *bullshit* you have to say about my mom!" My hands clench and unclench of their own accord, itching to throat-punch this cunt.

I don't get time to think about anything else before his hand snaps out, grabbing my throat and tightening his grip to the point of pain. Gone is the cocky bastard of a few moments ago as his eyes harden, gleaming with a monstrous ice void of everything but hate. I notice the skin of his neck has started to mottle.

"Check your mouth in my presence, dear daughter!" he says through gritted teeth, squeezing my neck harder.

I can't breathe properly—my lungs are burning under the pressure, protesting for air.

"Now be a good daughter and listen to the story of how you came to be." Pushing me away with a shove, he releases his hold.

I take a deep lungful of air, coughing and spluttering, and say nothing.

Pushing away from the desk, he strides over to the far corner of the room, staring out of the massive window that seems to take up most of the wall in the otherwise-featureless room barren of personal touches.

I get a good look at him from this angle, and decide I wouldn't have guessed he was a *Bratva* boss if he hadn't told me. He doesn't look like the typical Mafia boss, that's for sure—not that I would know what one looked like outside Mafia films and episodes of '*The Sopranos*'. He wouldn't look out of place in a big business building on Wall Street if it weren't for the scars cutting across his neck saying it all.

Glancing through the window over his shoulder, I see that it's close to dusk and the sun has started to come back down.

Never taking his eyes from the window, Vadim breaks the silence that has settled over the room. " You see, your Mom wanted to come to America to chase the American Dream and have a new life of prosperity so she could send money back to her family. I offered to get her into the country for a price, telling her she had to pay it back some way. I took what I wanted from her. She wasn't very responsive at first, but with a bit of encouragement, I got her going—she needed at least a couple of goes to get her nice and wet. Anyway, shortly after we started our arrangement, an unfortunate event happened—in my line of work, it's to be expected. Sadly, my house was raided and I was arrested before I could collect your Mom and keep her with me."

My stomach rolls and I feel like I'm about to spew up that lump of bread that I forced down my throat, the bile bubbling and burning in my stomach at his words. I know they can't be true.

Mamá said that my *Abuelo* brought her to America when she was small, and she would never lie to me once, let alone for the whole of my life.

This old man needs to just fuck off…

"I was raided by the FBI while I was in Russia on business matters," he continues. "The rest of the women were taken to refuges or sent home to their families, I believe, but when I got information about your *Mamá*, I found out she was still in America with young FBI agent Jacob Davidson—or should I say Jacob Davis."

"You're lying! About my Mom, and about my Dad. He's not an FBI agent! He's a…"

"Police officer in Cookeville." we say at the same time.

He turns around to meet my eye, his face stoic and unemotional. "*Printsessa*, how many police officers do you know who can afford the scale of your parents' property? Haven't you ever thought about his lack of police uniform?" he enquires condescendingly as a smug look graces his ugly face.

My heart seizes at the words, but I don't believe them…not completely. I know my parents; I know who they are…but my gut tells me I can't deny that there is some truth to what he's saying.

Oh fuck, he just wants to get into your head! Don't let him!

"Kelly…dear sweet *doch'*, do you want me to prove it further? I can tell by your face that you still do not believe me. If I hadn't bedded her, how would I know that your sweet mother has a nasty oil burn on her left thigh? How would I know that she's allergic to latex? That is how you were conceived, after all. How would I know that she purrs like a lioness when she comes around my cock? Ah, she was a feisty one in bed, always clawing at my back to get away. In the end, my men had to hold her arms down so I could get back inside her."

"SHUT UP! Shut up! Shut up! You lying piece of fuckin' scum! You're lying, you could have got most of that information about my mom from the hospital, and be bullshitting the rest. You're lying, you're lying! I don't believe you! I am not the child of a Mafia boss, or some revolting, rapist pig! I don't believe you! I don't! I don't!"

I end my tirade on a sob as my heart starts to crumble, wanting to curse at him and call him a motherfucker, but the words die on my lips.

Bile is bubbling at the back of my throat now, making me retch. I try to crouch down, but Mikhail's strong hold on my arms is stopping me, so in the end I just vomit down my new deep red top I chose especially for my date with Dagger.

As I spew the orange-yellow bile, my top grows darker and darker like this whole affair.

This is all some dark nightmare I can't escape…

Even after I've brought up my stomach's contents, the thought that I may have been fathered by this psychotic rapist cunt sickens me.

My heart, head, and my gut war with each other, but I can't keep my heart at the forefront in this situation. I need to fight him and get free like my mom did, and I have to cut out my heart to find the truth—I can't ask my *Mamá* about it, only this merciless, inhuman, vicious animal.

I rub my lips on a clean-ish part of my shirt, even though I'm most likely smearing some of the vomit on my cheek. Lifting my head, I glower daggers at the man who professes he's my father and ask the question that's been whirring around my head since his revelation.

"If you're meant to be my father, why find me now? Why not when you first found out my mom had had a child? I mean, a man of your power would have known for years; it can't have taken you long to track her down."

His face shifts slightly, revealing the tiniest smile that graces the corner of his lips. Most people look nice when they smile, but not this man. It looks unnatural, devilishly inhuman and inhumane all at once.

"Ah, so like me, always asking the right questions. I only found out about you when one of my men brought me some evidence about your mother about two years ago or so. On your birth certificate—which I doubt you have ever seen a true copy of—it states that the father is unknown, but your mother was married to Jacob, and the maternity records state he was there at your birth. Doesn't it strike you as odd that she would do such a thing if he were your real father?"

I don't respond to his first sentence. I'm numb from all this, and I want it all to be over and go home, but I refuse to believe that what he says is true.

"I've seen my birth certificate, and it has my Dad's name on it, so that's completely false, and anyway, you have to have a name on the birth certificate," I bite back, still struggling in Mikhail's tight hold, under which the fingers of my left hand have started to go numb.

*What a fucking great time this is turning out to be—
my life's apparently a complete lie, and I'll probably lose
my fingers, a hand, or worse by the time I get out of this.*

"Ah, you see, that is where you are wrong, sweet
Printsessa. If a father's name is not on the birth certificate
he has no legal rights to the child. Although he may be
the *biological* father, he is not the legal father because
his name has been omitted from the legal document. It is
perfectly possible not to name a child's biological father
on their birth certificate, as it is perfectly possible to falsify
a birth certificate to hide your daughter's true parentage,"
he argues, his accent getting thicker by the minute.

*Am I getting to the big bad rapist Russian Mafia boss!
Good!*

"So what do you want with me? Why did you need all
the theatrics to get me here to speak to you? Why have
your *'daughter'* abducted, drugged, and shoved into a
cage like a fucking animal if you just wanted to see and
get to know me?"

"Ah, another right question. You see, I had to go to
great lengths to find you and pick the perfect time to bring
you to me. I do not regret drugging and abducting you to
get you here, you needed to know about your parentage.
What I want from you is not for me; you are merely here
to join the family."

"Join the family? What, I'm going to forget my life and
join you just because you claim to be my father? Why
would I do that?" My fury is rapidly reaching the point of
no return, but just before I blow up, he spits his response
through clenched teeth as his face and neck turn
crimson.

The next words to cross his lips have my entire world crumbling around me, my whole heart sinking into the abyss that has been laid out before me.

"You will, because if you don't, your dear *Mamá* and *Dad,* your friends, and your biker boyfriend will be exterminated. You will create your own family to replace them by joining it with mine. Oh, and you need to get better acquainted with Mikhail, as tomorrow, dear *doch'*, you will be marrying him."

~ Chapter 29 ~

Dagger

22 hours missing…

"It will be another 15 minutes until we can land, Mr. Giordano," the voice of the pilot announces over the speaker.

I've never been in a private jet before, but this is definitely not how I envisioned having my first ever experience on one—there are things I would rather remember than flying to Florida rescuing my woman from a disgusting *Bratva* boss.

Fuck, I just hope she's okay…

We still don't know what he wants with her—even though I can guess based on the dossier containing details of what they found over 20 years ago during a raid they did on his house in Miami.

My stomach turns at the thought of all those women raped and bleeding from every hole, their fingers missing from apparent disobedience.

Things like that give my tastes in the bedroom a bad name…

I look in front of me and see Bear twitching like crazy, his leg bouncing up and down.

"Not a fan of flying, brother?" I enquire, trying to find anything to distract me from the world of pain I'm churning up inside of me. My plan is to dampen it down to a manageable level, then get it ready to unleash on the world once I find my woman.

Glancing over his shoulder, I stare out of the window as Florida comes into view, then look back at my brother, anger shining back at me in his eyes. It's not aimed at me—it's the anger we all feel when one of our family is under attack.

"What? Ah, no not really. It's just that I made a promise to Jade and Jenna when we left that I intend to keep."

I nod in agreement at him. It's the same promise all the women made my brothers and I promise—bring Kelly and Mags back and kill the motherfucker Mikhail. As we promised Matteo, he gets Vadim for whatever reason he hates him for.

I glance back at the Mafia boss as he stares out of the window during what I think must be the first time he's not been in a suit since he was a baby. Instead he's wearing all black—black cargo pants, a black long-sleeved t-shirt, and blacker boots. Even though we're all wearing the same outfit, I thought he would look the most alien wearing it given his usual tastes, but he wears it as well as one of his expensive suits.

Looking to his right, I see his right-hand man Leo going over the plan. Axe sits opposite him, the two men talking at a low volume, Nico is sitting next to Bear, and Lorenzo is sitting on my side. Both Italians closest to me have their heads reclined back and their eyes closed.

Brains is set up at the back of the plane, needing the most space thanks to all the gear and laptops he brought with him.

After a perfectly smooth landing with barely a bump, Matteo turns to us all—but mainly Axe—to inform us of the plan.

"We will be meeting Ramírez on the tarmac. He has an informant that has information we could use. He came to me with some information about Vadim, and when I asked him what he wanted in return for this favor, he said guns. That's when I got in contact with you regarding the gun deal we did with him. Maybe this was a twist of fate, no?"

"Fuckin' A! Giordano, you could have given me the heads-up on this information before now!" Axe shouts at him from his chair, fixing him with a glare.

"Easy Axe, remember your place!" Leo informs him, fixing him with his own stare.

"*Va bene,* Leo. Axe, it was best this way. We help each other, your man gets his girl, and I get Vadim's head."

"Fine. I don't have to like it. If it means getting Kelly and Maggie and killing the scum who took my brother's woman, then that'll have to do."

"*Bene.* Now, shall we go and meet Ramírez and end this hell for your women? *Si?*"

***

11:30pm - 26 hours missing...

Gasparilla Island, Florida

"Nico and Lorenzo are going to be at the front of the house causing a diversion which will lead most of the guards to the front of the property. That will probably leave two guards at the back, and if we take them out, we can go through the basement to access the house that way," Leo informs us, showing us the route with his finger on the blueprints.

The informant gave us the address to Vadim's huge-ass mansion, and here we are. Raúl is standing with Matteo, talking to him in hushed tones as he eyes the property in front of us. Most of the lights are on upstairs, but only two are on at the front of the house. According to the blueprints, they're reception rooms, and Vadim's office and bedroom are at the back of the property directly above the basements.

My eyes scan back over the house, my stomach rolling at the thought of being mere yards away from my Kitten.

Fuck, if she's hurt in any way, I'll be clawing my way upstairs to fight Matteo and kill Vadim and his men myself, agreement be damned.

"Are you ready to go, *Capo*?" Tomma asks Matteo.

Matteo swivels on the balls of his feet and strides towards us, his eyes black with rage.

"*Sì, pronto!*" he barks back at Tomma.

"*Capo,* Brains will shut off the electricity across this part of the island so they don't suspect anything. As soon as he does, Nico and Lorenzo will be there distracting the guards, and we'll be around the back of the property. Brains is going to listen out for any radio conversations, then we enter the back. Tomma will go with you upstairs to end Vadim."

"No. Tomma stays with you, I go on my own."

"Not happening boss, he stays with you," Leo says defiantly, to which Giordano just fists Leo's t-shirt.

"*Ricorda il tuo posto*, Leo! Tomma will come with me but wait outside that bastard's room until I say otherwise. *BENE?!*"

"Hold up, Brains is calling," Axe says.

As Axe digs his cell out of his pocket, Bear clasps his hand over my shoulder. "Brother, we got this. We'll find her and get her out," he informs me with determination in his voice.

I can't answer him; I'm already close to burning this place to the ground just to get her back in my arms. Fuck all this Mafia vendetta shit!

"Yes Brains, what is it?"

"I'm pulling the electricity in 5, 4, 3, 2, 1…GO!" he screams down the speaker.

At the same time, we see the lights in the mansion and throughout the whole block of houses on the street go off, including the streetlamps.

Perfect!

As we run across the overgrown land of Vadim's property to meet Brains, we hear the gunfire going off at the front of the building—Lorenzo and Nico's distraction.

We can just about make out the shadows of a group of guards running towards the front entrance upon hearing the gun shots at the front of the building, leaving two at the back on either corner of the house just as Leo said.

"Just what we wanted," Bear says to us all.

"Well, this will make it a helluva lot easier," Brains speaks up to the side of us where he's hiding behind a massive tree. The next thing I see is him jumping up from his hiding place with his Glock in hand, shooting each guard at point-blank range.

Fuck! He could give Tinhead a run for his money.

"It's been a while since I did some ground-work. Let's go do this, then get the hell out of Florida!" Matteo bellows at us all, smacking my arm in encouragement with a flick of his head.

Leo takes the lead, starting to run towards the dead guards as the nightfall and our black clothing cloaks us from view. We have become the darkness.

If I don't find my Kitten, I will drown in despair with corruption in my heart, and I know for fuckin' sure I will succumb to it willingly.

Leo points his gun towards the thick, heavy locks on the basement door and shoots three times just to make sure.

He pulls the door free, and we head into a dank, dark hallway. Leo has the blueprints in one hand and a torch in the other, and follows behind me, with Axe, Bear, Matteo and Tomma close behind. The passage ahead of us splits into two paths; one leading further into the basement, and the other leading to the door to the main house. A putrid smell drifts down the basement path, and as much as it pains me to think about what that might mean, my gut is leading me that way.

Coming up is the fork, Matteo and Tomma brush past us all, heading up to the front as Leo turns the torch on the blueprints, showing them the way into the house.

Before they leave, Matteo turns to me, even though I'm only able to make out the shadow of his face in this light. In his heavy accent, he says, "I hope you find your woman. We will meet back at the cars. Good luck. *Ciao.*" With that, Tomma and Matteo turn and run towards the door to the house.

As we run down the opposite fork, the stench of blood, urine, and tears hangs heavy in the air, clinging to me and layering my skin and beard with itself. The heat inside this basement is extreme to say the least, and it only makes the odor more pungent. I can only imagine that this is what the Dark Ages smelt like; the scent of fear, despair, and death…

I scan the room for a familiar face—anything familiar, really. Sobbing echoes silently from all angles, the black of the night cloaking my vision so I have only the wall under my fingertips to guide me around the darkened room. Each step I take sounds louder than the last, my boots vibrating off of the cement floor. My eyes are trying to adjust to the darkness, but when it's pitch black outside and even darker inside, what hope do I have? I focus on getting what I came for and leaving.

I turn a corner to my right with one of my brothers behind me. I'm not sure who it is—none of us have said a word since we came in, and we can't even turn a light on. We just need to get in, do what we have to, and get the fuck out of here. Too much bloodshed has and will happen tonight, more than I've seen in half a lifetime, but without Matteo's help we wouldn't be here. We owe him one; but at what cost?

As we round the corner, I feel a whoosh of heat from above me. Squinting up at the ceiling, I can just make out a huge industrial air vent. I know we're close; I can feel it in my bones.

As I slide to a stop, I slam into the back of Leo, knowing it's him purely because he's a bigger fucker than me and Bear put together. He's quiet like me, but pretty okay for a mobster. Leo twists slightly and signals with two fingers back and forth and then back again in front of him. I sidestep away from the wall to get a better look at what he's pointing at and see a faint strip of light on the floor that looks to be streaming out under a door…

Fuck, a door!

The pungent stench of urine and shit gets stronger as I approach, and Leo then leans over my shoulder and points with his two fingers over to the far corner next to the door. I see a familiar blinking red light.

Cameras? That figures, the sick bastard…

"We have to move," Leo's deep voice says softly in my ear.

I turn in Axe's direction. "Boss, we have to go, now! We can't fuck around; we don't know if there are more men coming."

A set of footsteps quicken, drawing closer behind me, and Axe pats my arm to talk.

"Dags, I know, brother, but we can't go off half-cocked. We need to make sure the coast is clear."

"Leo says we have to go now! Boss, we have to GO!" I declare, not caring about the rare hint of desperation in my voice. As much as I respect my boss, there ain't no man who is gonna lay their hands on what is mine without sufferin' for it. So help me God, I'll slit his fuckin' throat.

Axe glances over me and Leo and obviously sees exactly what he needs to see, because he flicks his head at us.

"Move, now! Now, NOW!" Leo orders. Not needing to be told twice, Axe, Bear, and I run up to the door as Axe fires at the camera and it explodes.

We try the door—it's locked. Not waiting another second, I shoot the lock off, kicking the door in with a swift strike. It falls back into the room, and as soon as it does, the smell is enough to put you off going to a public restroom for eternity—a gut-churning stench that burns my nose hairs and makes my eyes water. The putrid smell makes me gag, but the sight in front of me is what makes my stomach roll like waves crashing against rocks—harsh and angry.

The dirty desk lamp in the corner closest to the door illuminates the pure desolation and filth in this small, cramped room. Cages upon cages are lined up against the walls, running the length of the room. The sound of whimpering and crying coming from them increases as we move more into the room. For all intents and purposes, this place is a fuckin' pen, except for the fact that each and every single cage holds not a dog or any other animal, but a woman. Women fill each of the metal cages, even though there's barely enough space to sit on the floor without the top of the cages touching their heads. They all press their bodies right up against the back walls of the cages and ball up into the smallest shape they can. I can't see any of their faces; they're hiding them by tucking them between their chests and stomachs.

I can't breathe, but I don't dare open my mouth; I can feel acidic bile bubbling up the back of my throat, dying to get out. I swallow to force it down. I can be sick after, not now.

Coming further into the room, I start searching at one end, though I don't recognize any of the girls that are cowering and shivering in their cages. My eyes flick from cage to cage, and I notice for the first time that the girls inside are half-naked. I stalk down the room with more urgency in my step than ever now, impatient to get what I came for and get the hell out of this shit hole.

Stopping dead in my tracks, I see the one thing I would know anywhere—the lioness tattoo on that caramel skin. Everything else surrounding me falls away as I zone in, unable to tear my eyes away from it.

If there's one thing I know for certain, it's that I ain't leaving without what belongs to me.

I just hope I'm not too late to save her...

***

Kelly

Maggie tries to remove herself from me, but there's no room for me to pull back. I've been lying on top of her since I got dumped back in the cage. The guards forgot to turn off the lamp in the corner when they left, making it just about possible to see all the girls in the room even though it's still nearly dark.

Giving up, Maggie instead shifts her body to cover more of mine and wraps her arms around me, protecting me.

'There's no need!' I want to scream out, 'It's too late, they can do what they want now!'

The fight within me has finally been extinguished. In 8 hours, I will be married to Mikhail and shipped off to Russia. Well, to be accurate, Vadim said that me and Mikhail will marry, consummate the marriage in front of him, then go to Russia to live. My friends, my family, and Dagger will all be gone, but I won't risk their lives, no matter how hurt and enraged I am at my parents for possibly lying to me for years.

Part of me still doesn't want to admit that I'm not who I thought I was, an 'unknown' like my real father on my birth certificate.

The more I think about it, the more I'm forced to admit that Vadim might be telling the truth about being my father.

When he mentioned my *Mamá's* burn on her thigh, I knew the one he meant—she did it as a little girl while helping her *Mamá* to cook. The latex allergy is right too, she has to be careful with what gloves she buys and wears for cleaning or else she comes out in hives and lumps.

But my Dad, an FBI agent? I don't know what to believe, but the lack of his police uniform makes sense if that's the case. I remember asking where it was years back; I was told they get washed at the police station, and that was the end of that. Then there's the big house and the flashy new car every time I got told Dad got a bonus or a promotion...lies upon lies upon lies, twisted like threads in the tapestry of my life.

And then there's Dagger. I can't believe I'm never going to be able to tell him I fell in love with him. He was my entire world; he grounded me and loved me so much in his own way, whether he believed he could or not. He showed me how he felt with trust and how he treated me like I was his entire universe. He even altered his worldview to realize he was capable of love all along.

It dawns on me that I'm never gonna get to see that smirk he saves for me again as I gaze down in disgust at my half-naked body, my new red shirt now soiled from the dirt on the floor and puke over the front and barely hanging on. My jeans are torn right across my thigh, the tattered denim leaving my tattoo on full show.

I feel like I will never be clean again, both because my hands are so filthy from walking on them in this cage, and because the dirty marks left on my soul from this whole ordeal are killing me inside. At least I know I can use that hurt, pain, and desolation to get through a life without Dagger, biding my time until I can claw my way back to him and everyone else, even if it kills me to try.

All I can do now is accept my fate for now…

"Kelly…Kel'," Maggie whispers at me.

I don't reply, and I don't think I could if I wanted to. After kicking and screaming that I wouldn't marry Mikhail, I got shown by my dear father what happens to his daughter when she's insolent. He punched me straight in the stomach, and then got Mikhail and my brother Ivor to hold me face down over his desk while he tore my top straight down the back lengthways and lashed my back a dozen times with his belt buckle. When Mikhail yanked me upright, my whole body doubled on itself. Glancing up, I could see his clear arousal at my state pushing up his pants, the sick fucker…

The welts on my back pulsate painfully at my recollection, the blood rushing up to the surface of my skin. I'm lying on my side facing the wall, staring at the black and slimy surface on the back of our cage absentmindedly drawing circles in the scum.

"Kelly…Kelly!" Maggie whispers more forcefully this time as she shakes my shoulder, tugging me towards her. She gazes down at me, her eyebrows crinkling with worry that's clear as day. "Kel', do you hear that? I think I just heard banging upstairs, and now I can hear what I think Is running. It sounds like it's getting closer!"

"What?" I mutter. Just as the word escapes my mouth, I hear another bang and a man yelling. A gunshot rings out maybe 30 seconds later, along with heavy-booted footsteps. There's a rattle as the doorknob tries to turn but doesn't budge, then another gunshot straight at the door, making me and Mags both jump as she clutches onto my body and pulls me onto my side to protect me, wrapping her whole body around me like a cocoon as both our bodies tremble in fear.

Her fingers bite into my hips as the door gets kicked in with a huge bang, the force making it rebound off the wall. I just cling on for dear life to Mags' little body as I hear several feet come into the room, starting at one end and systematically working their way down before a pair stop next to our cage.

My heart's racing, and I feel Maggie's vibrating against my chest, her breaths raspy with terror. Squeezing my eyes shut, absolutely petrified, I hear a shuffling noise followed by the voice I'd hoped I'd hear again a billion times since I was taken but never believed I would—*Dagger!*

"Kitten…baby, I'm here."

The dehydration and hunger must have gotten to my mind, but even if this is a dream, it's the best kind of dream I could wish for.

Even my brain's manifestation of his voice calms me, soothing the terror inside of me.

"Axe! Here! They're here!"

Weird, why is Axe in my dream?

I hear a few more sets of feet at our cage and cling to Mags as she clings to me too.

"Kelly, I'm here. Stay where you are, I'm going to shoot the lock off. Don't move," my Not-Dagger's voice tells me.

With that, another gunshot is fired at the corner of our cage making me and Mags scream out. I tug Maggie closer, pulling her into the far corner. I sit up to shield her, and that's when I see him; my man, my Dagger.

My whole world stares down at me like a starving man looking at a hot meal and reaches in, offering his hand.

I dislodge myself from Maggie, then practically launch myself at Dagger, but as soon as I feel his hands wrapped around me, I hiss out in pain. I sob into his t-shirt—the one he was wearing the night he claimed me in Wrench's room, which feels like a lifetime ago now. I take deep breaths of his scent, drinking in my life, my soul, my other half. I let out another broken sob as I gasp out, "You came...you came for me!"

Once me and Tomma leave the other men, he takes the lead, silencer already in hand

Pop! Pop! he shoots the door lock.

"Stay behind me, boss," he tells me. I was going to anyway, but it doesn't matter; once I find Vadim, I'm going to have to leave him. He gingerly and carefully opens the door, the sounds of the house echoing around us as we run down the hallway, hearing shouts and shooting from the other end of the hall.

Exiting into the house, I notice we are in a kitchenette of some kind, although it's hard to see properly in here.

"Boss...over here," Tomma whispers.

Swiveling on my heel, I jog over to the far side of the room. The door that's wide open across the hall is the entrance to what we know is Vadim's office. Shadows pass across the pool of light shining from it.

"*Capo,* stay here. Let me make sure you're not walking into a trap." Tomma cautiously leaves me just inside of the kitchenette, hiding behind the door flush to the wall and peeping through the crack. Tomma checks left and right as the gun fire carries on at the front of the house; a good sign that so we won't get disturbed unless Ivor is with Vadim...

Doubtful; he's as spineless as his Padre, I think to myself.

As I hear running coming toward me, I aim my own gun, ready to shoot. As Tomma comes rushing through the door, I've still got my gun pointed right at his skull at first, but when I realize it's him, my body relaxes.

"Tomma?" I hiss, making sure.

"Clear *Capo,* go! I've got your back!" he snaps at me as he checks everything is clear.

Walking round him, I check again and make a beeline for the door that the monster who has destroyed so many people's lives waits behind. I grasp ahold of the door handle to step into the demon's lair, pushing the door open with such force that it bangs off the wall—I always was theatrical. I step through the entryway without hesitation, gun aimed right at the man who I've wanted to kill for many years. His maniacal stare holds the look of surprise I have been chasing after for years.

I'm going to savor and enjoy every delicious moment I have to do this, so I saunter over to him, ready to capture my prey.

"Giordano…I didn't realize we were due a reunion. Will you please lower your gun? There is no need for this," he tells me, appearing calm, but his voice wobbles on the last words. He's always feared me, but it never stopped him from waging war on my territories.

Foolish old man! He has this coming.

"Vadim, I do not think so…You may have weaseled your way into my *Padre's* business, but that's where it ends." He starts to back towards his dark wood desk as I prowl towards him, ready to pounce. "Stop right where you are, you dirty *Russo!* You have a debt to pay, and I'm here to collect," I grind out.

My eyes are painfully wide, and I feel fury and rage ripping through me that I have had bottled up for years. I am the eye of the storm, destroying anyone in my path.

Death and destruction are my forte, my favorite pastime, I was born and bred this way; my *Padre* saw to that.

Vadim steps to the side, quickly trying to scramble to open his top drawer; I can see from here that a gun lays inside.

Pop! Pop!

He collapses on the floor, wailing and squealing like the pig he is. *"Grebanaya vlagalische!"*

I shoot him in the hand twice, the bullet cutting right through his palm like he's being prepared for a crucifixion. The juxtaposition is sick; he is definitely not a savior.

"Calling me a fuckin' cunt isn't going to save you, Vadim! Be careful what you say; one thing my *Padre* taught me was to learn a lot of language. It's one of my many talents. You should have never underestimated me! You did so at your peril, old man! Before I kill you—because it will be *you* who dies tonight—I could make you suffer like you did *Luciana*..."

Pointing the gun straight at his throat, I shoot. He tries to scream for help, but it comes up a gurgled cry as the blood pours out of him. With no hesitation, I point my gun straight at his dick and shoot off his cock.

The gurgling and spray of blood intensifies as he tries and fails to scream for help.

"These will be the last words you hear from me before I kill you," I tell him, crouching down so I can say the words that disgust even me I'm calm and collected on the surface, but underneath, my heart thrums with excitement, mimicking a hummingbird hovering. I can nearly taste his blood on my tongue. I've wanted this for too long...craved vengeance and justice for the wrongs in my past.

"*Si muore ora, Padre! Scusi,* where are my manners, I forgot you can't speak Italian. You die now, father!"

I watch the shock shimmer in his eyes, but waste no time digging the gun straight into his head.

"This is for *mia madre!*"

With that, the last shot rings out, sending his head jolting back with the force. Chunks of his brain and skull splatter across the back of his desk like a sick painting.

People speak of not feeling better after getting revenge, but a feeling of happiness washes over me and fills my soul—if I have one. Most say not, but I can't be worse than *mio padre!*

It's only what he deserves...

***

2 hours later...

As I recline in my soft private jet seat beginning to relax after all the pleasantries of meeting Dagger's woman Kelly and her friend Maggie—who seems to be clinging onto Kelly and completely oblivious to my men; especially Leo, who for some reason keeps looking up at her with a mix of fascination and interest. I have only seen Leo interested in women if they are either paid for or present at the many bars I own across the world.

After Vadim's death, we rescued the rest of the girls—they were wary of all of us at first, but as soon as Maggie and Kelly reassured them, it took no more than ten minutes to get them out of that awful basement that smelt like nothing I have smelt before In my whole life—although some parts of *Napoli* could probably rival it on a bad day, as much as I love my home.

We eventually got all the women in Ramírez's van, and he took them straight to the *Polizia,* while we looked on to make sure he did. He may have been the reason we were able to save them at all, but just because he got me Vadim's address doesn't mean I trust him. The only people I have ever trusted are my men and *mia madre.* Giving the jet a final sweep to check everyone is okay, I recline just in time to see Nico doing the same on the double seats opposite me on my far left. We can relax for now…

***

45 minutes later…

I'm such a light sleeper that I'm surprised I got any rest on the jet, I've never done that before. Perhaps it was the exhaustion…or perhaps it was due to the fact that I have now purged the world of one more serial rapist and sex trafficker.

I hear whispering coming from in front of me, and opening my eye a crack I see Kelly and Dagger talking in hushed tones. Dagger has given her one of his spare t-shirts he left on the jet, which absolutely swamps her petite figure.

She sits in his lap talking animatedly, her hands waving around, I can't quite catch what they're saying, but Kelly suddenly bursts into floods of tears, anguish clearly written across her whole body as it crumples in half. Dagger's face is full of rage, and I can tell he's close to the edge. He's dynamite, and Kelly is mere moments away from lighting the fuse with her pain.

I turn my gaze away from them, closing my eyes again as we have another 30 minutes until we land.

Seconds later, I overhear something that has my ears pricking up.

"He…he told…told me he's my father, Dagger!" Kelly gasps out between sobs.

"Who, Kitten? Mikhail? That's sick!"

"No…not him…but if you didn't get to me when you did, I would have been m-married off to him and shipped to Russia."

"So who then, baby?" I hear Dagger growl.

Kelly's next words seize the air out of my lungs and make my heart stop.

"Vadim. Vadim is—or *was*—my father!"

~ Chapter 31 ~

Kelly

I still can't believe I fainted on Dagger after he found me. After he traipsed across America to rescue me, I greeted him by *fainting* on him.

Wow, seriously, Kelly!

Relief washes over me as I find myself waking up cocooned in his warm, strong arms. Maggie's hand is still holding onto mine tightly, but Dagger hasn't even tried to separate us.

He holds on tight to me, whispering soothing words in my ears. "You're never getting out of my sight again, Kitten. You hear? You're going nowhere."

As soon as the familiar deep timbre of his voice hits my ears, head, and my heart, my body instantly relaxes. Peeling one eye open, I gaze down, seeing that I'm now wearing the Harley Davidson shirt from his 40th birthday. Feeling my skin prickle as the hair lifts on my arms, I take the chance and finally risk a look up at the man who makes me feel the safest I've ever felt—even safer than if I had two hand guns and a canister of pepper spray in my purse. He's the man I need and want by my side, always.

As I finally lay my eyes on him, I see that those mesmeric green and golden brown ringed eyes—the eyes that cut through all the bullshit, that would burn intensely enough to make a grown man shit themselves, that show me how much he desires me—are staring down at me.

But right now, in this moment, the fear and relief I see shining back at me are tenfold what they were before, as is the depth of the worry line that graces his forehead.

Before we even breathe a word to each other he bends his head slightly to lean against mine. The instant his skin touches mine, that spark between us comes flooding back into my system like an electric current shooting through my blood, giving me new life.

"To answer you, yes I did come for you, I will always come and find you. You're mine, Kelly Davis. I ain't ever fuckin' gonna forget it, and you definitely shouldn't either."

Hearing his voice crack as he utters the last sentence makes my heart ache, my own voice wobbling as I consider how close I was to never seeing him again. It absolutely guts me.

"God, Dags...I really truly believed...th-that I was never gonna see you again. I can't believe I'm actually here with you."

As soon as I breathe the last words, the tears that I was holding back for dear life rush forward to make my vision a completely blurry mess.

I blink them away, not giving a flying fuck that they fall down my face, catching the still-open cuts there as they descend, the sting of pain reminding me that this right here and now is real. I don't have to close my eyes to dream of him or remind myself of his face as he's right here with me.

"Dags, I'm just so happy to finally be here with you and have Mags safe too. I'll never ever be able to show how grateful I am that you found us. Thank you, so much," I tell him as I reach and rub my palm lazily over his dark ginger beard. He never takes his eyes off me as I do. Just as I burst into tears again, he wraps his arm around me tighter, forcing me to have to let go of Maggie's hand. Dagger sinks his face into the crook of my neck, whispering words of comfort that I soak up.

"Shh, Kelly, just close your eyes, darlin'. I got you. I've always got you."

I don't need to be told twice, sinking my own face into the crook of his neck and breathing him in, savoring his unique scent mixed with its signature salty undertone. Just like a balm, it soothes and rejuvenates my soul, allowing my sore, tired eyes to give out.

***

20 minutes after...

As I extract myself from Dagger's neck, I can't help but notice I have drooled a little bit on his shoulder. Stretching my neck out and rubbing my eyes—which still sting like a motherfucker—I straightening up in my seat, looking over to see Mags slumped over towards me, with Leo reclined and statue-still opposite her, looking like he's ready to pounce at any second.

I glance up at my man, deciding that I'm claiming his ass whether he likes it or not if he doesn't get his head out of his own ass and claim me first.

He shoots a curious look in my direction as he casts his eyes over me, but it soon softens after a few minutes of just drinking in each other in.

He tucks a lock of my hair behind my ear, and looking around the cabin again, I whisper, "Hey."

"Hey yourself, Kitten. How ya feeling?" he replies in a deep boom that's the best whisper he can manage.

"I'm okay, still tired. I have so much going around in my head I don't even know where to start with it all."

My heart sinks at the information overload going on in my head. I hope it won't be like this forever now.

"I have to ask—I have to *know*. Did they…touch you?" I don't miss the growl in his voice, or the nervous way he cracks his neck. I know what he wants to ask, and I can see he's fighting with himself over it.

As soon as I say the words he needs to hear, his body visibly relaxes and sags. "No. Well, not the way you think. It wasn't about that; this whole thing was about something else entirely…"

"How d'ya mean? You can tell me."

"I know I can…I just…I just don't know whether…" I break off, taking another look around the plane to make sure everyone is asleep, including Mags. I can't risk her hearing this before my parents. "I don't know whether to wait until I see my parents to say this, but my brain feels like its gonna explode if I don't."

"What is it, Kitten? Tell me and we can work this out together, whatever it is. I promise ya, darlin'."

"Well, it's nothing you can really help with, Dags… he…he told…told me he's my father, Dagger!" I gasp out between sobs.

"Who, Kitten? Mikhail? That's sick!"

"No...not him…but if you didn't get to me when you did, I would have been m-married off to him and shipped to Russia."

"So who then, baby?" Dagger growls.

"Vadim. Vadim is—or *was*—my father!"

***

Back Home...

We've just landed back in Tennessee, and Dagger and I exit the jet hand in hand. Dagger hasn't let me go for even a minute since we were reunited; I had to talk him down from coming in when I needed the bathroom on the plane, but he still stood outside just in case.

I don't blame him; my heart didn't feel whole for a single minute. I was torn away from the man I love. Glancing back at Mags, I see Leo trying to talk to her— he's fricking huge, poor Maggie! I go to go warn him off when Dagger shakes his head.

Strange...

"Where do you want to go first when we get back? Do you want me to take you to your parents'?"

I slip my hand from his and wrap my arms around his waist, resting my head on the side of his chest as we walk towards the club's truck. I'm about to tell Dagger we aren't all going to fit in it, but as I round the corner from the hangar I see his and Axe's bikes parked up next to the truck. Hoping he won't notice my lack of an answer, I give him a tight squeeze. This is the first time I have felt that giddy feeling of happiness since I was taken, and I don't want to go and see my parents and ruin it just yet. I need to try and get my head straight before I speak to them.

"Kitten, I was going to surprise you on our date night by turning up and taking you on my bike for the first time. I know you've been grinding my ass about getting on it," he explains, his chest rumbling underneath my ear.

I feel his eyes on me, and I peer up at him under my eyelashes. Even though he hasn't ever said the words, I can feel the love and adoration radiating from his eyes.

"Dagger…"

"Kitten, putting a woman on the back of your bike is a big deal for most bikers, but I've never had a single woman on the back before."

I've got goosebumps forming up and down my body, I step away from his side to stare up at him, then throw my hands around his neck, tugging him down to meet my face as that secret smirk that belongs to me blooms on his handsome face.

"What does this mean, Dagger?" I ask, holding my breath as I know this is big—massive, even.

"Kitten…Kelly, this means I'm claiming your juicy-as-fuck ass. This means you're gonna be my Ol' Lady. This also means I love you. I didn't even think it was possible for me to love anyone, but you showed me I can; I was just waiting for you."

My heart soars, and I can't actually believe the words coming out of his mouth, but they're exactly what I need right now. Dagger and our love are the balm that will help me heal.

Tipping my head up to meet his lips, I latch onto my anchor, who is holding me and keeping me afloat from the madness that surrounds my life at the moment. As he licks the seam of my lips, I let him in and savor every drop of Dagger seeping into my soul, allowing him to mend the shattered pieces.

Pulling apart from him, I dislodge myself from his hold, and he responds with a growl and grumble, walking after me as I stride up to the side of his bike and hook my leg over the seat. Staring into his eyes, I dramatically plonk my ass down on my Ol' Man's bike. I beam up at him with pure love as he leans down to steal another kiss.

Just before he does, he mumbles, "Little girl, you just sealed your fate. I ain't letting you go."

"Good, Mr. Thomas, because I ain't going anywhere."

"Damn straight, Kitten, damn straight." His lips latch onto mine, marking me again.

We're about to roll out and head back to the clubhouse when Matteo comes up to the bike.

Dags swivels his head around to face him as he does. "Thank you for helping me get my woman back. I'll be forever grateful."

"Speak nothing of it, Dagger. Would it be okay with you both if Kelly came to walk with me? I wish to speak to you alone."

Okay…this is weird, I have no idea why he would want to speak to me…

Dagger just looks back at me silently, but uncertainty is written all over his face.

Matteo is a strange man with a criminal background who I've only just met, and the knowledge sets my nerves on edge after all I've just been through, but part of me fights to push them down, reasoning that Dagger trusted him to get me home. He told me that without Matteo's help, it would have taken longer to get to me.

The thought of what that could have meant for me fills me with a terror as cold as ice that brings a shiver down my spine.

As my unease dissipates following that thought, I climb off Dags' bike and decide to walk with Matteo, following after his elegant strides and noticing for the first time that he moves like a wild cat in the jungle. We don't walk very far, stopping at a spot about halfway between his car and Dags' bike, just far enough away that we have some privacy.

I'm just about to ask him what he wanted to talk to me about when he meets my eyes. "I know you have been through a lot, and there is no easy way to say this, but I overheard your conversation with Dagger on the jet, and I need to tell you something. I wish our connection could have been built on something other than that *fica vile*, but our lives are entwined now nevertheless. Kelly, you are my sister."

"What?! What the fuck! What?! No. What?! " I hiss, angry and confused as hell.

I have another half-brother, but not just any half-brother; of course he had to be the boss of the fuckin' Italian Mafia!

My life has unfolded like a fuckin' movie over the past 48 hours, and I swear I have experienced every feeling possible to a human; shock, confusion, anger, hate, terror, joy, love, and now shock all over again. I would kill my sperm donor for the mess he has turned my life into in a matter of hours if he hadn't already been killed by my brother… which is entirely another level of messed-up that I have to deal with.

As I scrutinize Matteo, I can see something familiar in him that I first saw in Dagger—the reluctance to get closer. The shutters are down before I know it, and as of now, I don't have the energy to jam them open.

"How? What? This is so messed up…" I say instead, completely and utterly exasperated at the whole situation.

"All you need to know is that my *Mamma* didn't have a choice either, but her story is very different to your mother's," he informs me as he looks over at his Maserati.

"Is she okay, your Mom? Is she happy?" I enquire, now knowing what both women must have been through.

He doesn't answer straight away, and an awkward silence stretches in front of us until he breaks it.

"She is now. She has peace," he replies curtly, then turns on his heel to go and get into his car.

"Will I ever see you again?"

"I don't see why you would want to," he tells me over his shoulder just as he opens the back passenger door.

"In the space of a little over 24 hours, I have found out my whole life is a lie, my dad isn't who he said he is and my real dad is now dead, I have an evil Russian brother I knew nothing about and he's dead, the man who I had a few dates with months ago turned out to be one of my sperm donor's goons scoping me out, I nearly got forced to marry him but he is now dead, and to put the fuckin' cherry on top of a pretty shitty cake, I find out I have *another* brother who helped save me and my friend, but who happens to be a *fuckin' Mafia boss!* I think I'd like to stay in touch at least."

I finish my rant at him, then a tiny wave of worry comes over me as realization dawns.

I just shouted and swore at the Mafia boss...and he's my fucking brother!

I can see he's waging an inner war with himself for a moment, and even though I barely know him, my heart sinks when he finally breaks the silence to stab me with his words. "It's safer we don't. You have your life and I have mine."

As he turns to go again, I ask, "Do you have a sister already? Is that it?"

"No, I am an only child, but my life doesn't need any weaknesses in it."

"Ouch, 'Teo, that hurt. I just wanted to have someone in my life who gets it. I don't know who I am anymore; I've lost my identity," I say as my voice cracks, trying to will the tears in my eyes to stay at bay, but they are too close to the surface.

His initial lack of reaction is like a slap to the face. I watch him stare off into distance, the moonlight bouncing off of the inky black goatee he's sporting, then he walks away, but I see something shift in his eyes just before he gets into his expensive Italian car. Even from this distance, the distinct scent of soft leather and that new car smell wafts out. Sitting there a moment before snapping his fingers and grabbing something off of the man they call Tomma, he scribbles something onto it and strides back over to me, handing me a napkin.

"This is my personal number. Save it in your phone, then burn the napkin. You can't tell anyone we are related, Kelly; including your parents."

The curt response stings me, and the gut-wrenching feeling of dread at the mention of my parents returns. I push it down.

"I won't lie to Dagger; don't even ask me to. If he asks, I *will* tell him."

My stubborn streak is back in full force, and in this moment I don't care if he snatches the napkin back and I don't ever see him again. Of course, it will sting like a fucking bitch, but keeping secrets from Dagger is something I cannot and will not do. To my surprise, he relents, which makes the breath I was holding leave my lungs in a gust.

"Fine, but no one else. No one—*no one*—can know you even have my number, let alone that you're my *sorella*. It puts you at risk and makes me weak. I cannot have that."

"Okay. I get it, but will I see you again? I'm not asking you to come over for Christmas or anything…"

"I do not know, but there is a possibility. That is all I can offer you. My life is complicated and dangerous; more so than you will ever encounter—even being a biker's wife," he informs me, a grim, distant look in his dark eyes

"Wife? Ha! We aren't married!" I snigger.

"You love him?" he counteracts, an ebony eyebrow arched in question.

"Yes!" I say with no hesitation.

"He treats you *bene*—good—*Si*?"

"Yes! He's amazing!"

I love him, stupid… I add silently.

"Bene, bene. We must go; once the authorities find him, they are going to be looking at me. *He* didn't keep his hate for me quiet. Bye*, piccolina.*"

After ducking back into the car, he slams his door shut, and the car whizzes away just as abruptly as he came into my life.

Watching him leave the airfield in the opposite direction to us, I mutter, "Bye, 'Teo."

Looking down at the napkin, I fold it up and tuck it into my bra for when I get home.

Home…

Does that even exist anymore?

***

Matteo

I knew I had a half-brother, but a sister too? *Gesù Cristo!* It would make a good story if it wasn't so twisted. But everything in this life is…

My *Mamma's* and Kelly's mother's lives are both entwined with the dirty Russian *Bratva*, through no fault of their own…

My life isn't much cleaner or better, but sex trafficking is a red area I do not touch. My *Padre,* or at least the man I consider to be my father, dabbled too—the only thing he had in common with Vadim beyond my *Mamma* and his vocation.

Watching Kelly go off with Dagger sets my teeth on edge, but I push away the odd feeling seeing them together threatens to stir in me.

Age, ha! Means nothing as long as it's legal.

I think she was hoping for a warmer reception but what can I give her? What can I offer her by being in her life? Money, yes, security, yes, but love? No, I cannot do that. I'm capable, yes, but I shut that part of my body down years ago. Once you get made into this—the cold-hearted criminal— there is no coming back from the darkness and depravity or the wickedness and immorality that has occurred at my hand. It's all I know.

I thrive off of the darkness like a bat, always searching and seeking it out. I am not a complete bastard, so I will check in with my *sorella* now and then, but from afar. It is for the best for her and for me. She doesn't need to be associated with another Mafia boss. For now, I need a break from all this shit, and we need to disappear…

"Nico, *Andiamo a casa a Napoli ottenere il getto pronto ad andare stasera. Ciao,* America."

Chapter 32

Dagger

Three months after the abduction…

"What the flyin' fuck is this on your pussy?" I'm staring down at my Kitten's pussy, which has jewels at the top of it like a fuckin' sparkle fairy just spat on it. I can't tear my eyes off the pinks, purples, and golds shimmering and sparkling back at me.

"What d'ya mean? It's pretty, ain't it?" Kelly peers down over her perky tits, staring at me, but my confused frown doesn't waver.

"Is this shit gonna transfer? I don't want sparkly shit on my dick!" I grumble out. I know I'm being a dick, but fuck, why try to make something that's already perfect better? As I look closer, I can't deny it looks hot as hell on her—not least because she's written *'Dags'* in rhinestones with a tiny heart coming off it.

If that doesn't mark her like me cumming all over her face and neck, I don't know what will…

"Well, the…the man at the salon thought it would look good and you would like it."

My eyes snap up to hers, anger burning in my gut as I spit, "Man?! Did you just say another fuckin' *man* had his hands on my pussy?! What the fuck, Kelly? Are you serious right now? Who?"

Fuming, I jump up from the bed, grabbing my pants and stabbing my legs back into them, forgetting about the buttons I try and grab my t-shirt off of the bedroom floor.

"Yours? Since when has my pussy been yours?" Kelly sits up on her elbows, pinning me with a stare and raising one of those perfectly manicured eyebrows at me.

"Don't dodge the fuckin' question, Kelly! Tell me now! Which. Fuckin'. Man. had his hands on you?" I growl, grind my teeth at her. Her blasé reaction has just stoked the fire.

"Drake. His name is Drake," she tuts, sassing me.

This woman better not go there with that mouth.

"Who the actual fuck is Drake? Where the hell is this place?" I ask, finding my t-shirt under her leopard-print thong…which isn't helpful, as flashes of her peeling that down those thighs fill my head…

"Why? You want one too, baby?" she asks in a breathy voice.

Holy shit! That went straight to my balls…

I shove my t-shirt over my head.

"Like fuck I do! No, because I'm gonna go kill him!" I bite back at her, staring her down. My sincerity turns her look of amusement to shock.

"You will not, Dags!" she snaps at me as she tries to yank my arm back.

Fuck, my kitten's strong! I end up mis-stepping, tripping over my foot and falling down on top of her, her naked body pressed to my fully-clothed one. She wastes no time in targeting my weak spot.

"Don't distract me, little girl! Quit rubbing your pussy up against me!"

Fuck, I need to hold my ground, but I've been desperate to sink into her skin on skin since she told me earlier she's got an IUD. I've been eager to take her this way for so long that I can hardly stand it.

"Why?" she rasps breathlessly. Goosebumps travel up my arms towards my neck at the sound, making my whole body tingle like hell.

She thinks I don't know her tricks, but I know exactly what she's trying to do. I told her before about women and their tricks and games, but this woman here who owns my dick and my heart is the ultimate poker player, the perfect trickster!

"You need a hard spanking for letting another man touch you there!" I grind out, pushing my denim-covered cock up against the wetness of her pussy, making her gasp out words I wasn't expecting to hear. The admission gives me some relief, but she still needs to be punished.

"He's gay!" she giggles into my neck.

I just grumble back into hers, licking it and tickling her with my beard the way I know drives her fuckin' wild. "I don't care if he was gay, straight or bi! This pussy is mine and I know its magical gifts. It could make the gayest men want it! The dude would have to be blinder than I was when we first met to not want you. So, Kitten, turn the fuck over! Now!"

I sink my teeth right into the spot under her jaw, then whip my face away from her neck, which sends her mewling like the feisty Kitten she is.

She flips on her front, pushing that ass out. My fascination with this thing won't ever quit; even when she's older than I am now, I'll be still trying to pop beads and eggs inside of her. My thirst will *never* be sated.

I strip off my t-shirt, not wasting time with my pants beyond shoving them back down with force.

Seeing her present herself to me like this with her ass jutting out reminds me why Eve was tempted by that fuckin' apple. Her juices glisten and sparkle on her skin already, calling to me. I could sink into her over and over and never grow tired. "I'm gonna spank this naughty ass, little girl. Do you know why?!"

"Because I teased you, making you jealous." she squeaks out between gasps.

I stroke my palm over her plump ass as my fingers linger on her butt crack.

Hmmm…

I slide them just on the edge of her cheeks as her breath hitches and catches in the back of her throat, making my balls ache tightly.

Making her jump from the intrusion, I shove my fore and middle fingers straight into her soaking cunt, making her moan and gasp as she rides my fingers. I let her for a few seconds before tugging them out as Kelly tries to clench down on them to stop me.

I bring them up to my mouth, sucking on them, devouring them. If this right here were to be my last meal on Earth, I would die a happy man. I raise my hand and land a series of blows on her ass

Slap! Slap! Slap!

With each slap I hear the noises that could bring even a monk to his knees—Kelly's throaty cries of want. With each spank, the sounds grow louder, becoming breathless pleas as I refuse to let up long enough for her to catch her breath.

"Dagger!"

Slap! Slap! Slap!

"Fuck…Me!"

Slap! Slap! Slap!

"Take…Me!"

Slap! Slap! Slap!

"I'm. Gonna. Come!"

At these words, my hand falls away from her ass, my hand almost as red raw as its target, burning like fire.

The air in the room is thick and heavy with our arousal and desperation for each other.

Threading my fingers through her gorgeous long locks, I twist her head to one side see an on-edge Kelly about to explode.

"Hold on, little girl, because your Ol' Man is gonna fuck you, and it's gonna be quick!" I inform her in between gasps of breath.

True to my word, I don't let her respond or react as I slam right into her. There's no barrier, just us. As I feel the velvety soft inner muscles clamping down on my dick, I bite back a moan.

Sweet fucking God!

Without wasting another second, I rear back and slam into her over and over.

"Yes! Yes! Yes! Dagger!"

"Who. Owns. This. Pussy!" I grind my dick further into her as I bite down on the delicate flesh of her neck, pumping manically. Trying to find our releases, she pushes back on my dick, riding it fiercely and answering me with a scream just as she cums, wrapped around my dick.

"YOU! Always…you!" she rasps out.

"Good girl…remember that! I'm not finished with you yet. Your man needs to cum; roll over!" I grit out as I pump hard inside her again for good measure.

***

I look over at my sleeping woman after making her cum two more times, admiring the fact that she's all snuggled up on my chest looking just like a fuckin' angel—except this angel is 99% minx. When I don't think it's possible to love her any more than I do, she finds a way to make me fall all over again.

She has been wanting this for months, but next week she gets to meet my Ma, and I couldn't be happier to be letting her see the real me. She is the reason why I can barely think straight, she fits with me and my life, and everything is easy with her. She makes it easy to love her, even though she loves to push my buttons at the same time so I can take charge. We seem to ebb and flow effortlessly like that.

Fuck, losing her nearly broke me. When I saw her cowering in the corner like a scared little defenseless animal it near enough broke my heart clean in two. Seeing the headstrong woman who had pushed her way into my life, bed, head, and heart looking completely and utterly lost gutted me to my very core.

When she clung to me like a newborn baby to its mom when I found her and whispered the words, "*You came...you came for me!*" my whole universe shifted into crystal-clear clarity.

How the hell could I have ever fought everything I feel for this strong woman? She shifts everything back into perspective. It's like I'm always chasing due north and she's the compass.

Sometimes you don't realize what you want until you find what you need.

***

The night after…

"Yo-you're the reason why none of them in the past have come up with the g-goods."

It's barely 10 at night, but we have all decided to drink together; Kelly's on her first drink since she got home and she's already slurring her words.

She carries on with her speech, in which she's decided to give me a full breakdown of her initial feelings for me. "I knew, kind of what I wanted, but falling with—I mean for—you, I met my match when it came to the pusshh and pull. Kinda also helps you have a good sense of humor when yo-you're not alpha-ing my ass," she sniggers, shimmying her body between my seated legs. She has those black leather-effect pants on that she wore at my party, and she has stolen one of my old Harley T-shirts, which she's twisted and tied right around her waist like the sexiest biker chick you ever saw.

And she's all my crazy problem…that I intend on keeping…

I shake my head at her statement. "Kitten, don't get it twisted. You love it when I alpha your ass that's what made you fall for me," I point out as I take a long swig of beer.

"Naaaah, that wasn't it, it was the forearms, the moody face, your beard and your red hair…What can I say, red heads *are* hot! Asskk Jade…why do you think me and her are besties…"

She wiggles those damn eyebrows at me suggestively, then I watch her as she stalks off, her ass bouncing around.

Damn that woman! She gets my engine running; no matter how much I take her it will never be enough. I try and push my dick down.

"Kitten!" I shout across the room to her. She's standing next to the rest of the girls, and they all turn around at the same time.

"Yep?" her plump lips purse at me, those mischievous eyes sparkling with desire.

"You and Jade?" The confused look that was there before disappears and she slides her arms around Jade and Jenna, stroking their arms and whispering in their ears.

A second later, she shouts back over to me.

"Ohh yeah, totally!" she sniggers. Her eyes become heavy-lidded, blazing back at me and silently begging for me to come and get her—and I fucking intend to!

I jump off my bar stool, leaving the rest of my brothers at the bar and marching straight over to the woman who owns my balls. I growl when I reach her, then hook my arms around her legs and fling her over my shoulder. Spanking her ferociously hard, I snarl out loud enough for everyone to hear, "You're mine, Kitten! Remember that as I pull all those moans from you. I'm the only red head you're ever gonna let into your bed!"

***

Kelly

A week later - Meeting Dagger's Ma...

I'm sitting on the back of Dagger's bike, clinging to him tighter than a virgin as we ride over to meet his mom. He's already warned me that she's very stuck in her ways and particular about her home because she likes control. The apple not falling far from the tree comes to mind with the Thomas bloodline...

As we weave in and out between the traffic, heading over to the other side of town, I enjoy the feeling of my hair whipping around me as the wind snaps at it, setting it billowing around me.

My thoughts leaving Dagger's mom, my mind drifts to the last time I saw my parents. Things are still tense and strained between us. The first time I went over with Dags, my Dad didn't want him there, but I told them straight that either he was coming in or I was leaving.

There was screaming, crying, and shouting about everything that had been told to me by my sperm donor, but they didn't deny anything minus some finer details that *he* had left out about my *Mamá*. The fact she thought she was coming to America for an opportunity was right, but she arranged it on the Mexico side of things, and the people who agreed to help her actually sold her and other girls like her to the highest bidder.

She was sold to *him* when she was 20, and as soon as she arrived in the basement in Miami, she was raped continuously by *him*, gang-raped by his men, tortured, and used for some gut wrenching evil things.

Vadim was right about my Dad—his birth name is Jacob Davidson and he was an FBI agent, but he changed his name when he went into hiding with my Mom. While he was still serving, he and my Mom fell in love and got married, moving from Florida to Tennessee before I was born. He isn't an FBI agent any longer, but he does help them with freelance work occasionally and got a decent payout when he left.

When we went back over last week—this time to less protestation about Dagger—we went over it again. It's getting easier, it's just going to take time. At least the truth can't be erased now it's out in the open…

I follow Dags through the front door of the quaint one-story house, with a cute pale-blue porch swing in the far corner and large flower beds full to the rafters of every color possible. I decided to wear jeans and my new favorite t-shirt that Dags treated me to.

Even though I told him there was no need, he was adamant he wanted to get a Devils Reapers black fitted t-shirt made for me. It's plain on the front apart from the emblem over the left breast, and then on the back in a huge font the same style as the emblem, it reads 'Dagger's' in a semi-circle at the top and 'Ol' Lady' at the bottom. It's big and clear enough for anyone to see from miles around, and I fucking love it!

His arms wrap possessively around me as he marches us both straight towards the kitchen, the smells of smoked barbecue chicken cooking instantly soothing the butterflies in my tummy.

"Relax Kitten, you're perfect just as you are," Dagger says, reading my mind as he places a kiss on my temple, making the last of my butterflies disperse.

Leading me over to the curvy woman with short curly white hair cooking in the corner, he booms, "Ma, this is Kelly, she's my woman. Kelly, this is Ma."

I feel a familiar arm wind itself around my waist, fiercely protective over me. Ever since what happened with Vadim, we have hardly spend time apart and I love it. The club is officially our family now I'm an official Ol' Lady, which all the club girls grumbled about, but Wrench and Brains couldn't be happier. They have three girls to share, but Brains only has eyes for Candi, which leaves Wrench with Brandy and Jewel.

Looking up from the stove, Dagger's mom swivels around to meet me, an apron still tied around her waist.

Her eyes go straight to Dags with a hint of disappointment in them before she speaks up, "Oh, hello son! Derek, she's awfully young for you."

She scans me doubtfully. "You're not one of those club girls, are you?" she asks with detest on her face. "Don't you think you could choose someone your own age? You do know he'll be an old man soon, don't you? Are you up for that?"

Her words sting me, but I just lift my chin up at her.

"Yes, I do know that, and I don't care about his age, it's just a number. Dags knows I'm in it for the long haul, I'll be there every day no matter what: he's it for me and I love him."

I peer up at him as his hold pulls me tighter into his side. Never taking my eyes from him, I continue, "I've never been as happy as I am with him, and his heart belongs to me."

I turn my gaze back on his Ma and carry on my speech.

Screw it, this is who I am. She can like it or not, I don't give two fucks!

"If you think you're trying to scare me off, Ms. Thomas, it's not gonna work. I can see you're as stubborn as your son, but he will tell you I'm a helluva lot more stubborn, and I don't scare easily. He tried the same thing, and he found out I was right all along," I say smugly,

Your move; how d'ya like them apples!

She matches my stare and then glances at Dags as a small smile breaks out on her round face.

"Hmmm, I think I'm going to get on well with you," she says, nodding her approval at me.

"I like her, Derek, she's got fire in her belly."

She smiles back at me again. "You remind me of me in my heyday; I never took no for an answer either. You told me exactly what a Momma wants to hear about her child."

Dagger's Ma looks at his feet, frowning. "Did I raise you in a barn? What have I told you about traipsing in your dirty boots through my clean house?" she chastises him like a naughty boy, which only makes the smirk on my lips grow wider until I can't help bursting out in laughter, breaking all the tension in the room.

In the end, we all end up laughing, and Dagger speaks up, "I'm glad you like her Ma, as I'm keeping her. I've claimed her as mine. While I'm at it, I'm fuckin' 40, not a boy you know!"

Dagger's Ma responds by smacking him on the shoulder with a towel, "Derek! Don't say fuck! You cheeky shit! I'm glad you're keeping her.

She beams at me. "Now Kelly, tell me all about yourself."

~ Epilogue ~

Kelly

2 years later...

"Remind me why we decided to have babies again?" Jade pipes up from the other end of the picnic bench as we all gather around in the big town park on a beautiful fall day. She's a month further along than I am at 26 weeks. Dags starts grinning over at Tinhead, the smile reaching his cheeky eyes.

I shout down towards Jade. "If I remember it right Jadey, we had no say in it! Tinhead is the one who made you take the test after weeks of being sick, and as for Dag's, well, even his sperm are stubborn; they got through my IUD."

"At least you look pretty while you're pregnant. I look like a balloon just got inflated inside of me and I still have a month and half to go. Damn you, Dylan!" She purses her lips at him, either unable to stop fidgeting around from being uncomfortable or because drinking soda has given her indigestion again.

"Red! Quit talking about yourself and my child like that! You're beautiful; you're growing our child and making a perfect home for them until they want to make an appearance," he wraps his arm around her, tugging her to his side of the bench, then I hear her grumble something under her breath at him.

Watching them bicker reminds me of the fact things still aren't perfect with my parents, but I understand that they did what they did to protect me and *Mamá*. I think the fact that I'm going to be a Mama too has put things into perspective. Not only that, but Dags settling into parenthood has helped me see that your DNA doesn't define you, and it takes a real man to be a Dad.

"She's not wrong Kitten…you look so fuckin' sexy with my child growing inside of you. Fuckin' turns me on knowing I put them in there," Dagger rasps, his voice sending delicious tingles up and down my body, touching my nipples. I look through my eyelashes to where he sits opposite me as he continues, "I so want to bend you over this table and take you over the edge and then watch you cum over my fingers."

His eyes are on fire, shimmering with the hues of all the reds and oranges on the leaves hanging from the trees surrounding us.

"Stop it, " I protest lightly, shaking my head at him as I carry on drinking my hot chocolate, then gaze at him over the lip of my cup.

"You know that's never gonna happen, so don't even go there. You knew what you were getting when you got with me. I told you that when you first started chasing me."

"Excuse me, I think you're the one who's remembering it wrong. *I* saw what you were offering, and *I* still wanted you, you were just stupid enough to ignore your needs. Stubborn ass man." I jibe back at him with a hint of extra sass from the hormones. Taking another gulp of my drink then looking back up at him I see his face has a stoic look over it.

He grabs my cup, placing it down on the bench, and bending over at his waist, he claims my lips, drinking me in and taking what he wants and needs from my body. He can have it; he's owned it since I met him, and I give it to him willingly tenfold.

He dominates my mouth his tongue wrapping around mine, tugging my hair slightly to make us break apart on a gasp of breath, making me feel dizzy as hell.

"I was a stupid fuckin' asshole for rejecting you. You're right, Kelly. I love the bones of you, and I'll spend the rest of my days showing you and our child how much."

As my throat constricts with emotion, I can't help blubbing. I'm terrible at the moment, everything makes me cry; even the weird car commercial with the doggy. Right now, though, this moment here is worth crying for.

"I love you, so much," I cry out as I dash my fallen tears away.

"I love you too."

Dagger looks up. "Yo! You two! We better get going; we need to be back at the club. Axe said he wants us all there," he shouts over to Jade and Tinhead who are as wrapped up in each other as Dagger and me.

"What's it about anyway? It can't be that they're engaged, they got married last year…Oh I wonder if they're having another baby? Or…something else."

Chuckling at me rambling on, Dagger helps me off the bench. The combination of big donkey booty and pregnancy make me feel more out of proportion than before, not that my man seems to mind. He can't get enough of me, and I him.

"Why don't we go find out, hey?"

***

Dagger

Only Kelly and Jade could end up being pregnant together—always the dynamic duo in almost everything they do.

Walking back through the club, we see Jenna sitting down on the couch next to Sue and Dani, looking fresh as a daisy and beaming up at us. Even though she has some bags under her eyes, she doesn't seem to care one iota, wearing them like the little warrior she is.

I give her a peck on her cheek and go off to my best bud, who's facing and chatting to Axe. I clap him on the back to get his attention.

He turns, and if that ain't one of the best sights I've ever seen...

I grin at the big gruff biker wearing a gigantic shit-eating grin, his huge arms tightly knitted together holding a pink bundle.

I peer down at his and Jenna's daughter, who's fast asleep and completely oblivious to the crazy-ass world she's just been brought into and how fiercely she's loved by everyone in it.

"You look just like your Mama! At least you haven't got a beard like your Dada, little one," I chortle, earning a snort from Bear.

It feels surreal that this little one is even here; he and Jenna didn't even want to announce that Jenna was pregnant. Of course, we all knew, but they said they wanted a big celebration once they got home with their baby.

I tug Bear into a side hug. "Proud of you bro'."

He just can't stop smiling; I can see tears welling in his eyes as he gazes down at wonderment at his newborn baby daughter. He walks back over to Jenna as she gingerly stands next to him wrapping her arms around her family.

As I gaze around at everyone in this room, I know they have all touched my life in one way or another. I see Doc and Sue wrapped up in a hug standing near Jenna, the two of them beaming like proud grandparents.

Fuck, that gets me right in the chest…

I seek out my reasons for breathing, instantly wrapping my arms around Kelly's growing belly and placing a soft kiss on the crook of her neck, whispering the words that still surprise the hell out of me. "I love you, Kelly Davis."

She relaxes into my hold, and hearing her sigh makes me smile, but hearing the next words makes me feel like I won the lottery. Every. Single. Damn. Time.

"I love you too Dags."

Axe interrupts our hushed declarations as he bellows out as loud as he can without waking Bear's daughter, "Listen up! You're all here for a celebration in honor of one of my best buds and his Ol' Lady; Bear and Jenna. Bear?"

Axe steps back to go to Dani who's looking blissfully happy, as she coos over Zara and Flex's 6 month old son, Zain Benjamin Fletcher, born April 7th. Benjamin is Doc's real name, which he ended up being proud as punch about it, although he jokes that Zain got Flex's hair but Zara's baby blues.

A hush falls over the room as Bear clears his throat to start, "This is a day we didn't think we would ever get a little over two years ago, as you all know, but me and Jenna want to say a massive thank you from the bottom of our hearts for all the love, support, and occasional punch ups you guys give us."

He eyes me with a smirk, then carries on.

"You have no idea what it means to us, and we're so happy we get to enjoy all our family lives together and bring our miracle daughter into the most amazing club and family. So if you can all raise your drinks to…Hope Sophia Jameson, who always has her sister by her side."

There isn't a dry eye in the room, including mine. Wrench whoops and cheers, earning himself a glare from all the Ol' Ladies worried about the baby, Brains and Candi smile on with their arms wrapped around each other, and even Brandy and Jewel have their glasses raised up to our newest arrival.

"Hope Sophia Jameson!" everyone shouts in unison.

Kelly starts whooping as tears stream down her face, not caring that she drips her orange juice over her hands. My woman is gonna be the best Mama; she's as fierce as a lioness and has the most loving heart of gold I could have ever wished for.

"Who wants cake?" Jenna shouts, her face beaming like the sunshine on a summer's morning as her tears of happiness stream down her own face.

Just as my stomach starts rumbling, my woman gently shoves me aside.

"You aren't getting a piece before us ya know! Oi, Jadey! Why didn't you tell me your sister had the baby?" Kelly waggles her finger at Jade.

"Kellybean, I was sworn to secrecy! She was born yesterday; me and my Momma went up to the hospital last night. Don't hate me!" she pleads as she wraps her arm around my woman.

"I don't hate you, but you best tell me when you do, or I'll be making sure Tin doesn't get to put his special jizz sauce in ya ever again."

Kelly's words send the beer that I was drinking shooting out of my nose, and I choke on it. "Fuckin' hell Kitten, give me some warning won't ya!"

She peers up at me, her chin in the air and that stunning smile beaming at me from ear to ear. "Ooops. Sorry…" she teases with that naughty sparkle in her eye, which I love so much. I'm starting to see more of it these days, and I fuckin' love it.

She was offered counselling after what happened to her and Maggie, but she declined it, saying she just needed her man, friends, and family. I've been keeping an eye on her just in case, and when we started back up in the bedroom I threw all my rope out. She told me not to just in case she felt ready to use it, but I ain't ever risking her mental health like that, not for my own personal gratification.

I'm in complete awe of her. I can see she's upset Maggie isn't here, but since she got back she's retreated more into herself and away from gatherings like this. Kelly mentioned that Leo, Matteo's second-hand, calls her every now and then, but she doesn't answer since the first couple of times thinking about the Mafia boss in question, I drop down to her ear level.

"You heard or spoken to your brother yet?"

She freezes, then peers up and around us as the commotion carries on before tugging on my hand and leading me outside to the place where it all started—up against the side of the clubhouse.

As soon as we're there, she peers around to double check we're alone, then blurts out, "Yes… I spoke to him this morning, but it was just a general chit-chat, you know…it's like getting blood from a stone with him. I told him that I was pregnant, and he asked the due date. Well, technically I didn't tell him I was *pregnant,* I told him he was going to be a *Tío* —an Uncle. He's happy for us."

"He still hiding out in Naples?"

"Yeah…He said we could visit once all the heat has gone off him, although he'll probably be back in the US by then…"

"What is it, baby?"

"I don't know… I guess I feel sorry for him. He's alone. I mean, yeah, he has the money and his men, but he's so closed off."

"It's the way he is, and probably the way most Mafia men have to be, Kelly. Don't you try steamrolling him like you did with me," I laugh as I push her flush with my body, molding her to me.

She wraps her little arms around the back of my neck so I have to bend down to kiss her, which I do gladly. This right here is what it's all about—I have everything I could ever want in my bubble with this woman. I feel our little one move across her stomach as it touches mine, and it feels amazing.

Placing my hand on her growing stomach, staring down in pure amazement and hearing her soft sigh as I rub back over the spot where our baby is inside of her.

"Girl."

My palm halts just over what I think is our child's little butt—or head—then she repeats it again.

"We're having a girl! I know we said we would wait and see, but I called Dr. Swann earlier and she told me. You're not mad, are you?" she asks cautiously.

"Fuck, Kitten, mad? How could I be mad at you!" Emotion clogs my throat, but I clear it and carry on. "I fuckin' love you...oh *fuck!* She's gonna be just like her Mama; causing me nothing but trouble, pushing my buttons, and having no filter, ain't she?" I grumble as rub down my face,

Kelly starts giggling back at me, her soft silky voice tickling my ear. "Don't you mean, 'and have me wrapped around her little finger just like her Mama'?"

"Yeah, you got that right woman, and I'm damned proud of it!" I growl in her ear, needing to have my way with my Kitten again...

The End...

Thank you so much for reading *Dagger.*
I hope you enjoyed his and Kelly's story as much as me.
I hope people realize after reading it that taking that
chance at love is worth it! Even if you get burnt, it's an
experience we won't know unless we try. Just because
you haven't done it before doesn't mean you can't.
I do hope you loved Dommy Dags as much as me...

I would really appreciate you leaving a review on
Amazon or Goodreads, even if it's a one liner.

Thank you again,
Love and hugs
Ruby xx

* ~ *

Read more about the Devils men...

Devils Reapers MC Series

Axe: Book 1 is available now!

Flex: Book 2 is available now!

Bear: Book 3 is available now!

Tinhead: Book 4 is available now!

Come and follow me on

Facebook: https://www.facebook.com/rubycarterauthor/

Twitter: https://twitter.com/rubycarterauth1

Instagram:
https://www.instagram.com/rubycarterauthor/?hl=en

Printed in Great Britain
by Amazon